FROM LITTLE TOKYO, WITH LOVE

FROM LITTLE TOKYO, WITH LOVE

SARAH KUHN

VIKING

VIKING
An imprint of Penguin Random House LLC, New York

First published in the United States of America by Viking,
an imprint of Penguin Random House LLC, 2021

Copyright © 2021 by Sarah Kuhn

Viking & colophon are registered trademarks of Penguin Random House LLC.

Visit us online at penguinrandomhouse.com

LIBRARY OF CONGRESS CATALOGING-IN-PUBLICATION DATA IS AVAILABLE.

Printed in Canada

Hardcover edition ISBN 9780593327487
International edition ISBN 9780593403082

10 9 8 7 6 5 4 3 2 1

Design by Lucia Baez • Text set in Stempel Garamond

For everyone in Halfie Club—
I believe in your happily ever after.

Once upon a time, a beautiful princess lived in the magical kingdom of Los Angeles. Always alone, she belonged to no one—and no one belonged to her. She dreamed of one day finding someone who shared her passions, a handsome prince obsessed with monstrous mythical creatures and exploring all the weirdest corners of her kingdom.

Or alternately, she dreamed of kicking ass and winning the regional judo championship, which came with a really awesome trophy.

Neither of these things happened, so she revealed herself to be a nure-onna (an actual monstrous mythical creature), transformed into a snake, and ate everyone's faces off.

The end.

ONE

Never argue with the Nikkei Week Queen of Little Tokyo.

Auntie Suzy gifted me with this advice when I was six, and I probably should've taken it to heart. But "never" sounds like a long time when you're six, and I must have known deep down that there would be so many things I'd want to argue about.

"Ugh, Rika-chan, why won't you just *stop fighting with me!*" My sister Belle—the current Nikkei Week Queen of Little Tokyo—gives me an impressively regal glower. "You have the worst temper in the whole entire world."

"False," I say, even though it's kind of true. "I'm actually suppressing my kaiju-temper extra hard because I'm trying *not* to fight with you. Even though you're the one who's blocking my bedroom door and waving random bits of fabric in my face."

"It's a scarf!" she proclaims, flapping the floaty bit of

cloth she's been trying to tie around my neck for the last five minutes. "And you need it."

"I do not need a scarf," I retort, batting her hands away. "We live in LA—no one ever *needs* a scarf."

"It's *decorative*," she crows, her face screwing into that look that means I'm being a total pain the ass.

I would argue—see, again with the arguing—that *she's* the one being the pain in the ass, since she's keeping me from what I actually *need* to do. I have to get over to the dojo, where my fellow judoka are preparing for our big martial arts demonstration today. We always put on a show at the parade that kicks off Nikkei Week, the annual festival in Los Angeles's downtown neighborhood of Little Tokyo celebrating all things Japanese and Japanese American.

I'm *really* trying not to deploy my temper—Auntie Och calls it "Rika-chan's kaiju," or giant monster, after all the Japanese creature movies she watches on "the YouTube," holding her phone screen way too close to her face. I'd swear her tone sounds almost . . . admiring? But the truth is, my temper always gets me in trouble. It's somehow even more monstrous than Godzilla or Mothra or any of the titans rampaging across Auntie Och's screen, destroying entire miniature cities. It's one of the snarling beasts in the Japanese folklore stories I've been obsessed with since I was a kid, clawing through my blood and rattling against my rib cage, dying to escape and gobble up those who insist on provoking it.

Like the guy who thought it would be funny to "pretend choke" me after I tapped out during a sparring session in judo. I was only eight, so I bit him—and almost got kicked out of the dojo over it. Or the anime-obsessed white girls who frequent my Aunties' katsu restaurant and order me to speak to them in "an authentic Japanese accent." I once dumped a full can of Coke on Queen Becky, the Ultimate White Girl Who Just, Like, *Loves* Asian Culture, and it felt *so good*—until that particular Becky's mother started an online petition to shut down the restaurant, and Auntie Suzy wearily explained to me the need for our family to appear "respectable." (That one . . . did not happen when I was eight, by the way. That was last week.)

I don't want to be in trouble all the time, so I try to keep my kaiju-temper leashed.

But my kaiju-temper doesn't care about what I want.

Even now, I can feel it rising up, swirling through my bloodstream, tempted to bite at Belle for derailing what should be a big day for both of us simply because she hates my outfit.

Oh yes, that's what started this—my sister hates my outfit.

"Rika." Belle brandishes her decorative scarf again and gives me the imperious look that's made her the benevolent but unchallenged leader of the cool kid crew at Tataki High. "Seriously. All eyes are about to be on you at this parade and *that's* what you want to wear?"

"All eyes are about to be on *you*," I counter. "You're temporary royalty, ruling over the glorious smog of downtown LA. I'm merely one of your subjects—"

"—who just happens to be the reigning judo star of the Little Tokyo Dojo, about to kick every available ass in the Nikkei Week parade's demonstration." She gives me that imperious look again. "Don't act all modest, Rika-chan, I know you're proud of your fighty abilities."

Even though my temper's still simmering, a burst of warmth pokes through—like a tiny sparkle of a fairy trying to distract my kaiju. She's right, I *am* proud. I'm sparring in today's centerpiece match, the crown jewel of my dojo's demonstration. It's a chance to be part of the parade's magic—in a way that feels like *me*, rather than what my scarf-obsessed sister might want—and I can't even pretend I'm not thrilled.

"The dojo is the one place where I *can* be proud of my fighty abilities," I say, giving her a half smile. "And

I'm excited about today—for both of us."

Belle has dreamed of being crowned Nikkei Week Queen since she was old enough to say "tiara." Every year, six Japanese American girls are chosen from the local high schools and two from the middle schools and one is crowned queen. Belle was a junior princess in sixth grade, a princess-princess the summer before our junior year, and now that we're about to be seniors, she's achieved her dream. And as for me . . . well, I've worked my ass off to ascend from Rika the Biter to the top-ranked spot in my dojo, have pretty much made it my goal ever since Auntie Suzy put me in judo in order to channel my "aggressive tendencies" into something productive. I love the precision, strategy, and control of judo—they help me tame my kaiju-temper, or at least focus it on doing something useful.

"Belle-chan," I say through gritted teeth. "My outfit will be totally covered by my judogi anyway, so what does it matter?"

"You *need*! The! Scarf!" she cries, her voice twisting in that high-pitched way that always makes Auntie Och's ears hurt.

"Why is this scarf so important?" I snap, snatching it from her grasp and unfolding it to reveal . . . huh. It's a pattern, some kind of colorful embroidery forming a vague shape that kind of resembles—

"Wait a minute," I say, scrutinizing the embroidery. "Is this supposed to be *Nak*?"

"Yes, it's my precious puppy," Belle says, jabbing at the embroidery with her index finger. I can now sort of see that Nak (short for "sunakku," which means "snack" in Japanese), her tiny mutt of a dog, is embedded in some kind of pattern of interlocking swirls. "He's my mondo-koro, my crest—I designed it myself. You should wear it during your match—it will make you look *so* regal. And it will give you a meaningful way to represent—"

"I *am* representing in a meaningful way," I protest, gesturing to the ratty T-shirt I'm wearing, the one she hates so much. "This is *my* mondokoro."

My T-shirt bears an illustration of a nure-onna, one of my favorite monsters from Japanese folklore. She has the head of a woman and the body of a snake and bloody fangs, like she's just indulged in a feast of tasty humans. The nure-onna is my aspirational monster—she totally eats people, but she's cunning about it. She plots and plans before she strikes; she doesn't let her temper sweep her away and fuck everything up.

I still haven't mastered that part yet. But while Belle

was dreaming about all the princess things when we were kids, I was dreaming about being the nure-onna.

I bought the shirt for five dollars at Bunkado, a neighborhood gift shop that's been around for decades and is still run by the same family that opened it when they returned home after the Japanese American incarceration of World War II. Its eclectic shelves are crammed with stationery and teapots and vintage Japanese vinyl—and this amazing T-shirt, which was the only one of its kind. The saleslady gave me a major discount because she could tell I just *had* to have it.

I thought wearing this nure-onna shirt would show off my Little Tokyo pride. Totally appropriate for the parade. I've completed my look with roomy basketball shorts (excellent ventilation to keep me cool in the blazing late-August heat) and gold Adidas that are waiting for me by the door (kinda royal in their own way, no?).

I can tell from Belle's expression that she's not really seeing the crest-like power of the nure-onna, though.

"Listen," she says, rolling her eyes, "wearing this scarf is kind of the least you can do, since you straight-up refused to be in my court—"

"Oh—oh *no*!" I sputter. "I should have known: this is about princess shit!"

"*Everything* is about princess shit!" Belle explodes.

"And every girl wants to be in the Nikkei Week court. The fact that you *spat* on that honor—even though you could have performed princess duties in addition to your judo demo—is . . . just . . ." She shakes her head, like she's a robot short-circuiting.

"I'm not princess material," I say, crossing my arms over my chest and glaring at her. "We all know this."

"But you could be," Belle asserts—and now she's back to waving the scarf around. "If you would just be *open* to letting me do you up, like Cinderella—"

"Cinderella's stepsisters cut off their toes to fit into the glass slipper," I fire back. "That's the real story—not exactly happily ever after."

"Do. *Not*," Belle says, thwacking me on the arm with her scarf. "Cinderella's my main bitch."

I release a long breath, trying to shove down my temper—which is now slamming itself against my breastbone, wanting more than anything to get *out*.

It's not that I want Belle to give up on her fairy tales, with their sanitized happy endings. It's just that I want her to open up to *my* version of fairy tales, my melancholy stories from Japanese folklore. Where the endings are often bittersweet—emphasis on the "bitter." Where it's possible for, say, a girl with a dead mom and a deadbeat dad to triumph somehow, even if it means casting aside idealized notions of love and turning into a monster.

The nure-onna, after all, always gets a certain kind of happy ending—really, the only kind I can see for myself. Solitary yet satisfied. Fighty abilities top-notch. No prince in sight.

You'd think Belle would be open to all that after her umpteenth overly dramatic relationship imploded. (Belle dates, in her words, "hot people of all genders," but still hasn't found anyone who can successfully execute an Instagram-worthy promposal.)

"Why are you guys yelling?" Rory, our twelve-year-old sister, stomps into Belle's room. I've never seen someone stomp quite like Rory, who walks everywhere like she's trying to shake the ground. She insists this is her natural gait—all the more impressive when you consider her minuscule frame. "I can hear you all the way down the hall," she continues, cannonballing herself onto my bed. She lands with a *whump*.

"Ugh, you can hear *everything* in this apartment," Belle says, rolling her eyes dramatically. "Why bother having walls at all?"

"Rika, what are you wearing?" Rory sits up in bed, her cute little eyebrows drawing together.

"See!" Belle whirls around, her bright pink fingernails whipping toward Rory. "Rory thinks you should dress up more, too."

"Rory didn't actually offer an opinion, just a question," I say.

"Rory thinks the outfit is bad," Rory says. "Opinion given, no questions."

"Thanks for nothing, *Aurora*," I say, calling her by the full name that only gets dragged out when she's in trouble or when people feel like being overly proper. Sometimes I can count on her to form an alliance with me against Belle. As a math genius who hasn't felt challenged by the curriculum since kindergarten, Rory tends to be more practical-minded.

"You should look like a princess, too," Rory says. "To match us."

Oh, right. Even with the genius-based practicality, Rory still buys into that princess shit—she's a junior princess in Belle's court. Whenever she and Belle form their own alliance (#TeamPrincess), I get a little twinge that reminds me they're technically not my sisters— they're my cousins. Peas in a pod who were named after actual Disney princesses. I'm always supposed to match *them*, not the other way around.

Even though they're built differently—Belle is all

generous curves to Rory's spindly limbs—they both have the same perfectly straight manes of black hair and flashing dark eyes, the same flawless creamy skin, the same cute little round noses. When they stand next to each other, the effect is almost comical: as if Belle has somehow manifested a smaller, more serious-faced version of herself.

I, meanwhile, have always looked like the outcast cousin—so much so that Belle's and my teacher on the first day of second grade asked Auntie Suzy if she was "sure" we were both hers, giving me the suspicious side-eye, like I was trying to con my way into going home with people I didn't belong to.

"She's *half*!" Belle had declared, stomping her foot at the teacher as if that settled it. "And we claim her as a whole Asian!"

I have wavy, tangled hair a few shades lighter than the rest of my family—sometimes picking up brassy glints of red in the sun. And smatterings of freckles in various places, including across my wider bump of a nose. I do look Japanese (especially to all those Beckys who want to hear my accent, I guess), but it's in that way where, as I accidentally overheard the confused second-grade teacher say later, "You can tell there's . . . something else going on." When we were younger and less aware of stuff, Belle dubbed me "Asian Lite." We both thought this was funny until Auntie Suzy wearily informed us that it was not.

Auntie Suzy is Belle and Rory's actual mom, and she took me in after my mother—her sister—died in childbirth and my "white devil" father took off for who knows where. Belle was still a baby when all this happened, only six months older than me. To this day, the murmurs still run through Little Tokyo. How Auntie Suzy did her Good Asian Duty by taking care of family. How my mother was such a tragedy, she'd had such potential before she got pregnant at fifteen—so beautiful and charismatic, able to charm the pants off of anyone she met with a smile. How it must be tough on the remaining Rakuyamas since I look so . . . different. There's always that weird pause before "different," as if the greater community of gossiping Little Tokyo Aunties and Uncles are carefully assessing my appearance, clocking all the ways I look . . . well, Asian Lite.

Some of them simply refer to me as "a mistake." I'm not sure which is worse.

I refuse to buy into their Tragic Hafu narrative. But that's another reason I don't want to be a princess— because I'd definitely be the worst princess ever, and I don't need to stand out even more than I already do by being that bad at something. I know some of those gossip-mongers would have no trouble gossiping *extra loud* from the sidelines, vocalizing the thing that's always dancing around the back of my head:

What's she *doing here?*

I'm good—no, *excellent*—at judo. Sparring is one of the only times I don't feel like some kind of weirdo, bad-tempered Asian Lite mistake, trying to go home with families I don't belong to. It clears my mind and settles my restless body, and I can connect to the pure magic of Little Tokyo that I love so much.

In other words, the only time I feel truly at home is when I'm fighting something.

And if I push myself to be outstanding today . . . I mean, my judo teacher, Sensei Mary, told me there will be a UCLA scout in attendance, assessing our performances for scholarships.

I dream of ascending the college ranks, kicking ass on the competitive circuit, maybe even helping Sensei Mary run the dojo one day. Basically, this is my ideal future as the nure-onna, defeating all enemies who stand in my way and eventually settling into a life where my fighty-ness is an asset.

And if I can do the community proud, maybe the gossip, the whispers, the lingering stares will . . . stop. Maybe I'll finally feel like I belong here, to this place that flows through my blood as naturally as the sizzle of my temper.

"So, who do you think the grand marshal will be at the parade?" Rory says, snapping me back to the present. "And why is it always such a big secret?"

"It's for the *drama*, Rory, they do a big reveal every year," Belle says, rolling her eyes. "But honestly it's probably some boring old person we've never heard of — as usual."

"I have to go," I say, suddenly realizing my door is now unblocked and I can continue on my quest to the dojo.

"Wait!" Belle protests as I dart toward my exit.

"I'll wear it like this!" I shout over my shoulder, hastily using Belle's scarf to tie up my unruly hair.

"Rika-chan!"

I let out a yelp and jump back as my bedroom doorway is blocked *yet again*, this time by Auntie Suzy. She's swaddled in an old yukata with a fading sakura print and Adidas slides with socks, and she looks like this day has already exhausted her, even though it's barely nine a.m. Nak scampers around her feet, tail wagging.

"Rika-chan," Auntie Suzy repeats in a way that's probably meant to be admonishing but is, as usual, too absentminded. She reminds me of a kindly witch who can't remember what spell she's supposed to cast. "Are you girls fighting already?" Her gaze lands on me, and her nose crinkles. "And what is that . . . shirt?"

Nak gives me a scolding look, as if to agree with her, and trots over to Belle.

Okay, so *everyone* in this family disapproves of my amazing T-shirt. Even the dog.

"It's a nure-onna," I say. "A Japanese fairy creature who morphs into a half snake and seeks revenge on those who have done her wrong—"

"Mmm, why can't you like the *nice* fairy tales?" Auntie Suzy shakes her head.

"Fairy tales *aren't* nice," I mutter, twisting the hem of my shirt. Stubbornly, all of them being so against it makes me want to wear the shirt even more. "Anyway," I say, edging my way toward the bedroom doorway again, "I really need to get down to the dojo and warm up because—"

"No." Auntie Suzy's voice is sudden and firm—a marked contrast to her usual dreamy cadence.

"What?" I stop cold in my tracks, unsure that I've heard right.

Auntie Suzy deflates a little. "I'm sorry, Rika-chan, but you can't participate in the demonstration today. I need you to work at the restaurant—we're having a much bigger crowd than usual."

"But . . ." I shake my head, confused. My Aunties'

restaurant, Katsu That, is located right below our apartment, and their claim to fame is they will katsu literally any foodstuff. The whole family works regular shifts there, but I'd specifically asked for today off. "I've been training for this all year. I mean, really for most of my life, considering how long I've been in judo."

My voice is already rising, my face flushing, my temper bubbling to the surface.

"I'm sorry, Rika-chan," Auntie Suzy says again, but now my kaiju is *roaring*, threatening to consume my entire body, and I *have* to make her understand.

"I finally made the number one spot this year—do you know how hard that was?" I say, struggling—and mostly failing—to keep my tone even. "Natalie Ito and I have gone back and forth since we were nine, and she is a legit *beast* at sparring—she beat me out three times in a row for the regional championship, remember? But I finally did it, I beat her enough times in class, and now I get to lead warm-ups and be in the centerpiece match, and I can finally—" My voice catches, hot tears filling my eyes.

I can finally show everyone I belong here.

Auntie Suzy cocks her head at me, something I can't recognize passing over her face.

"Rika," she says slowly, "why must you make everything so *difficult*?"

Really, her weary tone is one of the most infuriating things. How can she be so unbothered, so dismissive of something so important to me?

"You wouldn't be doing this if I were a princess like Belle and Rory!" I blurt out.

"Technically I'm the queen," Belle murmurs.

"Because *that's* important, right?" I bulldoze on, ignoring her. "You *get* why that's important, them wearing fancy dresses and waving to the crowd, but when it's something that's important to *me*—"

"Your sisters are performing a service to the community," Auntie Suzy interrupts, her tone still flat. "You had your chance to do that, too, and you chose not to—so now you can be of service to your family—"

"I'm barely part of this family!" I spit out, my temper exploding. My face feels like it's on fire, and the tears are starting to run down my cheeks, and I'm just . . . so . . . *frustrated.* "None of you will even try to understand why I like my monster-woman shirt and why I don't want to be a princess, and by the way, part of this isn't *just* about my resistance to all things princess—I also don't want to deal with Uncle Taki death-glaring at me from the sidelines because he thinks only 'pure Japanese' girls should be Nikkei Week Princesses, and—"

"Ma Suzy." Belle's voice is soft and placating. I can

feel her sidling up to me, gently adjusting the scarf in my hair. I also feel Rory's hand take mine. "Rika is the best at the dojo. She's earned the chance to show everyone how good she is, right?"

I swallow hard and look at the floor, trying to shove the temper back down. But it doesn't want to go. When it's like this, it feels like it has *nowhere* to go. It's a blaze consuming my body, obliterating everything else.

"I'm sorry," Auntie Suzy says again—and now she really does look sorry, that sadness she always has about her brimming to the surface. "Your family needs you in the restaurant, Rika-chan."

Then she turns and shuffles out of the room.

I feel Rory squeezing my hand, Belle messing with my hair. I love them and I know they mean well—but they're trying to soothe something that can never be soothed, to slap a coating of princess over the messy remnants of my snarling monster.

I feel the distance growing between us—and there's that twinge again.

The one that says no matter what, I will never belong here.

And I will never belong to my family as fully as they belong to each other.

TWO

I escape to the closest thing I can find to a comforting dark corner—the floor of Auntie Suzy's dusty walk-in closet.

The closet is the only room in our apartment that feels big, even though it's stuffed to the brim with Auntie Suzy's collection of vintage dresses and kimono. As the story goes, Auntie Och—Auntie Suzy's wife—used her handyperson skills to knock down a wall between two smaller closets and make one giant one, back when they first got married and spent all their time being hopelessly in love.

Sitting on the cool floorboards, shrouded in a rainbow of crammed-together patterns and colors, you can almost feel the soft sweetness Auntie Suzy used to possess, before she was just tired all the time.

Also before she was so into crushing the dreams of her only niece.

I take a deep breath and worry the silky hem of a bright orange yukata between my fingers, trying to get my temper under control. I glance over at the mirror hanging on the closet's door, nearly hidden by all the kimono. Whenever I look in the mirror, I see the nure-onna staring back at me: bloody fangs, flashing red eyes, unadulterated *rage*. Ready to take down her enemies. I find it comforting, to be honest. It tells me the armor I've worked so hard to build up is firmly in place. That I can get through anything.

Although I don't quite feel like that right now.

I should be getting ready for my newly acquired shift at the restaurant, but my mind is stuck on the dojo, working furiously to figure out how I can still do the demonstration at the parade.

I *love* the parade, because it's the one day a year when all the magic bubbling under the surface of Little Tokyo comes out to play, amplified by the wonderstruck crowd of locals and tourists. The cavalcade of bright colors is more vibrant, the creepy hidden-away nooks and crannies are even darker, and the juxtapositions of things that shouldn't go together are just *more*. That crumbling, overstuffed souvenir shop crammed next to the modern swoop of the most elegant hotel in the city looks even more beautifully improbable. The blazing sun shines even brighter, illuminating the crimson and ivory lanterns strung through the air and making for a cheery facade—but that facade gives way to shadows lurking in grubby alleyways and abandoned warehouses.

Those soft, comforting shadows are what I sink into when my temper's about to explode.

It was at the dojo where I found the shadows. It happened the day I finally beat Natalie Ito for the very first time, when we were both nine. She usually won every single match, but that day, I somehow managed to get her into a kata-gatame hold and willed myself to *stay put*, staring resolutely at one of the shadowy spots where Sensei Mary always forgets to clean, little pockets of space populated by spiders and dust and wilting, discarded hand-wraps. These corners seem in direct contrast to the rest of the dojo, with its big, bright open space, its soft mats to catch your falls, its high ceiling with skylights that soften the relentless Little Tokyo sun. It's that juxtaposition of things that shouldn't go together but do. That characteristic that defines so much of the neighborhood.

Those dark corners are my favorite. As a kid, they always seemed to me like doors to other worlds.

I always thought that maybe if I stared hard enough at one of the dark corners, the nure-onna would emerge. She'd kick *ass* at judo.

My discovery inspired me to search out other magical dark corners in Little Tokyo. Whenever I felt my kaiju-temper flaring, I'd find one—I'd go hide under the biggest tree in the garden behind the community center or retreat to the back of Uncle Hikaru's ancient mochi shop on First. I'd crouch among the wild assemblages of plants and flowers or the unwieldy stacks of packaged mochi and dusty snack boxes and random trinkets. And I'd read one of my Japanese monster books until I felt better. Slowly, I'd be soothed and held by the shadows. I'd feel like I was *home*.

I sometimes wonder if my mother was like me, gravitating away from #TeamPrincess and toward tales of monstrous snake-women and hopelessly sad endings. Sometimes the whispers about me drift to the mysterious nature of her death. How there was no funeral, even—it was like she simply ceased to exist. Vanished into the ether. Some say it's because Auntie Suzy was ashamed, but I don't see how that could be. Auntie Suzy seems too exhausted and dreamy for that kind of shame—I think she was just *sad*. And still is, to some degree. Whenever I try to talk to her about my mother, she says the same stuff everyone says about how beautiful and charming Mom was, then changes the subject or finds some chore for me to do.

So I guess I'll never know.

I freeze in place as the closet door creaks open and light spills in, startling me from my thoughts. I try to make myself smaller, huddling more fully underneath the canopy of kimono. A pair of feet wearing mismatched socks—one has a stripy pattern, the other is covered in bright yellow cartoon Minions—shuffles in my direction.

"Rika-chan!" a voice bellows, and I nearly jump out of my skin. I should have known I couldn't hide from her.

"Down here, Auntie Och," I call out.

She kneels and moves the orange yukata out of the way, her stern face sizing me up. Auntie Och has the same incredible mane of jet-black hair as Auntie Suzy—but hers is starting to streak with white. Which just makes her more formidable.

"Almost time for the parade, ne?" she barks at me. Auntie Och can never seem to manage less than a bark. "What you doing down here?"

"I . . . um . . ."

"I need a kimono," she says abruptly, her gaze turning to the orange yukata. "I'm going to drive Belle and Rory through the parade in my Mustang."

"Oh . . . cool," I manage. Every member of the Nikkei Week court has to come up with their own mode of parade transportation—there's no central float. So it's usually some kind of family car where you can put the top down and wave to the crowd. Auntie Och has had her Mustang convertible since she was a teenager. Apparently she was quite the hell-raiser, back when she and Auntie Suzy met as princesses in the Nikkei Week court and Auntie Suzy fell for her rebellious charms. Auntie Suzy was eventually crowned queen—which is probably why she's always told me to "never argue with the Nikkei Week Queen of Little Tokyo." She was basically telling me not to argue with *her*.

I guess we can see how that worked out.

"Suzy always liked this one," Auntie Och says, rising to her feet and freeing the orange yukata from its hanger. "It was a special-occasion yukata, only for Nikkei Week." Her harsh features soften as she gazes at the yukata, lost in memories.

I'm also suddenly fixated on the yukata, but for different reasons. Because my overactive brain has *finally* worked out a way I can still do the judo demo and . . .

I gnaw on my lower lip. *Wait, is this ridiculous? Or . . .*

The pretty blue-and-yellow flower pattern cascading over the yukata's voluminous sleeves shimmers, as if encouraging me.

"Auntie Och," I exclaim, scrambling to my feet

before I lose my nerve. "What if *I* drive the Mustang in the parade?"

Her bushy black eyebrows draw together. "I thought you were supposed to work in the restaurant with Suzy."

"I . . . I am," I say. "But Auntie Suzy said something about me turning down the honor of being a princess, and . . . and it really got to me! I want to be in the parade with my sisters. All princess-y and stuff."

I give her what I hope passes for a winning smile. Her bushy brows are still drawn together, suspicious. I don't think she believes one single word I've said.

But then one of her brows quirks upward, transforming her expression to thoughtful. "I would rather work in the restaurant than deal with driving in front of the Watanabes' flower-shop float," she muses. "George Watanabe, he always yell at me for braking too fast. Even though I am a much better driver than him."

She hems and haws for a few moments, then nods decisively. "Hai. Okay. You drive the Mustang. I'll tell Suzy."

"Can you *not* tell her, actually? I mean. Not right away," I say quickly. "I want it to be a, um, surprise. Since she wanted me to be a princess so bad."

"Mmm." Auntie Och nods—but looks suspicious

again. She thrusts the orange yukata at me. "Wear this."

"Oh, but I'm already . . ." I gesture to my nure-onna T-shirt, anticipating how freaking hot and uncomfortable the yukata will be.

But Auntie Och shoves the yukata at me more insistently.

"You will wear," she says in that way that's definitely an order. "You want to be princess now, ne?"

I guess . . . I do? Even though I don't plan on being a princess for long.

I take the yukata with a smile, the kind I imagine the nure-onna flashing right before she strikes the killing blow.

❀

I emerge from our building to blazing heat. It's only nine thirty, but the sun is unrelenting. Downtown—and Little Tokyo in particular—is always hotter than most of LA thanks to the rays bouncing off all the tall, reflective buildings of the business district and baking the sidewalks. During the summer, the air seems to shimmer, casting a magical, muggy haze over everything.

There's nothing magical about the sweat patches already forming at the small of my back and under my arms, however. Even though it's a lighter cotton material than some kimono, the yukata is still an excess of fabric for this weather. Auntie Och finished it off with a giant purple obi around my waist, and I already know the stiff, clunky bow affixed to the back will shove me forward in the driver's seat, adding about a thousand degrees of difficulty to my task.

Luckily, I managed to escape before she popped geta on my feet, which would have made driving near impossible. My gold Adidas aren't quite covered by the yukata's length, but they'll be hidden by, you know, the entire car.

I asked Auntie Och to send Belle and Rory out once they're finished assembling their royal looks—but also asked her not to tell them I'm their new driver. I don't want to risk one of them letting it slip to Auntie Suzy.

The minutes before the parade starts are the only time this neighborhood is *ever* quiet. The charmingly cramped assortment of ramen shops, mochi emporiums, and that one slightly illicit-looking place that sells bootleg DVDs of martial arts movies and disintegrating old kimono are all closed for the parade. The neon CHOP SUEY sign that's been a fixture for decades and usually casts a wild rainbow glow over First Street is dimmed. And the temple across the street is deserted, silent, and a touch eerie—lending credence to the rumors that it's totally haunted.

It feels like the whole street is taking a nap.

When it's quiet like this, the shadows become more prominent, and I can truly sink into them. It's like that underbelly of Little Tokyo I love so much is singing to me.

My phone buzzes, and I do the clumsy dance of exhuming it from the yukata's cavernous pocket. This will be a fun game I get to play for the rest of the day.

It's a text from my judo buddy Eliza Hirahara (who is my third best friend after Belle and Rory, mostly because Belle and Rory would riot if I referred to anyone else as my best friend). She wants to know why I'm not at the dojo, getting ready for the demonstration. Eliza joined the dojo when we were both seven, and she's my exact opposite—quiet and calm, as even-keeled as they come. We were destined to become either mortal enemies or inseparable. We've gone the latter route, especially after my whole biting incident. None of the other kids wanted to spar with Rika the Biter, and some of their parents even demanded I be kicked out of the dojo. I'd resigned myself to staring resolutely down at the mat as my cheeks heated with humiliation while the other kids paired up, leaving me all alone.

Until the day Eliza toddled up to me and extended a hand.

She was so sweet, so *kind*. And she still maintains to

this day that she hadn't done that because she felt sorry for me.

"It was because you were so good, I didn't care what anyone else said," she always says, warm brown eyes sparkling with amusement. "I wanted a worthy opponent—not like Craig Shimizu, who cheats his way through."

It's probably a half lie, but I love her for it.

And once I had a regular sparring partner, other kids started wanting to spar with me again, too. Which helped me get started in my quest to work my way to the top.

Eliza's also excited about the UCLA scout today—we've been practicing extra hard the past few weeks, hoping we can both kill it and land matching scholarships and show Sensei Mary that all her hard work has paid off. She's been training us since we were tiny, and she's made sure the dojo feels like a second home to us. She's the one who's kept me from getting kicked out, even when other parents protested my Rika the Biter moments, even when my kaiju-temper got the better of me.

I text back that I have to join the judo crew mid-parade, and I'll explain everything later. Then I shove the phone back in my pocket.

I try to breathe deeply, to relax into the hazy heat.

Unfortunately, the sweaty patch has spread up my back and down my sides, and the yukata is clinging to me in a way that's about as far from relaxing as you can get. I reach behind me, trying to scratch a spot that's becoming unbearably itchy. My hand is instantly blocked by the obi, which I've decided is pretty much my nemesis.

I let out a sputter of indignation, my gaze going to the other side of the street, where Auntie Och's convertible is parked. The convertible is also supposed to be relaxing, preparing for its big moment in the spotlight. But instead . . .

I frown. There's some . . . *guy* hovering around the car, running his fingertips along the hood. A baseball cap obscures his face. We're the only two people on this supposed-to-be-napping street. What the hell is he doing?

"Hey!" I bellow before I can stop myself. I gather my yukata in my sweaty hands and race across the street, once again thankful that I managed to preserve the Adidas portion of my outfit. My voice is a strange, sharp note puncturing the soupy air. The guy's head snaps up, and he jumps back from the car like he's been caught doing something illicit.

I mean, maybe he *is* doing something illicit—maybe

he's a saboteur from another Nikkei Week Princess's camp, angry that Belle landed the queen title. Am I about to nab a would-be vandal? Will I be the savior of the Nikkei Week parade?

I try to imagine myself being feted, surrounded by Japanese American dignitaries and Asian celebrities, smiling as they clap for my heroic feat. Somehow that just isn't right, the picture won't cohere —

"*Yaaaaaaargh!*"

I've gotten so wrapped up in my fevered imaginings that my yukata slips out of my sweaty hands, and before I realize what's happening, I'm tripping over the hem and crashing headfirst into the possible vandal. I'm not sure who makes that bullhorn-like sound of distress. Maybe him. Maybe me. Maybe both of us at the same time.

We crash into the lava-hot concrete of the street in a tangled heap. He ends up on the bottom, so he bears the brunt of it, letting out a hearty "oof" as we hit the ground.

"I . . . sorry," I manage, trying to pull myself up. My hands are on his shoulders, attempting to avoid the blazing concrete. His hands have clamped onto my hips. His hat's gone flying and I finally get a good look at this possible vandal, who I have just apologized to for some reason.

He looks like he's about my age. His shiny black hair is doing that K-pop/J-pop thing, playfully mussed in a way that has to be on purpose, perfectly complementing his golden-brown skin. Sharp cheekbones contrast with dark eyes that hint at mischief—although they're currently overtaken by consternation.

"I mean . . . sorry for knocking you over, but not sorry for foiling your attempts at vandalism," I amend, trying to give him a stern look. I feel totally undercut by our awkward position and the fact that the yukata has decided to tangle itself around both of our legs, making it impossible for me to pull away from him.

"Vandalism?" He gives me an incredulous look. "What, why? I barely even touched the car!"

"But you were planning on it?"

"Shouldn't I be asking why *you* just crashed into me out of nowhere?" he retorts. He scans my face like he's looking for signs of malfeasance. "Are you some kind of Little Tokyo Citizens Patrol?"

"I could be," I say, trying to straighten up again. Any movement I make only seems to entangle me in my yukata/his legs further. "I could totally be on patrol."

For some reason, that makes his face relax a little,

a bit of that mischief sparking in his eyes. "Well, then, Officer," he says, "I'll confess: I wasn't vandalizing, I was *appreciating*."

"Oh?" I find myself scrutinizing his features further. He's a little too cute—the kind of cute that *knows* he's cute and uses it to his advantage whenever the opportunity presents itself. There's also something oddly familiar about his face, but I can't put my finger on it. Maybe he's one of Belle's vast, interconnected crowd of cool kids.

"Yeah," he says. "It's a '66 Mustang, right? You don't see a lot of those in such good condition."

"It's my Auntie's," I say. "She was wild when she was younger, but we all know if we get a scratch on it, we'll pretty much be murdered."

He lets out a surprised laugh, deep and rich—it's not the laugh I would expect from someone so focused on his own cuteness. It's too unguarded, too full throttle in its joy.

He's on the verge of a snort, even.

That laugh reverberates through my body. I mean, it's kind of impossible for it not to—we're still pressed together, tangled in my yukata. I suddenly feel even warmer than I did before, the sweat gathering at the base of my neck and behind my knees and other places I didn't even know you could sweat.

"Um, anyway," I mutter.

My face flushes as I yank my yukata free and scramble to my feet, silently thanking Auntie Och for tying the obi so tight. It's basically glued to my waist, and that's saving me from flashing the empty streets of Little Tokyo and this person who is apparently not a vandal. Belatedly, I remember he's still on the ground and offer him my hand. He quirks an eyebrow and gives me an amused look.

I stiffen. "I've laid out guys twice your size in judo," I blurt out.

God. Why am I blurting so many random and oddly defensive factoids to this too-cute-for-his-own-good stranger?

"I'm not smiling because I think you're incapable of helping me up," he says, his grin widening. "I'm smiling because you look so—"

He gestures to my ensemble.

"I look so *what*?" I say, my face flushing further.

"Never mind," he says, his smile getting so big, it's *absolutely infuriating.*

He takes my hand but doesn't really put any weight on it, leaping to his feet with catlike grace. His long limbs, ribboned with lean muscle, look dancer-y.

"I just . . . I like your outfit," he says, gesturing to my yukata. "Pretty unusual for an officer of the law."

"Not my regular day wear, really," I say, crossing my arms over my chest.

"You know that was a compliment, right?" He gives me an easy half grin. I can't help but think *everything* is easy for him.

Out of the corner of my eye, I see Belle and Rory emerging from our building. *Shit.* I need to send this Apparently Not a Vandal on his way before Belle starts crafting our fairy-tale happy ending.

"I don't have time for compliments," I say to him, waving a hand. "I need to get to the start of the parade route."

"You're a princess?" he says.

"Just a driver," I say, my tone more defiant than I mean it to be. I see Belle and Rory getting closer, two bright splashes of color floating into view.

"Ah, okay," he says, looking a bit skeptical. He points to me. "Not a princess." He points to himself. "Not a vandal. Nice to meet you."

And with that, he scoops his baseball cap off the ground and strolls away. I . . . wait, is he *whistling*? Like he's in some kind of old-timey musical? I tilt my head at his retreating form, trying to make sense of this . . . person.

Suddenly, Belle and Rory are screaming in my ear.

"Rika!" Belle yanks on my arm, jumping up and

down. Rory looks Rory-level excited, her little eyebrows waggling. "Do you . . . was that . . ."

"What?" I say irritably, shaking her off.

"That was *Hank Chen*!" Belle shrieks. "Remember, he was on that show we watched in middle school, about the traveling kids' show choir—"

"And then he won *Dance! Off!* last season," Rory chimes in, naming her favorite competitive reality show. "He had that routine with all the backflips and splits and—"

"Riiiiiight," I say, fragments of memory floating through my brain, images of some boy smiling and charming his way through a jaw-droppingly acrobatic routine, the sparkle in his eye never fading.

"Is he here for the parade?" Rory wonders, her brow crinkling.

"I dunno, maybe he's the grand marshal?" I suggest.

"Oh my god, *no*," Belle says. "Didn't you see? The identity of the grand marshal got totally leaked. It's . . ." She pauses for effect, dark eyes flashing with glee. "*Grace Kimura.*"

Oh god. As if I need more princess shit in my life.

Every little Asian American girl who dreams of fairy tale–worthy happy endings has grown up swooning as they watch Grace Kimura get hers over and over *and over* again. She's the reigning Asian American rom-com queen, one of the modern world's chief perpetuators of the whole happily-ever-after thing. She's starred in a seemingly endless cycle of rom-coms, running through countless airports and wedding ceremonies and rain-soaked streets to tell a string of blandly handsome men that yes, she *does* truly love them. She's gotten her heart broken onscreen dozens of times, only to have it mended by the end. Her hair is always shiny, her bold lip always on point, her mascara smudged in an artful way that never detracts from her perfect ingénue beauty. She's her own kind of princess, Belle's ultimate vision board come to life.

One of my family's favorite pastimes is to marathon her movies, gathering around the TV with fuzzy blankets and multiple flavors of shrimp chips, Rory oohing over the goopiest scenes, Belle mouthing along with the dialogue she's committed to memory, Auntie Suzy misting over whenever Grace Kimura cries. I can sometimes be tempted to join by the shrimp chips, especially if they get the spicy ones. But I always find myself getting twitchy once Grace Kimura starts running through the airport or whatever.

It's another thing that binds all the Rakuyamas except me.

"That's probably why Hank's here," Belle says, practically vibrating with excitement. "He's in Grace Kimura's new movie. Maybe he's supporting her. God, he's cute."

"We need to get this show on the road," I say, fishing around once again in my yukata pocket—this time for Auntie Och's car keys. We *don't* need to get into a full-on analytical discussion of Hank Chen's cuteness, and I know Belle well enough to know that's what she's just about to do.

"Wait, what's this 'we'?" Belle says, her eyes narrowing suspiciously. She studies me, clocking my outfit. "Why are you wearing that?"

"I'm your driver," I say, giving a little bow. "Finally embracing my inner princess."

"Bull. Shit!" Rory yelps.

"Rory, no garbage mouth," Belle says. "But seriously, what the fucking hell, Rika. That is so not what you're doing!"

"All right, all right," I say, holding my hands up in surrender. "The truth is, I thought I could drive y'all to that first big stopping point—where the ondo dancers do their routine? Then jump out of the car and book it over to the front of the dojo for the demonstration. I need to . . ." I pause, gnawing my lower lip. Now that my kaiju-temper isn't flaring, I can't find the words to explain to them how important this is.

"Rika-chan." Belle smiles at me. She looks every inch a queen—she's also wearing vintage from Auntie Suzy's closet, but her outfit's not from the yukata section. It's taffeta from the fifties, nipped in at the waist and decorated with obscenely large cabbage roses. She's added a frothy petticoat underneath to make the skirt even more cupcake-esque, and the whole thing fits her curves perfectly. "Of course we've got your back," she continues. "You deserve this."

For the second time this morning, my eyes brim with tears, and I hastily wipe them away.

"Thank you," I say. "Thank you for . . . wait a minute."

Now I clock what *Rory's* wearing. She's pulled her hair into two tiny Princess Leia buns and sprayed her whole head with glitter. Then added little white cowgirl boots and a short purple "dress" that appears to be . . .

I narrow my eyes, scrutinizing her more closely.

"Aurora," I say. "Is that *my nure-onna T-shirt*?"

She shrugs. "It looks better on me."

I open my mouth to protest, then close it.

The thing is, it really does.

THREE

The obi complicates driving even more than I thought it would.

Not only is its bulk pushing me forward in the seat, but it's tied so tight that it holds the yukata in place in a way that makes moving my arms a challenge. I have a limited range of motion as I steer the convertible, and I'm thankful that I don't have to make any sharp turns or parallel park or something. I mentally reverse my previous thankfulness to Auntie Och for tying the obi so snugly. Maybe flashing the streets of Little Tokyo and smug-ass Hank Chen wouldn't have been so bad. That thought makes me flush for some reason, and I order myself to refocus on the task at hand. I definitely don't need to be any sweatier.

I pilot the convertible forward in painstakingly slow fashion, mindful of the ondo dance group walking—and occasionally stopping and performing—in front of us and the float for the Watanabe family's flower shop behind us.

The car carrying Grace Kimura is in front of the dancers—top down, like the Nikkei Week court's cars, so everyone can bask in her beauty. Belle and Rory are practically beside themselves with excitement. Still, they're trying to carry on with their queenly/princessly duties. They're both sitting up on the back of the convertible, feet resting on the back seat, waving to the crowd. Occasionally, we catch a glimpse of Grace's brilliant smile when she turns her head, her glossy mane of raven hair swishing around her shoulders.

The sun has moved high in the sky and beats down on us with brutal intensity. I feel hot everywhere. It's like the sun is slithering its way into every possible bit of my being, down to the roots of my hair. The roots of my hair feel like they're about to catch *fire*, actually.

I'm going to take like ten thousand showers after this parade. Or maybe just roll around in ice cubes or something.

"Rika, stop!" Belle's voice jolts me out of my thoughts, and I hit the brakes. The stop is a little abrupt and jerky—I hear the people on the flower float behind us grumbling.

"Dance break," Rory says, gesturing in front of us.

The ondo dancers are going through their routine again, identical smiles in place. The crowd claps along to their steps appreciatively, and I can't help but wonder if any of the dancers have ever cracked and gone on a murderous rampage, fed up with having to smile and perform the same steps over and over again in punishing summer weather.

Why don't you like any of the nice *fairy tales?* Auntie Suzy says in my head.

I put the parking brake on so the car won't roll forward into the dancers. Auntie Och's convertible is not super reliable at the whole not-rolling-forward thing.

"Being a Nikkei Week Princess is boring," Rory grumbles.

"Rory!" Belle admonishes. "It's an honor to serve our community."

"A *boring* honor," Rory says. "I like *watching* the parade because we see everything and we see it once. Whereas *being in* the parade means we only see, like, two things and we see them over and over again. I thought being a princess meant I'd get to do *cool* stuff, like make my own all-you-can-eat mochi buffet or claim one of those warehouses on the edge of Third as my new kingdom."

I can't help but smile. Rory's logic is often indecipherable to anyone but Rory, but there are moments when it just makes sense. She occasionally gets close to envisioning a version of princessdom I could actually get behind.

"Let's liven it up, then," Belle says. "Let's try to get Grace Kimura's attention! Maybe she'll see how amazing we look and put us in her next movie."

"How?" Rory says, intrigued.

Belle, of course, already has a plan.

"Grace!" she calls out—loud enough to be heard over the clapping, not loud enough to disrupt the dancers. "Grace Kimura! Little Tokyo loves you!"

"You're our, um, queen!" Rory says, her voice less assured.

"I thought Belle was the queen," I can't help but add.

"Right, you're our *other* queen!" Rory attempts, getting a little louder.

"The whole point of a queen of any given area is that she's the only one," I say.

"Stop ruining our fun," Belle says, reaching down to swat me on the shoulder.

"Grace!" Rory yells, committing more firmly to the bit. "Queen Grace Kimura!"

"Queen! Grace! Kimura!" Belle cries out, giving it a rhythm.

I don't know how exactly it happens—these things *always* seem to happen when Belle decides to bend a large group of people to her will—but suddenly others take up this chant and then it syncs with the clapping and the dancers get in the same rhythm and it's like we're all part of a weird spontaneous flash mob with the sole purpose of getting Grace Kimura's attention.

"Queen! Grace! Kimura!" everyone yells, Belle's voice the loudest. "Queen! Grace! Kimura!"

Grace Kimura finally turns in our direction, because . . . well, how could she not?

She's still all smiles, charisma radiating from her every pore, beaming the full wattage of her beatific expression on us. Being on the other end of her smile really does feel like being showered in glitter and sunlight—you can't help but smile back. She gives Belle a wave and a gracious nod, like they're communicating in some special queen-to-queen language. Her gaze moves to Rory, and she gives her kind of an "aww" look—but not in a condescending way. It's like she's fully honoring Rory's adorableness.

"Oh my god," Belle gasps, and I hear Rory rustling around behind me, sitting up a little straighter.

Damn, Grace Kimura is really freaking good at being a movie star.

Grace's gaze finally wanders down to me, the sweaty person behind the wheel.

And the blood drains from her face.

I barely have time to register that before all hell breaks loose.

Because all of a sudden, Grace Kimura is definitely *not* acting like a movie star. Her smile has been totally wiped from her pale face, bright red lips turned downward. A shadow passes over her eyes. And then she's scrambling down from the car and leaping into the street.

"Holy *shit*," Belle says. "What is she doing?"

A bunch of people start shouting, the dancers stop dancing and look around in confusion. Someone on the flower float whines, "What is going *on*?" because they can't see. A man in a dark suit—Grace's bodyguard, maybe?—springs from the passenger seat of the car Grace was just riding in and takes off after her.

But Grace, in addition to being a movie star, is surprisingly *fast*.

She zigzags through the confused dancers, looking like she's effortlessly navigating an obstacle course. There's a bunch of confused murmuring among the dancers as they dodge this way and that, trying to get out of her path. Some freeze in place, unsure of what to do. Like should they try to stop her or . . . ?

The vibe from the crowd on the sidelines is similarly confused, but they're calling out to her: "Grace? Are you okay? Grace, what's wrong? Grace . . . Grace . . . Grace . . ."

The weird but genial flash mob we had going a few minutes ago has morphed into something else, threads of shared panic and worry and just *not knowing what to do* winding themselves through the air. Sweat prickles the back of my neck, the tips of my ears. Even now, sweat is finding all new fun places to take root. I hear someone in the distance call for security.

"Ms. Kimura!" yells the man in the dark suit, Bodyguard Guy, his voice commanding. "Please. Stop!"

But she doesn't listen. She darts past the last confused clump of dancers and barrels straight for our car.

Her face is still ashen, her eyes haunted. Her hair has somehow worked itself into a wild tangle. I lock gazes with her, unable to look away. In an instant, Grace Kimura has transformed from beautiful princess to monstrous wild woman. Something pings in my heart, a strange connection that forms as her eyes hold mine.

"Rika!" Belle hisses. "Do something!"

I snap to attention, reacting instinctively. I unbuckle my seat belt, throw the car door open, and catapult myself in front of Grace Kimura.

And for the second time today, I'm part of a unit of two people crashing into each other.

Only this time, I'm the one being crashed into.

Belle's and Rory's screams ring in my ears as Grace and I slam to the ground. I feel the impact of my backside on concrete and wince. She lands on top of me, and my arms fling themselves around her waist, as if trying to protect her.

Ow. I know how to brace my falls pretty well thanks to judo, but being unexpectedly knocked to the ground still hurts a whole hell of a lot.

Grace looms over me, her eyes searching my face. She looks like she's really panicking now, her breath quick and uneven.

She reaches out with shaky fingers and touches my face.

"Hey," I say, trying to sound comforting. "It's okay. You're okay. You . . ."

She shakes her head quickly, as if to indicate that she's definitely *not* okay. She leans in close to me and manages to push a single word from her lips, barely a whisper.

Then she slumps against me, passing out.

It all happens so fast, but it seems like time slows way down as Bodyguard Guy finally catches up to her and scoops up her limp form. Security guards for the parade are hot on his heels, and they swarm around him and Grace, blocking them from view.

"Rika-chan!" Belle is at my side, and she looks terrified. Rory's head pops up behind her. "Are you okay? Do you need a doctor? Should we take you to the hospital or call an ambulance?!"

I sit up slowly, totally dazed. I'm barely aware of the tears that have filled my eyes, and I don't register any of her questions. Because my brain has hooked itself onto one thing, and it's totally obsessing on this one thing, and there's no way anything else is getting in there.

Right before she passed out, Grace Kimura whispered one word.

It was my name.

FOUR

How does Grace Kimura know my name?

And why did she look at me like she'd seen an onryo—an extra-terrifying kind of Japanese ghost?

The whole thing is just too weird.

I replay the beyond-bizarre sequence from the parade as I make my way down the street to Suehiro, one of the prime sources of Japanese comfort food in Little Tokyo. My family's decided they want takeout (or, to be more precise, *Auntie Och* decided, waving a commanding hand at the rest of us and declaring, "I make katsu all day for parade-goers and then what happen? Bananas Hollywood lady make a scene, everyone lose their appetite. Someone else cook tonight, ne?"). I volunteered to go get it. I was kind of trying to get away from Auntie Suzy, who was *not* happy about the fact that I'd totally disobeyed her and gotten myself wrapped up in some sort of disruptive parade drama on top of it all. Definitely not "respectable." Definitely calling the wrong kind of attention to myself and rocking the boat.

If there's one thing Auntie Suzy hates, it's rocking the boat.

After Grace and Bodyguard Guy were swarmed by security, the parade was cut unceremoniously short. I'd thought Belle might sulk about her reign as queen getting overshadowed. Instead she'd been overly worried about me, attaching herself to my side and making concerned clucking sounds about how I needed to go to the hospital. I kept saying I was fine. I'd just have some bruises in really interesting places.

Because the judo demonstration never actually happened, Auntie Suzy never found out about my ruse—she bought my lie that I'd had a change of heart about being a princess. I'm disappointed to have missed my chance to impress the UCLA scout, and if this were an ordinary day, I'd be obsessing over it.

But it's *not* an ordinary day, and I have other things to obsess over.

I can't stop thinking of that moment when Grace locked eyes with me, her movie star persona giving way to something less polished. She'd looked almost . . . feral. And then she'd uttered those two syllables.

Rika.

I rewind the scene further in my mind, going back to the Belle-instigated flash mob. Grace turning to look at us: impressed with Belle, charmed by Rory. Her gaze finding me.

I frown, homing in on those brief few seconds. *That's* when her whole expression changed. When her dazzling smile vanished. It was when she saw me. She leapt from her car, bulldozed her way through an entire dance troupe, and ruined the whole parade because she was trying to get to *me.*

Why?

My brain simply can't wrap itself around what this could possibly mean.

I arrive at the restaurant and push the door open, the bell jangling in what usually sounds like a friendly greeting. Tonight it sounds different. Almost . . . creepy? Maybe because Suehiro is uncharacteristically deserted. It's usually packed on weekends. But everyone seems to have fled Little Tokyo post-parade.

I nod at the Auntie behind the counter. She recognizes me, gives me a curt nod back, and bustles to the kitchen to retrieve my order. I instinctively pull my phone out of my pocket, but realize I don't want to look at it. Eliza's been texting me all day—she, of course, saw all the social media pics with Grace crashing into me and is demanding to know what's going on. Sensei Mary has also been texting me, wanting to know if I'm okay and if I'll be at practice tomorrow.

I don't know what to text back. For some reason, when I think of anything involving the dojo, I feel so *guilty*. Like I was part of ruining the parade and am therefore responsible for the demonstration not happening, which was probably embarrassing for Sensei Mary and may have ruined . . . well, not just my chance to be seen by the UCLA scout but also *Eliza's* chance.

I also don't want to look at my phone because the Grace Kimura Incident has blown all the way up on social media, shaky phone-camera footage of her leaping from the car playing its way across all platforms. Someone managed to zoom in and get a close-up of her distressed face, mouth half open, hair flying everywhere. Her reps haven't commented yet, but of course everyone's speculating about what caused her to fling herself into the chaos of an in-progress parade.

Does the squeaky-clean rom-com queen have a secret drug problem?

Is she cracking under the pressure of the new movie?

Was it just, like, heatstroke?

Seeing the images from today juxtaposed against so

much breathless #discourse . . . I don't want to look at that. Weirdly, when I replay what happened in my mind, it feels private. Like Grace Kimura and I were suddenly the only two people in the world and experienced a brief moment of pure mind-meld. Even with the mob around us, I was the only one who heard her whisper my name.

I haven't told anyone about that part. What would I say? *Grace Kimura knows my name and looked completely freaked out at the mere sight of me! Yay!*

It's even weirder since, you know, I've never really cared about any of her movies. She should have had that mind-meld moment with Belle or Rory.

But Grace said "Rika."

I stuff the phone back in my pocket and cross the room to Suehiro's massive photo collage. Through the years, the restaurant's owners have taped a wide assortment of Little Tokyo snapshots to one wall. No frames, no explanatory text, and no discernable organizational system involved. The photos go back so far, however, that the wall has ended up being a kind of unofficial historical chronicle of the neighborhood. It looks to me like a wild, unkempt garden of images.

My eyes wander over the photos, some of them shiny and new, some of them faded and disintegrating around the corners. There's a snapshot of a little boy cramming taiyaki into his mouth, his eyes lit with glee. A worn photo of an elderly couple sitting side by side on the plaza—not touching, but giving each other a tender sidelong look that makes you feel the warmth of their companionship. It's that thing I always see when I look at Belle and Rory bonding, at my Aunties being all romantic. That connection and sense of belonging to each other.

And of course there are so many shots of Nikkei Week, smiling faces and the kaleidoscope of bright colors that is the parade. A particular color catches my eye, a flash of vivid orange. My gaze skitters to that photo. It's near the top right-hand corner of the wall, nearly covered by the other photos that have been taped around it.

It almost seems to give off a little extra shimmer, as if calling to me.

Two teenage girls beam at me from the photo, arms around each other. They're both wearing brightly colored yukata—it's the orange yukata on one of the girls that's caught my eye. I've looked at this wall collage thousands of times and that orange has never stood out to me before. It probably wouldn't have stood out to me *ever* . . . except that I was wearing the exact same color today. The fabric is identical, down to the intricate pattern of intertwining blue and yellow flowers. I'm pretty sure that *is* my yukata. Or Auntie Suzy's yukata. Most of her vintage kimono and yukata were inherited from various distant branches of the family. Maybe this is one of them?

I'm so laser-focused on the yukata, it takes me a minute to actually look at the girl's face.

When I do, my mouth goes dry.

How . . . can this be? How . . .

I swallow, trying to regain my bearings. I stare at the photo harder, willing it to give me answers. But it's so high up, I can't make out every detail. I am suddenly consumed by the desperate desire to see the photo up close, to be able to study it. To have just one thing today *make sense.*

I *need* to see more.

Normally I'd never even think of disrupting Suehiro's seating arrangement—the silent, judgy wrath of the Aunties is not something I want to be on the receiving end of. But all of that is overwhelmed by my need to see more of this photo. I don't think I've wanted something this much in my entire life.

So I grab a chair that's pushed into one of the tables, my hands shaking as I drag it over to the photo wall. The chair squeaks against the cheap plastic of the floor—a noise made all the more ominous by the restaurant's eerie quiet. The only other sound in the place is my labored breathing. I consider myself in pretty decent shape, but my need to see this photo ratchets up my nerves, makes my heart beat faster.

I climb on top of the chair and stand on my tiptoes, reaching out to graze my fingertips against the photo. Now that I'm closer, I can see it more clearly. And the thing that sparked my need to see it up close becomes all the more real.

The teenage girl on the left is *most definitely* a young Grace Kimura.

She's not quite Grace Kimura, Movie Star, yet—her hair is a long, unstyled thicket, falling artlessly to her waist. Her front teeth are a little crooked. And she's not wearing a speck of makeup. But the brilliance of her smile, the way it draws you right in, that undeniable charisma— that's all there. You can see the future Grace Kimura she will become.

It feels like my heart has dropped into my shoes, and I get all light-headed. I rest my hand against the wall to keep myself from toppling off the chair and crashing into the carefully laid out table setups—that would *really* make the Aunties mad.

The answer to the question in my head is floating around me in pieces. But I'm suddenly too scared to put them together.

I'm staring at Grace so intently, I almost don't see the other girl in the photo. When my eyes finally slide to her, I get the last piece I need.

"Rika-chan?"

I let out a high-pitched squeak of alarm, my heart catapulting into my throat, and whirl around to see the Auntie bustling in from the kitchen with my food. She gives me a quizzical look, her brows drawing together as she takes in the image of me perched precariously on a chair for no apparent reason.

"I was just, uh, checking something," I say, flashing her a bright smile.

She frowns but doesn't inquire further, facing the register to ring me up. While her back is turned, I snatch the photo from the wall and stuff it in my pocket.

I clamber down and put the chair back where I found it, taking extra pains to make sure it's aligned exactly right. Then I pay and hurry out of there, barely noticing that the Auntie is already readjusting the chair and tsk-ing at me under her breath.

Once I'm back out on the street, I pull the photo out of my pocket so I can stare at it some more. But all my staring doesn't change what the photo's telling me.

The other girl in the photo is Auntie Suzy. She must've been in her early twenties at this point, but she still looks like a teenager. The way she and Grace Kimura are embracing is undeniably sisterly—it reminds me of Belle and Rory. And Grace is wearing the very same yukata I was wearing today . . .

My phone buzzes in my pocket, and I yank it free, jamming it to my ear.

"Hello—"

"Rika!" Belle shrieks on the other end. "Where are you?! You left forever ago, and I'm worried you passed out because of your *injuries* and fell into a ditch and *died*—"

"There are no ditches in Little Tokyo!" Rory yells. They sound like they're on speaker. "And if she was dead, she wouldn't have answered her phone!"

"I'm not dead!" I squeak. "And I'm not in a ditch. And . . ." I pause and take a deep breath, the truth of the photo sinking into my bones. I can't stop myself from blurting it out. "I think Grace Kimura is my mother."

FIVE

"Get in here." Rory grabs my free hand and tows me inside, her face scrunched into a look of extreme determination. "Belle's creating a diversion," she hisses as I slip my shoes off and she leads me down the hall toward our living room.

"A diversion?" I say. In spite of my current state of total confusion about . . . well, *so many things*, I can't help but smile a little. Rory's in what Belle and I call Super Sleuth Girl Detective mode—so single-minded in her pursuit of whatever goal has captured her fancy that she starts going all Nancy Drew and shit.

"Yes." Rory gives me a curt nod as she continues stomping down the hall. "So we can have a *Sister Conference*."

"You didn't tell the Aunties, right?" I say, momentary worry skittering through me.

After I'd given Belle and Rory a blabbery, incoherent version of my conclusions over the phone, they'd told me to come home immediately so we could discuss. But I'd insisted they not say anything to Auntie Suzy and Auntie Och, because . . . well. I didn't even know where to begin.

I mean, if my theory's correct, Auntie Suzy has basically lied to me all my life about who my mother is and, you know, the fact that she *isn't dead*, and—

Ugh.

I can't think about any of this without my brain spiraling in a million different directions, my kaiju-temper threatening to flare up and destroy everything around me. No, I can't ask the Aunties about this yet. I feel like I'll *explode.*

"Hi, Moms!" Rory says loudly, stomping her way into the living room. "Rika's back. She has food."

Auntie Suzy and Auntie Och look up from their respective TV trays. Since our living room is also our dining room, everyone has their own TV tray, although we're not actually allowed to watch TV during dinner (an issue Rory vehemently protests every chance she gets). I meet Auntie Suzy's gaze and immediately look away. All I see now is that girl from the photo, smiling like she doesn't have a care in the world.

"Leave food here," Auntie Och says, tapping her TV tray. "Belle-chan needs you. She's in her room."

"Needs . . . me?" I say, my voice tipping up at the end.

"She is having some kind of crisis," Auntie Suzy says,

her brows drawing together. "A teenage crisis. That she couldn't talk to us about."

"So dramatic, ne?" Auntie Och says with a snort. "Everything is crisis. When I was younger, we shove it down, act like everything is okay. Then started plotting revenge on whoever wronged us."

"Come on," Rory tugs my sleeve, waggling her eyebrows at me meaningfully. They're bouncing up and down so much, they look like overcaffeinated caterpillars.

Oh—this must be Belle's *diversion*. So we can have a Sister Conference. Or Sister-Cousin Who Just Found Out Her Mom Is Possibly Alive and Also Possibly One of the Most Famous Movie Stars on the Planet Conference.

I allow Rory to drag me down another narrow hall in our apartment, to Belle's bedroom. Belle whips the door open just as we arrive. Nak comes trotting up to me, barking his tiny head off. He's wearing a pink doggie sweatsuit that's identical to the human-sized one Belle is wearing— probably part of an Instagram shoot. Belle is on a quest to make her dog an influencer and nobody's going to stop her. Except maybe Nak himself, who objects to the multitude of outfits and photo shoots his would-be stardom seems to involve. Even now, he stops barking for a second to gnaw at his sweatsuit's tiny sleeve.

"God, Rika!" Belle exclaims, pulling me and Rory inside and slamming the door behind us. "Rory and I had to work overtime to make the moms believe you hadn't been murdered or something. And then we had to set everything up *just right*."

"Set everything up for what?" I say. "I thought we were just going to talk—"

"Mostly, yes," Rory says, her eyes darting back and forth. "I have to go do one thing."

"I'm not even going to ask," I say, slumping on the bed as she stomps out of the room.

"Let me see," Belle says, holding out a hand.

I fish the photo out of my pocket and hand it to her. Her eyes get all big.

"Holy shit," she says. "That is totally Grace Kimura. And *Mom*."

She stares at the photo for a moment, her expression shifting as her world adjusts. After all, this means Auntie Suzy lied to her, too. Unless . . .

"You didn't know about this, did you?" I demand.

"Rika-chan." Belle's face goes deathly serious, and she sets the photo to the side. "Of course not. I would *never*." She reaches over to the nightstand and grabs the family iPad—a gadget of questionable repute that Auntie Och won in an eBay auction. Nak, apparently forgiving her for trying to make him a star, snuggles up next to her. "Also, do you really think I'd be able to keep my cool over the fact that I might be related to Grace Kimura?"

"Point," I murmur as she unlocks the screen.

It is weird, though, the way the whole family is obsessed with Grace Kimura. Did Auntie Suzy do that on purpose—like, get Belle and Rory way into those rom-coms at a young age so she could follow her sister's illustrious career? Does Auntie Och know about this, even? I mean, she must . . .

I guess that explains why my mother's death was so shrouded in secrecy, why there was no funeral, why it was like she *just disappeared*. Because she did just disappear—only to be reborn as Asian America's sweetheart.

What the hell?

I can't even begin to think of the level of *planning* that went into this. Maybe Auntie Suzy is a witch after all.

"Okay," Belle says, gesturing to the iPad. Her expression has shifted again—now she's all business. "We need to discuss your future."

"My *what*?" I look at the screen. Belle has assembled an Insta-worthy aesthetic collage of Grace Kimura photos. Grace in one of her most famous movie roles, running through the rain, eyes full of fake tears. Grace on the red carpet with a posse of other Asian American movie stars, smiling her most dazzling smile. Grace done up for a photo shoot as an actual princess, tiara sparkling against her raven hair.

These photos orbit the main attraction, though—a giant photo of me that Belle has placed in the center. She of course couldn't find one where I'm smiling or even making a borderline attractive face. I'm looking at something off to the side, my face twisted into a scowl. I am the grouchy sun in this thoroughly weird solar system.

That has not stopped Belle from photoshopping a tiny crown onto my head.

"Rika," Belle breathes, her voice reverent. "Don't you see what this means? You're *Hollywood royalty*. An actual princess. Which is hilarious, since you're so opposed to all things princess—"

"Yes, 'hilarious' is definitely the word I would use," I mutter.

"Grace is going to bring you into her world, you'll be swept into the upper echelons of Asian Hollywood," Belle crows. "*That's* your happily ever after!"

Her eyes are lit with glee as she runs her bright pink nails over the collage, and I know she's picturing all of this in her head, the sequence unspooling like the third act of her favorite movie. My skin airbrushed, my eyes wide and shiny with happy tears, my wardrobe suddenly brimming with fancy designers and diamond-encrusted headwear.

Before I can ponder that further, Rory stomps back in and triumphantly waves something over her head.

"Found it," she says. "Proof."

She marches over to the bed and inserts herself between Belle and me, passing me the two scraps of paper clasped in her hand. Nak grunts in protest, resettling himself.

One of the scraps is another faded photo—teenage Grace again, not much older than she is in the picture I stole from Suehiro. But this time she's wearing a blah hospital gown instead of a yukata, and she's holding a tiny smoosh-faced baby. She's still smiling, though, that Grace Kimura dazzle on display even though she looks tired around the eyes. The other is a crumbling piece of paper that appears to be my birth certificate.

And right there in the MOTHER column? Grace Rakuyama. Because of course Grace was once a Rakuyama, like us.

I feel light-headed again, the letters and numbers on the certificate blurring in and out.

"Where did you find this?" I finally manage.

"The locked drawer where Ma Och keeps her weed

stash," Rory says, sitting up proudly. "I taught myself
how to pick all the locks in her dresser last week. Figured that most forbidden drawer is where the moms keep
their most top secret documents."

"Nice work, Aurora," Belle says, giving her an appre-
ciative nod. "Now that we've determined the facts, we
need to talk about Rika's future."

"My *future*?" I spit out, my voice twisting on that
last syllable. "Y'all, this is not . . . *not* . . ."

I shake my head, frustration welling in my chest. How
do they not get that this isn't some kind of fun game for
me? It's not a mystery for Sleuth Rory to solve. A fairy
tale for Queen Belle to preside over. It's learning that my
entire existence is a lie. That the foundation of my life is
something totally different than what I thought it was.

It feels like there's an earthquake in my heart.

Once again, that wall goes up between me and my
sisters. Cousins.

They're exchanging looks now, looks that say they
don't understand why I'm freaking out, but they know
they have to play it cool. They have to *handle* me, because
I'm being difficult, as usual. Their undeniable connection
snaps into place. They belong, as always, to each other,
and communicate all of this through their sister telepathy.

"I don't want to be a Hollywood princess," I say, trying to make my voice measured, even. Still, it cracks. "I just want to . . ." To what? I gnaw on my lower lip, considering.

"To talk to her, right?" Rory says. "Get all the answers about the mystery of your existence."

"Something like that," I mumble.

"Then let's figure that out," Belle says, her demeanor back to all business. She gives me a sidelong look, like she's trying to gauge my reaction. She still doesn't understand why I'm freaking out. I guess if Belle found out Grace Kimura was her mother, she'd be too busy celebrating and posting Insta collages to think about anything else.

"Hmm," Belle says. "That's odd."

"What?" Rory leans over, peering at the iPad in Belle's lap. Belle has navigated away from her Asian Hollywood Royalty collage and is now tapping her way through various social apps so fast, her fingertips are a blur.

"All of Grace's feeds are gone," Belle says, her eyebrows drawing together. "No Insta, no Twitter. The usernames don't exist anymore."

"Maybe her, uh, people took them down," I say. "After today's disaster, doesn't it make sense to go dark on social?"

"Go dark, yes," Belle says, tapping her way over to TMZ. "But usually that means posting a hiatus message and leaving it be. Maybe locking, if you want to get extreme. But not deleting entirely." Her brow furrows further as she scrolls through various news stories and paparazzi footage. "Even weirder: Grace's reps still haven't issued a statement. No one's seen her since she fainted at the parade."

"So she's missing?" Rory says, her eyes widening at the hint of yet another mystery.

"Probably just lying low, but all of this is bizarre," Belle says. "There should have been a statement by now, at the very least. Something about how she was exhausted and the sun got to her and she's resting, can everyone please respect her privacy at this time. Blah, blah, et cetera."

As she and Rory continue discussing the particulars of this weirdness, I take the iPad from Belle and focus on the story she's pulled up. It features a single photo from earlier in the day, someone's phone camera shot blown way up. It's actually pretty clear—maybe one of the dancers took it? Grace has that wild woman look again, her eyes desperate, her hair swirling around her.

I flash back to right before Grace collided with me,

her eyes locking with mine. That moment when I felt so connected to her. Like we were communicating with our own version of telepathy.

I have to find her, I realize. Even if she's lying low, even if she's gone into hiding, even if she's deleted all her social accounts and wants to pretend like Grace Kimura, Movie Star, doesn't exist.

And not just to unravel the mystery of my past. I have to find her because for that brief moment when her eyes locked with mine, I felt a flash of connection with another person that was so powerful, it brought tears to my eyes. Maybe, like me, she doesn't belong to anyone.

Maybe we could belong to each other.

Once upon a time, a peasant girl lived in the quaint village of Little Tokyo. She was a tragic orphan, an oddity people whispered and gossiped about. She tried to blend in as best she could and to perform various tasks as a dutiful member of her remaining family. Then, one day, she discovered her mother was in fact a beautiful and beloved queen, and the peasant was orphaned no more. There was much rejoicing throughout the village, and the peasant felt that perhaps she had finally found answers to questions she'd harbored all her life.

However, the queen suddenly disappeared without a trace, not even having the courtesy to leave an away message or a forwarding address or an "on hiatus" tweet.

Seriously, what the hell, Mom?

SIX

I've come up with the worst plan ever.

I should have known it was the worst plan ever, because it hit me at like three a.m., well after Belle, Rory, and I had exhausted every other possibility. We'd tried calling Grace's agency—no answer, it was the middle of the night on a Saturday. We'd scoured the internet for further hints—but Grace was still MIA, no statements from anyone, just tons of speculation, most of it involving some form of rehab. Belle started a #WheresGrace hashtag and got it to trend locally. But even with her infinite Belle powers, we hadn't gotten any clues as to where Grace had gone.

I'd tried to sleep, but it was impossible, and I'd ended up staring into the darkness. My bedroom is covered in various drawings Rory and I had done of yokai— Japanese monsters—when we were goofing around one afternoon, and I couldn't help but think they were gazing back at me, trying to help.

So I'd gotten my phone out and scoured the internet *again*, trying to find some morsel — *any* morsel — that would lead me closer to Grace Kimura. I'd come across a lot of articles about her latest movie: another big, splashy rom-com called *We Belong* that was set to come out next summer. They were almost done filming, but Grace was still on the job, still had a few more weeks of shooting to go.

Said movie is the one co-starring Mr. Not a Vandal, Hank Chen — who my extensive research tells me is seventeen, the same age as Belle and me. He's nabbed himself a "potentially scene-stealing" role as Grace's irrepressible younger brother. Much is being made of the fact that this is Hank's first "real" acting role, the first time he'll have to do something other than look cute, smile, and dance. It's apparently kind of a surprise that he got the role in the first place, and the more uncharitable entertainment gossip sites are salivating at the idea that he's about to totally mess up and make a giant fool of himself and be banished to endless rounds of being a coach on *Dance! Off!* before fading into the obscurity reserved for all the Disney kids and boy band stars who never manage to shed their former image.

My brain hooked into this part of the Grace Kimura saga, and it was ultimately the genesis of my terrible plan. It led me to looking up Hank's Instagram and sending him a delirious-sounding three a.m. message, and that's why he's now sitting across from me in a cramped booth at Katsu That, my Aunties' katsu restaurant.

I have to admit: when I woke up this morning feeling less delirious, I thought there was no way I'd hear back from him.

But here he is.

He still looks too cute, that bit of inherent smugness impossible to suppress. But there's something less assured about him today—a wariness that creeps into his dark eyes every now and then. Or maybe people just look different when you're not crashing headfirst into them and getting all tangled up in your own yukata.

An unexpected warmth flashes over my skin as I think back to our meeting the day before. I shake it off.

"So explain this to me," Hank says. "You need to find Grace Kimura because—?"

I fold my hands on the table and school my features into what I hope is a starstruck look.

"Because I am *definitely* her biggest fan ever, and when she ran into me yesterday at the parade, her bracelet got caught on my yukata and I need to get it back to her. And it would be amazing to really meet her, you know? Without the crashing-into-each-other part."

He stares at me for a moment, studying me intently. Then he lets out that laugh again, the one that's snort-adjacent.

"That," he says, "is the biggest load of bullshit I've ever heard."

"Excuse you—" I huff, indignant.

"You are an interesting person and a terrible liar," he interrupts, cocking one of those too-cute eyebrows. "You were so insistent yesterday about not being a princess. And anyone who's that averse to being called a princess is most definitely *not* a Grace Kimura fan. She's princessdom personified."

"Really?" I say, a little too quickly. Something stabs at me, a burst of pure longing. "What's she like? I mean, in real life."

"Oh no," he says, raising a finger. A bit of that mischief has crept back into his eyes, that infuriating smugness on full display. Like he's just so *amused* by everything. "You are not getting any more information out of me until you tell me what this is *actually* about."

Auntie Och chooses this moment to slam two steaming plates of katsu down in front of us. Mine is a fairly traditional pork cutlet, but Hank's gone for the experimental side of the menu: cheese katsu. Kind of like a big mozzarella stick. My eyes go instinctively to the food, the freshly fried panko bread crumbs glistening in the light. Mmm.

"Here. Eat," Auntie Och says, waving a hand and giving Hank a suspicious look. I told her he was a "friend from school" and that we were working on an extra credit summer project together. Auntie Och's eyesight is just bad enough, I hope she won't recognize him from all of Rory's *Dance! Off!* viewing.

"Arigato," Hank says, with a perfect accent. Rolled r and everything. Show-off.

"Ah, good boy, speak Japanese," Auntie Och says, her suspicious gaze turning to something more curious. "You not Japanese, though, ne?" Her eyes narrow as she scrutinizes him. "Filipino?"

"Filipino-Chinese mix," he says, grinning at her.

"Mmm, a mutt like Rika," Auntie Och says. It is unclear from her tone whether this is a good thing or not. Then she sweeps away from the table with no other pleasantries.

"This looks great," Hank says, inhaling the fragrant, greasy steam wafting off the katsu. "Good god. I haven't had carbs in *months*." He glances around surreptitiously—like, what, he's expecting paparazzi at Katsu That? Then he very carefully picks up a piece of katsu with his chopsticks, the cheese oozing out of its panko shell as he pops it into his mouth. "So," he continues, gnawing on his katsu. I try not to stare at the little bit of cheese that gets stuck to the corner of his mouth—or the striking fullness of his lips, the way the lower one is just a little bit fuller than the other. Even his imperfections are interesting to look at.

Not that I'm interested. In anything.

"You were saying?" Hank says, making a "go on" kind of gesture with his chopsticks.

"Right." I assess him, trying to block out the imperfect perfection of his features and get a read on his gullibility. What lie can I tell that will get him to help me? What lie would the nure-onna tell? What lie will be *believable*?

Then I realize: the freaking *truth* isn't believable. So I might as well go with that.

"Hank—"

"Henry."

I blink. "What?"

"Henry. Is my actual name. When I was starting out, my reps thought Hank sounded more . . ." He gestures vaguely with his chopsticks.

"Henry," I say. I don't know why, but this tiny change seems to focus him. Like he just got a little bit clearer before my eyes or someone removed the Instagram filter or something. "I think Grace Kimura is my mother," I continue. "Like, I think she had me as a teenager and then left me with her sister and it was all a big secret and . . . well, I don't know the rest. Because of the big-secret part. That's why I need to find her."

I tell him about yesterday's discoveries in a garbled burst, my katsu getting cold in front of me as I recap what happened, the evidence Rory found in Auntie Och's weed drawer. Everything we think we know—which isn't much. I show him the photos of Auntie Suzy and Grace, of Grace and me when I was a baby. And some more recent pictures on my phone of Auntie Suzy, to really sell it.

"See," I say, jabbing an index finger at a current photo of Auntie Suzy that I've positioned next to the picture I stole from Suehiro. "This is obviously the same person. So—"

"You don't need to show me all this stuff—I believe you," he says, waving a hand.

I blink at him again. "You do?"

He flashes me that easy grin. "Like I said, you're a terrible liar. These sound like the first true words you've said to me since we met."

I bristle. "That is *not* true—"

"So you really are the Citizens Patrol of Little Tokyo?" His grin widens. Ugh, so very annoying. "I do have one question, though." He rests his elbows on the table and leans forward, meeting my eyes. "How has the truth of Grace's identity remained a secret for this long? Has no one else in Little Tokyo recognized her? Because she still looks"—he taps the photo of young Grace—"so *her*."

I lean back in my seat, considering. "That's part of this whole mystery, I guess. But to be honest—Little Tokyo has a lot of secrets. And people keeping *each other's* secrets. Grace getting pregnant when she did was probably seen as shameful. If she was, like, banished or something, and then went on to become one of the most successful and beloved Japanese American celebrities on the planet . . ."

"Then no one would want to admit they'd banished her in the first place," Hank—er, Henry—says, pointing at me with his chopsticks. "Yeah, I gotcha—shame, duty, family, community secrets. I'm familiar with all of these things thanks to growing up in not one but *two* Asian cultures. Do you think everybody's just pretending they don't recognize her?"

"Maybe," I say. "But the more pressing issue at the moment is that it seems like Grace has dropped off the face of the earth. And I really need to find her. I know you guys did that movie together, so . . . have you talked to her? Since yesterday?"

Henry takes his sweet time answering. He pops another bite of cheese katsu in his mouth. Sets down his chopsticks. Brushes away that wavy lock of hair that keeps falling over his eyes. Looks at me in a considering way, like he's trying to figure out if what I just told him is also a big ol' load of bullshit.

"No," he finally says, drawing the word out slowly (which makes me stare a little too long at his mouth again). "I came to the parade to show her some support—my part of the movie's wrapped, and I haven't seen her in a couple weeks. She did check in once last night with Asian Hollywood—"

"Asian . . . Hollywood?" I sputter, leaning in, trying to make sure I heard him right. "That's a thing?"

"Oh yeah," he says, cracking his charming smile. "We have a group chat." He brandishes his phone. "Grace is usually on it a lot, actually. She's Chiitan."

I shake my head. "What?"

"Chiitan—the otter mascot from Japan? The one who's always doing those wild stunts? That's her avatar." He shows me the phone screen, featuring a cascade of tiny avatars. One of them does indeed look like a cartoon otter wearing a devilish expression and a pink turtle for a hat. "She checked in late last night," he continues. "Said she was okay and she didn't want any of us to worry, but she has to go off the grid for a bit. I dunno how they're working that out with the movie since she's got a couple weeks of shooting left, but yeah."

"And you just *believed her*?" I shake my head again. "What if she's been kidnapped or something?! What if that's her captor feeding you *lies*—"

"Whoa, what's with the instant conspiracy theorizing?" He holds up his hands. "Or is this another one of your Citizens Patrol duties? She actually sent us this secret code we came up with in the group—the one that means 'I'm okay.' It's a code no nefarious kidnapper could ever hope to get out of her."

"And that is . . . ?"

He raises an eyebrow. Amused again. "A secret. Hence the name 'secret code.' "

"Wh-why does Asian Hollywood need a secret code?" I say. "Is kidnapping that much of a regular occurrence?"

"It's usually used in more mundane situations," Henry says, chuckling a little. "It's like a shorthand. Say you're out at an event and some garbage story with big scandal potential breaks—like that you're having an affair or your public meltdown was caught on camera or the paparazzi got a horribly unflattering photo of you cramming an entire Egg McMuffin down your throat—"

"*That's* a scandal?!" I scoff.

He hesitates, something passing over his face that I can't quite get a handle on. It's the ghost of a shadow, a flicker of . . . uncertainty, maybe? No, that can't be right. This boy has nothing to be uncertain about—that is the one thing I *am* sure of. Then he shrugs and presses on.

"Just an example. So anyway, everyone in that group is about to start spamming up the thread with 'Are you okay?!' messages. Instead of typing back some long-ass reassurance, you send that one little code word. This is also useful if you need to go off the grid and don't feel like getting into all the gory details—but also want to make sure people aren't worried about you. Seems like that's what Grace is doing." He shrugs again and pops the last bite of katsu into his mouth.

I crumple my napkin in my fist in frustration, curling my fingers tightly around it, feeling it get all hot against my palm.

"But still," I say, "don't you want to make *sure*? If she's your friend and all?"

"She needs to do her own thing right now. I'm giving her space to do that. As a true friend would." He flashes me a genial grin, and I ball my fist more tightly around the napkin. How can this infuriating stranger remain so *calm*?

My kaiju-temper claws at my insides, heat rising in my cheeks. He's acting like this is no big deal, like for me it isn't *the biggest deal ever.* I flash back to his easy smile from yesterday, me thinking about how *everything* must be easy for him. Is this how you act when it's all just that easy for you, like you don't have to worry about the fact that the mother you've imagined as a hazy, lost figment all these years might possibly be . . . found?

What do I have to say to get him to help me, to find the one person in the world who might . . . might . . .

"Won't it be kind of disastrous for you if she *stays* MIA?" I press.

A ghost of a frown pulls at his lips. "What?"

"If she doesn't come back, if she decides she *likes* being off the grid," I say. "That movie you guys are doing—like you said, she's not done yet. They need her to finish it?"

"Yes—"

"What if she doesn't come back and they *can't* finish

it? It might never come out. And then you wouldn't get your shot, right?"

His brow crinkles like he's confused—but I can tell he knows what I mean.

"Your chance to prove yourself," I continue. "To show the world that you're more than a cute smile who can do the splits. If you are, in fact, more than a cute smile who can do the splits."

That last bit sounds snarkier than I intend it to, but I can tell it hits. He leans back in his seat, his brow creasing further. His smug, carefree facade has dropped entirely now, and he looks downright perplexed. Well, good. Maybe I got him to see how serious this is. For me *and* him.

"You know," he finally says, drawing each word out slowly, "you could've just asked for my help."

Now it's my turn to look perplexed. "What?"

He rests his chin on his hand, a hint of that self-assured smile returning. "You want to find your mom. That's a very understandable thing."

"But . . . I *said* that . . ."

"Right. And then you proceeded to run through various elaborate reasons why I should help you, like that maybe she was kidnapped or that helping her also helps my career ambitions—"

"You need a reason to help me, no?" I sit back in the booth, crossing my arms over my chest.

"Sure." His smile returns fully, and I try, yet again, not to stare at his mouth. It really is . . . at the peak of its power when he smiles like that. "But that reason could be a lot simpler than you're making it: you need help, I'm in a position to offer help. It's the right thing to do."

I am actually speechless. Is this "Aw, shucks, I'm just so *decent*" thing part of his aspiring Hollywood heartthrob persona?

"I'll help you," Henry says simply.

"Okaaay," I say, my eyes narrowing with suspicion. "And what do you want in return?"

He hesitates for a long moment, then finally says: "How about some more cheese katsu?"

"I can do that," I say.

"You remind me of her," he says abruptly.

I shake my head. "What?"

He leans in, his eyes searching my face. I squirm a little, even though it's not an intense kind of searching—more like he's trying to memorize my features, to map them to hers.

Hmm. Actually, that *is* kind of intense.

"You remind me of Grace," he says.

And goddammit, my eyes fill with unexpected tears.

"Because I'm angry?" I manage.

"Because you're *passionate*," he says. Then he gives me a mellow smile—as if he's trying to take us back to a casual vibe, as if he knows anything more is too much for me to take right now. "So, do we have a deal?"

I nod and gesture to Auntie Och to bring more katsu, blinking away my tears. I don't trust myself to speak.

I can't make whatever happens next mean anything less than everything.

SEVEN

You would think that what happens next would be super dramatic, stuffed full of intrigue and mystery.

Instead, smug-ass Henry Chen insists on butting in on the Nikkei Week mochi demonstration.

It's the day after our lunch at Katsu That. We left it like this: Henry would put some feelers out in Asian Hollywood to see if anyone had more information on Grace's whereabouts. I'd see if I could find anything in our apartment from the past, anything at all that might give me a clue about what happened all those years ago, when my mom fake-died. But Rory's super-sleuth lock-picking skills didn't yield any new information. The birth certificate and the photo appear to be the only remnants of Grace's presence on the apartment premises.

It's like Grace herself is the onryo, the ghost. She'd vanished into the mists of tragedy all those years ago, only to reemerge as something more powerful, ready to wreak vengeance on all who wronged her. Or that's what the onryo would do, anyway. I don't know what Grace would do. Because I still don't know my mother at all.

I didn't tell Belle and Rory about my new . . . hmm, I guess "partnership" with Henry. I just said I'm "making inroads with people connected to Grace" and we should still keep our investigation from the Aunties. They didn't protest, I think because their Nikkei Week court duties are now kicking into high gear.

Today is the mochi demonstration, wherein all the princesses gather in the big room connected to the garden at the Japanese American Community and Cultural Center, and Uncle Hikaru leads them in a demo of wrapping fresh mochi around blobs of anko—red bean paste—and then rolling it into balls.

The modest crowd that gathers is mostly old Aunties who relish telling the princesses they're doing it wrong, with a couple of white girls who are "so into Japanese culture" sprinkled in. I make a note to sit on the opposite side of the room so none of the Beckys will try to talk to me in loud, halting Japanese or ask me where I'm *really* from or explain why they just *feel* "so Asian" on the inside.

As I'm heading over to that side of the room, though, I notice yet another person I don't want to deal with— Craig Shimizu, the biggest asshole at Belle's and my school. Well, actually he graduated two years ago. These days he makes a lot of noise about going to "business school," but mostly he works for his father, who does some kind of fancy investment banking and heads up the Nikkei Week board—the committee that organizes, manages, and administers the festival every year. The Shimizus wield a lot of power in the community, and Craig likes to make sure everyone knows it.

He's actually the kid I bit in judo when I was eight, and I'm still not sorry (unlike Auntie Suzy, who reminded me once again that I needed to try my hardest to *not* rock the boat and *not* cause disruptions and *not* stand out in a bad way). That incident really kicked the Legend of Rika the Biter and Her Uncontrollable Kaiju-Temper into the stratosphere, tripling the intensity of all the disapproving looks and whispers that were already being thrown my way. Like Craig was some noble prince, unfairly attacked by a vicious monster.

I change course and scuttle to the very back of the room, wedging myself between two Aunties. Belle told me I should at least act like I'm participating in Nikkei Week activities so Auntie Suzy and Auntie Och don't get suspicious. So here I am. Participating.

Before things can even begin, Uncle Hikaru is pissed off at Belle because she's insisted on bringing Nak.

"No dogs," he says, slicing a hand through the air. "Unsanitary. Plus, no dogs allowed in the JACCC, period, so you're double breaking the rules, Belle Rakuyama."

"Nak is part of my royal entourage," Belle says, drawing herself up tall and pulling the dog more tightly to her chest. Nak lifts his nose in the air and stares Uncle Hikaru down, as if trying to prove Belle's point. "And I am the Nikkei Week *Queen*, am I not?"

I can't help but admire Belle's willingness—I mean, that's not even the right word, it's more like a *desire*—to make a complete spectacle of herself. And here I am trying to go to the shadows so my temper won't act up and destroy everything around it.

"Guh, fine," Uncle Hikaru snorts. "Just try to keep him hidden under the table. If any of the Nikkei Week board members come in here during our demonstration, I know nothing."

Great—Craig is *so* reporting this to his dad.

I hear disapproving mutterings among the audience of Aunties as Belle gives Uncle Hikaru a regal nod and settles in behind the long table that's been set up at the front of the room. Completely disregarding Uncle Hikaru's orders, she keeps Nak clutched to her chest, his little paws resting on the tabletop, precariously close to the blobs of mochi. Rory sits next to Belle, the rest of the court taking their places around her as Uncle Hikaru starts barking instructions.

"Mmm, our famous Hollywood grand marshal is a no-show," the Auntie next to me murmurs, frowning at the empty seat at the end of the table. "I *told* the Nikkei Week board not to choose some flighty actress. Not that they *ever* listen to me. And now look: she's disrespecting our traditions, hmm?"

"What do you think happened yesterday—nervous breakdown?" the Auntie on my other side says, talking over me like I'm not even there. "Mmm, I thought only white actresses had those."

"Who knows, but what happened was very disruptive," the first Auntie says.

And then both Aunties give me major side-eye. Like it's all my fault that the parade was disrupted.

In a way, I guess it *was* my fault. But they don't know the whole story. Still, I find myself shrinking into my seat, trying to disappear.

"Some people are like that, always disrupting things," the second Auntie says, her side-eye intensifying. I shrink even more. "Are they gonna appoint someone else? We can't have no grand marshal! It's Nikkei Week!"

"No one's asked me what I think," the first Auntie sniffs. "But they should replace her. How will it look if we have no grand marshal at the gala?"

Nikkei Week always ends with a big gala at the Japanese American National Museum, and the grand marshal is expected to give a speech and take photos with everyone. But now that the grand marshal's MIA . . .

"This year's Nikkei Week is cursed," a loud, braying voice at the end of the row says.

I swivel to look—and inwardly let out a huge groan. Somehow, Craig Shimizu must have sensed my presence and the fact that I was trying to get away from him and has moved so he's sitting closer to me.

"Didn't everyone read that letter Uncle Taki wrote to the paper?" Craig continues, naming one of the cranky old men who seems to have lived in Little Tokyo forever—no one knows where he came from or who he's related to, but everyone knows him all the same. "He said only pure Japanese girls should be Nikkei Week Princesses. Because Nikkei Week is a festival that's supposed to celebrate everything *Japanese*."

"Japanese and Japanese *American*," I blurt out without thinking, my temper flaring. So much for shrinking. Now the Aunties are side-eyeing me again.

"And Japanese American can mean a lot of things. Anyway, what does that have to do with anything? Belle is one hundred percent Japanese."

"She's related to *you*," Craig counters, his sneer deepening. "And you're only half. Therefore, she's tainted by association."

"Uncle Taki writes that same letter *every year*," I snap. "My Auntie Och says he does it because it's something to do—otherwise he's got *nothing* to do except boil so much fish that his white neighbors complain about the smell."

"My dad says your Aunties or moms or whatever are living in several kinds of sin," Craig says, latching on to something else he can needle me about. "So—"

"So *shut up!*" I explode, leaping to my feet. My hands curl into fists, my face flushes bright red, my kaiju-temper *roars*—

Craig regards me smugly, a sly grin spreading over his face. Because he's gotten to me, *really* gotten to me, and that's all he wanted. He leans back in his seat, his grin getting wider by the second. "Machigai," he murmurs—the Japanese word for "mistake." "Your whole family." He jerks his chin toward Belle. "Maybe you *all* should be banned from Nikkei Week."

"Do *not* talk about my family," I snarl, my fists curling so tight, I can feel my fingernails scratching tiny crevices into my palms. "You listen to me, Craig Shimizu, if you ruin this for Belle and Rory, I will *end* you—"

"Ahem. Rika Rakuyama. Please stop whatever you are doing." Uncle Hikaru clears his throat and glares at me.

The Aunties are also glaring at me.

Even Belle is glaring at me from her perch up front.

Stop, she mouths at me.

I breathe deeply, forcing my temper to quiet. When it just *explodes* like that, it feels like it's consuming my entire body, burning me up from the inside. I lose all awareness of my surroundings, which means I didn't notice how loud my voice was getting or how the room has gone totally quiet and everyone is staring at me.

That's exactly what it was like when I bit Craig all those years ago. I could only feel *rage*, and before I knew it, my teeth were sinking into his forearm.

The second Auntie's words echo in my head: *Some people are like that, always disrupting things.*

Face still flaming, I sit down in my seat again, trying to make myself small. I picture myself as the nure-onna, strategically stowing her anger away so she can strike when it makes sense.

Everyone goes back to whatever they were doing—

Uncle Hikaru yelling orders at the princesses, the Aunties casting judgmental looks his way, the princesses valiantly attempting perfect mochi. But I already know this *incident* will spread through the gossip grapevine of Little Tokyo, yet another unruly blowup from Rika the Biter.

I only hope Belle won't be too mad at me for ruining one of her queenly moments.

My gaze wanders to the garden connected to the room. I've loved this garden since I was a kid, its bristly shrubs and stout rock formations offering so many of those magical shadows for me to sink into. I try to mentally sink into them now, to breathe deeply and calm myself.

One time when I was twelve, I snuck in while the garden was technically closed, nestled myself under the twisting limbs of the biggest tree—I'm not sure what kind it is, but it's always looked to me like it came from another world, its long flowering branches flowing to the ground and forming an enchanted canopy to hide beneath. I sat there and read about onryo well into the night—until Auntie Och hunted me down and yelled at me for disappearing without telling anyone and nearly giving Auntie Suzy a heart attack.

I'd been swept up in my stories—I was fascinated by the fact that so many onryo were women, so many of them were truly wronged in life, and so many ended the story by getting the vengeance they sought. Their long, tangled waves of hair reminded me of the branches of the big canopy tree, flowing and curving in all different directions, wild and unrestrained. From then on, I referred to that tree as "the onryo tree."

And it's still one of my favorite hiding spots, honestly. It absorbs my temper like nothing else.

I'm so caught up in thinking about the tree and onryo and how Grace is her own kind of onryo that I don't even notice when freaking Henry Chen sneaks up behind me and whisper-yells, *"Hey!"* in my ear.

"Blagh!" I yelp, nearly jumping out of my seat.

Uncle Hikaru shoots me another admonishing look. Belle murmurs something soothing to Nak, while Rory rolls a ball of anko and mochi between her palms, her brow furrowed in intense concentration.

I whip around and glare at Henry Chen.

He's sitting in the seat directly behind me, wearing a baseball cap pulled so low, it nearly conceals his eyes. Guess he's doing the incognito-celebrity thing again. And it seems to be working, since the Aunties around us are paying him barely any attention. (Now they've forgotten about Grace and how disruptive I am and are mostly waiting for an opportunity to speak up about the clearly subpar mochi-making going on at the front of the room.)

"What are you doing here?" I hiss at him.

"Come outside with me," he says, giving me one of his smug-ass grins.

"What?!"

"Rika, look!" Rory calls from the front of the room. "I got it to be perfectly round!"

I turn back around to see Rory proudly brandishing her mochi ball. I give her a thumbs-up.

"It's still too big," Uncle Hikaru sniffs, scrutinizing her work.

"Perhaps if you could get the mochi to be the proper texture, Hikaru," one of the Aunties heckles from the audience. "Then she would not have to roll so much together to get it to stick."

"Or if your anko was *real* anko and not premade paste from the market," another Auntie chimes in. "You should always make it from scratch."

"I *did* make it from scratch," Uncle Hikaru growls.

"Well, I thought this one was pretty good," Rory mutters, looking down at her apparently very controversial mochi ball.

"No." The first Auntie shakes her head. "Too big *and* lumpy. You might as well start over."

"*I* think it looks perfect!" I cry—attracting a death-glare from nearly everyone in the audience.

Okay, I really need to stop with the disruptions. But god, I hate it when stompy little Rory looks even a tiny bit discouraged. I want to turn myself into an onryo, float up onstage, and wreak vengeance on everyone making her feel bad. (And maybe there will be a little vengeance left for Craig Shimizu, if the onryo has time.)

"Come outside with me." Henry Chen is now leaning forward so he can whisper directly at my head, his breath tickling my ear. I picture his annoying, constantly amused grin, and my cheeks warm. "I got something. From Grace."

My stomach drops, and all thoughts of mochi balls and busybody Aunties evaporate.

"Okay," I mutter back. "But we have to be stealth about it, or all everyone will be talking about for the next week is how I was involved in *multiple* disruptions of the mochi demonstration, just like I was involved in the total disruption of the parade—"

"No worries," Henry says, his voice easy. "I got it."

I hear rustling behind me as he leans back in his seat

and mutters to one of the Aunties sitting next to him: "Is that *dog* eating the mochi?!"

My eyes go to Belle. Who is just straight-up feeding Nak mochi now. He looks like he's in heaven.

"Hikaru!" the Auntie behind me bellows. "Are you letting dogs participate in our sacred tradition?!"

"What?" Uncle Hikaru whirls around to look at Belle. "Belle Rakuyama, I *told* you . . ." He shakes his head and turns back to the audience. "You all *heard* me tell her—"

But it's too late. The Aunties explode with disapproving activity, some of them rising and bustling up to the table.

"Really, Hikaru, if you cannot keep control of this demonstration—"

"You've become so permissive over the years, the shame of it all—"

"I *still* think you bought that anko from the market—"

I hear Belle exclaiming, "Nak is part of the *court*!" over the din.

"Come on," Henry says, jiggling my shoulder.

As the chaos rises, he grabs my hand and pulls me out of my seat, dragging me toward one of the exits.

"Wait!" I bark. "You don't know where you're

going!" We switch course, *me* pulling *him*, so we can escape out the other exit, into the garden. I pull him behind the onryo tree so we'll still be hidden from view when the chaos dies down.

"That wasn't stealth at all," I say, shaking my head at him, the flush rising in my cheeks. My kaiju-temper flares—it does *not* seem able to keep itself under control when confronted with Henry Chen. "The demonstration was still totally disrupted."

He shrugs. "But it wasn't disrupted because of us leaving and it wasn't disrupted because of *you*, which seemed to be your primary concern. So basically a win?"

"Your definition of 'win' differs from that of every Asian elder out there," I say. "And it was already disrupted because of me, so I was trying to avoid—ugh, you know what, never mind. Tell me what you got from Grace."

He raises an eyebrow and gets that annoying amused look.

"You seem mad," he says.

"I always seem that way," I retort.

"I'm just wondering why you're mad . . . at me?"

"I . . ." I draw in a deep breath, some of my aggravation dissipating. I'm not mad at him, I guess, I'm mad at . . . everything else? When my anger overtakes me that way, all the things I'm mad about get piled together in one big lumpy mess and there's nowhere to put it. It just *sits* in my chest, eager to lash out at the first thing that comes its way. "Um, no. I'm not mad at you. I just . . ." I pause, trying to clear my brain. "Some stuff happened before you got here, and I . . . I'm sorry. I appreciate you helping me."

He looks like maybe he wants to say something else, but doesn't. Instead he just nods, pulls his phone from his pocket, taps the screen, and hands it to me.

Displayed is a single photo that looks like a very pretty pattern. The close-up of some kind of mosaic, perhaps? Bright splashes of green and yellow and blue that appear to be etched onto tiles. Is it a floor? Or . . . something else with tiles?

"What is it?" I murmur, almost to myself, turning the phone around—as if the image will make more sense upside down.

"I asked around last night, but no one in the Asian Hollywood group text seemed to have any idea where Grace is," Henry says. "So I decided to go straight to the source. I was thinking about what you were saying about making sure she wasn't kidnapped or something. How I should be a good friend. Grace has been helping me with something—"

"What something?" I say, my "this person is using vague language to hide their nefarious intentions" antennae going up.

"Just something," he says, a resistant and obstinate thread creeping into his easygoing voice. "Anyway, I sent her a message directly, outside of the group text. Asked her to send me proof of life—please. She sent back that photo."

"Did she say anything else?" I scroll down on the text thread, but it's just Henry gently asking Grace a few more questions regarding her whereabouts. She never responded.

"I'm trying not to scare her off," he says, gesturing to the screen. "But maybe I can keep getting her to send me those photos? Use my natural charm." He grins at me.

I scrutinize the photo harder, bringing the phone closer to my face.

I don't know what it is about Henry Chen that makes me want to immediately dispute what he just told me: that Grace sent him this photo after going off the grid so fully that the general public still has no idea where she is. Maybe it's that thoroughly irritating smugness he has going on. Or maybe it's the fact that this whole situation is just so bizarre, so unbelievable, that every step feels like it's infused with a strange sort of magic. Everything I learn, everything that leads me closer to my long-lost mother, feels so *momentous*.

And this photo is so ordinary. So mundane.

It feels like something I was looking at the other day wandering through LA, like something I can remember glancing up and seeing—

Then it hits me.

That's *exactly* what it is.

I search back through my memory. And I realize this image probably feels so mundane because I've seen it before.

"This is an extreme close-up of one of the tile art pieces at the LA Central Library," I say, tapping the screen, a spark of excitement igniting in my chest. "Have you been there? It's one of the most beautiful buildings I've ever seen—"

"Probably because you've never been to New York," he says, his amused grin turning teasing.

Maybe that's supposed to make me laugh, but I find myself glaring at him anew. "Oh god. Are you one of those 'New York is the best city ever, and glitzy, fake-ass LA cannot ever hope to compare' snobs?"

He gives a loose shrug that tells me everything I need

to know. "Is the Citizens Patrol of Little Tokyo about to tell me I'm wrong?"

"The Citizens Patrol was about to feed you local tacos as absolutely irrefutable proof that LA is superior," I say. "But with that attitude, you don't deserve tacos, so let's keep to the task at hand. If this is Grace's proof-of-life photo, that means she was at the library—when did you get this?"

"This morning," he says. "I sped over here to show you."

"When you could have just texted me and *not* interrupted the mochi demonstration," I say. "Yes, that makes sense."

"If I'd texted you, we wouldn't have been able to immediately go to our next obvious investigative step," Henry says. "Which is—"

"Go to the library," I say, completing his thought. "Maybe she's still there. Or will be there again. Or maybe somebody saw her and will be able to tell us something. Or . . . or . . ."

I can't even vocalize my next thought. Which is that maybe standing in the same place Grace was standing, picking up on whatever spirit or energy she left in the air, will help me figure out where she's going next. My gaze wanders up the twisting branches of the tree, and I imagine them morphing into the twisting hair of an onryo.

"So?" Henry says. He gestures to the garden's exit. "I'm parked in the Aiso Street garage. We could take my car?"

"It's not that far—we can walk. Or are you one of those New Yorkers who thinks LA people don't walk anywhere?" I give him a scathing look.

He grins. "You said it."

"But you thought it."

He just laughs. "Berate me if you must, Citizens Patrol—last I heard, you can't arrest me just for thinking something."

EIGHT

I'm pretty sure I know the exact tile art in Grace's photo. If you zoomed out, you would see a marvel of blues and greens forming the image of a wildly growing plant. There's a striking blue vase at the plant's base, but it can't contain all the curving leaves, or the bright yellow flowers sprouting at the vine-y tips.

It's a vivid portrait of life contained in a small space, in this series of tiles.

Every inch of the Los Angeles Central Library is crammed with these beautiful details—it is absolutely packed to the brim with hidden and not-so-hidden art. And I know all the corners of the place, each of its nooks and crannies, thanks to my addiction to gigantic Japanese folklore tomes. I still check them out by the stack.

I'm on a mission to get to the tile art from the photo, striding into the building with purpose. But before I can complete my mission, Henry grabs my arm.

"Hey, uh . . ." He gestures to the library gift shop.

"You want to get a baseball cap or something?"

I stop in my tracks, crossing my arms over my chest and cocking my head at him. "Why? I live here. I don't need a souvenir of our visit. Is my hair too . . ." I brush away a reddish tendril that keeps flying in my face—the glints of red in my hair get especially bright and brassy in the summer, and I've always been self-conscious about that. I tried to dye my hair straight black when I was younger, but that annoying red always pokes through somehow. Maybe it's offending his precious celebrity eyes.

"No, no," he says quickly. "I, uh . . . I like it."

Um, what?! But before we can linger on whatever that was, he barrels on.

"I just . . ." He hesitates, his eyes returning to the gift shop. There's something going on under all that breezy confidence again. Like there's A Thing he wants to say, but he knows saying it will make him sound like a megadouche.

"Sometimes . . ." He pauses again, then gives a little shrug, as if trying to reclaim some of his bravado. "When people recognize me, they take photos or post on social media and—"

I can't help but laugh. "Are you serious? You're worried about getting recognized? At the *library*?"

He gives me a smile that's a tad too close to a smirk. "You'd be surprised. Anyway, I'm not so much worried for myself as I am for you—all the photos and stuff are particularly intense when I'm out with . . . a person. Hence the camouflage." He taps the brim of his baseball cap.

"I don't need camouflage," I say, rolling my eyes and sweeping a hand through the air. "I'm not famous. And I'm perfectly capable of taking care of myself should we meet"—I lower my voice, make it extra dramatic—"your *public.*"

"Fine," he says, his smirk widening. Whatever oddness was lurking underneath that easy confidence has vanished now. Maybe it was never there in the first place. "So where are these tiles?"

I lead him to the escalator, and we go up to the second level. I'll admit, I kind of take him the long way, making sure we go through the crown jewel of the building: the rotunda. I'm gratified when he stops for a moment in that glorious airy open space—craning his neck to drink in the beauty that's all around him.

"Whoa," he says softly, taking in the impossibly high curving ceiling, the endless tiled murals that cover the walls. Even the floor is a sea of marbled tiles. My favorite part, though, is the fixture that hangs from the very center of the ceiling, a globe encircled by a ribbon of lights.

It looks like absolute magic, suspended midair.

And somehow, this beautiful space is always perfectly quiet, even though the library's status as a very historical, very beautiful building makes it a prime tourist attraction. Today there are three different tour groups, chattering softly among themselves, being walked around the rotunda by enthusiastic guides.

I gaze at the lit-up globe and feel the quiet and the sheer *bigness* of this place deep in my bones. When I'm tired of being in the real word, when the shadows of Little Tokyo aren't enough, I know I can come here and feel utterly transported.

"Not bad, eh, New York?" I murmur to him.

"Are the tiles from Grace's photo here somewhere?" Henry asks, his voice reverent.

I try to hide my smile. "You'd think so, but no. Those particular tiles are somewhere slightly less, um, epic. Come on."

I lead him to the side of the rotunda—past the Teen'Scape library-within-a-library, with its comfy couches and lovingly curated displays of YA books—to one of the little nooks I know so well. It's where the tile art of the wild plant is, displayed over—

"A drinking fountain?" Henry says, his voice skeptical.

"This whole building is stuffed with art," I say, trying to sound all superior even though that was kind of my reaction, too, when I first saw these tiles. "Not every display can be as majestic as the rotunda. Doesn't mean it's not beautiful."

He leans in, scrutinizing the tiles more closely. They're set back in a recessed part of the wall that serves as a little nook, a colorful backdrop for the drinking fountain—close enough to admire, far enough away that you have to lean quite a bit to touch this precious art. "So what should we do now? Just stare at this until it gives us more clues?"

"I . . ."

Hmm. That's exactly what I was planning on doing. But it sounds ridiculous when he says it out loud like that. I buy some time by leaning over the fountain and brushing my fingers against the tiles, like I'm trying to communicate with them. I lean so far, things get a little precarious, me hanging over the fountain—but I really want to *see* . . .

"Rika." Henry's fingertips graze my waist, trying to steady me as I nearly lose my balance. "Be careful!" My shirt has ridden up during my fevered leaning, so his hand brushes over bare skin and I get all goose-bumpy.

I mean. Probably because the air-conditioning is so intense in here.

Ugh. This all feels so haphazard. I don't know what I was expecting. That I'd get here and look at the same tiles my mother gazed upon just a few hours ago and I'd instantly feel this mystical, magical connection—

I freeze as my fingertips make the most cringeworthy scraping sound against one of the tiles.

Scrreeeeppp.

"What was that?" Henry says, leaning in closer, his hand leaving my waist for the moment.

I run my fingertips over the same tile again.

Screeeeeeeppppp!

Same hideous noise. And something about this tile feels . . . different. My heart starts beating faster, thwacking against my breastbone so loudly, I'm convinced the whole library's going to hear it. Very, very gently, I poke at the tile.

It shimmers a bit—and then it comes loose.

"Holy shit!" Henry exclaims. "I mean, uh . . ." He lowers his voice to a library-appropriate whisper. "Holy shit."

As carefully as possible, I pull the tile free, revealing a hollow space in the wall behind it. There's the tiniest bit of blue missing from the vase now, the one that's valiantly trying to contain the plant.

And in that hollow space is a scrap of paper.

My heart speeds up, my vision narrowing to this one small spot behind the wall. Henry's saying something in my ear, but I don't even hear him. My hand shakes as I reach out to grasp the scrap of paper—this tiny thing that *must* be a clue and therefore *must* contain the secret to my entire existence. I shimmy back to a standing position, the paper in my hand. It's folded over and over and over again until it's barely anything, and my hand shakes even more as I try to unfold it.

I'm still picking at the stubborn folds when I hear a voice behind me scream:

"Oh my god. It is *so totally* her!"

Here's the thing about the rotunda: it is vast and beautiful and usually silent. But when someone screams like that, it creates an echo effect that bounces off every gorgeous tiled surface. It basically triples any scream.

Henry and I both turn around, as if in slow motion.

A girl around my age stands behind us, phone raised, snapping away. She's part of one of the tour groups. And her scream has attracted plenty of other people in *all* the tour groups.

My brain is processing all this very slowly. My brain is, to be honest, still focused on the folded scrap of paper clutched tightly in my sweaty fist.

The girl lowers her phone a fraction of an inch and

beams at me, her eyes wide and shiny. "You're that girl," she screeches, her voice bouncing off the rotunda again. "The one from the parade—the one Grace Kimura crashed into!"

The more she screams at me, the more people gather behind her. There's kind of a mini mob going on, and now they're all snapping photos of us. I blink at the screaming girl, my fist getting tighter and sweatier around my scrap of paper—like I'm worried she's going to steal it from me.

"Rika," Henry murmurs, and I swivel to look at him. His face has gone pale underneath the brim of his baseball cap, and his breathing is unnaturally rapid. It's a complete transformation from his usual carefree, confident demeanor. He looks almost . . . scared.

"Oh my gaaawd, and that's *Hank Chen*!" Screaming Girl bellows, instantly swiveling her phone to capture Henry's terrified face.

"What are you guys doing at the library?" someone else calls out.

"Do you know where Grace is?!" yet another person yells.

"Are you, like, *together*?!" Screaming Girl helpfully chimes in.

Suddenly everyone's yelling questions and snapping

photos, and the mini mob presses closer to us. My face is hot and my fist is getting even sweatier and I can't think . . . can't think . . .

I pivot to the right and spot a small hole in the mob, next to the side entrance into Teen'Scape.

I grab Henry's hand and run.

"Rika . . ." His voice is all shaky, his breathing still rapid and uneven.

Lucky for him, I know this library like the back of my hand. I yank him into the side entrance of Teen'Scape, snaking us around the rotunda and popping us out by one of the library's sweeping side staircases—like a secret passageway. I am extremely aware that some of the mob has caught on to my sneaky ways and is clattering behind us, still shouting questions.

We reach the bottom of the staircase, and I pull him sharply to the left, taking us up the escalator to the third floor and ducking through the entrance to the popular-fiction section. I hear the mob behind me, their voices echoing up the escalator.

"Which way did they go?"

"Why are they running like that?! You're not supposed to run in the library!"

"Were they holding hands?!"

I can't afford to look behind me, so I just keep pressing forward, winding us through the shelves and shelves of books. The din of the mob seems to recede the farther we get into the maze of shelves, the book jungle.

Slowly, the beautiful silence of the library begins to restore itself.

I pull Henry into another one of my favorite nooks, a corner in the very back of this section of shelves, conveniently located right next to a tall, narrow window that looks out onto the city. It lets some light in, but not enough to disrupt my beloved shadows.

Now I can't hear the mob at all. My breathing slows, and I try to let this dark, silent corner soothe me.

"I think we lost them," I say. "But we should probably stay here for a few minutes." I turn to face him, expecting him to make some smartass wisecrack or give me one of his amused grins. Instead I do a double take. Because now he looks . . . well, absolutely awful. His golden-brown skin has a gray cast, his eyes are glassy and blank. And his breathing is still way, way too fast.

"Hey," I say, reaching out to touch his arm. He flinches, and I drop my hand. "Henry. Are you having a panic attack?"

A bit of recognition flashes in his eyes, disrupting his blank look. Like he's trying to bring himself back to the present moment.

"It's okay," I say softly. I reach out more slowly this time and brush my fingertips against his palm. "You're here, all right? In the present. All those, uh, people . . . are gone. And I'm here with you."

His hand closes around my fingertips.

"Can you breathe with me?" I say.

He nods. So I start doing the breathing Eliza taught me. Big breath in through the nose. Hold it for several counts. Long, slow breath out through the mouth. Steady, steady. My eyes never leaving his.

"My friend Eliza gets panic attacks, too," I say, my voice still soft. "She says sometimes it helps to think of something specific to ground yourself. Like, um, pugs."

He raises an eyebrow, still doing the breathing.

"Yeah, that's random—she just loves pugs," I say, laughing a little. "So if you think of, like, a big room full of pugs, and they're all, I don't know, wearing matching bow ties or something, does that calm you down?"

That just makes him raise his eyebrow even more.

"Okay, so not a pug enthusiast," I say. "Well, look around. Maybe there's something here that will ground you."

He nods again, still doing the breathing with me. Still clasping my fingertips.

Then his other hand drifts up and he touches that

bright red strand of my hair that keeps flying in my face. And, very gently, tucks it behind my ear.

Our eyes meet again and the silence of the library feels extra heavy, like it's pressing against us. I am suddenly both hot and cold all over.

He shakes his head and drops my hand, his eyes finally losing that glassy look. His breathing also seems to return to normal.

"Sorry," he says, sounding like Henry again—but a somewhat more subdued, less smug version of Henry. "I didn't mean to . . . something about your hair . . ." He gestures vaguely around my face. "I haven't had one of those in a while. But that screaming girl, that crowd of people . . ." He tries for a half smile and mostly gets there. "It was a lot."

"Agreed," I say, trying to shoo away all the hot-cold feelings that seem to have suddenly seeped into my bones. My voice comes out like a little squeak, and I clear my throat. "Um. Are you hungry?" He tilts his head curiously. "'Cause I am," I barrel on. "Let's go get something to eat."

I try for my own half smile—and, I'd like to think, mostly get there.

"But first, let's stop by the gift shop," I say. "I need to buy a baseball cap."

NINE

I take Henry to Grand Central Market, the bustling collection of food stands housed in a giant warehouse-like thing right in the middle of downtown. There's always a crowd here, but everyone's hyper-focused on the sizzle and pop of food cooking, on the mingling of delectable scents, on getting the eats they want to inhale as soon as humanly possible. I suppose it feels like we're all focused on the same goal, and it's therefore way less scary than a mob chasing you through a usually peaceful building full of books.

We manage to nab a table right next to one of the market's most Instagram-friendly spots, a giant multi-colored neon sign for Bulleit whiskey. The sign is a graffiti-like collage featuring all kinds of doodles lit up in bright colors—a mermaid, a skeleton in a top hat, a palm tree.

"That's cool," Henry says, gesturing to the sign.

"My favorite part is the pickle," I say, adjusting my brand-new LAPL baseball cap and pointing to a nonsensical illustration of a humanoid pickle lady wearing a bow and high heels and standing on top of a downtrodden-looking male pickle. *Watch your pickle back*, she says.

"Of course it is," he says, grinning. "Hey, I just realized: in all the commotion, we never looked at that thing you found behind the tile."

"Oh my god, I can't believe I forgot about it," I say, fishing around in my pocket for the scrap of folded paper that seemed, at least for a few seconds, like the most important thing in the universe.

I manage to unfold it and see that it's an old, faded photo, its edges dog-eared and torn. The photo features younger versions of the same two girls from the picture at Suehiro. Grace and Auntie Suzy. Arms around each other again, big smiles in place. This time, they're posing in front of a sun-blasted rock formation topped with wild greenery. But there's something *off* about the rock formation. Its edges are square, like building blocks.

"I think . . ." I frown at the photo, trying to scour for whatever clues it might contain. "I think this is the old Griffith Park Zoo. It was abandoned when the zoo moved locations in the sixties, but they left all the animal enclosures and added a few picnic tables, and then nature"—I gesture to the wild greenery, curling around the rock formations like unruly vines—"just kind of grew in around it. These rock formations are the old animal enclosures. It's like LA's version of ancient ruins."

"Sounds fun," Henry says.

"Yeah, it's one of those oddball LA things, apart from what people usually think of—the Hollywood sign, Beverly Hills, celebrities. It's more ordinary, yet also totally weird. It has its own kind of magic going on," I say.

I flip the photo over—and my heart does a somersault.

Scribbled on the back are the following words:

Tomorrow, seven p.m.

"Oh my god!" I exclaim. "Is this . . . did Grace leave a message for me?"

We both stare at those words, as if more will magically appear if we wish hard enough.

"So this is an actual clue!" Henry says.

I turn to look at him. His dark eyes are lit with glee, his mouth tipped into one of his charming smiles. But there's something more genuine about this smile—it's like the visual version of his almost-a-snort laugh. Like he can't contain the sheer goofy giddiness rushing through him.

Honestly, I can't either.

"It *is* a clue," I say, scarcely able to believe it. "Maybe she wants to meet up with me and explain everything."

"Then we have to go tomorrow!" he says, his goofy grin widening.

"I . . . wow." I set the photo down and shake my head, trying to get a handle on the roller coaster of emotions rushing through me. Am I actually going to meet my mother? Who I didn't even know was my mother until, like, two days ago?

My phone buzzes, snapping me out of my whirlwind of emotions.

"Eliza?" Henry says, leaning over to read the name flashing on my phone screen. His breath tickles my ear, and I flush—then move the tiniest bit to the side, putting space between us. "The same pug-loving Eliza who gets panic attacks?"

"Yeah, she's one of my best friends," I say. "We do judo together."

"You do judo? Oh, that's right, you told me when you were *not* arresting me." Henry gives me a teasing grin. "That's so awesome. I've never studied any martial arts. What's it like?"

"Um . . . it's, uh, cool," I say, scrutinizing the text.

Normally I could talk for *hours* about judo, but right now I can only feel the immense guilt that overtakes me whenever I think of the parade disaster that ruined everything with the demonstration and the UCLA scout and . . .

Eliza's been texting me nonstop since the parade, but

I've only responded a couple times to reassure her I'm fine, just busy with . . . things. I also sent Sensei Mary a bunch of excuses for missing practice this week. I'm not sure when or how I can face them—especially after all they've done for me. Maybe I can't.

I dismiss the text.

"You're ignoring a text from one of your best friends?" Henry says.

"Not ignoring it. Just, uh, I'll respond later," I say. I tap the photo of the old zoo. "Right now, my mind is way too occupied by our actual clue."

"This clue calls for a celebration," Henry says, slamming his palm on the tabletop, like he's Thor or some shit. "You stay here, basking in the glow of the pickle. I'll go get us food. Lots of food!"

He jumps to his feet, that dancer's grace flowing through his every move. How can he make something so mundane look like I'm suddenly front row at the ballet?

"Wait!" I call out as he dances—like, literally *dances*—away. "You don't know where anything is!"

"I'll figure it out!" he calls back. "One of everything that looks good, right?"

"That means literally one of everything here," I say. "We'll be eating *forever*."

He's already too far away to hear me. But as I gaze

down at the writing on the back of the photo once more, I realize I'm smiling too much to care.

✿

Henry brings back . . . well, basically one of everything. Sizzling steak in garlicky sauce, lovingly ladled over a bed of sticky rice. A gooey egg sandwich, yolk perfectly runny. Handmade pasta with luscious, meaty Bolognese. Lumpia, fried to crisp deliciousness. And tacos so spicy, they'll make you sweat.

I'm pretty sure the table's about to collapse under the weight of all this food, and we haven't even started exploring dessert options yet.

I notice Henry surreptitiously glance around before we start eating, pulling his baseball cap lower so it hides his face better. I look around, too, but everyone else still seems to be wrapped up in their own food adventures.

"We're okay," I reassure him, attempting to make my tone light. "No fan mobs."

I expect him to flash me that easy grin, but he gives me a tense head-bob, scoops up a taco, and takes a very small bite.

And then the tension melts away as a look of *pure bliss* spreads over his face.

"Ugh, so good," he groans, cramming the rest of the taco into his mouth with unabashed gusto. He chews and swallows, then gives me a sly smile. "I'll concede these are way better than anything in New York."

"*Anything?*" I challenge. "You're really willing to forsake your beloved city over tacos?"

"They're awesome tacos," he says. "And all your talk about the 'magic' of LA is winning me over. Pretty soon I'll have gone full Californian—wearing flip-flops as formalwear and talking about nothing but freeways for, like, *hours.*"

He lengthens his vowels on those last two words, affecting an exaggerated Valley girl–type voice.

"I *never* talk about freeways," I say, trying to sound imperious—but an irrepressible smile's playing around the corners of my mouth, and that just makes him smile even bigger. "But I do think LA is magic, yes."

"How did that even start?" he says. "You do not seem like the type to, um, see things that way."

"I think . . . hmm." I pause and take a bite of my own taco, that potent mix of fresh spices exploding on my tongue. No one's ever asked me that before. "Maybe it has to do with growing up in Little Tokyo," I say slowly, trying to figure it out. "I know people think everything in LA is . . . new? And, like, made of cheap plastic or something. No sense of history or culture." I give him a

pointed look, and he shrugs and grins, like, *Yep, guilty.*
"But Little Tokyo . . . it has *so much* of that history, that
culture. It's been around since the early 1900s, and it's
been through a lot. It used to have the largest Japanese
American population in North America. And then so
many people were forced to abandon their homes and
lives because of incarceration during World War II. But
they rebuilt after. When I walk those streets . . ." I pause,
a surprise lump forming in my throat. I fan myself with
a napkin, trying to stave off unshed tears. "Whew, these
tacos are spicier than usual."

"Mm-hmm," Henry says, sounding like he doesn't
buy that for a second.

"When I walk those streets," I continue, "I can *feel*
that. That sense of history and community and struggle
and passion. There are so many stories jammed into every
block—the whole neighborhood feels so *alive.* And then,
of course, there's Mr. Sherman."

"Mr. *Who*?" Henry says.

"Mr. Sherman!" I say, my grin reinstating itself. "He's
this ancient cat who's guarded one of the neighborhood
boutiques *forever.* No one knows exactly where he came
from or how he's lived this long or why he has eyes
that legit look like human eyes. But he's always there.

Flopped in the doorway and shooting haughty cat glares at everyone who passes by. Tell me that's not magic."

"It absolutely is," Henry says, nodding vigorously. "All right, fine. Between Mr. Sherman and the tacos, you've convinced me: LA is an enchanted wonderland!"

"Thank you," I say. "But *how* have you been out here this long and not had good tacos?"

"I've really only been out here for work," he says with a shrug. "The kids' show I was on—the one with the choir?—filmed in New York. *Dance! Off!* and the movie with Grace were here, but I'm working so much, I don't really eat anything except the very sensible salads production orders for me."

"Gotta maintain that hot-guy physique," I say, cocking an eyebrow.

I expect him to laugh, but his smile gets more forced. "Yeah, well . . . when you're known for something . . ." He shrugs again—but that seems forced, too. And for some reason, I feel bad.

"But now you have the chance to be known for something else, right?" I say, trying to sound encouraging. "This movie with Grace—if we can find Grace."

"As you so helpfully pointed out to me during our first meal together," he says, giving me a slight smile.

Shit. Now I feel *really* bad. The nure-onna isn't supposed to feel bad about anything.

"It's true, though, there are a lot of layers to this role," he says, his demeanor going back to perfectly smooth—like he's being interviewed on the red carpet or something. This bothers me, and I can't quite articulate why. "I get to be funny, I get to be serious. I get to have a really emotional sibling-bonding scene with Grace. And I'm grateful they cast me, period. I'm usually too brown or not brown enough or people just don't know what's going on here." He gestures to his face. "They always ask—"

"'What are you?'" I finish, smiling slightly. "I'm very familiar."

"Like we're trying to trick people or something," he says, shaking his head. "'Cause, y'know, Guess the Ambiguously Ethnic Person's True Background is a fun game to play."

"For everyone except the Ambiguously Ethnic Person. Man, you'd think, in this day and age . . ." I realize I don't even know where I'm going with that. Or how I can complete that thought and actually believe it. I'm trying to make some grand statement, but my own experience doesn't back it up.

"You have your own stuff, too, right? About not fitting in?" he says, as if reading my mind. Something more genuine sparks in his eyes, and I can't help it—I feel warmed.

"I mean, it's not weird to be a half-Japanese girl in Los Angeles these days," I say slowly. "But it *is* weird to be a half-Japanese girl with mysterious, scandalous parentage living with her full-Japanese relatives and not totally looking like them. There are a lot of stares. A lot of . . . questions." I self-consciously tuck that strand of red hair into my baseball cap. His eyes follow my every move, lingering a little on the hair.

"And you don't talk about this with anyone—this not fitting in," he says. Not as a question. He just *knows*.

I open my mouth to tell him that of course I don't talk to anyone about that. I'm the freaking nure-onna, goddammit. I retreat to the shadows. I plot my revenge. I don't think about *feelings*.

But . . . he's looking at me so earnestly and openly.

And suddenly I find myself saying a bunch of other stuff instead. Stuff I don't usually say out loud.

"My Aunties have it tough anyway," I begin. "They haven't always been accepted by the community either. I don't need to be complaining to them. About my, um, feelings. My temper gets the best of me enough as it is—I almost got kicked out of judo once because of it." He smiles a little at that. "And anyway, even if I did talk to them—or my sisters—they wouldn't . . ." I trail off, something catching in my throat.

His smile turns gentle. "They wouldn't understand," he says.

I look down at my food, blinking back the tears that want to spill out and fuck up our tacos.

"I get it," he says. "The mixed-kid thing—it's both totally weird and totally normal. I'm an only child, but people never believe I belong to either of my parents—"

"Wait, you're an only child?" I say. "My family's small by most Asian American standards, but—"

"My family's *tiny*," he says, holding his thumb and forefinger mere millimeters apart to illustrate. "My grandparents—both sides—weren't super keen on my parents' marriage, and my mom and dad are both only children, too. So. It's really just us." His expression turns wistful. "It's cool that you have Little Tokyo, that community—the way you talk about it is so . . ." The corners of his mouth lift. ". . . joyful. I wish I had something like that—my parents kinda kept to themselves after dealing with all that disapproval. And then I started working so young, I sometimes feel like, I dunno, I don't have those connections?" He shrugs, trying to play it off, but I can tell this bothers him. How could it not? "But do you ever feel . . . well, not quite part of it? 'Cause when I think about my experiences with communities that should be mine, I also feel like maybe I'm not welcome. Like I'm not *enough*, y'know?"

"There are certainly people who *want* me to feel that way," I say. Craig Shimizu's smug face floats through my brain. "I guess it is weird sometimes. There are definitely Japanese people who think I'm just, like, white with a little sprinkle of soy sauce. Or some kind of aberration, an unfortunate dilution of pure Asianness. But it's not like white people look at my face and think I'm one of them." I think of all the Beckys who want to hear my accent, all the fetishizing white guys who have said truly disgusting things to my face, all the grown adults who compliment my English and use the word "exotic" to describe me. "It's almost like . . . you're seen as someone who can never *really* belong anywhere."

"And everyone projects all kinds of things onto you," Henry says, nodding in recognition. "You're a mongrel—a mistake. You're a watered-down diet version of something else."

"Like a fraction," I say. "A thing to be claimed only if the community deems you worthy."

I flash back to Belle and me in second grade, her screaming "She's *half!*" at the teacher who didn't believe we were related. She'd been trying to stand up for me. But something about that had still cut deep—as if I could never be a *whole* version of anything.

"Yeah," Henry says. "Or you're a great savior, here to unite two worlds in peace."

"Like Aquaman," I say.

He lets out a surprised laugh—and this time, he *totally* snorts. "Hey—*Aquaman* was *tight.*"

I don't know what it is about that that makes me start laughing. Maybe it's the way he says it, with so much sincerity and gusto. Maybe it's the fact that he's grinning at me while lit by a neon pickle wearing a bow. Maybe it's . . . oh, I don't know.

But I do laugh. Long and hard. And he's right there with me, snorting all the way.

"I just want to be able to exist as myself, you know?" Henry says, as we're catching our breaths. "Not a savior, not a tool, not a mystery to be solved. Not someone who has to be described using fractions."

"Just a whole *you*," I murmur.

"Yeah," he says, smiling. "I really hope you get to meet Grace tomorrow. I think you *could* talk to her. About all this. She's really empathetic?"

I nod, picking up another taco and nibbling at the corner. I don't want to interrupt, hoping against hope that he'll keep going, tell me more.

"She . . ." He meets my eyes, his brow furrowing. *Wow.* I don't think I've seen Henry Chen's smooth brow furrow, ever. I didn't know it was even capable of such things. "She talked to me about the panic attack stuff," he finally says. "Had her therapist refer me to someone. *That's* what she's been helping me with. She has an anxiety disorder—she's talked about it a lot in interviews—and she helped me understand that that isn't, like, a shameful thing. That I don't have to shove it down and pretend I'm okay. Which is what my parents would prefer."

He snags the last bit of sticky rice, his more confident expression sliding into place. I'm beginning to understand that that's the expression he puts on when he's getting truly uncomfortable, when he's *done* talking about something. So I don't push it.

It hits me that *I've* just talked quite a bit to this near stranger about things I never share. I should be feeling weird about that, uncomfortable. And yet, talking to

Henry about all this stuff feels like the most natural thing in the world.

"I hope you get to meet her," he says again, shoveling the sticky rice into his mouth.

I give him a tentative smile. "Me too."

Something I don't want to put a name to has taken up residence in my chest—a tiny light, a flutter of hope. A little fairy thing that's about as far from the nure-onna's vengeance-loving ways as you can get.

I can actually see myself meeting Grace in front of one of these old zoo rock formations. Her embracing me. Both of us teary. It must be said that the whole thing—finding this scrap of a photo behind an old library tile, the mysterious inscription directing us to a legendary LA location, the potential reunion—feels . . . well, like a fairy tale.

With a happy ending.

Wait, am I starting to believe in happy endings now?

Belle will never let me live this down.

Once upon a time, there lived a handsome . . . no, cute. No, adorable prince. (Ugh, did I really just use the word "adorable"?) He was gifted with an enchanted smile and the magic of dance and used his charms to entertain everyone in the land. But his dancing feet masked so many more magical abilities that were far less appreciated—a genuine empathy and a goofy laugh and the talent for eating multiple delicious spicy foods all in one sitting.

Not to mention the magical ability to totally distract the nure-onna from her very important mission.

What was I talking about again?

TEN

"Rika . . . Rika-chan! My hair's on fire and you're the only one who can put it out!"

"That's nice . . . wait, *what*?" I whirl around to see Belle cocking a quizzical eyebrow at me. I'm standing atop a small stepladder in the cramped kitchen of Katsu That. I've been counting down the minutes—the *seconds*—until five p.m., when I can finally leave and set out on my quest to the old Griffith Park Zoo. Henry is supposed to meet me outside the restaurant, incognito baseball cap firmly in place. After the library debacle from the day before, we're determined to be *discreet*.

I've been distracted all shift, my brain whirling around what this rendezvous might hold. In just a couple short days, Grace Kimura has grown into an epic figure in my mind, an exiled queen unfairly cast out from her kingdom. Or maybe she's more like a fairy godmother who will wave her glittery magic wand and make me whole.

Ugh. Did I really just think that? My fantasies are

getting so *flowery*. The nure-onna does *not* do bibbidi-bobbidi-boos.

The nure-onna also does *not* do whatever my brain is doing with Henry Chen. I can't explain it, but in the midst of me spinning various scenarios about my impending Grace reunion, he keeps popping into my mind. I hear his dorky snort-laugh as I shred cabbage for salads. See his smile—the soft, genuine one, devoid of smugness—as I tote plates of piping hot katsu to customers. Remember his fingertips brushing against my skin as I leaned precariously over the water fountain, and how I got all goose-bumpy—

"Rika. Chan!" Belle claps her hands on her hips and stomps her foot to get my attention.

I snap back to the present and blink at her a few times, trying to remember what I climbed onto the stepladder for.

"You want to bring that Worcestershire sauce over here? And really, no reaction to my hair being on fire?"

I slowly turn to look at the bottle in my hand. Oh, right. I was getting the Worcestershire so we could make more katsu sauce. The restaurant has been chaos all afternoon. Nikkei Week is always extra busy, but today's positively off the charts.

"Your hair looks beautiful," I say, hastily clambering down from the stepladder and passing her the bottle.

"You're the only person I know who could pull off fire."

"Hmph," Belle says, somewhat mollified. I'm relieved that she seems to have forgotten yesterday's mochi demo debacle, but that's Belle—she's on to her next royal task, no need to dwell on the negative. She pours the sauce into a bowl and starts mixing in the other ingredients. "What is going on with you today? Your face is very *red*."

I reach up to touch my cheek and realize it's even warmer than Katsu That's un-air-conditioned kitchen. Actually, my whole body feels warm, suffused with an inexplicable flush that's crept from my toes to the roots of my brassy hair, which is currently contained in my brand-new LAPL baseball cap.

"Are you sick?" Belle reaches over to feel my forehead, and I bat her hand away.

"Not sick," I insist. "Just . . ." I trail off, trying to think of what lie I can tell her. Because I definitely do not want to say: *Just can't stop randomly thinking about this maddening boy who's helping me find my long-lost mother and how it felt when he sort of touched me—not really in a sexy way, it was all very accidental, yet my brain cannot seem to stop itself from playing these three seconds of footage over and over and—*

"Ah, of course," Belle says, snapping her fingers. "You're preoccupied with your Mom Quest! I'm so sorry I haven't been able to help much the past couple days, Rika-chan. My queen duties have been keeping me so busy, but rest assured I'm still ready for your entrée into Asian Hollywood—"

"Rika!" Auntie Och strides into the kitchen, her bushy eyebrows drawn together. Belle's and my heads snap up from the half-finished katsu sauce. I feel a little flutter of something deep in my gut—and am surprised to realize it's disappointment that Belle didn't guess what I was *actually* thinking.

But . . . why? Did I want us to have some kind of sisterly bonding moment over my obsessive thoughts, which sound like they belong in a rom-com? Don't I *hate* rom-coms?

That confuses me and sends me down all sorts of spiraling thought paths I definitely do not like, so I focus on Auntie Och. "Go take table four's order," she says, jerking her formidable mane of hair toward the dining room. "They asking for you."

"Me?" I say, my brow furrowing in consternation. Has the queen of the Beckys, the one I dumped soda on last week, returned for her ultimate revenge?

"They want 'the girl with the red hair,'" Auntie Och says, her tone brusque. "That must be you, ne?"

"I . . . right," I say, exchanging a puzzled look with Belle. "Okay, then."

I dutifully straighten my apron, make sure my hair's tucked securely under my hat, and check my watch. It's only a few minutes to five—I can make this my final task of the shift. And even if it involves the Return of Queen Becky, well, I can suck it up, grit my teeth, and ignore her pleas for an "authentic Japanese accent." Because right after that, I'll be set free—ready for the fateful meeting with my mother. I imagine myself as a princess escaping the suffocating confines of her castle, gleefully tearing through the woods, her long thicket of hair streaming behind her—

Wait, why am I imagining myself as a *princess*? I have literally never been able to get that image to appear in my mind. Not even when I was little and had a very brief moment of wanting to join Belle on #TeamPrincess.

I glance at my reflection in the big metal doors leading out to the dining room. I still see the nure-onna: fangs bared, ruby eyes flashing. Ready to snap at anyone who looks at her funny. I pause as the image shimmers in and out, those brilliant eyes staring back at me.

And I'm not sure why, but that weird sense of disappointment flashes through me again. Like maybe I was hoping to see something different this time?

I shake it off, stuffing that wild curl of red hair that keeps escaping back under my baseball cap. Then I reach into my pocket and touch the three photos I've stored there: the pictures of young Grace and Auntie Suzy and the one of baby me being held by new-mom Grace. They're like a talisman, calming me. Reminding me of my ultimate goal.

I imagine my nure-onna armor rising up and enveloping me, that essential layer of protection. Then I straighten my spine and push through the double doors, emerging into the chaos of the dining room.

The long table in the middle is taken up by the usual assortment of raucous Uncles, who come in every week for brunch and spend endless hours gossiping, downing Sapporos, and commending Auntie Och for weaseling a liquor license from the city's nefarious clutches. This is, quite honestly, all part of Auntie Och's brilliance—she knows the Uncles love to spend their days getting absolutely tanked, and an abundance of Sapporo gives Katsu That a huge advantage over other would-be brunch places.

But the Uncles aren't the only ones causing a ruckus today. Every booth is *packed*. And as I scan the faces, I realize I don't recognize most of them.

That's odd. We usually get a handful of new folks popping in during Nikkei Week, but for the most part, I know all the clientele.

"What's this, people waiting?" Auntie Och emerges from the kitchen, nearly barreling right into me. My gaze follows hers to the front of the restaurant, where a small line has formed. "Hmm." Her brow furrows. "Strange. But good, ne? I will go start a list!" I watch as she bustles toward the front, ready for battle. It *is* strange. We're usually busy, but not so much that we need a wait list. What on earth—

"Rika-chan!" Auntie Och barks over her shoulder. "Table four!"

"Right," I say, snapping out of my reverie and aiming myself at table four, a cozy booth stuffed in the back right-hand corner.

I scan the customers as I approach, activating my nure-onna armor even more. Three white girls have crammed themselves into the booth, which is really more of a two-person situation. They're looking at their phones, whispering among themselves, giggling. As I approach, one of them glances my way and her eyes get all big. She whispers something to the girl she's crammed next to, and then they're *all* looking at me and . . .

What the hell is going on?

I don't recognize any of these girls—why are they already laughing at me? Did Queen Becky warn them about Rika the Soda-Dumping Bandit? Or was it Craig Shimizu, who loves nothing more than recounting the long-ago tale of Rika the Biter?

Angry heat creeps up the back of my neck, and I shove it down. I *cannot* unleash the rage right now—not when I'm so close to something I want so badly. I have to be the nure-onna *before* she strikes, strategic and cunning. I only have to get through this last table, and then I can go find my mother.

I touch the photos in my pocket again.

Then I force my face to be pleasant, eager smile in place.

Just. One. *Table.*

The whispering and giggling quiets as I reach the table and take out my order pad, but they're all still staring at me with big saucer eyes, unsettling grins in place. They're like tricksters, ready to present me with three riddles—get all three right and I win a pot of gold. Get one wrong and I *die*.

When you get down to it, all fairy tales are pretty savage.

"Hi there," I say, pencil poised over pad. I am relieved to hear my voice sounding smooth, helpful. "What can I get for you?"

"Ummmm." One of the girls flashes me a big toothy grin and glances down at the menu as if she's seeing it for the first time. "I'll have the, um, chicken."

"Breast, thigh, or karaage?" I say, pencil still poised.

"Oh, um . . ." The girl looks at the menu again, frowning. Like she had no idea that question was coming. The girl sitting next to her whispers something in her ear, and they giggle again, sneaking glances at me as they pretend to study the menu.

I clench my teeth into a pleasant expression and tighten my grip around the pencil. What is up with these girls? They're acting like I'm some kind of zoo attraction. I clench my teeth harder, try to make my smile even brighter. Tell my kaiju-temper to stay put . . .

And it's right then that I turn a little to the left and see the third girl at the table trying to surreptitiously take my picture.

"Hey!" I spit out before I can stop myself. That heat blazes through my entire body now, kindling that's burst into wild flame. "What do you think you're *doing*—"

"*Rika!*"

I whip around to see Rory stomping through the restaurant, waving her phone around. The rest of the chaos quiets as everyone turns to look at her. Even the brunching Uncles pause, sweaty bottles of Sapporo clutched in their fists. Auntie Och frowns in our direction—and even though Rory's the one making all the noise with her stompy little feet, I can't help but feel most of that frown is for me. The center of attention in a bad way, yet again.

Rory comes to a stop in front of me and brandishes her phone.

"Rika," she says again—and the restaurant has gone so quiet, her voice seems to reverberate off the walls. "What. Is. *This?!*"

I take the phone from her, trying to ignore the flush that's creeping up the back of my neck again—only now it's not angry, it's embarrassed. I can feel the stares of every single person in this restaurant, including my table of bad orderers, who are snapping pic after pic with their phones.

I wish my fairy godmother would swoop in and save me.

Not that the nure-onna needs saving.

But maybe just this once?

Rory's screen displays an Instagram post, a blurry

photo of . . . oh *god*. It's me and Henry. At the library, right before we made our daring escape. We're standing in the rotunda as the crowd presses in on us. I look angry, of course, my face screwed into an expression that's somewhere between confusion and total fury. My hair is flying everywhere, that blazing red lock unfurled like a flag of pure rage. Henry stands a bit behind me: his face pale, his expression verging on terror. I am a wild monster girl, protecting a handsome prince.

I look up from the phone, my gaze sweeping over Rory's indignant expression to the rest of the restaurant. They're all just staring at me now, and I want to sink into the ground. A smattering of whispers bubbles up, each word scraping against my skin like sandpaper.

"That's *her* . . . the girl with Hank Chen . . ."

"Are they a thing?"

"Why would he be a thing with a *waitress* . . ."

"*Rika!*" Rory hisses, snapping my attention back to her. She taps the phone screen with her index finger. "This post says you were with freaking *Hank Chen* at the library yesterday—and someone in the comments figured out who you are and where you work and . . ." Her gaze shifts to the table of white girls, who are still taking photos of me. To the Sapporo-loving Uncles, who are openly watching us. And to Katsu That's entrance, where a line has started to form and is already snaking its way down the block . . .

The rage that was rising up inside of me morphs into a small, hard knot in my stomach.

This is the third day this week I've managed to make a complete spectacle of myself—all while I'm trying to *discreetly* find my mother and keep my Aunties from learning about my quest and—

I'm jolted out of my thoughts by an earsplitting scream from the street. Auntie Och instantly snaps to attention, narrowing her eyes at the increasingly unruly line outside.

The thing is, that didn't sound like a scream of distress, it sounded more like . . . excitement? Like—

"Sorry, no, I'm just trying to get inside, I—"

Suddenly, Henry Chen is . . . well, some combination of falling and being shoved through Katsu That's front door. His face is flushed, his expression flustered. His incognito baseball cap has been knocked askew and is doing nothing to hide his too-cute face.

A scandalized murmur runs through the crowd. The bad orderers at table four actually *gasp*. And the line out front—which is very quickly turning into a mob—

presses itself up against the window, snapping pictures and screaming for Hank Chen.

Auntie Och plants herself in front of Henry, hands on her hips.

"Hey! You! Gotta wait in line like everyone else, ne?" she barks, making a shooing motion. "No cuts."

"Auntie Och!" Rory waves her spindly arms around, her face lit with more excitement than I've ever seen on her. "No! He's, like . . . he's . . ."

"He's coming with me," I blurt out, finally unfreezing from the temporary spell the sheer absurdity of this situation has cast over me and marching authoritatively to the front of the restaurant. I try to block out all the whispers, all the stares. All the attention that's pressing down on me, making me feel like the walls are closing in.

I find myself focusing on Henry—his perplexed dark eyes, his flop of mussed hair, his terribly interesting mouth, now quirked into an expression of total confusion. Focusing on him and only him . . . it grounds me in a weird way. Makes me feel like nothing else matters.

This is not something the nure-onna approves of, but it works for now.

I reach him, grab his hand, and tow him toward the kitchen.

"Hey, waitress—red-haired waitress!" one of the girls from table four yells. "You didn't finish taking our order!"

"I'll take your order when you stop whispering about me and taking my picture and figure out which kind of freaking chicken you want!" I snarl, dragging Henry through the kitchen doors. "There are only three kinds— it's not. That. *Hard!*"

"Wow, *rude!*" one of them calls after me.

"*There* you are," Belle says, as I storm back into the kitchen. "I was starting to wonder if the Beckys had managed to take you down, but to be honest, I can imagine no possible scenario where that . . . happens . . ."

Her mouth falls open as she zeroes in on the boy I've dragged in behind me.

And, for perhaps the first time in the seventeen years she's been on this planet, Belle Rakuyama is rendered speechless.

Auntie Och and Rory bustle in after us, talking over each other.

"Rika-chan, why you insult customers like that? We cannot afford—"

"Hank. Chen. *The* Hank Chen?! God, I have *so many* questions—"

"Everyone stop talking!" I yell, waving my hands around.

Surprisingly, they listen. The kitchen goes absolutely quiet—which only makes it easier to hear the chaos from the dining room.

I take a deep breath. Look at each of them in turn. Try to think of what comes next.

I finally settle for: "This is Henry. Henry Chen. And he's kind of famous."

Auntie Och's eyes narrow as she steps closer to Henry, sizing him up. To his credit, he doesn't flinch.

"You're that boy from the other day," she says slowly, like she's some kind of TV detective putting all the pieces together. "The one doing extra credit with Rika."

"No, Ma Och," Rory hisses through gritted teeth. Her little face has gone all red and she looks like she's about ready to die of embarrassment. "He was on *Dance! Off!*, remember? He *won!*"

Henry gives Rory a small smile—and she looks like she's about to disintegrate into a pile of heart emojis. Something about his smile tugs at my heart, too—and I realize it's because the primary feeling he's beaming out is *grateful*. Like he's thanking Rory for saving him from Auntie Och, even though he doesn't exactly need anyone to save him here, especially not a moony-eyed twelve-year-old.

"Um, yes," I say hastily, snapping myself back to the

present. "I mean. Both of those things are true. Henry just moved here for an acting gig, and he's going to be starting school with us in the fall, so he asked me to, um, tutor him."

I studiously avoid Henry's gaze, because I just know he's looking at me with one of his smiles. I don't know which one—smug? Earnest? Thankful?—and if I look at him, I'll get too caught up in deciphering that, which is 100 percent not productive right now.

"And then I guess some people saw us in the library while we were, um, studying, and they figured out where I work and . . . well . . ." I gesture toward the dining room.

Out of the corner of my eye, I see Rory sidling up to Belle and showing her the phone screen, the picture of Henry and me.

"Rika went *viral*," Rory murmurs, her voice full of awe. "Twice if you count the Grace photo, but no one was really focusing so much on Rika-chan in that one."

"Wow, you guys are *studying* really hard," Belle says, arching an eyebrow as she looks at the picture. I can practically see the gears in her brain turning—remembering how I was so flushed and out of it earlier, trying to speculate on the reason for my spacinesss . . .

Thinking about that only makes me flush more. I try

to shove it down, to will my cheeks to *not* turn bright pink.

"Yeah, so," I say, trying to make my voice as nonchalant as possible, "my shift's about over, and we actually need to go study some more—"

"No." Auntie Och shakes her head vehemently, her laser-like gaze homing in on me. "Rika-chan, we have way too many customer, we need you to stay! Suzy is at the weekly Little Tokyo business owners meeting, and those things always last forever because George Watanabe drone on and on and on."

"But . . ." I shake my head and try to calm the flash of temper that's already rising in my chest. I have a *plan*. I can't let anything mess it up, not when I'm so close. "My shift is over. And I *really* need to study. You've got Belle and Rory—"

"I'm really good at making the salad," Rory boasts, grinning eagerly at Henry. "It's kind of my specialty."

"Surely you can handle . . ." I spare a glance out the kitchen door's tiny window, and my heart nearly leaps out of my chest. Henry's adoring public has apparently tired of waiting outside, and the massive line is trying to pack itself into Katsu That. We're in serious danger of violating the fire code. And maybe some other codes as well.

"W-we have to close," I sputter. "We can't handle this.

I'm not sure we even have enough panko for this crowd—"

"No." Auntie Och glares at me. "We cannot turn away customers, Rika-chan, we must rise to the occasion. This kind of . . . mmm, what you call it? *Publicity.* Doesn't come around very often."

"But . . ." My voice is plaintive, desperate. My rage has somehow morphed into panic, the realization that I could get stuck here and miss Grace flashing through me like a lightning bolt hitting me square in the chest.

I can't miss this chance. I *can't.*

But I also can't tell Auntie Och what I'm up to.

I shake my head, furiously trying to get my brain to turn on, to come up with some miraculous solution that will allow me to claim this thing I want so badly—

"I can help."

Four Rakuyama women whip around in unison to gaze upon the source of that remark—Henry Chen.

"I can help," he repeats. "With getting through this rush. The faster we get through all these customers, the sooner Rika and I can go study. Right?"

"Hmm." Auntie Och squints at him, her naturally suspicious gaze somehow turning even more suspicious. "What experience do you have, fancy TV star? You know anything about working in a restaurant?"

"Not really," Henry says cheerfully. "But I cook dinner with my parents all the time when I'm home in New York. I can probably pick some things up."

"That's so *wholesome*," Belle murmurs.

"Mmm." Auntie Och sizes him up some more, then seems to come to a decision. "Okay—hai. I run across the street to the store and get more panko—if I send one of you, I know you will get the wrong kind. Rika, you and Belle take turns waitressing and making the katsu."

"And I'll do the salad!" Rory sings out, dancing over to the counter that's designated for salad-making, already covered in the piles of cabbage I shredded earlier.

"Henry Chen, you help Rory with the salad," Auntie Och says hastily—because Rory, despite her proclamation, is actually *completely terrible* at making the salad. "Then help Rika and Belle with waitressing as needed. Maybe take pictures with your fans, ne? Tell them to tag Katsu That. And location tag, too, very important."

"Of course," Henry says, giving her one of his movie star smiles.

Auntie Och smirks slightly to herself, and now I can see *her* wheels turning—realizing that even though she doesn't know who Hank Chen is, all of these customers *do*. And his presence can only mean good things for Katsu That.

As she bustles off to get more panko, I grab Henry's

arm and pull him aside, trying to ignore the blatant stares from Belle and Rory.

"Hey," I whisper, scanning his face. "Are you sure you're okay with this?"

"The goal is to get out of here as quickly as we can, right?" he says, his eyes drifting to my baseball cap—and the bright red curl that has come loose yet again. "So we can make the meeting with Grace?"

"With *hopefully* Grace," I correct. "I just . . . that crowd out there. Isn't it bad for your anxiety?"

"Are you worried about me?" he says, his voice light—but there's something underneath, something charged I don't want to think about. Before I can respond, he switches back to his easy grin and gives me a shrug. "It's actually better for me when I have a job, something to do. I can focus on that—on each piece of the task, even if it's something as simple as smiling for the crowd. I'll be fine, and we'll be outta here in no time."

"Okay," I say, but he's already marching over to Rory's salad-making station. She's dumped all the ingredients for Auntie Suzy's signature miso dressing into a big bowl—in what looks like all the wrong quantities—and is mixing them together with fervor, her brow furrowed in intense concentration.

"Hey," Henry says, smiling at her. "Rory, right?"

"Aurora," she corrects, preening a little.

"Aurora," he says, not missing a beat. "I guess I'm your assistant, huh? Wanna show me how to make this famous salad?"

"It's all in the dressing," she says, brandishing her bowl. "Ma Suzy spent years developing her special recipe. Wanna taste?"

"Sure," Henry says, grabbing a spoon. He dips it in the bowl, takes a taste . . . and then turns absolutely green around the gills. "Oh, that's, uh . . ."

I smother a laugh. The dressing is, no doubt, drowning in salt, which Rory always adds with way too much vigor. Whenever one of us tries to gently suggest that she measure the ingredients, she righteously points out that Auntie Suzy never measures anything. And she's right—but one of Auntie Suzy's witchy powers is she doesn't need to. Her food always comes out perfectly delicious.

Rory did not inherit this power.

I'm about to step in and fix the dressing—like I always do—but Henry quickly swallows his terrible bite and reinstates his winning smile.

"Incredible," he says to Rory, somehow sounding like he isn't totally lying. "But you know what I think would make it even better . . ." He swipes a lemon wedge from the counter and holds it over the bowl. "May I?"

he asks. "Final decision is the chef's, of course."

"Ohhhh, I totally forgot about the lemon!" Rory yelps, her eyebrows quirking upward. "Yeah, squeeze it in there."

He squeezes the lemon in while Rory gazes at him adoringly. I find myself suddenly transfixed by the way muscle ripples up his arm, the way his plain white T-shirt hugs his broad shoulders and accentuates his golden-brown skin—

"Rika-chan!" Now Belle is hissing in my ear, startling me out of my very important study of, um . . . whatever I was just studying. "What's going on?" she demands, jerking her head in Henry's direction. "I know this isn't about"—she draws her words out suggestively—"*studying*."

"He's helping me with the Grace thing—he *knows* her," I hiss back, all too aware that my face is now several shades brighter than a fire engine. "And we might have a chance to meet her today, if I can actually get out of here."

"Okay, I really need to know *everything*," Belle says, swatting me with a kitchen towel. "I can't believe you've kept all these important developments to yourself."

"There hasn't been a ton of time to share," I say. "I'll tell you everything later, but right now I have to . . ." My overactive brain grinds to a halt. So much has happened in the last ten minutes, and it feels like there are *so many things* I have to do, but I can't seem to remember where I'm supposed to start.

Part of the problem, I suppose, is that my eyeballs are still glued to Henry Chen's biceps.

I tear my gaze away from him—all too aware that Belle is tracking my every move—and aim myself at the dining room. At the very least, I can go see if the Becky table is finally ready to order.

The dining room is still in chaos when I emerge, and I let myself sink into it—the noise, the clatter of plates, the irresistible scent of fried panko wafting through the air. The Uncles have gone back to their drunken carousing. The line outside is now more orderly. People are still peering through the window, trying to get a glimpse of Hank Chen. But now that Henry's been spirited away to the kitchen, some of the rabid frenzy seems to have died down.

The Beckys huddle around their table, combing over each other's phones with great intensity, probably trying to find the perfect candid shot of Henry to post. Or of me. I wonder how rage-y I look.

I take a few deep breaths, touch the precious photos in my pocket, and remind myself of my quest: all I have to do is get through this late afternoon rush, take some orders, and be borderline pleasant. And then I can go to Grace.

I can do this.

I paste what I hope is an extra-serene smile on my face and march over to table four yet again, pencil clutched in my sweaty hand like a sword.

"I'm back!" I declare, making my smile even wider and infusing my tone with over-the-top brightness. Unfortunately, my attempts at being cheerful make my voice sound completely unnatural and I can't *quite* squelch that thread of annoyance that keeps rising up, so my offer of help seems more like I'm threatening to bite their heads off. The girls recoil. I try to tell my face to freaking *relax*, but—

"Waitress! Hey, waitress!" A loud, sneery voice cuts through my thoughts. I whip around to see none other than Craig Shimizu snapping his fingers at me, smug grin firmly in place.

I see red before I can stop it, then sternly order my kaiju-temper to stay leashed. The goal is to get out of here, not start a brawl.

"Excuse me for a sec," I say to the table four girls.

I tighten my grip around my pencil—my sword—and cross the room to Craig Shimizu. His smug look never falters.

"Can I help you?" I say through gritted teeth. My

tone is not *completely* pleasant, but at least I don't sound like I'm about to bite his entire head off. Yet.

"Yeeeeah," he drawls, lazily tapping the plastic-coated menu. "Can you explain the cheese katsu?" His nose wrinkles. "Doesn't seem very authentic."

"It's basically as described," I say, my shoulders stiffening. He clearly wants to start some shit, and I have to remind myself *not* to take the bait. "Cheese, covered in panko, fried. It's for our more adventurous customers. There are plenty of very traditional offerings on the menu. As you know, since you've been here before. Many times."

"Hmm." He makes a big show of examining the menu. I tap my pencil against my order pad, trying to breathe through my full-body annoyance. "Maybe I'll have a salad. But please ensure that it's made by an *adult* who knows what they're doing—not that brat who over-salts the dressing until it's inedible—"

"*Hey,*" I snap, rage stabbing through me. "Do *not* talk about Rory—"

"You're right," he says, his smile getting even bigger. "It's not her fault she was born into such a mega-freak family. Maybe if she had better role models—"

"May I take your order?" I interject loudly, doing everything in my power to keep my voice steady. I press my pencil to my order pad so hard, the tip almost snaps off.

"*There's* that temper," Craig says, his eyes narrowing shrewdly. "I've always thought that must be your white side coming through—*you're* probably the reason Rory's all messed up, huh?"

I reel back, all the blood draining from my face.

"I . . ." I swallow hard. My voice is wavery, on the verge of tears. I feel like I'm about to explode. Why does he have to do this? Why does he have to choose *today* of all days to do this?

"Is there a problem here?"

I nearly jump out of my skin, then turn to see Henry standing behind me, toting two big plates of katsu. Without missing a beat, he sets them down in front of two elderly Aunties at the table next to Craig's. The Aunties gaze at him adoringly, then turn their attention back to me.

And suddenly I'm very aware of the fact that *everyone* is looking at me. I'm causing yet another *disruption*. The Becky table chatters among themselves and snaps pictures. The drunk Uncles openly stare at whatever drama's about to unfold.

"No," I say to Henry, collecting myself. "Everything's fine. Go back to the kitchen and help Rory with, um . . ." I swallow again, trying to squelch the flush that seems to be overtaking me, the red haze that's fallen over my vision. I know my nure-onna fangs are out now.

An excited murmur sweeps through the restaurant, everyone buzzing about Hank Chen's hunky presence and the rage-y girl who cannot seem to keep herself from becoming the undesirable center of attention these past few days.

"Oh, how nice," Craig gloats. "The half-breed orphan's found herself a mutt guard dog."

"*Honestly*," I blurt. "Did your mother just never teach you any manners ... or ... or ..."

He grins as I sputter. Then he leans forward in his seat and locks his eyes with mine, sounding each word out very deliberately.

"At least I have one."

His retort hits like a slap. I take a step back, trying not to give in to the unleashed rage thrumming through my veins. An avalanche of words clogs my throat, making me choke, and unexpected tears fill my eyes. I blink them back furiously, trying to get a handle on the emotions blazing through me, but they won't stop, they just ... won't ... *stop* ...

I'm out of control again. I'm about to fucking explode. I'm ... I'm ...

Henry studies me, his expression unreadable. I know everyone in the restaurant is still staring at us, but they all seem to fade away as my vision narrows and the blood roars through my ears.

Henry turns back to Craig and tilts his head. He looks so *unbothered*. Like Craig is a gnat, barely worthy of his interest. He crosses his arms over his chest and gives Craig a placid grin.

"That was extremely rude. I think you should leave."

"I'm a *customer*," Craig says, relishing every syllable.

"A customer who's being *rude*," Henry says, that placid grin never faltering. "Therefore no longer a customer."

"My father is very important in this community—head of the Nikkei Week board," Craig sneers. "I know you might not realize that, being an outsider and all. And I really don't think you should talk to me that way."

"Then maybe he should come down here and explain *why* you're acting like an asshole," Henry says—and I marvel at how he still sounds so *pleasant*.

Craig splutters for a moment. The more worked up he gets, the calmer Henry becomes.

"Fine," he snarls, scrambling to his feet. He starts to move toward the door, but Henry lightly places a hand on his shoulder.

"Before you go—apologize," he says.

Same pleasant tone, same placid grin. Like he's giving Craig tips on flower arranging or something.

"Excuse me?!" Craig spits out.

"Apologize to her," Henry says, nodding at me.

Craig's gaze goes to Henry's hand on his shoulder. Then to me.

"I don't think so," he says.

Henry's expression never wavers. I notice his hold on Craig isn't firm or menacing at all; he's just resting his hand lightly on Craig's shoulder, almost like he's trying to reassure him of something. Craig could probably easily shake that hand off and storm out.

And yet, he doesn't.

There's something about Henry's posture, the way his gaze never wavers from Craig that makes it seem impossible to do so. Maybe it's his natural movie star charisma, turned all the way up. He's so *in control* of the situation. I am envious—because I'm never in control of any situation. Once my temper comes unleashed, everything spirals and destruction is inevitable.

They stand that way for a moment more, frozen, everyone watching. The restaurant has suddenly gone deathly silent, the weight of everyone's gaze making the air thick and soupy.

"Henry," I murmur. "It's all right. It's—"

"It's not," he says.

Craig finally breaks the spell, shaking Henry's hand off.

"Sorry," he mutters in my general direction. He huffs out of the restaurant with as much dignity as he can muster, which isn't very much.

Henry watches until he's gone. Then he turns to me.

"Are you okay?" he asks, his eyes searching my face.

"I—yes," I say, feeling my nure-onna armor reinstate itself. "Why did you . . . you didn't have to make a scene. I can handle myself. I don't need someone else to fight my battles."

He takes a step closer to me, his gaze probing in a way that makes me squirm. This isn't movie star Henry or joking Henry or too-cute-for-his-own-good Henry. It's something clear and heartfelt, something I can't quite process.

"I know you can," he finally says. "But you don't always have to fight alone."

ELEVEN

By the time Henry and I get to Griffith Park, it's nearly seven. I find myself wishing really hard that somehow Grace *knows* I'm coming, that our magical mother-daughter bond snapped into place the moment she crashed into me at the parade.

My nure-onna nature tells me that's impossible. That I never wish for things, because I know they can't come true. That I need to prepare myself for my typical sad ending yet again.

That's all that's possible. That's all that's *ever* been possible. Why am I even entertaining such fantastical flights of fancy?

"This is beautiful." Henry's voice cuts into my thoughts.

I'm so distracted, I can only respond with an off-handed "Yeah."

It really *is* beautiful, though. Griffith Park is a huge sprawl of green and flowering wildlife wrapped around one end of the Santa Monica Mountains. It's big enough to be at least three parks, and I love all the ways it transports you to different worlds. It's like a fantastical kingdom with a selection of doors—portals that will take you on an endless array of adventures.

The gorgeous hiking trails winding up into the mountains give you stunning views of the city. Its majestic observatory—featured in a cavalcade of movies that never seem to do it justice—takes you to the stars. And the deeper you hike into its wild clusters of nature, the more untamed and overgrown it gets. It feels like entering a magical hideaway, cut off from the smog and urban bustle of the city.

Because it's summer, I know all areas of the park will be hopelessly crowded, so I have Henry park in the big lot near the famous merry-go-round—that means we'll have to hike a bit to get to the abandoned zoo area, but that will be way faster and less frustrating than trying and failing to find parking in one of the tinier areas closer to where we're going. The tinkly music from the merry-go-round gives us a somewhat eerie-yet-festive fanfare when we exit the car.

Henry can't seem to stop looking around excitedly as we hike farther in, his eyes lit with genuine awe.

"Do you come here a lot? It's incredible."

"I do," I say, trying to brush all thoughts of my imminent reunion from my mind—even as the fluttery feeling in my gut remains. "I'm kind of surprised at *your* reaction, though—don't you have cool parks in that ever-superior New York of yours?"

"We do," he says, his eyes doing that twinkly thing that means he's just oh-so-amused. "But this is something else. I didn't realize such *grandeur* was possible in LA."

"Well, get ready, because there's way more where that came from," I say, gesturing to the gloriously clear early evening sky. "Once we get to the old zoo, I'm expecting you to be fully dazzled."

I have to say, this amorphous stretch between day and night always feels extra weird during the summer, when the sun hovers in the sky for longer and the light fights off the encroaching darkness for a few extra hours, refusing to give an inch. The heat also lingers, although out here it's not quite as blistering as downtown. All the green tempers it—there's that scrap of shade from a lazy palm frond, that soft breeze feathering over our skin. I know summer is a time a lot of people associate with pure fun—freedom and possibility, a season when things both end and begin. But I've always seen it as hopelessly melancholy. The sun and the heat try so hard to stay, to hang on to those last gasps of daylight before sliding into the cool gloom of fall.

It's not just summer that's weird and melancholy right now, though—there's also this off-kilter energy between me and Henry. After Craig stormed out, things mostly got back to normal—whatever this afternoon's version of "normal" is. We cycled through our customers, Henry took pictures with all his fans, and we left Auntie Och gleefully tallying up the day's impressive earnings.

And Henry and I have snapped back to our usual dynamic—his happy-puppy energy bouncing off my permanent scowl and resulting in snipey bickering. But right now there's something about it that feels hollow, like we're playacting exaggerated versions of ourselves, wearing costumes that suddenly feel too big.

I can't help but flash back to our afternoon at Katsu That, to that moment when he met my eyes and very seriously asked if I was okay—

"Rika, is everything all right?" Henry says, as if reading my mind.

And those simple words bring up that wild swirl of untamed feelings all over again. I feel my face get hot, my chest tighten. I don't know why I'm having all these *emotions* over such a basic question.

"Fine," I say briskly, quickening my step.

God, we're about to be late. Part of me wants to turn around and go home. There's no way she'll wait for very long—is there? Will she fight as hard as the sun to stay here? Will she fight as hard . . . for me?

I can't stop that tiny flutter of hope skittering through my gut, wanting so desperately to believe that we'll arrive at those jagged rock formations and see Grace Kimura, her brilliant smile lighting up the whole damn park as she throws her arms wide to greet me. "We're coming up on seven way too fast, and since she never responded to your texts, we have no real way of communicating with her, and I just . . . I hope . . ." I trail off, the words thickening in my throat. I can't even vocalize my hope. It feels too much like . . . well, a fairy tale.

"She'll be there," Henry says, the sureness in his voice sending a flash of warmth through me that has nothing to do with the hazy sun. "But I meant, like, are you all right after what happened with that rude asshole—Craig?"

"Oh," I say, my voice tipping up in surprise. "I mean . . . yeah. Of course. He's always doing shit like that—saying shit like that. I'm used to it."

That last bit comes out way snappier than I intend, and I bite my lip, as if trying to stuff all the words back into my mouth. Henry's quiet for a long moment, and the only sounds are our feet rustling against the soft cushion of the grass as we continue to tramp toward the abandoned zoo.

When he finally speaks, his voice is so quiet, I have to strain to hear it.

"That doesn't make what he said okay."

I . . . *what*? I have no idea what to do with that, so now it's my turn to be silent. I find myself walking faster, moving ahead of him. Like I'm trying to outrun both the slow set of the sun and any further conversation.

But Henry being Henry, that's not the end of it.

"That guy's a dick," Henry says with great conviction. "And you're so *you*—"

"What is that supposed to mean?" I say, my face flaming.

"Just . . . you never have any problem telling me when I've done something . . . displeasing," he says, a hint of amusement creeping into his voice.

I walk even faster, farther ahead of him, my face getting hotter with every step. I don't want him to see how red I'm getting.

"So why don't you let that Craig dipshit have it?" Henry continues.

"I did—once," I say. "Well, two times. When we were kids in judo together. I was eight, he was ten."

"I definitely need to know this story," Henry says.

"That's basically it. The first time, we were sparring, and he didn't release me when I tapped out—so I bit him.

The other time, he was being obnoxious, saying a bunch of shit about my family. He made Belle cry. I saw red, and I charged him. I don't know what I was thinking—he was so much bigger than me. Auntie Suzy scooped me up by the back of my judogi before I even got to him."

"I can picture exactly what you must have looked like," he says—and I swear I can hear his smile. "So small, yet so fierce."

"People in the community didn't see it in quite such an adorable way," I counter, keeping my steps brisk. "I almost got kicked out of the dojo over the biting—the whole Rakuyama clan nearly did. And that's how the Legend of Rika the Biter and Her Uncontrollable Kaiju-Temper got started in Little Tokyo." I try to revert to a lighter, more jokey tone. Like I'm delivering an especially epic movie trailer voiceover instead of talking about myself.

But Henry doesn't laugh.

"I dunno," he says. "It sounds like Rika the Biter was *provoked*. By an older kid who wasn't playing even close to fair. Maybe that incident should've started the Legend of Craig the Big Bully Asshole instead."

"Not how the story goes," I say, waving a hand. "But it's cool. I aspire to one day transform from Rika the Biter to full nure-onna."

"Nure-onna?" he says. Perfect rolled r again.

"She's a mythical creature from Japanese folklore—a badass snake-woman," I say. "Only she's able to be *calculated* in her lashing out. I . . . my temper. It *destroys* things. It's like this monster, living inside me. I have to shove it down, keep it all chained up. I already bring a lot of the wrong kind of attention to my family just by existing. If I let loose on Craig, if I totally let the monster out . . ." I shake my head. "The consequences could be a lot. His father is really powerful in the community—they could get people to boycott my Aunties' restaurant if they really wanted to, or ban all the Rakuyamas from Nikkei Week."

"Is that how you see yourself?" he asks, his tone genuinely curious. "A monster?"

"Always," I say. "When I get into a rage about something, it's bad. It's like this thing, pounding against my chest, dying to get out. And when it does get out, it wants to bite things. Dump full cans of soda on people. Or . . . see that family over there?" I gesture to a happy family lounging in a picnic area: Mom, Dad, two little daughters. All perfect and blonde and wearing coordinating outfits. The girls both have red balloons, floating lazily above their heads. "When I was a kid, we were out on the Japanese Village Plaza one day, and I saw a picture-perfect family like that with these two little blonde white girls holding Hello Kitty balloons. They were about the same age as me and Belle. Belle *really* wanted a balloon—it was pink and sparkly, after all—and Auntie Och said no, it was a waste of money. Somehow, those white girls overheard and started making fun of Belle. Talking about how she couldn't even afford a freakin' balloon, laughing at her little homemade princess dress. They said she couldn't be a real princess anyway, because she didn't look like one."

"Because Asian," Henry murmurs.

"Yeah. They started calling her Mulan. In a way that was definitely *not* meant as a compliment—and Belle always wanted to be Cinderella anyway, so she started crying. So I, um . . . I popped their balloons."

"What?" Henry hoots, shaking his head. "Just like that?"

"I mean, they were already deflating, getting lower to the ground—it wasn't that much work to run over and stomp on them. That 'pop' was *so* satisfying. Of course they started crying, and I got in huge trouble, and Auntie Och hustled us back home. Belle was pissed at me for ruining the day."

"Sounds like she should have *thanked* you," Henry says. "You were a brave little knight, swooping in to avenge her honor. Personally, I think your inner nure-onna should be proud of that."

"Belle definitely did *not* see it that way," I say, my voice wry. "I was destructive. An angry monster, ready to attack, fangs bared."

I quicken my pace, wanting to get away from the perfect blonde family. Will my mother also see a monster? Or will she understand? She's a beautiful princess, a *queen*—and yet I swear I saw something so familiar in her eyes that day at the parade.

I'm so set on my determined march—eyes forward, not looking at Henry at all, focused on getting to Grace—that I nearly jump out of my skin when I feel his hand grab mine.

I freeze in my tracks. Like if I pretend to be invisible, I won't feel that crackle of energy running up my arm.

I'm still in front of him, my arm stretched out behind me, and he catches up so he's standing right next to me. Now our arms dangle between us, loosely connected at the point where he's taken my hand.

"You keep talking about your temper—and it seems like people in your family, your community like to bring it up a lot, too," he says. I'm still frozen in place, my eyes trained straight ahead, not looking at him. It feels deeply weird. It also feels like moving so much as a millimeter would be even weirder.

So I just keep looking off into the distance.

"I . . . I don't really see anger," he says, his words coming out in a rush. For some reason, I think he's flushing, too, and that only makes me flush more. "I see *passion*. I see that you care so much about things—about your family, protecting the people you love, not wanting to hurt them in any way. But I think sometimes that's hurting *you*."

Tears spring to my eyes, unbidden. I *definitely* can't move now.

"What that Craig guy said to you wasn't just, like, teasing," he continues. "It was cruel. You said you're worried about destroying things, but some things *need* to be destroyed. That doesn't make you a monster. Not in the way you're thinking, anyway."

We stand there for a moment, frozen in time. I am acutely conscious of the sun beating down on us, the sweat beading the back of my neck, the scent of jacaranda wafting through the air. And, of course, of his hand holding mine. His touch is light, his grip is loose—I could easily pull away if I wanted to.

And yet, I don't.

Henry's the one who finally breaks the spell, giving my hand a little tug forward, then dropping it.

"We should get moving," he says, his voice overly

bright—back to wearing that too-big costume. He walks ahead of me, his stride long, his steps jaunty. I almost expect him to start whistling. "I have no idea where I'm going," he calls over his shoulder. "You gotta take the lead again."

I shake myself out of my frozen stupor—as if an evil witch has released me from her curse—and jog back in front of him, self-consciously brushing my unruly hair forward so that, once again, he can't see my face.

✱

It takes us ten minutes more to reach the site of the old zoo, but it feels like ten *years*. We're definitely about to be late. The sun is hazy in the sky now, the full power of its brightness beginning to dim. It bounces off those jagged rock formations in dreamy patches of light.

This old site has always fascinated me—there's a sense of abandonment and decay, all too apparent from the fading slashes of graffiti sweeping over some of the old sun-bleached orange-brown animal enclosures and the rickety picnic tables covered in the gossamer film of spiderwebs. And yet, there is also something about it that's indisputably *alive*—the air feels heavier when you enter the space, the chorus of bug chitterings seems to get louder, and I always half expect all that graffiti to come to life, leap off those surfaces, and envelop everything in its bright web of jagged lines.

It's almost like the old zoo is begging not to be forgotten, even though it no longer serves its original purpose and never will again.

The area is fairly deserted as Henry and I approach—there's a mom trying to get her kids packed up and outta there, an old man taking a meandering walk with a sack of oranges slung over his shoulder . . .

And then the old man moves out of the way to reveal a slim figure in a wispy white summer dress with a flowing mane of raven hair. Her back is to us, and she's standing very still.

Waiting.

My footsteps slow, even as my heart speeds up. And I swear a glow surrounds this figure, calling out to me. My heartbeat is so loud, I can hear it in my ears, pounding relentlessly through my bloodstream, syncing with each step forward.

I imagine mere milliseconds into the future, the figure turning and seeing me, her eyes lighting up as the glow emanating from her surrounds us both—

"Rika," Henry says—and he sounds as excited as I feel. "I think that's . . ."

Then she actually does turn. And her face does light up—for the man rushing toward her and sweeping her into a romantic embrace.

It's not her.

It's not Grace.

My head gets the message before my heart does, stopping me dead in my tracks once again.

And then my heart gets it, too, plummeting back through my chest, my stomach, right down to my shoes.

It's not her.

"Oops, false alarm," Henry says. "It really looked like her from the back, though."

"Let's go," I say, my voice spilling out in a way that I want to be brisk and businesslike but sounds way too much like I'm trying not to cry. "It . . . it's just like I thought. We're too late, she's not here, and . . . I already knew she wouldn't be, I don't know why I let myself . . . *hope* . . ."

"Hey." Henry moves in front of me so I have to look at him instead of remaining fixated on Not Grace off in the distance. "Just because *that's* not her doesn't mean she isn't here, period. I did some research into the old zoo last night—aren't there other areas, like . . ." He gestures at the rock formations. "Inside? Or behind? That we can explore?"

"Yes," I say, forcing my mind to focus, to stop my heart from wailing at me about its dashed hopes. "But why would she go deeper inside if the whole purpose is to meet up with me? Why would she *hide*?"

Henry purses his lips and turns to the rock formations, assessing their every crevice. "Maybe she doesn't want anyone else to see her—since she's gone off the grid and all. But also, this whole situation is weird, right?" he says. "Just flat-out, does not make sense, sounds like a totally made-up story *weird*. I don't think we can apply logic to any of it. You said the zoo is like LA's ancient ruins. So we have to consider ourselves true adventurers—explore every possibility."

He grins at me—and his gaze is so earnest, I can't help but feel that little flutter of hope rise in my chest again.

"I . . . okay," I say, turning back to the rock formations. "So, yes, there are more parts of this we can explore. These enclosures were kind of built into a giant hill, and there's this area that's sort of *inside* the formations, that leads you to the upper part of the hiking trail—that's where the graffiti game *really* comes out. It's kinda hard to maneuver in, though—you might be a little, um . . . tall . . ."

Why does a word as mundane as "tall" make me blush all of a sudden? *What is wrong with me?*

"I can handle it," he says, his grin turning sly. "I've got moves, remember?"

And then he dances ahead of me, that balletic grace of his on full display. The kids being swept off by their mom titter among themselves, pointing in his direction. He notices, makes a goofy face at them—and dances even more.

I find myself laughing, too, as I jog to catch up with him, wondering how someone can be so . . . unrestrained. Unselfconscious. I am always so *aware* of how my body is positioned, what I look like, what people might say about me.

But he doesn't care. He is so utterly and completely himself.

"It's this way," I say, jogging ahead so I can lead him. I gesture to the entryway of one of the formations—a big jagged-edged hole that looks like a gaping mouth. "See, I think this entryway used to be covered in glass, so you could see lions roaming around inside. And then we go over here . . ." I step inside the formation, into the cavernous darkness. In front of us is another, much smaller hole revealing a narrow series of concrete steps bordered on each side by rocky stone walls—a tunnel, basically. A set of iron bars hovers over the entrance to the steps, presenting an additional challenge—the space we have to crawl through to get to the steps is so tiny, we'll both have to crouch down. And Henry will have to crouch down so much more.

Because, you know . . . he's so *tall*.

"Really—we can go in?" Henry says, cocking a skeptical eyebrow. "This looks like the kind of forbidden area kids sneak into in movies and then end up either getting arrested or dying horrifically after awakening some kind of ancient curse."

"I love how those are our only choices," I say, rolling my eyes. "But, no, this is safe—part of the ruins that people explore all the time. These steps are what leads us to the upper part of the trail—see how the sunlight is coming through? And if you get really scared, I'll protect you."

I half expect him to protest, all manly-like, but that's not Henry—he just grins and gestures for me to go first.

I crouch under the iron bars, crawl through the opening, and carefully begin making my way up the concrete staircase—another portal, transporting me to another magical part of Griffith Park. I spare a glance behind me and see Henry ducking under the bars, graceful as a cat.

The stairs are slanted, oddly steep, and the passageway is so claustrophobic—but for some reason, I've never been afraid of falling. Even though scraps of sunlight filter in from the trail, I still feel like I'm surrounded by shadows. Like I'm *home*.

This expanse of gray concrete might look pretty depressing if it weren't for the wild splashes of bright graffiti covering nearly every inch of space. This is a prime spot for the artists and taggers of the city; their work never gets washed away or "cleaned up"—people keep adding to it. Now it's an elaborate mural that feels like a decades-in-the-making chronicle of this part of the city—vibrant, always in motion, always alive.

"If we go up these steps, it leads to this whole area of old cages," I say, my voice echoing down the chasm of the staircase. "Lots of people like to wander around up there. Maybe Grace is one of them? I dunno, is this her kind of thing?"

My voice gets too loud and too high on that last syllable, as if I'm trying to hide the fact that every question I ask about Grace is weighted with bottomless yearning.

"I think she'd dig it," Henry says slowly, as we very gingerly pick our way up the staircase. "She's so . . . hmm, how can I describe it? She *relishes* life so much. She's always trying to dive fully into every experience, to wring every drop of joy out of it."

"So . . . not like me, then," I say, trying to keep my tone light. "Not trying to suppress her feelings and go to the shadows because she's scared of destroying everything around her."

"Mmm—actually, I think she *is* like you. Or you're like her. Like I said, she also has that *passion*."

I am suddenly glad for the catacomb-like atmosphere, because he can't see me blush again. I really need to get a handle on the blushing. Maybe I should get an on-purpose sunburn so no one can tell.

We reach the top of the staircase, duck under another forbidding set of bars, and reach the hidden world of the old zoo.

"Whoa," Henry says, his voice echoing a bit off the walls. "This is *so cool*."

He smiles in wonder, taking in the jagged concrete walls, the hollowed-out spots that were once animal enclosures, and that endless, uncontained rainbow of graffiti. The upper part of the old zoo has different "rooms," little secret spaces that feel like whisperings from the past, fitted together in a nonsensical puzzle. Once you step outside these rooms, you hit an old-fashioned chain-link fence with big holes cut in it. Pass through one of these holes, and you'll be transported to the sun-drenched hiking trail—another world, yet again.

The area we've emerged in actually has my favorite bit of graffiti, dreamy strokes of brilliant turquoise punctuated by silvery swirls that glint in the few rays of sunlight streaming in.

But today, it does nothing to calm me.

"It *is* cool," I say, my gaze sweeping the desolate space. "It's also empty. She's not here, either." I feel a pinprick of frustration, just potent enough to make me itchy.

"Let me try texting her again," Henry says, pulling out his phone. "Ahh, no service." He stuffs the phone back in his pocket. "What if we just wait for a minute?"

"For *what*?" I say. That frustration is clawing at my insides now, the itch spreading over my entire body. "Even if she was late, too, how would she know we're up here? How would she know where to look? I still don't even know that the message on the photo was meant for me. I don't know . . . what to do . . ." I sit down hard on one of the concrete benches jutting out from the wall, all the air leaving my body in a dejected *whump*.

For a moment, there's just silence—the eerie quiet of this tucked-away pocket pressing down on me. I look at the floor, at those wild splashes of paint so many graffiti artists have left behind. I hate the way hope sends you careening after something, ignoring all the practical signs that it's just not going to fucking happen.

Eventually, I hear the soft trod of Henry's footsteps, feel him settling in next to me.

"Tell me what you like about this place," he says.

My head jerks up. "What? I'm having an existential crisis and you want me to give you a guided tour?"

"Sort of?" He laughs a little. "Actually this is something Grace taught me. Sometimes if I'm in pre-panic-attack mode, she'll ask me to tell her a really specific story—something about a restaurant I've gone to, or a moment when I remember falling in love with dancing. It helps my mind focus on the details—it grounds me. And the emotions I was feeling before that were so frustrating kind of . . . evaporate."

"That sounds . . . okay, fine," I concede, as the frustration roars through me, louder with every passing second. "Why not? It's not like I'm doing anything else." I blow out a long breath and stare at the silver swirls. They shimmer, as if encouraging me. "Auntie Suzy brought me and Belle and Rory here when we were little. All those wide-open spaces outside—it meant we could run around all we wanted. Plus, it was a free activity. I remember she brought us here once after Belle begged and begged to go to Disneyland to see all the princesses. Auntie Suzy told us this was *like* Disneyland—but, you know, something we could actually afford." I smile slightly at the memory, at Belle's indignant face when she realized her Disney princess dreams were definitely *not* coming true that day. "I guess we were about ten? Belle thought it was ugly. Rory was indifferent, mostly because Rory's favorite activity at that point was grabbing as many blades of grass as she could hold in her tiny little fist. And I . . ."

I close my eyes, remembering that day. Auntie Suzy looking tired as usual, slumped at one of the picnic tables with Rory plopped on a blanket at her feet. The way my heart skipped a few beats when I saw those strange rock formations that looked like a half-finished villain's lair. All the dark corners and shadows waiting for me, as if calling me home. I'd explored every single one of them. And then . . .

"I came up here," I say, recalling the way I'd skulked into the rock formation and found that ominous tunnel. "I almost tripped on my way up the stairs, but eventually I ended up *here*. And I was so . . ."

"Scared?" Henry says.

"Enchanted," I say, giving him a wry grin. "It felt like the nure-onna's lair. Like a place with *endless* shadows. I fantasized about moving here, setting up my own little home. Just me, all by myself."

"What an enterprising ten-year-old," Henry says. "Your aunt must have noticed you were gone, though—did you scare the shit out of her?"

"Sort of," I say. "She was so busy trying to keep Belle entertained and Rory from toddling farther into the grass, she didn't notice I'd completely disappeared until it was time to go. By then, I'd been up here for like half an hour."

"Were you stoked?" Henry says, amusement creeping into his voice. "For a whole half an hour, you got to live out your ultimate secret-lair dreams."

"I suppose I was. But I also . . ." I trail off, falling back into that moment in time that feels so long ago. I remember being excited, then kind of bored as the minutes ticked by. I remember making plans for how I was going to decorate my lair, and how maybe Auntie Suzy wouldn't look so tired now that she only had two kids to look after.

How my whole family could finally escape the shadow of Rika the Biter, Rika the *Monster*, who always seemed to cause trouble for them no matter what.

"But you also . . . what?" Henry prompts.

"Nothing," I say hastily, but now the memories won't stop. They're crashing over me, as loud and endless as the graffiti on these concrete walls. "I . . . I told myself I was happy. And at first, I was. But then I started getting bored. I started feeling . . . lonely." The word comes out jagged, broken. "And deep down, I wished . . ." My voice catches and I press my lips together, determined not to let any more words out. But somehow I know Henry can hear the rest.

I wished someone would come for me.

Which is what I'm doing now, hanging out here and hoping Grace will magically show up.

I am nothing more than a pathetic girl, sitting in a hidden-away part of the world, waiting for someone to want her.

"Let's go," I say abruptly, springing to my feet and scraping a hand over my eyes. "She's not coming, the park's probably about to close, and we're wasting time on nothing."

I stalk back down the staircase, putting a little of that Rory stomp in my step. Henry follows behind me, his footsteps quiet. Always so quiet.

We emerge to a dusky sky, the sun finally losing her battle and sinking into the earth. It's not cold—LA is almost never anywhere near cold in the summer—but there's a slight breeze in the air, and I stuff my hands into my pockets for warmth.

And that's when I realize . . . there's nothing in my pockets. They are empty, useless. The photos I've been carrying around with me like some kind of talisman are *gone*.

"Oh . . . oh *no*," I whimper.

"What?" Henry says, his brow furrowing with concern.

"Th-the photos," I manage. "The ones of Grace . . . they're gone."

"Maybe you dropped them in the ruins—let's go back," he says, turning to the entrance.

"No." I shake my head vehemently—and to my horror, the tears I managed to suppress earlier rise up once more. "I . . . the last time I remember having them was at the restaurant. They could have fallen out at any point. During my shift. While we were hiking. In the tunnel. Th-there's no way to know, it's pointless to even look . . ."

"Rika . . ." Henry's voice is so gentle, my tears spill over.

"Everything's ruined," I say, my voice breaking. "I . . . I don't know what I was thinking. This is playing out just like I thought it would. I can't find my mother, and now I've lost those stupid photos, and . . . and no one is coming for me. It *is* like a fairy tale. My kind of fairy tales, with the sad endings. Only—"

I can't say the rest.

Only this time, maybe I didn't want it to be sad.

My tears are flowing freely now, and I'm too lost and upset to even be embarrassed by it. My kaiju-temper pounds at my rib cage, demanding to be set free so it can fuck up this beautiful park.

I turn on my heel, wrap my arms around myself, and start stomping back to the trail.

Then I feel Henry grab my hand.

"Rika," he says again, more firmly. He's behind me, just like he was when he grabbed my hand the first time. I stop in my tracks and am angry to realize that once again, I don't want to pull away.

He moves in front of me, never letting go of my hand. I look at the ground. I absolutely *cannot* meet his gaze. It's too much.

"You can't give up," he says. "*We* can't give up."

"I don't understand," I say, my head all mixed up and muzzy from the emotions spinning through me and that little bit of electricity that hits right where our palms touch. "This day was a complete disaster, and our whole quest is an overall disaster so far. How can you have so much hope?"

"Look around," he says, his voice lit with that sense of wonder—the one I found so annoying earlier.

But I do lift my head, because I am suddenly hit by a jolt of longing so deep, so *potent*. In spite of myself, I desperately want to see what he sees.

I look up and witness the hazy Los Angeles sky turning dreamy orangey-pink, like an artist's streaked it with paint. The sun setting in the distance, casting whispers of light over the rock formations. The fuzzy shadows, settling in for the night. It looks unearthly, not of the human realm. Wild and weird and magical.

"All this beauty in the world," Henry says. "How can you *not* have hope?"

I tear my gaze from the enchanted sky and meet his eyes. He's smiling at me so openly—in that way that's so *him*. I'm too overwhelmed by my tornado of emotions to put up my usual defenses. To tell myself that I don't like the way his eyes light up with so many things or the perfect imperfection of his mouth or the way he looks at me with such . . . *such* . . .

I don't even know what to call it. I've never been looked at this way before.

He's not ready to give up on this thing I want so badly, this thing I *need* to feel whole. He believes so hard, even when it seems impossible.

I soak in that delicious breeze floating through the

air, infused with the scents of green and summer. I look at the pink sky and the enchanted shadows flickering around us.

Something shifts in my chest, and it feels like the world shifts with it. I feel so *moved* by all this beauty—and this boy who won't give up.

"Henry," I whisper, my voice shaky.

He squeezes my hand and leans in closer.

"Yes?" he says.

And suddenly I'm not looking at the pink sky anymore. It all melts away, and I can only see him—that hair I want to brush off his forehead, those eyes I want to stare into forever, that mouth I want to . . .

"I . . . you're right," I manage, my words tripping over themselves. "It *is* beautiful."

"It is," he says, his eyes never leaving mine.

He reaches up and smooths my tangle of hair away from my face, his thumb stroking leftover tears from my cheek. I shiver.

"Rika . . ." he murmurs—and it feels like he's asking me a question.

I answer by leaning in and pressing my lips to his.

They're soft at first, gentle and warm—then more insistent, his hands sliding into my hair and urging me closer.

All I can feel is how good this is. All I can think is . . . nothing. All I want is to stay frozen in this moment, with this boy.

I want him to keep kissing me forever, kissing me with so much *intent* as the sun sets behind us, rendering the pink sky velvet black.

TWELVE

Unfortunately, we can't stay locked in that moment forever because the old zoo area of the park closes promptly at sundown. The rangers shoo us to the exit trail, and we hustle back to Henry's car without saying more than two words to each other.

I'm happy to have a task to focus on, because otherwise I'd probably be spending way too much time thinking about what just happened, obsessing over it, overanalyzing it until I convince myself it's a mistake and I have absolutely no interest in Henry Chen *that way* and I need to turn myself into a monster and bite his head off so he won't hypnotize me any further.

Instead I am flushed, giddy, almost *giggly*. I can practically hear the nure-onna snarling at me, telling me we don't *do* giggly.

But I can't deny what I feel, any more than I can deny that I desperately wanted Grace to come find me.

That I secretly hoped for a happy ending this time.

"I can't believe this is your sweet celebrity ride," I say, as we get into Henry's dented old Subaru. I don't know why I even say that. Maybe it's a half-hearted attempt to snap us back to something more comfortable. But seriously, for someone who was so into Auntie Och's Mustang, it's weird that he has such a basic car—and one that's definitely seen better days.

"It's my parents' old car," he says, fiddling with one of the falling-off knobs on the console. "They gave it to me when I came out here."

"They're still in New York?" I ask, puzzled. I'd assumed his parents moved with him.

"Um, yeah," he says, giving me a rueful shrug. "I live in this kind of dorm thing for actors—it's like boarding school. I have roommates and stuff. Not very slick. So . . . should I take you home or . . . um . . ."

It's too dark to tell, but I swear he's flushed bright red. Neither of us wants to go home, but we're both afraid to say it. Saying it out loud might destroy the delicate, awkward crackle of energy that's simmered between us since we broke our kiss and were rushed out of the park. It's like we're both dancing around an electric fence, the desire to reach out and touch it irresistible, the knowledge that we can't irrefutable.

"I . . ." I stare at him for a moment, unable to do anything else. I shake my head, trying to wake myself from this all-new and exciting spell that's been cast over me. "I don't want to go home," I finally make myself say. Well, more like *confess*.

Henry's mouth curves into a tentative half smile. "Me neither."

We are thankfully saved from the electric fence by Henry's phone, which lets loose with a series of chimes.

"Oh," he says, tearing his gaze from mine and picking up the phone, "looks like we're back in the service area. And looks like I got some texts . . ."

I glance at my phone. *Oh, shit.* I also have *many* texts. From Belle and Rory, demanding more details on my "studying" with Henry. From Eliza and Sensei Mary, asking about the flood of pictures from today's star-studded lunch hour at Katsu That—and also wondering when I'll be coming back to practice.

I dismiss all notifications and turn my phone facedown.

Henry's brow furrows as he studies the screen, and I try not to stare obsessively at every single one of his features, lingering especially long on his mouth . . .

"Yes!" he murmurs, tapping on the screen. He looks up and grins at me. "There's an Asian Hollywood meetup tonight at this Thai place near . . . hmm, that area where Thai Town and Koreatown and Little Armenia sort of mush together."

"Very LA," I murmur.

"Aaaaaand . . ." With great fanfare, he flips the phone around and waves the screen in front of me, even though I can't really make out any of the individual messages. "There's a rumor that none other than Grace Kimura will be there!"

"What, really?!" I exclaim. "Are you sure that's something that could happen?" I try to order my heart to get itself under control, but it's exploding with newfound possibility. "If she's in hiding, why would she come to something so public?"

"The Asian Hollywood meetups aren't really public," Henry says, tapping a message back to someone. "They're supposed to be a safe space, no social media allowed. We usually rent out a place so we have it all to ourselves. It would actually make sense for Grace to go there, of all places, because she knows we'll offer her support and actually respect her wishes to stay off the grid."

"So . . ." I take a deep breath, trying to get my thoughts in order. I'm so scared to let this new possibility truly take root, and yet . . . I can't stop the excitement flooding through me, making me feel like I'm about to burst. "Can we go there?"

Henry gives me one of his big, goofy grins. "Of course we can." He reaches across the gearshift and takes my hand. "See? Didn't I tell you to have hope?"

I want to refute him. To say that our having "hope" isn't what magically made this happen.

But as he starts the car, I am shocked to find that I actually *do* have hope. Maybe for the first time ever. Like, in my life.

And as we take our meandering drive to the Thai Town/K-Town/Little Armenia mush, he holds my hand the whole way.

❧

The restaurant we're going to—Jitlada—is crammed into one of LA's corner strip malls, improbable collections of businesses bunched together in a mishmash of rainbow awnings and glittering neon lights.

These strip malls always have exactly three parking spots, none of which are wide enough to position an actual vehicle in. Sometimes in the evening, there's also a valet outside—as there is tonight. But Henry breezes right by the valet, turns the corner, and squeezes his car into a nearly invisible slip of a spot on the street.

"Wow," I say, as he aligns his wheels precisely. "That is some *smooth* parallel parking."

"Are you swooning over my *parking*?" he says, giving me an easy grin—but this one's relaxed, genuine. Not like the smug easy grin from before that unsettled me so much. It's like . . . he's comfortable with me.

"What if I am?" I retort.

"How Angeleno of you," he says, his grin widening. "Come on."

We exit the car and walk up to the strip mall. Jitlada has a bright red-and-yellow awning, proclaiming its name in both English and Thai. Its windows are festooned with cascading twinkle lights, little strings of colorful beads, and a maze of handmade signs advertising the day's specials.

"I've never actually eaten here," I muse, taking it all in. "But I keep hearing about how good it is. Especially the southern pineapple shrimp curry—it's supposed to be so spicy that your mouth goes numb. Auntie Suzy's always talking about it because she wants to try developing this certain kind of gyoza for Katsu That that *also* turns your mouth numb . . . what?"

Henry has stopped in his tracks and is just kind of staring at me.

"Come here," he says, grabbing my hand and pulling me around to the side of the building.

It is fully night now, and we're plunged into deep shadows. I lean against the pebbly, cold concrete of the restaurant, barely able to make out his features. But I notice his breathing is uneven.

"Are you okay?" I whisper—even though there's no one around to hear us. The valet is positioned on the other end of the lot, so far away he doesn't even know we're here. But something about the shadows, those soothing swoops of darkness I love so much, feels . . . private. Intimate. Like anything louder than a whisper will shatter our bubble.

"I'm fine," he says quickly—then leans in so his lips are perilously close to my ear.

I want to move my head just a millimeter, so they'll touch . . .

I also don't want to move at all.

"I want to kiss you again," he says—and I flush all over, suddenly unable to move anyway. "Is that okay?"

"Yes," I manage to breathe out.

I expect him to just go for it, but instead he pulls back, his eyes searching my face in the dark. I can barely make out his gaze, the hint of that imperfect mouth I can't stop thinking about. I expect it to be tilted up, giving me one of his smiles. But he looks so *serious*, studying me so intently—like he's trying to commit every piece of me to memory. He reaches down and touches that bright red strand of hair that won't stay off my face, running it between his fingertips and then—very gently—tucking it behind my ear. He does all of this so slowly, so deliberately—like he's getting ready to perform open-heart surgery or handling some extra-rare, crumbling old document.

Like he's touching something precious.

His hand cups my cheek—again, so very *carefully*—and I don't know why my heart is beating so fast, why my mouth is suddenly so dry, why . . . *why* . . .

We've already kissed once. Why do I feel like I'm about to come apart?

He dips his head and takes my mouth with his.

My whole being sighs, nearly melting against the cold wall of the building. He nips at my lower lip, teases my mouth open, strokes my tongue with his . . .

I gasp against him. I feel too hot. I feel too cold. I feel too . . . *everything*.

His hands slide from my face to my hair, his fingers tangling in the unruly waves. He really seems to love my hair. My knees go all wobbly, and my hands shoot out to grasp his hips, a desperate attempt to keep myself upright. My fingertips brush against the bare skin just underneath his T-shirt, and he makes this *sound* in the back of his throat that makes me want to . . . to . . .

Oh, I don't know. I'm so swept up in this kiss, cradled by the shadows, feeling wild and free, consumed by him . . .

I've been kissed before. But never like this.

When we finally pull apart, I think it's because both of us need to fully *breathe* again.

"I . . . sorry," he says, his voice husky.

"What for?" I whisper.

"I really wanted to do that again," he manages.

"Me too," I say, grinning a little—and hoping he can see it. "And you asked me if it was okay. So what's the problem?"

"I just thought it would be somewhere more romantic," he says, chuckling and leaning in to press his forehead to mine. "Like, somewhere worthy of an epic story you could tell your sisters. Not in some weird, shadowy alley next to a strip mall. But I couldn't wait."

I run my hands over his hips and up to his chest, trying not to openly freak out about the fact that I'm finally touching those muscles I've become so obsessed with.

"I love this alley," I say. "I could stay here forever. It's totally epic."

He laughs again and—reluctantly, I think—pulls back, standing up straight.

"Not forever," he says. "We need to go inside and see if Grace is here—see if we can complete your *actual* epic quest."

"Okay," I say. And am shocked to find I'd sort of forgotten that's why we came here in the first place? How could I forget about my quest, my mother? How is he distracting me *this much*? "But first . . ." I grab the front of his T-shirt with both hands and pull him close again. "Can I kiss *you* this time? Because I want to do that again, too."

"A thousand times yes," he says.

And then, even though I initiate the kiss, I'm swept away all over again.

When we finally break apart and hustle ourselves to the restaurant's entrance, I have no idea how much time has passed. We could have been in that alley for ten minutes. An hour. A *year*.

The swinging glass door to Jitlada sports a festive handmade sign that says PRIVATE PARTY, surrounded by all the other decorative ephemera I noticed earlier. Not only do the lights and beads and notes about specials make the place seem homey and welcoming, but they also block the windows—meaning no one can see the cavalcade of Asian Hollywood royalty swanning about inside.

"You ready?" Henry says, reaching for the door—and I nearly jump out of my skin. His mouth is just *so close* to my ear again.

I manage to compose myself and nod, and Henry ushers me inside.

I am immediately hit by a raucous wall of noise, roaring laughter and impassioned chatter surrounding me. It's so overwhelming, I freeze in the doorway, trying to grow accustomed to it all. The place looks like someone's very beloved tchotchke-stuffed living room, crammed with scuffed, elaborately carved wooden chairs and tables swathed in mismatched bright pink and gold silks. The scent of spicy curry winds its way around every cluster of people, tickling my nose and making my mouth water.

The place is packed full—I guess this is Asian Hollywood. I can't help but feel that Belle would be a little disappointed at the lack of opulence, of *majesty*. Even though I recognize some of the faces sprinkled throughout the crowd, it looks like a pretty normal, no-frills kind of party. Or a massive family gathering.

I don't see Grace, though, and I feel a prickle in my

gut—the one that says I'm about to be disappointed again.

"Hey, my dude!" Suddenly, a whirling dervish of a man is hurricaning his way up to us, clapping Henry on the back. He's on the shorter side, a little scrawny, with medium brown skin and a big toothy grin. "You made it."

"Wouldn't have missed it," Henry says, giving the guy a genial half hug. "Rika, this is Mason Choi. Mason, this is—"

"Ahhhh, your new *friend*," Mason says, shaking my hand and giving me a broad, cartoony wink. "I've seen the socials, I'm up-to-date." His brow furrows as he takes a step back, sizing me up. "Are you an actress? Comedian? Do you do any storytelling gigs? I've got a YouTube channel where I spotlight all kinds of Asian American and Black creatives. You might have seen this one short we did that went viral—"

"Yo, don't bombard her with the sales pitch," Henry says, chuckling. "This is her first time here, let her take it in."

"Okay, okay," Mason says, holding up his hands. "You know how it is—I get excited about the prospect of new talent. Especially since . . ." He cocks his head at me, scrutinizing my features—like a lot of people do when they first meet me. But it's not in that way where

I'm a puzzle to be solved. It's more like he's looking for a connection he already knows is there. "You're mixed, too, yeah?" he says, then points to himself, flashing that toothy grin again. "Blasian here—Black and Korean!"

"Yeah, Japanese—and some white stuff on the other side," I say. "I don't know exactly what white stuff because I don't actually know my dad, but, um . . ." I bite my lip, realizing I've blurted out something extremely personal to a total stranger.

But Mason takes it in stride. "Aww yeah, Halfie Club *unite!*" he crows, clapping Henry on the back again. "I love it."

"Mase, we were actually wondering if Grace is here," Henry says, his eyes scanning the crowded room. "I heard she might show? I, uh, need to talk to her. About the movie."

"Haven't seen her," Mason says, lifting one shoulder in a careless shrug. "But hey, let's go ask Diya—she usually does the RSVP list."

Mason beckons for us to follow him into the crowd. I take a deep breath and wade in. Mason waves to nearly everyone we pass by and seems to have a personalized greeting for each person—a complicated high-five/handshake here, an indecipherable nickname there.

As we push through, I feel a light touch against my lower back and realize it's Henry—guiding me, making sure I don't get sucked into the mass of bodies. My cheeks warm and my nure-onna instinct is to pull away, to tell him I'm perfectly capable of making my own way through a crowd.

But I don't want to. I *like* the way his hand feels there. *Ughhhhhhhhhh.*

Mason finally reaches our destination—a table with two women tossing back very full glasses of wine and laughing uproariously. Like Mason, they appear to be in their twenties. One has glowing brown skin and the most brilliant smile I've ever seen—actually, she looks kind of familiar, and I wonder if I've seen her on TV before. The other is pale with a smattering of freckles across her cute upturned nose and wavy dark brown hair pulled into a messy ponytail—and my heart skips a beat when I realize she also looks like she's in Mason's "Halfie Club." Specifically *my* brand of Halfie Club.

"Heya," Mason says to the women, slipping into an empty seat at the table. "Look who showed up." He gestures to Henry.

"Baby Hank!" the woman I may or may not have seen on TV shrieks. "You came just in time—we ordered a whole mess of that pineapple shrimp curry!"

She grabs Henry's hand and tugs him insistently into another empty seat. I slide into the last empty seat at the table, already wondering how quickly I can get the story on this "Baby Hank" business.

"And you're *that girl*!" the woman exclaims, her eyes lighting up. She drops Henry's hand and reaches for mine, pumping it up and down enthusiastically. "I'm Diya Dey, and this is Joanna Raine." She gestures to the other woman, who smiles warmly at me. "And we need to know all about whatever's going on *here*." She waggles her finger—tipped with a perfectly pointed red nail—between Henry and me.

"Ease up, DD," Mason says, rolling his eyes. "Give the kids some room before you start planning their wedding. This is Rika—" He gives me a prompting look.

"Rakuyama," I fill in.

"Ah, Japanese?" Joanna sets down her wineglass and claps her hands together. "Me too!"

"Yesss, Halfie Club!" Mason says with a fist-pump. "Diya is an actress—you may have seen her in such illustrious roles as—"

"—as Convenience Store Owner's Wife and Distraught Indian Woman Number Three," Diya says, affecting an exaggerated Apu-on-*The-Simpsons*-type accent. "Just wait,

I'm gunning to be the actual Convenience Store Owner next time. Maybe Distraught Indian Woman *Number One*, even."

"*Also* known for a turn or two in my YouTube sketches," Mason says, grinning at her. "And Joanna is a writer, a novelist—she writes this awesome fantasy series that's being made into a TV show, so she's currently going through that nail-biting process."

"Wherein step one is answering the question, 'But why can't they all be white?' over and over again," Joanna says, toasting Mason with her wineglass.

"Holy shit," I blurt out. "You're all so cool."

"Trying to be the change," Mason says, sounding halfway between serious and sarcastic. "But it's hard out there in the mean representational streets of Hollywood, so Diya and I started this meetup. It helps all of us to have a safe space to commiserate."

"And by 'commiserate,' we of course mean 'bitch out the system while downing mountains of awesome curry,'" Diya says, letting out an explosive laugh. "Baby Hank is one of our youngest members. We're trying to make this world a little more welcoming for him and all the babies who come after." She gives Henry a maternal pat on the cheek.

"Baby Hank has been in this industry since he was

an *actual* baby," Joanna snorts. "He has more experience than any of us!"

"Ahh, but he's still so innocent!" Diya says with a smirk. "So earnest, so happy all the time—always believing the best of people! The rest of us are bitter old crones."

"Speak for yourself, crone," Mason says, rolling his eyes. "My youth is eternal."

I sneak a glance at Henry as the group dissolves into good-natured bickering. He hasn't really said anything, just let them rib him and joke among themselves. But he has the biggest grin stretched across his face, and he's leaning back in his seat, his broad shoulders relaxed. He is at ease. He *loves* this—this place, these people, the community they've built.

I look around the room, all these Asian faces. These incredibly varied, happy Asian faces. No one's shrinking or trying to hide, no one's threatened by Beckys or elders who think they're a mistake or a blight on their people.

No one's acting like they have to . . . I don't know. Apologize for the fact that they exist?

"This is so great!" I say—then realize I said that out loud, not just in my head.

Four heads swivel in my direction, and I immediately feel self-conscious.

"Sorry," I say. "I, um. I stick out? In my community.

For a variety of reasons." My cheeks flame. I don't need to be getting into my tragic backstory with total strangers. "But you all seem so, I don't know, comfortable in your own skin? Happy, even?"

"Are you expressing shock over the fact that we're all Asian, but we don't hate ourselves?" Mason says, cocking an eyebrow.

"Oh . . . oh, sorry, no!" I sputter. "God, I . . . I was only speaking for myself—*I* always feel like . . . um . . ."

"Mason, give her a break," Henry says, squeezing my hand protectively.

"Seriously!" Joanna says, swatting Mason's shoulder. "You know we've all fought, like, literal *battles* to get to where we are. Between racism, white supremacy bullshit, pop culture stereotypes, family pressure, intercommunity prejudices and politics, the fact that so many people still don't even know what 'Asian American' actually means . . . I mean, the messages we're fed about ourselves from *birth*, both from the outside and the inside, isn't that why we're trying to 'be the change' and all? So the next generation is less self-hating and grows up totally well-adjusted and comfortable in their identities?"

"Well, yeah," Mason says, rolling his eyes. "I was teasing—I swear, y'all never get my humor."

"Ooh, girl, don't even listen to him." Diya pats my

hand, her eyes dancing with amusement. "Jo is right, we've all fought hard to get here. And we all stick out in our own ways—trust me. There's plenty of purity-policing in all of our communities. So many East Asians like to tell me I'm not *actually* Asian because apparently brown-skinned girls don't fit in with their idea of what that should look like." She harrumphs, tossing her glossy mane of hair.

"And don't even get me started on the anti-Blackness in the Korean side of my family," Mason says, slouching back in his seat. "Fuck that, we're all Asian—and here, we celebrate that." He flashes me a charming grin. "Consider yourself celebrated, eh, Rika Rakuyama?"

I smile back, something soft and warm lighting my heart. My nure-onna hisses, urging me to shove that softness down as hard as possible. But the thing is . . . I don't want to. I want to bask in this warmth. This joy. This *celebration.*

"Speaking of celebrating," Henry says, releasing my hand and resting his elbows on the table, "you said Diya might know if Grace is stopping by?"

Oh, right, Grace! Ever since we left the old zoo . . . ever since we kissed . . . and then kissed again . . . I seem to keep getting *distracted* from my primary mission.

"Girl hasn't been on the text thread at all," Diya says, her gaze darkening a bit. "Truth be told, I'm worried about her."

"She said she'd send up a flare if she needed our help," Mason says. "But she also said she needs space right now." He shakes his head. "Trying not to be like my parents, all up in the land of boundary violations."

"Pfft, stop insulting your ancestors—I have no boundaries," Diya says, whipping out her phone. "I'm texting her *right now* to make sure she knows we're here."

"God, I haven't even gotten to meet her yet," Joanna says, toying with the end of her ponytail. "Though maybe that's for the best, since I'll probably melt into a pile of incoherent goo when I do."

"Really, you're a fan?" I say, tilting my head at her curiously.

"Of course!" she says, her smile widening. "Look, I'm an easy cry—if I start telling her what *Meet Me Again* meant to me the first time I watched it, seeing an Asian American woman as a legit rom-com lead . . ." Her eyes flutter dreamily as she brings a hand to her chest. "Forget it. I will lose my shit."

"Sweet Rika, are you saying you're *not* a fan?" Diya

says, drumming her red fingernails on the tabletop—and somehow I just know that "Sweet Rika" is my nickname in this circle now, just like Henry is Baby Hank. Obviously an *incorrect* nickname—Diya doesn't know me very well. "Do you not swoon every time our Grace gets her man?"

"Dude, even *I* swoon," Mason says. "And I'm the most unsentimental bastard you'll ever meet."

"Oh, I just . . . her movies aren't really my thing," I say, trying to brush it off. "I don't believe in happy endings like that."

"Excuse. Me?!" Diya levels me with a shrewd look, sizing me up through her long lashes. "Baby Hank, have we not raised you right? How are you treating your girl? Why is she so anti-romance?"

"Oh no—no!" I say hastily. "It's not because of Henry. It's just . . . the way I am." I give them a valiant smile, hoping maybe that can be the end of it.

"No," Diya says, shaking her head vehemently. "Big fat *nope*, I refuse to accept this, Sweet Rika. I saw that light in your eyes when you took in our little celebration. There is a soft heart in there, just waiting to be beaten to mush by the last ten minutes of *Meet Me Again*."

She turns to Joanna, looking for support.

"Yes, agree," Joanna says, her eyes sparkling as she gets into it. "That ending . . ." She puts a hand over her heart again.

I stifle a groan. *Meet Me Again* is one of Belle's favorite Grace Kimura classics, the movie that really cemented Grace as Asian America's sweetheart. She plays a sweet, hapless photographer who has a meet-cute with some jerky guy who runs his dad's old camera shop—but inexplicably hates photography and knows barely anything about it. He accidentally knocks her camera into the lake they're both hanging out next to, replaces it with an even better model from his shop . . . and you can guess the rest. In the climactic moment, after they've seemingly broken up, Grace's character asks to meet at "their" spot—the lake—not knowing if the guy's going to show.

But of course he does. It wouldn't be a Grace Kimura movie if he didn't.

I've never understood why she wanted to smooch on some asshole who destroyed her most prized possession, but I am clearly not the audience for these kinds of happily ever afters.

"It's *beautiful*," Diya declares. "She puts it all on the line—her heart! There's that achy moment, when she's looking out on the lake . . ."

"Probably thinking about her destroyed camera," I mutter.

". . . and you think maybe—just maybe—he's not gonna show," Diya continues.

"But then he *does*!" Joanna squeals. "She's walking away, she thinks he's not coming, her heart is broken. And then suddenly he's running after her . . ."

"Which would be really alarming in real life," I can't help but say.

"It's *romantic*," Joanna swoons.

"It's not what would actually happen," I retort.

"It could," Henry says, grinning slightly at me. "Are you telling me you *never* get swept up in that moment?"

I shrug. "I don't like the idea that she needs him to 'save' her. She's successful, creative! What exactly is he saving her from—because it's sure not the idea that women need to drop everything for the first loser who shows any interest in them."

"I don't see it as saving," he says, leaning forward. "I see it as showing up—they're both there for each other, no matter what. They'll both show up at that lake, every time."

"I don't believe that!" I say, throwing up my hands. "Even if she *did* want that, I never *believe* the moment when he shows up. I just feel like he wouldn't—the real ending of that movie is, like, her sitting there all alone. Waiting and being annoyed that she doesn't have her original camera. No happy ending."

Henry cocks his head to the side, his gaze turning strangely serious. "I think he'd show up for her. Always."

"Aww, Baby Hank." Diya smiles at him affectionately. "You're the biggest mushy heart of all."

Henry blushes a little and shrugs, casting a surreptitious look my way.

"Anyway," he says, "we actually really need to find Grace. Are there any sightings, rumors? Stuff that wouldn't be out there on social media?"

"Mmm, let's ask everyone's favorite gossip factory," Diya says with a wink. She whips her head around and barks in the general direction of one of the chattering clusters of people. "*Clara Mae!* C'mere, we need your wisdom!"

A twentysomething woman sporting a platinum crewcut and blinged-out sneakers peels off from the cluster and scampers over.

"Gawd, what is it, DD?" she says, narrowing her eyes at Diya. "You're in a very yell-y mood tonight."

"I'm *always* in a yell-y mood," Diya corrects. "Have you heard anything about the whereabouts of our illustrious Ms. Kimura? Baby Hank needs to find her."

"Ahhh, so stealthy," Clara Mae says, whipping her phone out. "I dunno if our Gracie is secretly a world-class superspy or what, but she's been very adept at avoiding any kind of exposure." She studies the screen for a moment, her brow furrowing. "That said, I have heard *something*. According to my pal who works on the Pinnacle lot, they're finally doing those last bits of shooting for *We Belong*—the sets and the crew are all ready to go, and it's just a matter of our Gracie actually showing up." She stuffs her phone back in her pocket and gives us an elegant shrug. "Supposed to be happening this week. That's all I know."

"Always there with the hot goss, Clara Mae—thank you!" Diya yells after her as she bounds back to her friend cluster.

"There ya go," Mason says, making finger guns at Henry. "A *tip*."

"A tip we can't exactly follow," Henry says, leaning back in his seat and frowning. "Security around that set was tight as hell."

"But you're *in* the movie," I pipe up, trying to work it out. "Maybe you could get us onto set that way?"

"I don't think so," he says, his face screwing up with frustration. "My part's done, and they locked that shit down. I can't see it working."

"Mmm," Mason says. "There's *another* way you can get on the Pinnacle lot, though, Baby Hank."

"Nope," Henry says, slicing a hand through the air. "Not gonna happen. Already decided."

"Ooh, yes!" Diya says, her eyes widening. "How could I forget!"

"Forget what?" I say, looking from Diya to Henry and back again.

"It's nothing," Henry says, waving a hand.

"Not *nothing*," Joanna says, leaning forward. "More like a possibly life-changing opportunity."

Now they're all staring at Henry. Three sets of eyes, locked on his every move, willing him to say something.

I turn and study him, too. He looks . . . hmm. I'm not sure how he looks. His eyes have gone to the floor, what I can see of his face is blank, his shoulders are stiff, and he's lightly drumming his fingers against the tabletop— almost like he doesn't even realize he's doing it.

It's interesting to observe these different shades of him, these slight nuances in mood that color him in. When we first met—god, was that really just *four days ago?*—I only saw the one face, the one extreme. Then I saw a few more. But this sort of deflection . . . he looks so *uncomfortable*. I wonder what's going on.

"Baby Hank, you have *got* to tell your girl about

this," Diya says, rolling her eyes affectionately. "Maybe she's having a hard time believing in romance because you're keeping such important things from her." She clucks her tongue disapprovingly.

"It's an audition," Mason volunteers.

"*Hey*," Henry barks, looking genuinely irritated. Wow, *irritated* is definitely a color I haven't seen on him before.

"No, she needs to know about this—maybe she'll talk some sense into you," Joanna says, downing the last of her wine. She sets the glass down on the table and leans forward, her gaze lasering in on me. "Henry landed a *huge* audition. It's the lead!"

"A Hot Guy starring role in a big action movie," Diya chimes in. "Perfect for our sweet Baby Hank. His star will absolutely *explode* if he gets it."

"And that'll be good for all of us," Mason says, nodding vigorously. "Oh, man, the *rep*. Henry, you'll be a credit to us all."

"Maybe I don't want that," Henry says, still looking at the ground.

"What are you talking about, of course you do!" Mason says, slapping his palm against the table. "I would kill for a part like that. Hell, I'd kill just to get the *audition*."

Henry doesn't respond, and his face is still blank. His fingers, I notice, have stopped drumming against the tabletop and are now curled into loose fists. And while I don't know him super well, I am sure of one thing: he is *really* freaking uncomfortable right now.

"Um, we should probably get going," I say, making my tone light even though what I'm saying is totally awkward.

"Noooo, you can't!" Diya insists. "Look, our food just came!" She gestures to the server, who is carefully setting down a silver tureen of bright yellow curry. Steam curls upward, and I can see little sparks of hot peppers swirling through the curry's depths, beckoning me.

It smells so good, I might cry.

"I have to be at a, um, place later," I say, forcing my eyes away from the curry. "I mean, just home. That's the place. My Aunties will murder me if I'm late."

"Ahh, can't risk the Auntie rage," Diya chirps, grinning at me. "I know it all too well. But hold on, take some of this to go, you *have* to try it!"

Somehow, a to-go container has already materialized next to Diya, and before I know what's happening, she's spooning curry into it and wrapping it up tight in a brown paper bag that she presses on me.

I reach over, slip my thumb into the curl of Henry's fingers, and tug gently.

"Come on," I say softly. "Let's go."

He seems to snap out of whatever trance he's gone into, his head jerking up, his eyes meeting mine. As we stand, our hands loosely clasped, he never stops looking at me.

Right as we're about to make this hasty exit, I realize that I really, *really* have to pee. I will *not* make it back to Little Tokyo on LA's crowded snarl of freeways in time.

"Um, I have to pee," I murmur. "Meet you outside?"

"Okay," he says robotically, looking like he's about a million miles away. He absently takes the curry from me so I don't have to cart it to the bathroom—even zoned-out Henry is somehow still considerate.

"Lovely meeting you all," I say, smiling at Diya, Joanna, and Mason.

As I book it to the bathroom, I realize that I truly mean that. Despite the sudden weirdness with Henry, I'm having an amazing time. I feel light. Free. *Celebrated*, even.

A giddy smile overtakes my face as I push through the heavy wooden door to the teeny bathroom.

When I emerge, Joanna's leaning against the wall,

looking like she's thinking about something very hard.

"Oh, hey!" she says, flashing me a smile. "Sorry, you said you had to pee and then I realized that *I* really had to pee, and . . ." She trails off and shrugs, her smile widening. "Did I just make this awkward? Do we have to say a second, extended good-bye now?"

"Really, no worries," I say, returning her smile. "Usually I'm the one making things awkward, so I appreciate it when someone else steps up to the plate."

"Ahh, I gotcha," Joanna says, throwing me a wink. "I knew you were a kindred spirit. Keep in touch, okay? I'm on all the socials."

"Will do," I say, giving her a little wave.

Joanna nods and puts a hand on the door—then stops and turns to face me, her brow crinkling.

"Hey. Sweet Rika. When you said you don't believe in happy endings . . . I think I know why."

"You do?" I say, taken aback. I'm so surprised, I can't even protest, can't point out that we just met and she barely knows me at all. She has *no idea* about my tragic backstory.

She lets her hand fall from the door and takes a step closer to me, her eyes searching my face in an uncomfortable way. Like she can see right through me. Like she absolutely *does* know my tragic backstory.

She rests a hand on my arm. Gives me the gentlest smile I've ever seen on anyone. And leans in close, like she really wants me to get it.

"Yes," she says. "It's because you think you don't deserve one."

THIRTEEN

Henry's waiting for me when I emerge from Jitlada. He flashes me a big smile that doesn't quite reach his eyes.

"You should take all this curry home!" he says jovially—but his voice is too bright, too loud. His smile gets that smug quality I was so irritated by when we first met. "Bet your family will love it."

"Okaaay," I say, looking at him curiously. "Why are you being weird?"

"I'm *not*!" he says, his smile straining so hard, it looks like his face is about to break in half. "Come on!" He turns and starts marching toward the car, his steps defiantly jaunty.

What the hell is happening here? It's like the real Henry—the one who went rigid with tension when his friends started teasing him—has been replaced by a smirking alien.

"Henry." I plant my feet and cross my arms over my chest. "What's going on?"

"Nothing—why would anything be wrong?" he says—so loudly that the valet turns and shoots us a quizzical look. "I'm fine."

"You're not fine," I counter, still refusing to move. "Whatever you are, it started back in there"—I jerk my head at Jitlada—"when that big audition came up. You got all *tense*."

He shrugs, his bizarre smile faltering. "I'm fine," he repeats, sounding like he's trying to convince himself. He throws me a smarmy wink. "You don't need to worry about me, Sweet Rika."

Ew. What was *that*?

"Stop saying you're fine!" I shoot back, frustration curling in my gut. "Why won't you just talk to me?"

A million and one emotions play over his face, and he's trying with all his might to keep that big, weird smile in place. But eventually he loses, his shoulders slumping, his face falling.

"Because I don't want to," he snaps.

I reel back like I've been slapped. "But . . . but I . . ."

He starts walking toward the car again. "Come on, let's go."

Somehow I manage to get it together and follow him, jogging a little to catch up. In my haze of confusion, I realize my kaiju-temper isn't slamming against

my breastbone, demanding release. Instead I just feel . . .
hurt. Even though he told me to come with him, it's like
he's walking away from me, his back stiff and straight.

"I . . . I've told you *everything*," I say, the words
pushing themselves from my throat. "Like, stuff I never
tell anyone. Stuff I don't talk about . . . hell, stuff I try
not to *think* about. And then we . . . in the alley . . ." I
trail off, that frustration rising in my chest again. The
words are getting all mixed up in my brain, and I don't
even know what I'm trying to say.

"And that means I owe you something?" he fires
back, stopping in his tracks and frowning at me.

"N-no," I say. "That's not what I meant, I just . . .
you got all weird and—"

"And what? That ruins your perfect fantasy of whatever it is you think I am? Whatever you . . ." He shakes
his head, like he can't find the words either. "Well, I'm
sorry. I'm sorry this isn't the photo op you wanted, and
I'm sorry it's not going to bring more excited customers
to your Aunties' restaurant, and I'm sorry I can't be so
fucking perfect all the time—"

"That's not fair," I snarl—oh, *there* she is. One kaiju-
temper, coming up. "You know I'm not like that. I barely
even knew who you were before we . . . *we*—"

"Rika!" He whirls around and marches the last few

steps to the car. "Just . . . stop. Stop being so *difficult*."

Difficult.

That's what everyone always calls me, whether I'm popping balloons or refusing to wear a scarf or letting my temper explode all over Craig Shimizu and ruining the mochi demonstration.

But Henry never called me that. Henry acted like he saw something else. Sweet Rika, the girl with the potentially mushy heart.

I guess the key word here is "acted." He's an *actor*. He knows what to say, what to do . . . how to look at a girl right before he kisses her in a moonlit alley, so she totally falls for it.

And Sweet Rika doesn't even fucking exist anyway.

"*Fine.* Let me remove this *difficulty* from your life," I growl at him, turning on my heel and stomping in the other direction. "I can walk back to Little Tokyo."

I will *not* look behind me to see how he reacts. I just keep stomping.

He doesn't call after me, doesn't start running like he's chasing me through the airport at the end of a goddamn Grace Kimura movie.

A moment later, I hear his car engine start.

And hot tears gather in my eyes.

What the hell?

Did I actually *want* him to chase me?

No. No way. That's exactly the kind of so-called happy ending I don't believe in. And this just proves that it doesn't exist.

I keep up my stomping even as tears stream down my cheeks—from anger, I tell myself. That's the remnants of my temper getting out. Nothing more. I don't know exactly *how* I'm getting back to Little Tokyo, which is most definitely not within walking distance. I wish I could call an Uber or something, but Auntie Suzy is always lecturing us about how we can't afford such luxuries, so I don't even have an account.

I'm still rage-stomping when I hear my name being shouted through the night.

My head snaps up, and I see Henry Chen's dented Subaru pulling up next to me.

"Rika," he says, slowing the car to a crawl so he can keep pace with me. "Please. You can't walk all the way back to Little Tokyo—"

"Yes, I can," I insist, my head held high—even though I was just thinking the same thing.

"Get in the car," he says. "Come on, I—"

"No," I snap. "I don't want to sully your night by being *difficult.*"

Of course my voice cracks on that last word, completely undermining the badass aura I'm trying to project. Why can't I just turn into the nure-onna, dammit? She wouldn't care about any of . . . whatever this is.

"I shouldn't have said that," he says. "Just . . . please. Get in the car. I . . . I have curry!" He takes one hand off the wheel and brandishes the brown paper bag, waving it around desperately, like he's trying to tempt me. That delectably spicy smell wafts my way, tickling my nose, reminding me of those little sparks of hot peppers . . .

Goddammit.

I feel like a cartoon fox, lured by a pie left out on a windowsill.

"Fine," I concede. "But only for the curry."

One side of his mouth lifts, his eyes softening—and now he looks like the real Henry again. I firmly order my heart *not* to skip a beat over that. But it doesn't listen.

"Only for the curry," he agrees.

❧

Once I'm in the car, Henry pilots us back to the same tiny side-street spot and maneuvers the Subaru into it. I do *not* swoon this time.

I peek inside the brown paper bag and can't help but laugh—momentarily forgetting that I'm still mad at him. "How did she do that?" I murmur to myself.

"What?" Henry says.

"Somehow Diya packed not just the curry—but also utensils, napkins, and rice," I say, marveling at how everything's expertly wrapped and fitted together. "Max Auntie skills."

"I'm sorry," he says abruptly.

I cock an eyebrow at him as I pull out the curry and rice.

"I shouldn't have exploded on you like that," he continues, his words falling out of his mouth like he can't say them fast enough. "I shouldn't have . . . said what I said. You're right, I got uncomfortable back there"—he jerks his head in Jitlada's direction—"and then I tried to act like everything was okay because . . . well. Because that's usually what people want from me. A big smile, no complaints, nothing more complicated than that. Just happy to be here." He affects the cheesy, jovial grin I was so confused by.

I pop open the rice and spoon a little curry on top. "When you say 'people'—"

"I mean literally everyone," he says. "My agent, who thinks I should be grateful for every stereotypical two-line gig that comes my way. My white actor roommates, who like to tell me I should be stoked that diversity is so 'trendy' right now. Everyone I've ever tried to date, who only wants the Prince Charming cheeseball they see onscreen. My parents—"

His voice catches, and he swallows hard. "They straight-up refuse to even talk about my panic attacks. They just want me to act like it's not a thing."

"I know a lot of old-school Asian families aren't super up on how to best handle mental health," I say, stirring my food so the curry mixes with the rice. The all-encompassing spicy smell makes both my mouth and my eyes water. "But do they really not know how common anxiety disorders and panic attacks are? Have you talked to them about any of the ways Grace has been helping you, how that's made you feel like you can . . . I don't know, start to handle what you've been going through?"

"No," he says flatly. "Because I know what the response would be." He hesitates, drumming his fingers against the steering wheel. I offer him a bite of my curry/rice combo, which he gratefully accepts. "Neither side of the family ever accepted my parents' marriage," he says slowly. "So they've always tried to hold me up as some kind of proof that it's actually perfect. Because *I'm* so perfect." He flashes that fake smile again. "And whenever part of me doesn't fit with their idea of 'perfect' . . . " He shrugs, his smile turning bitter. "I love them so much.

But sometimes I feel like they only want a certain version of me—not who I really am."

"You want to be a whole you," I say, remembering his words from our Grand Central Market meal.

"Yeah," he says, giving me a rueful smile. "But I'm sorry I shut down and blew up like that. I took all that out on you, and you're the last person I should be angry with."

"I don't want the Prince Charming cheeseball," I say. "I was totally repulsed by the Prince Charming cheeseball, remember?"

He laughs, surprised. "That's one of the things I liked about you. Immediately."

I'm glad it's dark so he can't see me blush. I pop another spoonful of curry into my mouth and luxuriate in the explosion of flavor—and the intense amalgam of spices, which do indeed turn my tongue numb.

"I shouldn't have blown up on you, either," I say, mixing together a perfect bite. "I just, um. I'm never this . . . open. With anyone. It makes me feel so, like . . . exposed? And I don't usually . . . " My blush deepens. "I'm having a lot of new experiences tonight."

Spilling my guts to a near stranger.

Going to an Asian Hollywood meetup.

Kissing Henry Chen in an epic alley.

"Tell me about this audition," I say, shoveling more tongue-numbing curry into my mouth.

"Ah." He laughs a little. "You are relentless."

"Difficult," I say, sounding out each syllable.

"I think more like . . . tenacious."

"Passionate?" I say.

"Whatever you are . . . I like it."

We let that sit between us for a moment, my blush raging. I wonder if his is, too.

"Those people in there—the Asian Hollywood gang," I say slowly. "They seem to really love the whole you. When you said you wished you had something like the community in Little Tokyo . . ." I jerk my head toward the restaurant. "I think you do. I think you found it."

"Maybe I have," he says softly.

"And they seem very invested in this audition. So yeah, I want to know more."

There's a long pause. I just keep eating my curry. I want him to feel like he can word vomit on me as freely as I've been doing with him.

"This audition," he finally says. "I actually really want it. I want the part."

"Hot Guy Hank Chen, Action Star," I say, giving him a small smile. "I can see it."

"Yeah, it's just . . ." He shakes his head. "I think if

it was *just* that, I'd be fine. I'd go in and read and listen to people tell me why my 'look' isn't right, or ask me to put on an accent, or show off my abs and do splits like I'm some kind of trained monkey. But with this one, they've said they're going to tailor the part to who gets it. I could actually play a specifically Chinese-Filipinx character for the first time ever. And it's the lead. I could show people . . ." He trails off, his gaze going unfocused as he stares out the windshield.

"You could show people who you really are," I finish. "That whole you."

Beyond Hank Chen, Prince Charming Who Can Do the Splits. Hank Chen, Vapid Pile of Muscles and Nothing More. Hank Chen, Perfect Pan-Asian Son and Living Proof of His Parents' Perfect Marriage.

He turns to look at me, his mouth quirking into a half smile.

"Yes," he says quietly. "It's a *huge* opportunity. But the stakes are so high. I'm scared of not getting it and letting everyone down—or even worse, *actually* getting it and letting everyone down by not being good enough. Or not being Chinese enough. Or Filipino enough. Or . . . *anything*."

He turns back to the windshield and grips the steering wheel, idly running his palms over the cracked vinyl.

"And as for my parents—all things considered, they've been really supportive of my acting," he continues. "And I've been able to help them so much, send them money—I don't want them to have to worry. About anything. I . . . I'm happy I've been able to basically support them the past few years."

I nod, studying him and his ancient car console. I wonder if this is why he drives this old Subaru instead of splashing out on something nice for himself.

"But that's extra pressure," he continues. "I don't want to let them down, and I don't want to suddenly *not* be able to support them. And yeah, I can't help it, I don't want to give them anything less than their perfect son. So what if I get this gig—a bigger spotlight than anything I've ever done before—and suddenly become a disgrace to my community? Or embarrass my parents? Or just . . . am so *terrible*, I get blackballed by every casting director ever?"

"That won't happen," I say with conviction. "Forget all this—what do you *want*?"

"I . . . want this part," he says. "But all of this triggers my anxiety in a big way. I can't seem to get past it. Whenever I even think of the audition, I freeze. I can't remember any of the lines, *nothing*. Grace was helping me, but now that she's gone?" He shrugs, then rests his elbows on the steering wheel and leans forward. "I don't know if I can do this. I think I'm gonna tell my agent to cancel."

"No," I blurt out.

He swivels to look at me. "What?"

"You *can't* cancel," I say, meeting his gaze. "Henry. This sounds incredible. Of course it's making you nervous, that's a shit-ton of pressure. It's like you can't even bear to hope for this incredible, potentially life-changing thing because *not* getting it would be way too devastating. But then actually getting it could *also* be devastating, in different ways. You don't want to feel that way, so you're trying to avoid it by feeling . . . nothing."

My voice is getting louder, and my face is getting hot, and he's still looking at me, a slight smile playing over his lips.

Oh . . . *oh*.

Probably because I'm *also* somehow talking about myself and all the things I'm afraid to want. And he can tell. Of course he can.

"My mom says that hope is like opening your heart," he says, his eyes searching my face. "But that means you're opening it up to *everything*. To so much hurting."

I set my now-empty curry container aside, trying to picture my own heart: a closed-tight door, shrouded in darkness. No hope let out. *Definitely* nothing coming in.

Only that's *not* the image that comes up. Instead I see a door cracked open the tiniest little bit, a barely perceptible smudge of light spilling out.

"Henry," I say slowly. "When we were at the zoo today. When—"

When we kissed for the first time.

"When I wanted to leave," I say hastily. "I was so ready to give up, but you made me hope. You made me feel like I *could* hope for something that still seems so . . . ridiculous. So fantastical." I reach over and tug one of his hands from the steering wheel, twining my fingers through his. "You're not giving up on this," I say firmly. "I'll help you however I can. I'll hope enough for both of us."

"Rika," he murmurs—and I shiver a little, just hearing him say my name like that. "I . . . that's so . . ." He can't seem to find the right words, so he squeezes my hand. "Thank you," he says fervently. "But there's another problem—I'm supposed to show off some martial arts moves. Literally any martial art since they don't know exactly what this character is yet. And I absolutely do *not* have those skills. Maybe they expect me to, because—"

"Because Asian," I say, grinning a little. "Yeah, yeah, I know—Asians who can do martial arts are *so* stereotypical."

"I didn't mean you," he says. "Or, you know, any

actual real Asians who can do any kind of martial arts. But usually when you hear about a part like that, it *is* super stereotypical. The fact that they want to make this character a full-fledged human being, with all kinds of other traits and passions and everything—that's part of why I want it so bad."

"I can help with this," I say, perking up. "Martial-arts-loving Asian right here, at your service."

I meet his eyes and give him what I hope is an encouraging smile.

"I can show you a few basic judo moves, stuff that isn't hard at all. I'm sure you'll be able to pick it up right away, you're so . . ."

Graceful.

My face flames again. There is something about that word that is suddenly *way* too intimate, too specific, like it really gives away how intensely I stare at him whenever he decides to do one of his impromptu dance recitals.

"Um, so *athletic*," I amend. "When's the audition?"

"The day after tomorrow," he says.

"Then tomorrow we should go to the dojo," I say— but I realize the problem with that as soon as the words are out of my mouth. "Or . . . well, actually it's probably gonna be full up with classes, but I'm sure we can find a spot . . . somewhere . . ."

"I'm really touched by the offer," he says. "But I've noticed that whenever you talk about judo—or anything related to judo, like your friend Eliza—you seem like you're avoiding something. Or avoiding *her*, maybe."

I look down at our intertwined fingers, gnawing on my lower lip. How does he always *see* so much? I'm not used to anyone seeing me that much—the me that exists beyond the bright hair, the explosive temper, the face that never fits in right. I don't even see that person most of the time.

My nure-onna self wants to hiss, to shove him away. To deflect and say he's imagining things and change the subject.

But I can't do that to him. Not after he was so open with me about something he clearly doesn't want to talk about.

I imagine the door to my heart cracking open just a little bit more.

"I think you're right," I say, my eyes still trained firmly on our clasped hands. "The dojo was supposed to do this demo at the Nikkei Week parade. Sensei Mary called in a bunch of favors to get a UCLA scout to come, and Eliza and I put in all these extra hours practicing so we'd be at our absolute best. It was going to be the pinnacle of everything we've worked for, ever since we were kids. And then I . . . I ruined it."

"Rika," Henry murmurs again—but this time, I tell myself not to shiver. I can't allow the magic that is my name on his lips to wash over me.

"Sensei Mary has *always* been kind to me," I press on, dismayed to feel the beginnings of tears pricking my eyes. "She stood up for me. She's the reason I never got kicked out of the dojo, even after I bit Craig and all the parents complained. She never looked at me like I was some kind of wayward orphan freak. And Eliza was the only kid who would spar with me after the biting incident. She's sort of my only friend I'm not related to. She's so *kind*. She never sees anything bad in anyone— not even me. And I *know* there's a lot of bad there."

"I disagree," Henry says. But once again, I block it out. Act like I can't hear him.

"They've both been there for me," I say, blinking hard so my tears won't fall. "Even when they had no rea- son to be, even when it was actually bad for them to back me up at all. And I totally let them down. So now I feel like . . . I can't talk to them. I don't even know what to say. Maybe it's better if I don't, if I just—"

"What, never talk to them again?" Henry says. He

reaches over and cups my face, gently tilting my chin up so I'm looking at him. All I see in his eyes is warmth, *caring* so potent, all I want to do is look away and maybe never talk to him again either. "*How* did you let them down? You didn't stop the demonstration from happening, you didn't disrupt the parade—"

"But I'm the *reason* for the disruption," I insist. "Grace was trying to get to *me*—"

"So, what, it's your fault for being born?" Henry says.

Yes, my brain says viciously. I swallow the word.

"I let them down," I repeat. "Why would they ever want to talk to me again?"

"You're always so ready to not belong," he says, leaning in closer and locking my gaze with his. "It's like you think people are going to, I don't know . . . throw you away. Over the smallest things."

I feel a rogue tear slip down my cheek. I want to break away from him, heave myself out of the car, run far away. But I can't seem to take my eyes off of his.

"And now it's like you're throwing yourself away first," he says.

"Maybe I'm doing them a favor."

"No." He shakes his head vehemently. "That's not how friendship works. That's not how *love* works. And these people . . . Rika, they love you. I can tell by the way you talk about them."

I swallow again, trying to keep those fucking tears from falling.

Joanna's voice echoes through my head: *It's because you think you don't deserve a happy ending.*

What did she mean? It's not *that* so much as . . . I just think they don't exist. Not for girls who get called "mistakes." Not for girls who wait for someone to want them. Whether or not I *deserve* one seems like another question entirely.

But . . . do I think that?

I definitely don't deserve Sensei Mary's and Eliza's love. My kaiju-temper always destroys everything in its path. Somewhere deep in my gut, I've always known I'd destroy them, too.

"I think you should talk to them," Henry says.

"I . . ." I trail off, studying him. Those sweet, hopeful eyes I can't seem to get enough of. He wants this so badly for me, just like he wanted me to meet Grace at the zoo. How can I say no to that? "Tell you what," I say slowly. "If we go to the dojo tomorrow together—if I talk to them and show you a few moves—will you keep your audition? And, hey—what you're saying about love.

Don't you think it could apply to your parents, too? Maybe you should talk to them. About how you feel."

He grins, surprised—and maybe a little bit amused.

"You're very strategic sometimes. Cunning."

The nure-onna at her finest, I think, smiling back.

"Okay, deal," he says, nodding vigorously. "You talk to your friends, I'll keep my audition."

"And talk to your parents?" I push.

He laughs. "What did I say before? *Relentless.* I'll . . . I'll think about that one. Maybe if you show me these slick moves of yours, I can overcome all this pressure I'm feeling."

He squeezes my hand one more time and turns back to the steering wheel, finally ready to start the car and maneuver us out of this tight parking spot.

"Overcome that pressure *and* win the part you want," I say, trying to pump him up.

"Oh, and get on the lot and try to find Grace!" Henry exclaims. "Even more incentive."

I smile at him, even though I totally forgot about the Grace factor. She's been slipping further and further from my mind all evening.

"That's the multitasking spirit," I say.

"Excellent pep talk," he says with a chuckle. "Hey, if we *are* in a fairy tale—are you my handsome prince, swooping in to save me? You did it at the library, you did it tonight at the meetup, extricating me from an awkward conversation, and now you're doing it again." He waggles his eyebrows in a way that is probably meant to be suave but mostly just comes off as dorky.

I can't help but laugh and am about to respond with something tossed-off and snarky . . . but before I can, a bunch of images flash through my mind.

Henry agreeing to help me on my Mom Quest, even though he had no reason to.

Henry resting his hand on Craig Shimizu's shoulder, telling him to apologize to me.

Henry at the zoo, asking me not to give up, to look at all the beauty the world has to offer.

Henry trailing after me in his car, unwilling to let me stomp off into the night.

Henry touching me with so much care, kissing me with so much passion . . .

"I think we've saved each other—a few times," I say. "Maybe we're *both* the prince in this scenario."

Once upon a time, *a pair of noble war-riors set out to slay their respective dragons.* They both had quests they desperately wanted to com-plete, if only they could vanquish these fearsome beasts that stood in their way. They both spent most of their lives in an endless cycle of fighting, losing, and returning to the dragon. Only to be defeated once more.

And yet, neither of them could seem to give up.

One fateful day, they decided to team up in the hopes that their combined noble warrior skills could take down their dragons once and for all.

Both knew it was a risky proposition—if they were to be defeated again, as they had been so many times before, perhaps it would be the last time. Perhaps they would both crumble into dust, the dragons reigning over all the land.

But if the warriors emerged triumphant, it could be the start of something new. Something truly beautiful.

All they had to do was remember to never give up.

FOURTEEN

"Just go inside. That's all you have to do. Worry about the rest as it comes. Live in the moment. Oh god, now I sound like one of Belle's wannabe influencer captions."

"Rika?"

I whirl around to see Henry approaching, head cocked at me in a quizzical manner. I'm standing outside the dojo, letting the relentless summer heat of Little Tokyo beat down on me. My hair sticks to my sweaty neck, and I can already feel those little bits of perspiration gathering in the crooks of my knees and other weird places.

I thought I could do this. But going inside the dojo, entering this space after the parade disaster, suddenly feels like trying to scale the most skyscraping of mountaintops. I am a mere speck at the bottom, looking all the way up.

Henry drove me home last night, and we agreed to meet at the dojo in the late afternoon, right when I know classes will be winding down. I was conflicted when he dropped me off. Part of me wanted to kiss him again—could pretty much think of nothing else. The other part told me to eject myself from the car as quickly as possible—and that's what I ended up doing. I didn't want to ruin the pure magic of our kiss in the alley, of that giddy feeling that surged through me . . .

Ugh. Listen to me. Maybe Sweet Rika has a mushy heart after all.

Everyone was asleep when I'd let myself into the apartment, and I'd managed to slip into my room with no problem. Then I'd worked a bustling morning shift at Katsu That, which still seemed to be reaping the benefits of Henry's appearance yesterday. Luckily, there was not a Craig nor a Becky in sight. And Belle and Rory were busy with their courtly duties, so I managed to avoid them as well.

That hasn't stopped Belle from blowing up my phone, demanding to know all about what I'm "studying" with Hank Chen.

I meet Henry's eyes and flush, the memories of the "studying" we did yesterday flashing through me *most vividly.*

"Rika?" he says again, his brow crinkling. "Are you okay? Were you just talking to yourself?"

"Yes," I squawk, my flush deepening. "I'm, um . . ."

Thinking way too much about your mouth.

". . . still nervous about going inside," I say, brushing the other notion away. "I thought I could do this, but . . ."

I turn back to the dojo, its stately arched entrance framing a wide set of heavy wooden doors with a series of kanji carved into them. Sensei Mary told me once how these doors are the only part of the building that survived LA's massive earthquake in the nineties. These kanji are all scratched up and faded now, and I can't make out what they say. But Sensei Mary always tells me these doors and these kanji are like symbols of what you have to go through when you're training hard in judo. You get knocked down, you pop right back up. You may not always be able to *stay* standing, but you don't break. Not ever.

I feel like I will *absolutely* break if I set foot back in that dojo.

"Hey." I'm still laser-focused on those damn doors and their indecipherable kanji when I feel Henry take my hand. "Try the breathing," he says.

I turn to face him, jolted out of my reverie about doors.

"What?" I say, confused.

He gives me one of his warmest smiles, and I feel that awkward crackle of electricity between us yet again.

"The anxiety breathing," he says. "Even if you're not on the verge of a panic attack, it can still help kind of center you so you can come back to the moment and feel like you're ready to"—he nods toward the big doors and squeezes my hand—"step inside."

I open my mouth to protest, to tell him I don't need that, I can take care of myself, I can put on my mental armor and blaze through those doors just as I have so many times before.

Then I stop myself. Meet his eyes again. And we go into the breathing, like it's the most natural thing ever. Big breath in through the nose. Hold for several counts. Out through the mouth. Steady, steady, steady.

I find myself lasering in on the most specific of sensations. The sun pressing down on my neck, tendrils of heat slipping under my skin. Our palms brushing against each other, making me overly aware of what his skin feels like against mine. The fluttery snippets of sound wafting from the dojo, hard *smacks* against the mat and Sensei Mary's sweet voice calling out words of encouragement.

I breathe. I stare into his dark eyes, because there's simply nowhere else to look.

And I find myself feeling grounded, like my feet are more firmly planted on the earth than they ever have been before. I remind myself how much I want to help

Henry, this boy who's been so stalwart in helping *me*.

"Let's go," I say, making my voice as steady and confident as I can manage. The nure-onna, I think, would be proud of me.

"You sure?" Henry says, jiggling my hand.

I nod emphatically. "Yes. We gotta get you some new moves."

I wiggle my hips, my basic approximation of dancing.

"What was *that*?" he guffaws.

"These are *my* moves," I say, shaking my hips a little more. "Um, my non-judo moves. My dance moves."

"Those are *not* dance moves," he teases, amusement lighting his eyes. "Doesn't the Nikkei Week gala involve dancing? Has no one ever intervened on your behalf?"

"I don't go to the Nikkei Week gala," I say, rolling my eyes at him. "Or any places where I will be required to dance, really."

"Hmm. Things can change," Henry says, his hand drifting to the small of my back.

He keeps his hand there as we enter the building, but it's not like he's guiding me or trying to steer me in a certain direction. It's more like he's reassuring me? Letting me know he's there?

Why am I blushing *again*?

I bow as we enter the space, and he follows suit. Sensei

Mary doesn't really adhere to all the traditions and rituals of judo in the strictest sense, but she does like us to bow when we enter and exit, a show of respect.

In many ways, the dojo is exactly as I remember it when I first set foot inside as a kid. The high ceilings still capture the echoes of students training and Sensei Mary's constant encouragement. The sunlight still pours in from the big skylights, casting an otherworldly glow over the space. And those dark corners still beckon to me, their shadows and cobwebs shrouding forgotten hand-wraps.

Classes have finished for the day, and Sensei Mary is leading her three p.m. session of five-year-olds in a series of unruly tumbling passes—she says it helps the kids burn off their excess energy after working so hard to focus for an hour. I remember I used to get stuck on the first somersault, my brow crinkling in frustration as I tried to get it *right*. Sensei Mary kept trying to tell me that it wasn't about being "right," it was about having fun. But that never seemed to stop me.

"Ohmygod, *Rika*?!?"

Before I know what's happening, Eliza Hirahara is barreling toward me and sweeping me into a monster hug.

"Eliz—*oof*" is all I manage to get out before she's slamming into me. Eliza is tall and wiry with close-cropped dark hair that sits like adorable tufty peach fuzz atop her perfectly shaped head. Her mom *hates* that hair, but Eliza is never short on admirers of all genders. Since a few of those admirers have already proclaimed themselves future doctors, her mom's kind of let it go. For now.

"Where have you been?" Eliza demands, hugging me harder. "I've been texting you! I keep seeing all these photos of you on social media and . . ." She pulls back and makes an exploding gesture next to her head. "Mind *blown* by these adventures you seem to be having. Oh, hi, I'm Eliza." She turns to Henry without missing a beat, extending a hand.

"Henry," he says, laughing a little as they shake. "I've heard so much about you."

"Interesting, since I've heard absolutely nothing about *you*," Eliza says, side-eyeing me.

"Sorry," I blurt out. "I'm sorry. Eliza, I—"

"Rika-chan!" Now Sensei Mary is gliding toward us, her face lit with a welcoming smile. Sensei Mary is always so elegant—the way she moves through the world is so thoughtful, so *deliberate*, like she's being very careful to respect every single solitary object she might come across. It is the complete opposite of my destructive kaiju ways.

Sensei Mary envelops me in a hug—a softer hug than Eliza's, but she holds me for just as long.

"Kiddo," she says, giving me a little shake. "We've been worried about you."

"I'm sorry," I murmur, even as surprise tears prick my eyes. She's called me "kiddo" since I was six. I feel like she'll still be calling me that when I'm sixty.

"I'm sorry," I say again, pulling back and facing them. "To both of you. I totally disrupted the parade and ruined the demo, and I know you worked really hard to get that UCLA scout to come out, Sensei Mary. And, Eliza, I'm sorry you didn't get your shot to show off for them, I just . . . I was afraid to talk to either of you or even text back because I feel so ashamed about what happened. Like maybe you should have kicked me out when I bit Craig Shimizu. And . . . yeah. Sorry."

I hang my head, my cheeks blazing as my eyes go to the floor.

"What the hell, Rika!" Eliza cries. "Er, heck. Sorry, Sensei Mary."

"I *know* you all swear," Sensei Mary says, and I can practically hear the eye-roll in her voice. "Just try not to do it around the littler ones."

"Rika," Eliza says, her voice urgent. "Why on earth would you think we were mad at you about *that*?"

My head snaps up. "Because I ruined everything?"

"Oh, for goodness' sake," Sensei Mary says, shaking her head at me. "None of those things were your fault—unless you somehow hired Grace Kimura to jump out of a car and crash into you, and even then . . ." She studies me, like she's trying to make sense of it all. "Nothing was ruined, kiddo. Nikkei Week is still happening. The parade will go on next year. And I'm talking to the scout about setting up a time for a demo do-over so you and Eliza get your shot. That's why I've been texting you nonstop—I wanted to find out what your schedule might be like for that, and if you were up for squeezing in a few more practice sessions."

"Oh" is all I can manage to say. I guess, deep down, I thought she was texting me so she could finally kick Rika the Biter out of the dojo after all these years. But why was that my assumption? Sensei Mary has always defended me fiercely, has seen certain potential in me when no one else has.

"Who would get all petty about that anyway?" Eliza scoffs. "Oh, wait, I just listened to those words come outta my mouth and realized that Asians are *masters* of being petty, so of course we would. But I never thought any of that, Rika—I thought you were mad at *me*."

"N-no, of course not," I manage. I can't actually

think of what to say. My instinct is to now apologize for trying to apologize, which doesn't exactly seem like the thing to do.

"Rika-chan." Sensei Mary gives me another smile and squeezes my shoulder. "We were *very* worried about you. Please respond to our texts next time."

"Yeah," Eliza says, nodding emphatically. "I really don't want to worry that you've fallen headfirst off a cliff or something. Or that you're off having amazing adventures and have suddenly decided you don't need your best friend anymore." She throws Henry a pointed look, and he just gives her a genial smile. He's been quiet this whole time, giving me space to do whatever it is I'm doing.

I turn back to Eliza and Sensei Mary, who are both smiling at me in a way that's so open. It reminds me of the trust-fall drill Sensei Mary had us do when we were little, wherein your sparring partner stands behind you and you have to fall backward, hoping they'll catch you. I'd stand there for at least a few full minutes, my body tensing up, unwilling to take the chance. No matter who was standing behind me, I was always worried I was about to land flat on my ass. How could I just *know* someone was going to catch me?

Eliza used to call out: "Don't worry, Rika, I *will* catch you! Just let yourself fall!"

I could always *hear* that same open smile in her voice. It's what gave me the courage to let my feet slip from under me, to experience that terrifying moment of being weightless in the air.

And Eliza *did* catch me. Every time.

Looking at them now, hearing what they're saying . . .

I *matter* to them.

Maybe it's weird that I never quite realized it before. Henry's words float through my head: *it's like you think people are going to throw you away.*

But seeing those smiles on their faces, I realize: they've both been trying like hell to hold on to me. They're still going to catch me—every time.

"I . . . sorry," I say, laughing a little—I can't help but apologize for my apology, it seems. "Thank you for checking up on me, and I'm sorry I didn't respond to your texts. I did not fall off a cliff." I gesture to my clearly-not-falling body. "But the last few days have been *a lot*. And I promise to tell you everything *later*," I say, as Eliza opens her mouth to protest. "But for now, I need your help with something." I step a little to the side and make a sweeping gesture toward Henry. "This is Henry. And he needs to learn judo."

"Honored to meet you, Sensei," Henry says, giving a slight bow. It's so dorky, I have to stifle a laugh.

"I think we can take care of that," Sensei Mary says, her gaze narrowing as she sizes Henry up. "I have a beginning class for older teens and adults. It meets weekly—"

"We actually need something a little more, ah, immediate," I say hastily. "Henry has an audition tomorrow where he'll need to show off some martial arts moves. I thought you could teach him a couple basics? Like, right now?"

"Mmm, I can do that," Sensei Mary says, still studying Henry very intently. "But he'll need a sparring partner so I can instruct and correct his form."

"Oh . . ." I turn to Eliza, who is still in her judogi.

"I, um, have to go!" she says brightly, giving me a shrewd look and an overly grand wave. "Sorry. But I'm sure *someone* here can spar with Henry."

Before I can respond, she's skipping off, still waving merrily at me.

"It's all you, kiddo," Sensei Mary says, gesturing to the mats.

"Oh, I'm . . . I'm not dressed right, I didn't bring my kit," I say, motioning to my hapless outfit. I'm wearing an old Katsu That T-shirt and basketball shorts again. Plus I haven't done anything resembling judo in the last few days, so I'm not exactly at my best. My muscles feel cold and stiff, like they don't even remember exactly what they're supposed to do.

"There's no one else," Sensei Mary says, gesturing to the now-empty dojo. The five-year-olds have all been scooped up by their parents. "Come on, this is an informal-type lesson, take your shoes off and get on the mat—we'll warm up."

"I . . ." I gaze out at the mat, which suddenly seems weirdly intimidating, a vast expanse of soft blue foam.

"Rika." Henry clasps my hand again. I try to quell my blush, but I can feel Sensei Mary's eyes on us, taking in our every move. "Come on, help me—please. We can do a trade: you teach me how to spar, and I'll teach you how to dance so you can be ready for the gala."

"Oh, thank god," Sensei Mary says, rolling her eyes skyward. "*Someone* needs to teach Rika-chan how to dance. The attempts we've witnessed over the years are, uh, really something. You'd be providing a great service to the Little Tokyo community."

"I'm not going to the gala anyway," I mutter. But I grudgingly slip my shoes off, bow, and get on the mat.

Why am I being weird about this? I'm confident in my sparring abilities. It is perhaps the *only* thing I'm confident in. Yes, his frame is bigger and taller, but my experience should more than make up for that. This is just another way of helping Henry, which is why I came here in the first place.

Henry follows suit, slipping off his shoes, bowing, and joining me on the mat. Sensei Mary has us do a few warm-ups—stretches, jumping rope—then stands in front of us, sizing us up.

"Okay," she says briskly. "We're gonna teach you a simple shoulder throw. Not *too* hard, but looks impressive to people who don't know any better."

"Is Rika gonna throw me?" Henry asks, his gaze sliding to me. "Because I have to be honest, I find that prospect absolutely terrifying."

"You're going to throw *her*," Sensei Mary says, her expression turning amused. "Trust me, the thrower looks more impressive than the throwee in this scenario. But you are correct to be intimidated by Rika-chan's throws—they're the stuff of legend."

"I'll bet," Henry says, his eyes never leaving mine.

I tear my gaze away and move closer to him, positioning my body so we're facing each other.

"Rika-chan's going to put her hand on your chest," Sensei Mary says, her tone as businesslike as can be. "She's attacking you—if you were wearing your judogi, she'd grab the front of your garment."

I obediently reach out and place my hand lightly on Henry's chest—and immediately have to order myself to *not* get distracted by the warmth of his skin radiating through the thin cotton of his T-shirt, or the fact that I can feel those ripples of hard muscle that were pressed up against me last night in the alley—

Goddammit. I'm already failing.

"Now you're going to grab her arm," Sensei Mary says to Henry. "One hand on top, right above the bend of her elbow. Other hand should shoot out and grasp her near the armpit."

"Okay . . ." Henry says, his brow furrowing as he tries to concentrate. He does as Sensei Mary instructs, his arms shooting out gracefully, his touch light.

"Mmm, you are a dancer, yes?" Sensei Mary says, nodding. "You have that natural grace in your movements. But in judo, you have to be firm—your moves should be decisive, almost choppy. If you telegraph too much, your sparring partner will be able to counter very easily."

"Got it," Henry says, making his hold a touch firmer.

"Now pull her forward and spin around on your front foot," Sensei Mary instructs. "You'll still be holding her arm, but now this hand"—she taps the hand in the crook of my elbow—"will go to her wrist. And bend your legs—it should look like you're trying to carry her over one shoulder."

Henry does all this, slowly working through each movement. He goes out of his way, I notice, to make his moves more exaggerated, more decisive. But it's all working counter to his natural grace—there's still a *flow* to what he's doing that is not quite right for judo.

I allow myself to be pulled toward him, and then he spins around and bends his legs so I'm kind of half-flopped over his right shoulder—like a baby koala.

"Okay," Henry says, sounding like he's concentrating super intensely now.

I'm pressed lightly against his back, the arm still in his grip draped over his shoulder. I can feel his breath, rapid and heavy. Hmm. That's odd—we've only just started, we haven't been exerting ourselves that much yet, and he's in such good shape—

He turns his head to look at me, his eyes scanning my face.

"Are you okay?" he says, his words coming out wheezy.

"I . . . fine," I say.

And his breath speeds up even more.

I realize then that my face has gotten all hot, that my entire body is basically pressed up against his, that this is . . . possibly the most intimate position we've been in? Suddenly, all I can hear is our rapid breathing, synchronizing and echoing through the empty dojo. Giving the space an uncomfortable heartbeat.

Sensei Mary clears her throat, and Henry's head whips back around to face her. I try to hide my blazing face in his shoulder, feeling like a kid who's gotten caught cheating on a test.

"Now," Sensei Mary says, "Henry, you need to lower your shoulder a bit, and flip her over so she lands on her back. It's kind of a circular motion."

"Oh . . ." Henry freezes, his muscles tensing up. "Won't that . . . I don't want to hurt her . . ."

"That won't happen," I say, regaining a teeny bit of my bravado. "I know how to be both thrower and throwee, I know how to land right—and these mats are cushioned. Anyway, weren't you saying how scared you are of me?" I raise a teasing eyebrow, even though he can't see my face.

"I am," Henry says—but he still sounds nervous, like he's worried he's going to Hulk out and crush my delicate girl body. "Okay, let's do this."

He bends his knee and slowly—so *very* slowly— drags me over his shoulder. I relax my muscles and brace myself, but then he also takes his sweet time flipping me, as if trying to take utmost care with every single movement. Like we're suddenly in slow motion or something. When he finally throws me onto the mat, it's so deliberate and gentle, it's more like he's . . . setting me down.

Like I'm some kind of super-breakable porcelain doll.

Which he should know by now that I'm *not*.

"That was *not* a throw!" I protest, scrambling to my feet. "That won't look impressive at all if you're trying to show off for the casting people!"

"I'm sorry!" he exclaims, holding up his hands. "I *really* don't want to hurt you—"

"*You're* the beginner!" I retort, my defensive armor rising up. "You're in way more danger of getting hurt than I am!"

"And I don't know what I'm doing!" he says. "That's *why* I'm trying to be so careful with you—"

"You don't have to be careful *at all*!" I snarl, practically snapping my nure-onna fangs at him.

"Enough." Sensei Mary holds up a hand and steps closer to us. "Henry: that was not a bad start. You have the general idea of the motion, but you're too trapped in your head, worried about getting it wrong. And perhaps"—her gaze slides to me—"allowing other things to distract you."

My blush is just a constant state of being now. But I can also feel the more familiar thrum of my kaiju-temper beating against my breastbone, raging through my veins, demanding to be set free. There's something comforting about it—like I know *this* state of being way better and am therefore more comfortable with it and trying desperately to hold on to it with both hands.

But . . . why am I suddenly so mad? There's no reason for it. He *was* trying to be careful. As careful as he was when he kissed me last night.

I take a few deep breaths, trying to calm my kaiju-temper and focus on what Sensei Mary's saying.

"Judo is all about contrasts, bringing seemingly conflicting ideas together," she says. "You want your form to be precise, your movements to be calculated—but there's also an element of going with the flow, allowing your body to instinctually fuse with what you are doing. If you're too rigid, your opponent will be able to take advantage of that."

Henry nods, his brow tightly furrowed—like he really wants to get this.

"Rika-chan," Sensei Mary says, amusement flickering in her eyes, "remember to be patient with beginners. Henry will learn, we just have to drill it over and over again and encourage him, mmm? We must be as patient as I was with you when you were small."

"Yes, Sensei," I murmur, looking down at the mat.

"Go again," Sensei Mary says, clapping her hands together.

We resume our positions, facing each other. This

time, Henry makes his movements firmer, faster. When he hauls me over his shoulder and tries to flip me, it's still awkward and his movements are still too slow—but he doesn't try to second-guess or soften my fall. I brace myself and land with a satisfying *whump*.

"Better!" Sensei Mary calls out. "Again."

"How many times before I master this?" Henry says, giving me a rueful half smile as we face off.

"Master it? Probably like a million," I say. "But I think we can get you to 'looks like he mostly knows what he's doing' reasonably fast."

"This is way harder than it looks," he says, as I reach out to put my hand on his chest.

That makes me want to bristle again—like, what, he thought this thing I've dedicated a good chunk of my life to would be easy? But that flash of irritation has no real heat behind it. It's an instinctual response, a thing my nure-onna self wants me to pounce on and lash out with and hold close to my chest until nothing but fire blazes through me.

That fire will keep me from feeling anything else.

"I think that's what's so cool about it," Henry continues. "Like, people always tell me I make dancing look *effortless*—but that's cause I'm putting in a whole lot of effort to make it seem that way."

"Yeah," I say slowly—and my anger just . . . dissipates. I tentatively smile back at him.

"All right," Sensei Mary says, clearing her throat again. "Let's go, kids."

We drill the move again and again, Henry flowing through it a little more easily every time. His brow gets less furrowed, his grip becomes more assured. He's less hesitant when he flips me, that combination of technique and instinct slowly beginning to fuse together.

We start drilling faster, falling into the calming repetition of the movements. After a bit, we stop talking entirely, developing an unspoken routine. He throws me, I get back up, and we face each other again. Over and over and over again, the *whump* of me landing on the mat giving us a rhythm. Sensei Mary falls silent, ceasing her corrections and stepping back so we have more space to work.

When I fall for what seems like the umpteenth time, Sensei Mary finally claps her hands together, and Henry and I both jump. We'd gotten so into our rhythm, I'd sort of forgotten she was there.

"Yes—good!" Sensei Mary says, beaming as she steps closer to us. "I think you've got it, Henry—you're a fast learner. So there's one stellar move you can show them, and if you need more help, please come back. I'm happy to teach you others."

"Thank you," he says, giving her a little bow. He's breathing hard again—this time from actual exertion and not because he's, you know, *distracted*. "Can we try it a few more times, though? I want my body to really *learn* it. I know I've got a dance move down when I feel like it's now housed in my bones or something."

"I actually have to head out," Sensei Mary says. "But you two can stay here and drill as long as you like—just make sure to lock up when you leave, Rika-chan. You know where the key is."

"Oh, of course," I say. "But . . . are you sure, Sensei Mary? I don't want to, um . . ."

I trail off, not sure what I'm trying to say. I do know where the key is—all the older kids do, in case there's an emergency. Sensei Mary keeps it underneath the little potted bonsai by the entrance. But this *isn't* an emergency, and I've never been entrusted with this task before. I've never been left alone in the dojo. Whenever the possibility of that has come up, I've imagined myself somehow destroying the whole building. I don't even know how, I just feel like my kaiju-temper would find a way. Sweet, even-keeled Eliza would be a more natural fit for this kind of responsibility.

But Eliza's not here.

"I trust you," Sensei Mary says simply. She flashes

Henry one last smile. "Nice to meet you—and good luck with the audition."

Then she's gone, gathering up her stuff by the entrance and heading out the door.

Leaving us alone.

My gaze wanders up to the skylight, where night has started to fall—the sun's trying so desperately to hold on again, but she's overruled by dusky shadows sweeping over the clouds.

"Shall we go again?" Henry asks me.

"Let's do it," I say, going to stand in front of him once more.

I place my hand on his chest, just like I've done a million times at this point. Only now that we've had a break in the rhythm—a *pause*—it somehow doesn't feel like something I've done a million times. And I swear I can feel his heartbeat speed up through the T-shirt that's now clinging to him in sweaty patches.

"So," Henry says, "I'm getting pretty good, huh?"

I meet his teasing gaze. "You're getting *passable*. At one move."

"And now I'm ready for more," he says, reaching out to grasp my arm. "You heard Sensei Mary—apparently I'm a fast learner."

"She was being polite," I say, as he twists around,

putting me in the baby koala position. "Don't let it go to your head."

"Hmm, I dunno," Henry says, his voice way too amused. "Sounds like you're worried about holding on to your top spot here."

"Never," I insist. "I'm never letting that go, especially not to a beginner. This is all kids' stuff, you're not ready for the real thing yet."

"You better watch out," he counters. "Soon we'll be sparring for real."

I want to retort, but suddenly I'm pressed up against his back again and he isn't flipping me yet—he's just kind of *holding* me there. I feel the heat of his skin through his shirt—so much warmer now that we've been drilling for so long. See the sweat beading his neck, drifting under his collar. His shirt is definitely *clinging* more to his biceps, his broad shoulders, and I'm so freaking close, I can't help but stare, my mouth going dry . . .

"What, nothing to say to that?" Henry says.

Then he does flip me. Only this time, I'm so fixated on his shirt and his heat and his stupid biceps that I'm momentarily caught off guard. I let out a loud yelp as I fly through the air, my sense of gravity disrupted, and then I'm landing flat on my back on the mat. I manage to brace myself just in time, but I still wince upon impact.

"Oh, shit," Henry says. "*Shit.* Rika, are you okay?"

"Fine," I manage, my breathing uneven. "I wasn't paying close enough attention."

Still grasping my arm, he leans down, frowning as he studies my face. "What . . . were you paying attention to?"

I really don't want to answer with "Your biceps, obviously," so I take advantage of his weakened position, ground myself firmly on the mat, and yank hard on his arm.

"Wha—" A look of utter surprise crosses his face as he goes tumbling down.

He lands on top of me, but because I'm ready, I use the momentum of his fall to flip us, so he's flat on his back and I'm straddling him at the waist. Kind of like the first time we met, only I'm not all tangled up in my cumbersome yukata. He gazes up at me, dazed, his hair sticking out in all different directions.

"And that," I say triumphantly, "is why you're definitely not ready to spar with me for real. You let your guard down and easily gave me the upper hand. And now . . ." I gesture expansively to myself and the dojo. "Winner. Undisputed number one champion of the Little Tokyo Dojo!"

He's still staring at me with that dazed look, like he's barely hearing anything I'm saying.

"Hey," I say. "Henry."

I flop forward and plant my hands on either side of his head, getting all up in his face.

"Are you okay? Are you listening to me?" I say.

He doesn't answer, just keeps staring at me in that weird, wide-eyed way. Almost like he's seeing me for the first time.

I am suddenly very aware of our breathing again—it's *so loud*, syncing up and echoing off the high ceiling of the dojo. And we're pressed up against each other once more, even closer than we were in the alley.

He reaches up, his fingertips grazing my cheek.

What would the nure-onna do in this moment? Probably kick him away, snarling and hissing. That . . . should be my instinct right now. That's what I would *normally* do.

But I don't do that. I do . . . well, the opposite.

I close those teeny, tiny millimeters of space between us and press my lips to his. He sighs, like he was waiting for it, and pulls me closer.

His hands run through my hair, down my back, finally landing on my waist. He shifts his weight and flips us in one fluid motion, so now he's on top.

"Now who's the judo champion?" he says between kisses, a little growl in his voice.

"This . . . is . . . not . . . *judo!*" I manage.

His mouth moves lower, trailing kisses to the delicate hollow between my neck and collarbone. He dedicates an amazing amount of focus to that spot, grazing it with his tongue, his teeth. Brushing the collar of my T-shirt aside so he can pay even more attention. That spot feels like it's on fire, the blaze radiating outward to consume my whole body.

I close my eyes and sink into that feeling. I want to touch him more, to slide my hands under his shirt and feel the muscles rippling over his back. But I can only manage to desperately cling to him, like he's some kind of life preserver.

And I still don't want to push him away. I want to fall into him, get swept up in the sensations crashing over me. I feel like the nure-onna again, but a nure-onna who's free to be unleashed, wild. Not afraid of her temper destroying everything around her.

When he kisses me, it feels like I *can* be that. It feels like I'm . . . safe.

Like he's standing behind me for the trust exercise, telling me he'll catch me no matter what.

And I believe it. I let myself fall.

FIFTEEN

I eventually come back to earth and remember that Sensei Mary probably won't appreciate it if she returns the next morning and finds that (1) I have not locked up, the one and only task she requested of me, and (2) I'm still rolling around on the mats with Henry Chen, and the stuff we're "practicing" definitely has nothing to do with judo.

So we disentangle ourselves and I *do* lock up, say goodbye to Henry, and walk home. We have our mission set for tomorrow. We're going to get on that lot, Henry's going to slay his audition . . . and maybe I'll finally meet my mother.

Henry and I don't really talk about what just happened between us. I guess I feel like saying anything will puncture the euphoria, that wildness I found myself so swept up in. But as I walk through the muggy evening air, reality starts to puncture my blissful-feelings bubble.

I felt *safe* with him.

What does that even mean? Why do I feel that now and so . . . naturally . . . when I've never been able to get anywhere close to that before, with anyone?

How can I trust it?

My head feels so mixed up. My heart is still swelling, carried away as it tries to store up every precious sensation — every kiss, every touch — to relive later. Both of these things are happening at the same time, turned up full blast, trying to drown each other out. I usually love that kind of wild juxtaposition, but this time? I most sincerely do *not*.

I let myself into the apartment, slip off my shoes, and pause in front of the mirror hanging in our entryway. I don't know what I expect to see. The return of the nure-onna? The beginnings of the princess?

But this time I just see . . . me.

My clothes are rumpled, the collar of my shirt stretched out to expose that tender hollow between neck and collarbone that Henry was so, um, interested in. My lips are swollen from all that kissing. And my hair is, of course, a mess — not that it's ever really anything less, but it's an extra snarly tangle right now, sticking out every which way, practically tying itself in knots.

I stare at myself for a moment, expecting the image to

shimmer, to change into something else. For my armor to reinstate itself and contain all of these too-big emotions that want to come spilling out of me.

It doesn't happen.

I stand there, shifting from foot to foot, considering. I could slip back to my room, wrap myself up tight in bed, shove everything down until all of these things roaring through my heart and mind quiet down. It's what I'm used to doing when I'm trying to control my temper.

But . . . I don't want to do that right now.

So. Where do I put all these feelings?

I find myself wandering through the apartment. The living room is empty—Auntie Suzy and Auntie Och are probably still feeding the hungry Nikkei Week crowds at Katsu That. I eventually end up in front of Belle's bedroom door, and before I can think too hard about why I'm doing what I'm doing, I knock.

"Come in!" she bellows over the perky K-pop beat blaring into the hall.

I enter the room and find her sprawled on her bed with Nak, both of them in their pink sweatsuits. Nak is once again trying to chew one of the sleeves off.

"Rika-chan!" she sings, sweeping out an expansive arm to beckon me closer. "Where have you even been? I've barely seen you since you brought your very special guest to Katsu That yesterday. Why haven't you responded to any of my texts with more than, like, one word? What's going on with the Mom Quest? And why won't you tell me what kind of *studying* you've been doing with Hank Chen?"

She sits up eagerly, jostling a put-upon Nak in the process. He gives her an aggrieved look and goes back to chewing his sleeve.

I sit down next to her on the bed, wondering where to even start.

"Henry's still helping with the Mom Quest," I finally say, thinking that this sort of encompasses both things she's asking about. "We've had some leads about where Grace might be, and nothing's panned out yet. But tomorrow . . ." A small smile plays around the corners of my mouth. "We have an idea of where she'll be, and I actually think it might work out?"

"Ooooh, intriguing!" Belle says, slapping her bright pink duvet. Nak lifts his tiny head to frown at her for jostling him again. "And very *mysterious*, Rika-chan."

"Not so mysterious," I say, laughing a little. "Henry has an audition on the Pinnacle lot, and we've heard Grace will be there for reshoots. So I'm going to sneak around until I find her."

"I love it," Belle says, her eyes flashing with eagerness. "Do you need me to come along? I'm *sure* I can convince any pesky security people you encounter that you are there on very official and important business!"

"Not necessary, but thank you," I say, laughing again. "I mean, technically we will be there on very official and important business—Henry's audition."

"Ah, yes, *Henry*." Belle cocks an eyebrow at me, her gaze turning sly. "Such a wholesome dreamboat. What *else* is he helping you with?"

I meet her eyes, studying her. Now is when I usually pull away, stuff everything I'm feeling back inside because I don't want her to see. I don't want *anyone* to see. And every instinct I have is screaming at me to do that. Because I know if I put these too-big feelings out there, it's like they become . . . real?

But this *is* why I came in here, isn't it? Because my feelings are too big for my body. Because I don't feel like stuffing them down this time.

So I take a deep breath and release them into the space between us.

"We . . . did some things," I begin, my face immediately heating up as the "some things" flash through my brain. "He kissed me. And then he kissed me again. And then I kissed *him,* and . . . I'm very confused. It's like my brain wants one thing, but my heart wants something else, and I've never really felt anything like this before—"

"Wait. Stop." Belle holds up a queenly hand, and I cease my babbling. Her eyes are dancing with barely contained excitement. "We need reinforcements for this." She picks up her sparkle-encrusted phone and starts typing. Nak lifts his head, trying to look at the screen. "I am absolutely *dying* here, but I don't want you to have to repeat yourself. You're going to have to share this with *everyone*."

"Who's 'everyone'?" I say, my voice tipping up with suspicion.

"Rory. Eliza." Belle taps on the screen and nods to herself, satisfied. "Your two *other* best friends. We're going to have a night out and help you with all these *feelings* you're having."

"Belle!" I grab for the phone, but she holds it just out of reach. Nak gives me a look like, *Why did you even try?* "Don't bother them! I . . . I just wanted to talk about this *quietly*, it doesn't have to be a whole production—"

"Rika-chan!" Belle shrieks. "*Of course* it's a production. You never admit to having actual feelings, and I am not going to let that go without some measure of fanfare." She grins at me and waves her phone in the air. "Anyway, I already sent the text."

"Gah." I slump back on the bed, defeated. "Fine."

"Now we just have to wait for them to respond," Belle says, her eyes narrowing at the screen. "But I don't want to hear one more word until we're all together— everyone should experience your epic telling of your emotions at the same time."

"*Fine,*" I repeat, throwing up my hands. I try to suppress the tiny smile that's tugging at the corners of my mouth again. When Belle gets like this, there's no sense in arguing. But just this once, I'm kind of enjoying it.

We sit there in silence for a moment, her staring resolutely at her phone, waiting for a response. I clamp my lips together, determined not to spill any more of my story until it's time.

After several minutes of this, she sets her phone down with a loud sigh and turns to me.

"They're taking forever. Wanna go try on some of Ma Suzy's old dresses while we wait?"

❋

Belle manages to get everyone into Auntie Suzy's vintage treasures before we leave the apartment. Then she herds us all out the door. We cross First and swan through the Japanese Village Plaza, our footsteps tapping lightly against the quaint brick path, lit by strings of glowing lanterns dancing overhead. When we pass by the Fire

Tower—a tall, majestic column composed of interlocking scarlet-orange poles—I look up, letting myself sink into the magical feeling this neighborhood always gives me.

Belle teases me for still being in awe of the Fire Tower, which was rebuilt in steel after the original version was demolished by termites. It's sometimes referred to as "Termite Tower"—not very majestic—and is also a prime spot for white guys to take photos with just-purchased samurai swords. But there's just something about it I find beautiful, a sense of history housed in its rebuilt bones. Tonight, there's not a termite or a faux samurai in sight, and the stars glitter around the tower's peak, giving us a show.

Belle guides us through the plaza and over to Bae—an extremely hip soft serve spot that specializes in charcoal ice cream. "Pitch-black—just like Rika-chan's heart," Belle always jokes.

Once again, I marvel at her ability to bend people to her will and execute a plan so efficiently. She really is meant to be a queen.

"Okay!" Belle says, smacking a hand down on our table at Bae. "It's *time*. Rika-chan is going to tell us all about her too-big feelings, and I, for one, have been waiting for this moment for *seventeen years*."

"So since you were born?" Rory rolls her eyes. "That's

not possible. Anyway, Rika didn't even exist when you were born."

"A technicality," Belle says, swooping an index finger through the air.

I smile and look at each of them in turn. Belle is swathed in a beautiful satin frock—this one emerald green, a stunning contrast against her creamy skin and midnight hair. Eliza, who doesn't really do dresses, discovered a brightly patterned blazer with swirls of blue and yellow that looks incredibly sharp on her long, lean frame. And Rory, who is too tiny for any of Auntie Suzy's grown-up clothes, simply grabbed a vibrant orange ruffled number and threw it around her shoulders like a cape. Belle managed to talk me into wearing a fitted silk sheath in the palest of pink. It's not something I would have immediately chosen for myself, but I have to admit I like the way the silk feels brushing against my skin, the way the soft color contrasts dramatically with my brassy hair.

"You look pretty," Belle cooed when I put it on. "But also like you could kill a man."

I'll take it.

Now we're all gathered around one of the tiny tables at Bae, eating black ice cream in our fancy outfits. This place represents another one of Little Tokyo's fascinating juxtapositions: unlike some of the more traditional, old-school spots, it's super modern and hopelessly hip, all black walls with flashing neon mini-signs that seem to exist purely for Instagram photo ops. The ice cream is similarly photogenic, black swirled with a more unicorn-appropriate rainbow of colors and topped off with cascades of sprinkles and sugary cereal bits.

It's also just so *delicious*. The special charcoal flavor of the day is pineapple, and I'm eating the pineapple-vanilla swirl, a perfect combination of tart fruit and soft sweetness. Those things that shouldn't make sense together but just magically do.

Henry would love this.

"Stop stalling, Rika-chan, eating your ice cream all slow!" Belle yelps, slamming her hand against the table again. "Tell us about Hank—*Henry*—Chen. Tell us about all the stuff you did." She waggles her eyebrows and takes a somewhat suggestive lick of ice cream.

"Um . . ." I begin—but then my eyes slide to Rory. Still a tiny innocent, happily eating her ice cream and being very careful not to drip it on her makeshift cape.

"Oh, stop, she's old enough to hear this," Belle says, rolling her eyes.

"Yeah, I'm *twelve*," Rory says with her mouth full of ice cream. "I know all about romance."

"Rika!" Eliza waves a hand in the air, like we're in class and I need to call on her. "What happened after I left you at the dojo? Did you and Henry, like"—she lowers her voice, her eyes shifting from side to side—"*do it on the mat?*"

"What!" Belle shrieks—not bothering to lower her voice at all. "If that's the case, it should've been the first headline you relayed to me, Rika-chan." She gives me a disapproving look. "Momentous both in terms of you losing your virginity and desecrating a historic Little Tokyo landmark."

"God, no," I blurt out, covering my flaming face with my hands. "We didn't . . . do that. We just . . ."

I take a deep breath and look at all of them again. They're all waiting. Eager. My nure-onna instinct is to stuff all these feelings down again, but they're just too big. I *need* for them to come out.

"We might've gotten . . . close," I admit. "Closer than I've ever gotten before."

"Oh my god," Belle whispers, her face lighting up.

I have been kissed exactly three times—well, three times before Henry—and it's never gone beyond that. The first time was Jack Fukuhara, who smashed his face against mine when we were thirteen and working on a bio project together. I guess he found all that talk of cells and blood and intestines super romantic. The second was Simon Jones, one of the only white guys in judo, who thought I was about to fulfill all his fetishy geisha-girl fantasies. The third was Chris Reyes, who asked me out on exactly one date and then was scared to come near me ever again. Probably because I shoved him away so hard, he nearly fell into the fountain at the god-awful outdoor mall he'd decided to take me to.

I shoved all of them away, actually. All three times, the kisses were like clumsy lunges with no warning and way too much saliva. I've never been kissed by someone as careful as Henry. Someone who will spend an endless amount of time fascinated by a very specific section of my bare skin . . .

"But wait, back up," Belle says, holding up a hand. "Why were you at the dojo? I need this entire sequence of events laid out for me, Rika-chan. Start from the very beginning."

So I lay it out. I tell them everything—rewinding as far back as the day of the parade, when we tumbled to the ground. I also catch Eliza up on my Mom Quest, how all of this ties together. I finish with our moment at the dojo—where we *did* kind of desecrate a historic Little Tokyo landmark.

"Unf," Belle groans, sitting back in her chair. "That

all sounds beyond swoony. Why are you freaking out so much, Rika-chan? Is it because you've never *done* this much with someone?"

"I . . ." I stop and think about it. And I swear that one spot he couldn't stop kissing *pulses*. "Actually, no," I say slowly. "Doing things with him, him touching me, us being together . . ." That spot pulses again, and I don't even want to know how red my face is at this point. I toy with the silky hem of my dress. "It doesn't feel weird at all. It feels *right*. It feels like . . ." I play with the silky hem some more, my voice lowering to the softest of whispers. ". . . we fit together."

The table falls silent. My cheeks burn, and I wonder if I've revealed too much, if they're all looking at me like I've completely lost my mind. I very slowly raise my gaze from my lap, expecting to be met by a trio of appalled expressions.

But . . . no. None of them look like that. Belle beams at me in a way that borders on smug. Eliza gives me a mushy gaze, like she's about to melt into a puddle on the floor. And Rory . . . well, Rory doesn't look appalled, but she is frowning at me in an accusing fashion.

"He was supposed to be *my* boyfriend!" she complains. "You don't even like *Dance! Off!*"

"He's too old for you!" Belle admonishes, whacking her arm. "We can find out if he has a younger relative of some kind. And anyway, Rika never likes anyone, so let her have this one!"

"Fine," Rory grumbles, slouching over her ice cream. "I *guess* that would be okay."

"Oh, Rika," Eliza says, reaching over to squeeze my hand. "This is so precious."

"Really?" I press. "It's not weird to feel that way about someone so fast? Like, I don't know, you belong with them and it's not hard to feel that way? It just works?"

"Well, *I've* certainly never felt that way in my many romantic escapades," Belle says, waving a hand. "But I don't think it's weird, no. Remember, that's how Ma Och says she felt the first time she saw Ma Suzy. Every person who was in that year's Nikkei Week court or involved with that year's Nikkei Week court or . . . I don't know, *in the vicinity* of that year's Nikkei Week court had some kind of crush on Ma Och. She'd just moved to the States from Japan, she was this exciting new face—and she was just *so* cool. But she says the minute she saw Ma Suzy, that was it. It was like a light went on. She felt that connection *instantly*, and she knew they belonged together."

I surreptitiously brush tears from my eyes. *Ugh.* Why am I crying? I've heard this story a million times. Maybe it's because this time I'm actually picturing it. Auntie Suzy, so beautiful in her princess gown, her smile the sweetest, brightest thing in the room. Full of hope, before she was tired all the time. Auntie Och, stopping in her tracks, completely bowled over. That connection snapping into place between them as everyone else in the room melts away. Just like a fairy tale.

Actually, I know exactly why I'm crying. It's because now *I've* felt that, too.

"I don't trust it," I say abruptly.

Eliza shakes her head at me. "What?"

"This *feeling*," I say, leaning forward and resting my elbows on the table. "Feeling like I fit with someone this way. It's too . . ." I give Belle and Rory a rueful smile. "You know—Team Princess. I usually feel like I don't belong anywhere."

I expect them all to object to that. I expect Eliza to tell me that of course I belong at the dojo. For my sisters to tell me that I belong with them, because we're family. I expect them to say all that and then for me to instantly reject the idea—because I *know* they're just saying that. I *know* I don't feel that way. It cannot be denied that I stick out like a sore thumb, and that their half-hearted protests are merely to make me feel better. They can try to "claim" me all they want, but I still don't really belong to any of them.

"I get that," Belle says.

My head snaps up. "Excuse me, what? *You* get that?"

She nods and pops the last bit of cone in her mouth. "Of course I do."

"What?!" I repeat. "No. There's no 'of course' here. Belle, you're the freakin' Nikkei Week *Queen*. One of the most popular kids at school. Your *dog* is an influencer—"

"Well, almost," Belle corrects. "I'm still trying to get his follows up to where they need to be."

"And you're so confident," I barrel on. "You're always so *sure* about what you're doing. How do *you* feel like you don't belong?"

"Rika-chan." Belle gestures expansively to her fabulous curves. "*This* is not what people think of as the perfect Japanese American girl body. Remember when Auntie Och tried to order us those cheap clothes from Japanese stores online? None of them fit me. I started getting boobs when I was *eleven*. I'm also loud. I talk too much. I date hot people of all genders. And I bring my *dog* to sacred Nikkei Week rituals." She gives me a sardonic smile. "The elders who disapprove of you so much are *not* holding me up as a shining example for our people—trust me."

"But . . ." I shake my head, my thoughts a tangle. "I *love* all of those things about you. And I've always admired how proud you are of them."

"I *am* proud," Belle says, drawing herself up in her seat. "*I* think I'm amazing. That doesn't mean I don't feel out of place sometimes, or that there aren't people trying to tell me I don't belong."

"Yeah, me too," Rory says. I notice that despite her best efforts, she's dribbled ice cream on her makeshift cape. "Everyone sees me as this math genius, right? Which, to be fair, I totally am. But I also like other stuff. Like dancing and drawing and coming up with costumes. Remember when we drew all those yokai pictures for your room, Rika? That was so fun."

"Yeah, I do," I say, smiling softly at her.

"I wish people would see that I'm good at that stuff, too," Rory says, her little face screwing into a look of consternation. "But people have already kinda decided who I am. The art clique kids all make fun of me when I try to ask them stuff, and the math club kids don't understand why I want to waste my time with anything else.

It's like no one sees *all* of me, exactly. Because no one wants to."

"I see you, Rory," Eliza says, giving Rory one of her sweet smiles.

"Thank you," Rory says primly, adjusting her cape.

"I feel that way, too, Rika," Eliza says, turning to me. "A lot of the kids in our class have teased me for being an 'Asian stereotype' because I'm good at judo. Even though I am in fact a real person, not some cartoon character. And they seem to feel extra comfortable teasing me because I'm so *nice*." She bites off the last word, glaring down at her ice cream.

"Wow, both kids and old people have the capacity to be massive assholes," Rory says.

We all laugh, needing the release. I look at each of them, taking this all in. It blows my mind that they *all* have felt this way. That *belonging* isn't as easy for other people as I seem to think it is.

That everyone, at some point, doesn't feel like a *whole* version of themselves.

I guess I've always seen them a certain way—like they were on one side of a fence, the side where you have exactly what you need to magically fit in. Belle's confidence. Rory's brilliance. Eliza's sweetness. I was always on the other side, bad-tempered and uncomfortable in my own skin.

But as it turns out, we were actually together—there was no fence. They can understand me. We can understand each other.

I feel that door to my heart cracking open a tiny bit more.

"Hey," I say. "I really love you all."

"Oh, Rika-chan," Belle says, reaching over to squeeze my hand. "Of course we love you, too. Now." Her eyes narrow shrewdly. "We've heard your plan for trying to track down Grace tomorrow. But what about your plan with Henry? Are you going to *do* more stuff?"

I laugh and glance down at my phone. I have a new text from Henry.

Just practicing my throw, it says. I used a pillow. But I wish I was throwing you instead.

My face flushes again.

I feel something bubbling up in my chest, something light and free, something that's become weirdly familiar the past few days.

I realize that it's hope.

Once upon a time, a beautiful princess was gifted with the keys to a glittering kingdom. As the prophecy foretold, it was there that she would finally be reunited with her long-lost mother—a great queen.

The princess could barely contain her excitement and hardly slept the night before her grand adventure, the keys to the glittering kingdom clutched tightly in her hand. Would the prophecy be everything she'd dreamed of? Would she and her mother share a long embrace, a fine meal? Would she finally feel found after feeling lost for all seventeen years of her lonely life? Would she be able to ask her mother all the burning questions she suddenly had about kissing and rolling around on judo mats with handsome princes and possibly desecrating historic landmarks?!

Unfortunately, there was nothing in the prophecy about that.

SIXTEEN

I can tell Henry's nervous. He doesn't *say* he's nervous, but the big smile plastered across his face when he picks me up is not that sweet, open one I've become accustomed to. It doesn't quite reach his eyes, which keep darting all over the place as his fingers drum an erratic rhythm on his car's steering wheel.

This time, though, that big fake smile doesn't bother me—because I know it's not a front for *me*. He's thinking ahead, to the people he has to impress.

He doesn't say much as he drives us to the lot. Which is maybe for the best, because I'm lost in my own thoughts. I'm thinking about Grace—allowing that little spark of hope to flourish. I'm thinking about the night before, the revelation that I'm not as alone as I thought I was. I'm thinking about Henry, his body pressed against mine on the judo mats, his lips seeking out that tender spot over and over again . . .

"Are you too hot?" Henry's voice cuts into my

thoughts, and I jump a little. "I can turn the air up." He reaches over and fiddles with the broken buttons on the car's console.

"F-fine," I squeak, my face flaming.

God. This is the part they don't put in fairy tales, the excruciating awkwardness that descends after you've crossed the threshold from *friends* to, you know, people who kiss. I'd really love to see the part of the story where Cinderella and her handsome prince are forced to make small talk while also wondering incessantly what the other person is thinking and if they maybe want to kiss you again.

We pull up by the security booth at the lot's entrance, and Henry offers his name, ID, and the reason he's here. The security guard takes his sweet time scrutinizing Henry's ID, then nods at me.

"Who's she?"

"Um, my assistant!" Henry blurts out, plastering that big smile on his face. "She goes everywhere with me! Part of my entourage. It's, um, necessary!"

I stifle the laugh bubbling up in my chest and give the security guard the most winning smile I can muster. I imagine myself as the nure-onna, transforming into a sweet, guileless princess right before his eyes.

The security guard side-eyes me for a few moments

more, making an extra big show of looking at Henry's ID. My heart beats faster—is he some kind of wizard-like gatekeeper, hell-bent on keeping both Henry and me from our happy endings?

But then he just shrugs and hands the ID back to Henry. "Park in the structure to the left," he says. "And here's a map—you're in Building H." He gives us a lop-sided grin. "Loved you on *Dance! Off!*"

"Thanks, man!" Henry says, giving the guard a little salute.

"Excuse me, your *assistant*?" I yelp as Henry pilots us into the parking structure. "*That's* my cover identity?"

"I had to think fast!" Henry protests. "What else was I gonna say?"

"I dunno, how about your trainer?" I counter. "I taught you all that judo shit, didn't I?"

He parks the car and turns to me, a more genuine grin spreading over his face as he studies me intently—in that way that makes me feel like he can see through my skin.

"You taught me a lot of things," he says.

And I blush—because of course I do.

"Apparently I didn't teach you how to *lie*," I huff. "Because you are truly terrible at that."

I'm trying to sound snarky, but there's no heat behind it. His grin only widens.

"We've already covered this," he says. "You are *also* a terrible liar, so I probably learned that from you, too. Now. Time to put all your lessons to work." He brandishes the map the security guard gave him. It's nothing more than a flimsy piece of paper with a blurry grid of boxes. Somehow I expected a little more effort from a fancy Hollywood studio. "I'm going here," Henry says, tapping one of the boxes. "And the sets for *We Belong* are over . . . here." He taps another box that's on the opposite side of the lot. "Soundstage Nine. Or at least they were a few weeks ago."

"What should I expect?" I say, wheels turning as I study this indecipherable grid. "Will there be, like, guards blocking off the area?"

"Not exactly," he says, a smile playing over his lips as he taps thoughtfully on the square. "You should see a cluster of trailers next to these two big soundstages— the sets are on the soundstages. Security's tight around the stages because that's where filming's gonna be. But there aren't really guards by the trailers. If you can find Grace's trailer, maybe you can catch her on a break. Oh—and the markers on the trailers will have character names, not actor names—look for the one marked 'Suzanne.' That's who Grace plays in the movie."

"Suzanne!" I exclaim. "Like Auntie Suzy."

"A sign!" Henry says, his eyes widening. "If you believe in that sort of thing."

"Maybe I'm starting to," I say. "Anyway, that plan sounds good and stealthy-like. Though my track record for being stealthy is *really* not great lately. What if I somehow cause a huge disruption that destroys the entire set and gets both of us banned from this lot for the rest of our lives?"

Henry laughs and holds the map out to me. "If you get to finally meet Grace? Then I think it would be worth it."

"How are you just so *decent* all the time?" I say, taking the map from him. "You're really saying you'd be fine with me tanking your career just for a shot at completing my Mom Quest?"

He shrugs. "It's important to you."

I meet his eyes and take a moment to revel in how good he is. It sounds dorky and cheesy, and Belle would have a field day if she heard me say that out loud. But it's true. He always does the most right thing, and it's never calculated—it's like an instinct. Whether it's helping Rory with the salad and making her feel like a star, or calmly eviscerating Craig Shimizu, or telling me he still has hope even when I've lost it completely.

"And this audition is important to *you*," I say. "So go

in there and crush it, okay? The part is gonna be yours—I can feel it."

And then, because I'm really going with the whole feelings thing, I impulsively stretch myself over the gearshift and kiss him. His hands tangle in my hair and he pulls me closer, and I feel myself falling into him again—

Until an earsplitting *HOOOONK* rings out through the parking garage and we jump apart, gasping for breath.

"Oops," he manages to get out. "I bumped the horn." He gives me a sly grin. "Look at you, already causing disruptions."

"Me?" I spit out, indignant. "*You're* the one who bumped the horn!"

"Because *you* distracted me," he says, leaning in again. He glances down at my shirt. "Hey, is that the nure-onna?"

"Oh . . . yes," I say, smoothing the front of my beloved T-shirt. "I wore it for luck."

"She looks cool," he says. "Like she's about to fight the good fight."

"I think she's actually about to eat people and have her revenge on all of humanity," I retort. He just grins at me. "But maybe she could do both," I amend.

He touches his forehead to mine. "Let's go accomplish our respective missions. I believe in us—and the nure-onna."

"Me too," I murmur. "Just don't forget to drop your shoulder when you're going into the throw, or you'll completely mess it up."

"What a pep talk," he laughs.

My heartbeat speeds up again and my palms start to sweat as we exit the car. Henry points me in the right direction and heads off the opposite way. I see him adjusting, trying to center himself, squaring his shoulders and muttering his lines under his breath. I watch him until he's a dot bobbing in the distance. The butterflies cascading through my stomach are for him, I realize—because I know he wants this so badly. And I know he's *scared* to want it so badly.

When he's finally out of sight, I turn and survey the lot in front of me. Just to my left is a small fountain, welcoming me to the stately, arched entryway with PINNACLE PICTURES emblazoned on it. Beyond that are rows and rows of soundstages—tall beige boxes that block out the sky. And to my right is an outdoor screen of some sort, a gigantic square of bright blue that seems to be serving as a backdrop for exterior shots.

I've never actually been on a Hollywood lot. Rory is always complaining because TV and movies that depict

LA are obsessed with showing approximately three elements of the sprawling city: the Hollywood sign, the gilded front of one of the many studio lots, and Rodeo Drive. "Why don't they show the *real* LA?" she'll say. "Like, the place where we actually live."

It *is* like watching a far-off glittering fantasy kingdom built on top of the city I love. These images people associate with LA have nothing to do with my actual daily existence. I remember some kids in my and Belle's class who moved here from the East Coast asking us if we knew any movie stars, like that was a normal part of life in LA.

Although . . . now I *do* know a movie star. My mother is a movie star. And my . . . whatever Henry is . . .

And here I am on an actual Hollywood lot, ready to find my happy ending.

I take a deep breath and step forward, passing under the entryway. I try to meander down the row of soundstages casually but with purpose, like I totally belong here and totally know what I'm doing. I am so focused on my extremely casual meandering, I almost bump into a man barreling my way, wearing a giant lobster costume.

"Oops, sorry!" I cry, scurrying out of his path. He waves an oversized claw at me and keeps on barreling.

As I continue my trek, I feel more and more like Dorothy getting her first taste of Oz, or a confused Alice right after she was plunked into Wonderland. I see various costumed people marching by, wearing all sorts of things. A woman dressed as a pancake, pacing back and forth and studying her lines. A trio of teen vampires who keep cracking each other up by trying to recite tongue twisters around their fake teeth. A very tall man dressed as some kind of scaly green alien, phone pressed to the foamy ear of his costume as he shouts about how he "just can't do this anymore!"

On my left, I see a path to what looks like a fake city street—facades of buildings that aren't actually buildings, a subway that doesn't go anywhere. Even the path beneath my feet appears to be made up of some kind of fake cobblestones, lovingly crafted to look real. Only their suspiciously shiny surfaces give them away.

I suppose I should be repulsed by all this, by this superficial kingdom dedicated to selling some version of reality that has very little to do with real life. Grace Kimura's happy endings.

And yet, as the gentle summer breeze and the laughter of the tongue-twisting vampires wash over me, I can't help but feel charmed. So many people's dreams are bubbling underneath the surface of these fake cobblestones. I imagine my mother, setting foot on this lot for the first time. Realizing the sacrifices she made led her here, that soon she would be catapulted into the glittering life of a Hollywood starlet beloved by millions. That she could at last escape her tragic past as a teen mother cast out by the community she once loved.

That she could be a princess in this kingdom built on top of my city.

I've gotten so lost in my reverie, I've actually come to a stop on the fake cobblestones and am gazing off into the distance, my eyes zeroing in on that fake subway station. I shake it off, reminding myself of my mission, and glance down at the crumpled map in my hand.

I was supposed to go . . .

I frown, turning the map over, and look up at the numbers on the soundstages. Then back at the map. Only now the map appears to be upside down . . . or is it? Sweat beads my brow as I turn it over and over, unable to make sense of it. I'm looking for Soundstage Nine, but I can't tell if it's to my left or up ahead or if I've already passed it. This janky-ass map seems to indicate that it could literally be in all three of these places.

I swallow hard, my brow furrowing. I'm lost. And I don't think I can just GPS my way to Soundstage Nine or ask the guy in the lobster suit . . .

"Hey, Rika? Sweet Rika?"

My head snaps up to see a familiar figure bustling toward me, swoopy ponytail twitching behind her—Joanna Raine. The writer from the Asian Hollywood meetup. The one who told me I thought I didn't deserve a happy ending.

"Hi," I say, suddenly feeling shy for some reason.

"Hey," she says, giving me an exuberant head bob. "What a nice surprise. The show based on my books is set to shoot a few soundstages over." She jerks her thumb in the direction of the fake subway. "What are you doing here?"

I belatedly remember that I'm not actually supposed to be on the lot at all. "I'm, uh . . . I just . . . I'm here."

"Oooh, wait, did you convince Baby Hank to go to his audition?" Joanna bounces on her toes. "That makes me so happy! I was worried he was going to, you know"—she gestures vaguely—"get in his own way."

"We're both pretty good at that, actually," I say, smiling at her. "Um, maybe you can help me with something, though." I brandish the map. "I'm trying to find Soundstage Nine. And I can't seem to figure out where I am or where it is or . . ." I trail off and gesture at the big row of soundstages, which are more and more indistinguishable from each other every time I look at them.

"Nine is this way—come on, I'll show you!" Joanna

says, pointing to a path that splits off to the right.

I follow her down yet another fake cobblestone path, marveling at her seemingly boundless energy.

"So what are you doing at Nine?" Joanna asks. "Is Henry's audition over that way?"

"Um, no," I say. "I'm, uh . . ."

Dammit. Henry's right. We're *both* terrible liars.

"I'm . . . looking for someone," I say.

"Oh, wait—you guys said the other night that you were looking for Grace Kimura, right?" Joanna snaps her fingers and beams at me. "Is Nine where they're shooting *We Belong*?"

"Yes!" I say, relieved that I can at least sort of tell the truth. "I, uh . . . I need to meet her. For reasons."

I expect Joanna to push me on that, but she gives me another sunny smile and we keep walking, our shoes clicking steadily along the fake cobblestones.

"Here we are," Joanna says after we've walked for a bit, sweeping an arm toward one of those giant beige boxes. This one has a big "9" emblazoned on it, and I breathe a sigh of relief. If Joanna hadn't happened upon me, I'd probably still be wandering around the lot, running into who knows how many people dressed as giant sea creatures. The soundstage appears to be all closed up, but there's a cluster of trailers set up near the entrance.

My heart starts to beat a little faster again—that's what Henry said to find. The trailers.

"Uh-oh," Joanna says, her brow crinkling. "It looks like no one's here—or at least they're not currently shooting. I guess Clara Mae was wrong about those rumors."

"That's okay," I say hastily. "I don't need to watch them shoot anything. Henry suggested I try to find Grace's trailer, maybe?"

Joanna tilts her head, studying me. She doesn't look suspicious, exactly. It's more like she's trying to take all this in, to figure out what I'm thinking. I shift uncomfortably, wondering if I've managed to totally bungle this situation already.

But then her gaze shifts back to the row of trailers.

"Okay," she murmurs, lowering her voice. "We'll have to be extra stealthy because even if no one's on the stage right now, there could still be security folks lurking around. Come on."

She beckons me forward, and we slip between two rows of trailers, practically plastering ourselves up against them in an effort to stay hidden. My heart is beating like mad now, and I should feel ridiculous—the way we're creeping around, eyes darting to the side, probably makes us look like a pair of extremely cartoony cat burglars. But my adrenaline is amped up way too high for me to think about anything except the possibility of reuniting with my mother. After these past few days, all our near misses, me feeling so close yet so far, me wanting it yet desperately wishing I *didn't* want it . . . is this really about to happen?

"Check the doors—we're looking for Suzanne, right? That's who she's playing?" Joanna hisses at me, tapping on one of the trailers. I see that each one seems to have a piece of masking tape affixed to the door with a character's name scrawled on it. This, much like the studio map, seems way jankier than what I would imagine for a fancy Hollywood production—when Henry said the doors would be marked with character names, I imagined some kind of engraved-plaque situation. I guess they spent all their money creating those fake cobblestones—the impression of reality is more important than actual reality.

I scan those scraps of masking tape on every trailer we skulk up to, adrenaline powering me forward, but none bear the name I'm looking for. They start to blur into nonsensical series of letters, puzzles I have to decode in order to gain the keys to the kingdom.

But then we reach a trailer at the end of the row, positioned right next to the soundstage. The sun trying to break through from behind the soundstage cascades over its brilliant white surface, illuminating this mundane piece of Hollywood like a glittering disco ball.

I *know* before I even see the masking tape on the door. I can't explain how.

And once I get close enough to actually see . . . there it is. That name, the one that's maybe a sign. Scribbled in that same basic marker as everyone else's. Yet the letters seem to pulse with an unearthly glow, calling out to me.

SUZANNE

I run my fingertips over them, reassuring myself that they're real.

"Yessss, you found it!" Joanna whispers, and I nearly jump out of my skin. I forgot she was there.

I try knocking—once, twice. Tentatively.

No answer. My heart sinks a little, and the glow around the name dissipates.

Is she really not here? Are we really having yet *another* near miss?

I don't know what possesses me, but I reach out and try the door. And just like that, it swings open.

"Wait, Rika!" I hear Joanna's urgent whisper behind me. "What are you doing?"

I can't answer because I don't actually know. But I also can't stop myself from climbing the little metal steps into the trailer and entering yet another space my mother recently inhabited. It's like some other force is guiding me, and I simply cannot do anything else.

The space is dark and cramped, and the stuffy air shimmers with dust motes and the beginnings of cobwebs. To my right is a teeny kitchenette-type area with a mini fridge. To my left, a very small couch and a makeup table with a mirror attached. Everything is so shrunken, it almost looks like doll furniture.

It's also very *empty*. If those cobweb whispers weren't enough to show me that this space has been abandoned for a very long time, the lack of anything beyond this weird doll furniture certainly is. When I walked under the big arched entrance of this lot earlier, I swore I could feel my mother's presence, could see her setting foot in her future kingdom all those years ago.

But now . . . I don't sense her at all. I can't picture her in this dark, sterile space. Shards of panic sliver their way through my heart. Have any of my feelings been real since this journey first started? Would I even know if they weren't?

"Rika?" Joanna sidles up next to me, her eyes shifting nervously to the side. "I don't think we're supposed to be in here—like, we're *really* not supposed to be in here. Maybe we should—"

"No!" I blurt out. My cheeks heat up as I realize how loud and weird and *angry* I sound. My kaiju-temper does *not* want to leave. I force myself to relax my shoulders and lower my voice back to a stealthy level. "I mean. I just need to, um, look around for a second. Please, Joanna."

She studies me again, that expression I can't quite read passing over her face.

"Okaaaay," she says, very hesitantly. "What are you looking for?"

"I'm not sure," I murmur, crossing the minuscule space to the makeup table. There's absolutely nothing on it, not even leftover traces of powder or lip gloss. It's bare, save for a thin layer of dust. I idly run my finger through the dust, just to see if it will actually leave a mark—or if this is all an illusion. My fingertips wander lower, to the single drawer built into the table. I give the handle a slight tug and am surprised to find it opens as easily as the door to the trailer.

And there's something inside. Something that's not dust or cobwebs or a blank expanse of absolutely nothing. A small square of faded colors, crumbling around the edges—another photo.

I sit down on the stool in front of the makeup table and pull the photo free. This one is just *her*. Grace Kimura.

She's young again, but she's not a child—maybe about

fourteen. She's sitting in a beautiful garden underneath the drooping branches of a big tree. I'd recognize all that green and that tree anywhere—it's the garden behind the JACCC. The onryo tree I used to hide under. The place that cradles me and gives so much comfort when I feel lost.

My mother is staring off into the distance. Longing for something.

"Rika?" Joanna crouches down in front of me, her face concerned. Once again, I'd forgotten she was there. "What's the matter?"

I look up from the photo . . . and realize my eyes have filled with tears. I freeze, making myself very still. Trying to imagine my nure-onna armor rising up and surrounding me. I sneak a sidelong glance at the mirror, but all I see is me.

That sad girl who doesn't want to admit she's sad. That girl who can't seem to stop waiting for someone to want her. That girl who knows the exact yearning in this photo because she's been feeling it in little bits and pieces every day for her entire life.

I look back at the photo, gripping it tightly between my fingers. My knuckles turn white. I've started holding my breath without even knowing it. Trying with all my might to be *still*. If only I can be still enough, maybe I'll disappear.

"Rika," Joanna repeats, her voice so quiet and gentle, it makes me want to let those tears fall. My fingers clutching the photo so tightly tremble. "There's more to this, isn't there?" she says. "More than wanting to meet a famous movie star?"

I don't trust myself to say anything, so I give her a tight head bob.

I expect her to press me for more, but she simply reaches up and squeezes my hands, which are still tightly clasped around the photo, then sits back on her heels. My gaze returns to the photo. I can't seem to stop looking at this girl Grace Kimura used to be. I feel such an instant connection to this girl—just like when we locked eyes at the parade. But she's so far away. So unreachable. Even though she's *right here*, in front of my eyes.

Frustration bubbles up in my chest, mixing with the potent rage of my kaiju-temper.

I just . . . I just *want* . . .

"I know what it's like," Joanna says.

My head snaps up, and I look at her quizzically—still not trusting myself to speak.

"To feel like you never totally fit in anywhere—or with anyone," Joanna says. "To love a community so fiercely, with everything you have—but to feel like you don't always belong there."

I look down at the photo again, at my mother. I blink hard, willing those tears to please, *please* stay put.

"When I said you don't think you deserve a happy ending . . ." Joanna trails off, and I feel her eyes boring into me again. "I know that was kind of . . . *forward* and weird. But I could tell you hurt the way I used to—the way I sometimes still do. That you have so much anger you're constantly trying to repress."

"I don't actually repress it that well," I murmur. "Or, like . . . ever."

"I think you do," Joanna insists. "I can tell it's sitting inside of you, getting bigger every day. That you're trying *so hard* to make yourself small."

I just keep staring at the photo. I don't even know what to say.

"I really wish so many of our communities would just, like, *acknowledge* that anger isn't always a *bad* emotion," Joanna continues. "Sometimes it's there to let you know when something's wrong or to protect you from being mistreated or to tell you that you care. You can't just reject it—you have to let yourself *feel* it, make room for it, or all that repressing will burn you up inside. You have to figure out a way to *channel* it. That's what I finally realized I had to do."

"How did you do that?" I manage.

"Lots of practice, lots of mistakes," she says, laughing a little. "But ultimately, I started listening to my heart more. Trusting myself. And I let that anger power me—every time someone told me no one would buy a dragons-and-swords fantasy series starring women of color, or a story starring more than one Asian, or that I don't look like someone's very narrow idea of what 'Asian' is . . ." She shakes her head. "I got mad. I felt that power, deep in my bones. And I used that to figure out what I really wanted and to drive me forward."

A single tear drifts down my cheek. I don't even know how to start doing . . . what she's saying. It sounds as far-fetched as the most candy-sweet of fairy tales.

"All this anger—it's a totally understandable response to the hurt," Joanna says, her voice very soft. "I know exactly what that feels like."

"Why?" The word escapes my lips, barely a whisper. "Why do I feel this way?"

"Because . . . some of the awful things people have said to you? You've heard them so many times, you secretly believe they're true."

I freeze, still blinking like mad. Staring at that photo.

I think of all the things Craig and some of the saltier Uncles have spewed at me. Being "claimed" by Belle, because otherwise I wouldn't belong to my family at all. All the times I've been called a mistake.

Do *I* think I'm a mistake?

I built up my snarling nure-onna armor so these words would bounce off of me. So I could throw them to the side and they wouldn't matter. And I fight everyone and everything to show just *how much* all of this doesn't matter.

But maybe, all this time . . . all I've been doing is absorbing these words, making them part of myself. Trying to consume them so they can never consume me.

Whenever I think of myself, it's always as this snarling, uncontrollable monster.

Joanna's telling me this monster could be so powerful . . . but I just don't believe it. I can't picture it. Currently, all I can see is the picture in front of me—my mother, longing for something.

I see myself in this picture, too. And this picture isn't angry at all.

This picture is sad.

"I have to go," I say abruptly, shooting to my feet and scraping a hand over my eyes. I don't even think about what I'm doing as I stuff the picture in my pocket.

"Wait," Joanna says, getting to her feet, too. "Rika,

you can talk to me about this. I understand—"

"No, you don't," I snap.

I push her aside and start to hustle toward the door . . . when I spy something else. A bit of blue-silver fluff, sticking out from behind the small couch. I change course, go to the couch, and tug on that bit of silver fluff. It leads to *more* fluff—the stuff just keeps coming and coming as I pull, like I'm a magician drawing an endless series of scarves from my sleeve. When I finally get the whole thing free, I shake it out and hold it up in front of me.

"Whoa," Joanna says, her eyes widening. "That is the most princess-y Cinderella dress I've ever seen in my life."

She's hit the nail on the head. There's really no other way to describe it. It's a fluffy concoction of tulle and silk, embroidered with cascading bits of sparkle that manage to glimmer in the dim light of the trailer. A bit of pure magic against its dull surroundings. Definitely a Grace Kimura Gets Her Prince kind of dress. A Happily Ever After dress.

We're both mesmerized by it. Frozen in place, watching the gentle sway of fabric, captivated by all that shimmer.

We're jolted out of the spell by a pair of voices bouncing off the trailers outside.

"Hey!" one of them calls. "Is someone prowling around

the trailers? Dammit, this area's supposed to be secure."

"Check 'em!" the other voice calls back. "You know fans manage to get on the lot all the time!"

And then there's the sound of footsteps getting closer . . .

"Shit!" Joanna yelps. "Come on."

She grabs my hand and pulls me toward the trailer door. For some reason, I don't let go of the dress. I *can't* let go of the dress. I don't know why, but there is *no way* I'm leaving this dress behind.

Joanna pulls me down the stairs of the trailer, then plasters herself against the side and looks around, trying to figure out where the voices are coming from.

"Oh, it's security," she whispers, jerking her head toward the opposite end of the row. I whip around and see two men in security-type uniforms, frowning and inspecting one of the other trailers. I turn back to Joanna, prepared to mimic her oh-so-stealthy movements. Unfortunately, the gigantic dress I've suddenly decided to steal gets caught on the trailer steps. I instinctively yank on it, trying to get it free . . . and then it makes a big *RIIIIPPPPPPP,* and then the security guards are yelling and Joanna is grabbing my free hand and telling me to run.

I bolt away from the trailers, following her back to

the fake cobblestone path, and we clatter away as fast as our legs can carry us.

I risk a glance over my shoulder and see the security guards yelling after us, telling us to come back, telling me to *drop the dress.*

Exhilaration thrums through my bloodstream, syncing with the jackhammer beating of my heart. I pick up the pace, sling the dress over my shoulder, don't think about anything except *getting away.*

We zigzag through another bank of trailers, dart through a narrow alleyway between two massive soundstages. Sweat beads my brow, and my heart beats even faster . . . and honestly, it feels *good.* It feels like relief, my tears clearing and my body responding to all this exertion like a happy puppy.

It's just like when I am fully enveloped in an intense judo session—I don't have to think.

We finally reach the entrance of the studio again—the arch, the fountain—and Joanna slows her pace, looking over her shoulder.

"Oh god," she wheezes, coming to a stop. "Okay." She doubles over in front of the fountain, hands on her knees. "You are in *much* better shape than I am."

"Where'd they go?" I say, looking around frantically

for the security guards. "Did we lose them? Are they making a report about us right now?"

"I doubt it," Joanna says, finally catching her breath and standing up straight. "They mostly just wanted to get us out of that area, and they did. If we cause any trouble on another area of this lot, it's another security team's problem. That said . . ." She grins and casts a pointed look at my stolen dress. "I'd suggest you get out of here as quickly as you can. Just in case they tell the other teams to be on the lookout for a girl running around with a gigantic Cinderella dress."

I laugh, the weirdness that engulfed me just moments ago melting away. It's not *gone*, but at least our impromptu chase took me out of the existential crisis I was about to settle into.

"Here." Joanna rummages around in her pocket, pulling out a business card and passing it to me. "Take my number. Call or text me anytime."

My instinct is to push the card back at her. We barely know each other—why would I want her number? But instead I take it. Yet another thing I can't really explain to myself.

Except . . . I can't deny that there's something about her that makes me feel instantly comfortable. And I'm used to feeling pretty much the opposite at all times.

"You remind me a lot of, well, me," Joanna says with a chuckle. "If there's ever anything you want to talk about, anything at all, please let me know. I'm always here."

"I . . . thank you," I murmur, tucking the card into my pocket. I know I need to get out of here before security comes crashing down on me, but I suddenly don't want to leave her. "Hey, Joanna. Thank you. For, um, helping me possibly commit an actual crime." I brandish the dress.

"I think that dress is yours," she says, running her fingers over the sparkles. "I could tell you didn't want to let it go."

"It's so not what I'd usually wear," I say ruefully. "I'll probably never even put it on."

Joanna's gaze turns introspective as she lets go of the dress, still studying all those sparkles. "You will," she says—and the certainty in her voice gives me chills.

"How do you know?" I can't help asking.

"I just do." She looks up from the dress and gives me a sly grin. "Maybe I'm your fairy godmother."

SEVENTEEN

Henry's waiting for me when I hustle back to the car.

"I was about to send out a search party," he says, flashing me an easy grin. "Or, you know, a text." His gaze lands on the dress clutched in my arms and his brow furrows. "Did you go shopping?"

"Not exactly," I say, glancing over my shoulder. "Let's get out of here. Quickly."

We get into the car, and I shove the dress in the back seat and attempt to hide it under Henry's jacket. Just in case the security guard at the front booth is checking cars for clearly stolen contraband or something. Henry raises an eyebrow but doesn't say anything further.

Luckily the security guard barely looks at us, just waves us through and goes back to tapping away on his phone. I let out a long, slow exhale of relief as Henry pilots us back onto the streets of Hollywood.

As we drive for a few blocks in silence, I text Joanna so she'll have my number. Now Henry's being *suspiciously* quiet. I give him a sidelong glance, trying to work out if he's, like, peaceful or if he's subdued because he's disappointed.

"So how did it go?" I say, turning to him. "Your audition. Did your sweet judo moves work out?"

"I executed that throw perfectly," he says, grinning at me. "Although I missed my sparring partner. They made me use this big, floppy mannequin. Not the same."

"And?" I swat his arm, impatient. "What does that mean? Did you get it?"

"I don't know," he says, his face falling. "I *think* I did well. I was really in it, you know? I felt like I was the character in the moment, and everything else just disappeared and . . . sorry, does this sound incredibly cheesy?"

"No," I say, giving him a small smile. "Not cheesy. *Passionate.*"

"Mmm." He smiles back at me in that way that makes me instantly blush. Talk about cheesy. "So," he continues, "what about you, what did—"

We're cut off by the blare of his phone—the ringtone sounds like a fire alarm.

"Oh, shit!" Henry exclaims. "That's my agent. I need to . . ." He looks around frantically, but we're stuck on a major, traffic-jammed LA thoroughfare, where there is most definitely no place to pull over.

"You have to answer!" I squeak as the phone continues to blare. It's ringing so hard, it's rattling around in the cupholder where Henry's placed it. "And do you *really* not have a dashboard mount? I thought you'd been in LA for months now!"

"I refuse!" he yells back. "I will not succumb to that particular bit of the Angeleno lifestyle!"

"Well, that makes it hard to answer your freakin' phone!" I snatch the phone out of the cupholder. I hit answer, then put the call on speaker. "This is Henry Chen's phone," I say, making my voice as authoritative as I can manage. "He's driving, but listening."

"Yeah, Hank," a brusque female voice barks over the line. She seems completely unfazed by the fact that some random girl has just answered Henry Chen's phone. "Great job in the room, buddy, *great job*."

I sneak a glance at Henry, but his eyes are glued to the road, his knuckles white as he grips the steering wheel. He has no idea what this lady who started a conversation as if they were already in the middle of one is about to say.

"I have a few deal points I want to push them on, but assuming they don't dick me around too much, the shoot will start in three months," she bulldozes on. "I assured them you're totally up for the physical demands, even if it means doing some extra training—"

"Wait." Henry finally manages to get a word in. "Are you saying I got it?"

"Well, yeah," the woman says, sounding like she has no idea why that would be in question. "Like I said, you killed it in the room."

"But . . . that's it?" he says, shaking his head. "No callback, no test, no chemistry read—"

"Hank." The woman sounds thoroughly annoyed now. "Do you want this or not?"

"Yes." He nods vigorously, even though she can't see him. "Of course I do."

"Faaaabulous," the woman trills. "Then I'll get to work. Lates."

And then she hangs up.

"Oh my god," Henry murmurs. He slaps the steering wheel a couple times, his face lit with total disbelief. "Oh. My. *God!*"

"Pull over!" I demand. "You're about to crash your completely-not-safe-for-LA car! Look, there's an alley just off Melrose—right there!"

Henry whips the steering wheel around, making a screechy, terrifying turn into the alley. He pulls up next to the curb, stops the car, and turns off the ignition. Then he reaches over the gearshift and sweeps me into his arms, pulling me tightly against him.

"Thank you," he murmurs into my hair. "This is all because of you."

"No," I say, pulling back from him. His arms are still around me, our faces inches apart. I reach up and run my fingertips over his cheek, my eyes roaming his face. I love being this close to him, just *studying* him. "*You* did that, Henry. You got that part. And I knew you could do it. I'm so happy for you." I brush my lips lightly against his and smile. "We should go celebrate."

"Wait," he says, shaking his head. "What about *you*? What . . ." His eyes drift to the Cinderella dress, still crumpled in the back seat. "What happened with Grace?"

"The same thing that usually happens," I say, tossing off a breezy one-shoulder shrug. "Absolutely nothing. The sets and the trailers were abandoned; there was no one there. I did run into Joanna, though." I disentangle myself from him and sit back in my seat. "So. Where should we celebrate?"

But of course, Henry doesn't let it go. Because he can never let *anything* go. A quality I find both infuriating and inexplicably attractive.

"Rika," he says, his voice heartbreakingly tender. "What really happened?"

"Like I said, she wasn't there," I say, throwing up my hands. "I found another old picture of her that she must have left behind. And that dress. And I suddenly had to have both of them—don't ask me why."

"This is bothering you," he says.

"Maybe it is—so what?" I say. "At this point, it feels like she doesn't *want* to be found. She doesn't want to meet me. It's like she's avoiding me on purpose. And maybe that's the way it's meant to be. She's the beautiful princess—the *queen*—who's disappeared into her far-off castle forever. We're star-crossed, never to meet. It's a sad, bittersweet ending—just like all of my Japanese fairy tales. And . . ." I swallow hard, trying to get rid of the lump that's rising in my throat. "And that's just how it is," I proclaim defiantly. "That's how it *always* is."

We sit there for a few moments in silence, me staring at my lap. Determined not to cry. I'm not even going to fucking *well up* this time. The silence grows heavy around us, an invisible force weighing down the entire car.

Then Henry reaches over the gearshift and takes my hand.

"But maybe this time," he says softly, "you didn't want it to be that way."

The silence grows heavier, pressing against me, making every single breath feel labored. Why can't I ever just say what I actually want?

"It doesn't matter," I say, trying to sound defiant again. "I think I got caught up in this idea of Grace Kimura being my mother—like we were going to have this tearful, perfect reunion and suddenly everything in my life would be fixed and I'd feel like I . . ."

Like I belong with someone.

I take a deep breath, trying to retain control. "And somehow, in that fiction, I guess I conveniently forgot that . . . I mean, I don't know exactly what happened, but no matter how you slice it, she *abandoned* me seventeen years ago," I say. "She left me behind and never came back for me. So why would she want me to find her now? I'm worse than Belle, dreaming of some kind of impossible Cinderella ending. I should have remembered that the nure-onna doesn't really do that sort of happily ever after."

Henry doesn't say anything, just squeezes my hand. And we sit in silence for a few moments more.

"I want to take you somewhere," he finally says. "One of *my* favorite magical spots in LA."

My head jerks up. "Excuse me? You know enough about LA to have a favorite spot? Please don't say Disneyland: that's not even *in* LA."

"Oh no," Henry says, a mischievous grin overtaking his face. He puts the key in the ignition and starts the car.

"It's definitely in LA. But I want it to be a surprise. Just sit back and enjoy the ride and don't try to pry any clues out of me." His grin widens. "You're gonna love this, I promise."

❀

"*This* is your favorite spot in LA?" I have to shout to be heard over the din of bleeps, blings, and screams emanating from the massive carnival swirling around us. "The Santa Monica Pier? One of the cheesiest tourist traps in the city? And by the way, Santa Monica is its own city, so it's not even LA, actually."

"Listen to you," Henry teases, throwing an arm around my shoulders and giving me a squeeze. "What a freaking snob. After all those lectures about LA's history and range and how I need to rethink my New York superiority complex, you reject *my* LA landmark?"

"Not exactly a landmark," I grouse. "Unless you think a rickety old roller coaster and a hot dog stand count as such."

"It's right on the beach," he says, sweeping an arm out.

The pier is a long stretch of weathered old wood that extends over part of the beach and just over the water. It's packed to the brim with concession stands, kiosks selling T-shirts and cheap souvenirs, and the raucous carnival. A cluster of old fishermen always inhabits the very end, throwing their lines out into the ocean and hoping to receive a bounty in return.

"That's your selling point?" I say. "The *beach*? You can get the beach almost anywhere along the coast of this area. And without all the excess noise."

"I know it's corny," he concedes, chuckling. "But I love it. All of it—the rainbow lights from the Ferris wheel, the loud noises from the boardwalk games, people looking for cheap thrills and fried food." He tugs the brim of his incognito baseball cap. "I feel like I can get lost here, escape into the crowd. It's hard to do that anywhere else."

"Hmm," I say, remembering the ruckus he caused at Katsu That. "I guess I can see that. So what's your celebratory fried food of choice?"

"Naturally it's the fried cheese at Hot Dog on a Stick," he says, his eyes getting a dreamy look. "Like a corn dog, only just cheese inside."

"You are quite the fried cheese connoisseur," I say. "People are usually scared of the cheese katsu at my Aunties' restaurant, but you went all in. Didn't even hesitate."

"I never hesitate when it comes to cheese," he says— and he suddenly looks so deathly serious, I have to laugh. "We need to strategize, though. Rides need to come *before* fried food. Unless you're the type of person who's more likely to get queasy on an empty stomach—"

"I don't do rides," I say quickly. "Especially roller coasters."

He drops his arm from my shoulders and whirls to face me, shock overtaking his expression. "Excuse me," he says. "But how, why, *what*? You're one of the most fearless people I've ever met. Are you telling me you're scared of *rides*?"

"Not scared," I protest, crossing my arms over my chest. "I just don't like them."

Now he crosses *his* arms over *his* chest, his eyes narrowing. "That's it?"

I shrug. "That's it."

He cocks an eyebrow. "Bullshit."

"Hey!" I yelp, falling out of my indignant pose. "That's not very celebratory."

"I don't want to celebrate if it means we're going to ignore how you're feeling," he says. "And I know you well enough at this point to realize when you say 'That's it,' it's pretty much never true."

"Okay, *ouch*," I say, clapping a hand to my chest, mock-wounded. "I thought this was supposed to be a fun time at the carnival, not some weird therapy session."

"It *is* a fun time at the carnival," Henry says, throwing an arm around my shoulders again. "And part of the fun is *rides*." He dips his head to whisper against my hair, his lips nearly brushing my ear. "Don't you want to be all pressed up against me on that roller coaster, holding on to each other for dear life?"

"We don't need a roller coaster for that," I mutter, my face flaming.

I study the scene swirling around us again. The rainbow of flashing lights bouncing off the dusky sky and the steady shimmer of the ocean. People laughing and stuffing their faces with cotton candy. And right in front of us, the most gigantic of the roller coasters, a rusting contraption of metal and the same generic "rock" song blasting over and over and over again as people scream their way through the series of loops and drops. The highest drop is, of course, the grand finale of the roller coaster's routine, and I watch as one of the little cars full of people trundles its way to the top. I can hear every squeak of the wheels against the track, every shift of gears that are badly in need of oil. It's like running sandpaper over my skin.

The car comes to a momentary stop, suspended above the drop, building anticipation. Its passengers are already waving their hands above their heads, eager grins splitting their faces. They're *ready*.

Then, just as the generic rock song reaches a particularly dramatic crescendo, the car releases from its perch, plummeting straight down. It's like watching people get unceremoniously thrown into the abyss.

But they all love it. Their screams signal *release*. The cacophony of voices is thrilled, a little bit terrified. They *want* to be scared.

I watch until I can't anymore, then bury my face in Henry's shoulder.

"Hey, Rika." His voice turns concerned. "We don't have to go on any rides if you don't want to—I was just kidding. But what is it? Are you scared of heights?"

"No." I shake my head against his shoulder, still unwilling to look at the roller coaster. "Not heights."

I take a deep breath and lift my head, meeting his gaze.

"I'm scared of . . . losing control."

He stares at me, looking perplexed.

"I . . ." I try to put the right words together. What is it about this boy that makes me want to *say* things? Especially things I'm used to shoving so far down that I forget they exist.

Maybe it's because I know he doesn't ask to hear these things because he wants to use them against me or make fun of me or tally them up as weaknesses. He genuinely wants to *know*.

"When you go on a roller coaster, there's always that moment when you lose control," I say. "You're in this situation where your body's thrown all over the place — you're basically being tossed off a cliff." I gesture to the new car of people reaching the top of the big drop. "And in that moment, you can't hold anything in — you just *can't*. Every feeling you've been having, every emotion you've been shoving down or holding so tightly comes tumbling out. You can't stop it. You *scream*. You *have* to feel things."

The rock music builds to its uninteresting crescendo yet again, the car releases, and everyone screams their heads off.

"My temper is always trying to get the better of me," I say, my eyes glued to this bumpy descent. "It takes everything I have to shove it down. But on a roller coaster . . . all that goes away. You can't shove *anything* down."

Silence falls between us as we watch carload after carload of people get tossed off the punishing drop, yelling all the way and loving every minute.

"Maybe that's what you need right now," Henry says.

I give him a look.

"I'm serious!" he presses. "You're dealing with this

whole snarl of feelings over all these things you can't control—like whether you ever find Grace or not. But you're holding on to them so tightly, they're about to eat you alive."

I can't help but remember what Joanna said—about all my anger, that tight ball in my chest that gets bigger every day, burning me up inside.

Henry turns so he's facing me, his hands on my shoulders.

"I'm not going to push you to do anything you don't want to. If you'd really rather keep it all locked up here"—he gestures to his chest, closing his hand into a tight fist—"we can skip the rides and go straight to the cheese. But I feel like maybe you *want* to let some of that stuff out? To scream? Maybe it would feel good, even."

I look at him for a moment, my eyes wandering from his hopeful expression to the coaster and back again. My stew of feelings—all that frustration that bubbled up earlier, all those tears I didn't want to cry in front of Joanna—is thrumming through my bloodstream, my kaiju-temper pounding eagerly at my breastbone. I imagine ordering them back, shoving them down once again. Letting my armor surround me and turning my back on the coaster. Going to eat fried cheese with Henry, allowing all that carby goodness to settle in my stomach, and casting my tight knot of feelings out to sea.

That thought should comfort me, this idea that I can reset myself so easily.

Instead it makes me twitchy. Like all these feelings rising up inside of me are my own personal onryo, and no matter how much I try to banish them . . . they'll always rise up again. I feel the same way whenever Craig says something awful to me. Whenever I feel disconnected from my family. Whenever I get called a mistake by the neighborhood gossipmongers or someone refers to me as a fraction or looks at me like I'm a puzzle instead of a person. It doesn't go away and it doesn't get better. It just *lives* inside of me, and it's like Joanna said—I start to believe it's true. The onryo that is my shoved-down feelings always comes back to haunt me.

"Let's do it," I say impulsively.

I grab Henry's hand and start towing him toward the roller coaster.

"What, really?" He lets out a surprised laugh. "Are you sure?"

"Yes," I say. "I'm not scared of a *carnival ride*. And this is how you wanted to celebrate, right? And . . . maybe I do want to let some feelings out. We'll just have to see."

I drag him over to the booth in front of the coaster, and we buy our tickets and get in line.

"So I told you why I don't usually do roller coasters," I say, shifting from one foot to the other. I can't believe I committed to this. What the hell am I thinking? "Why do you love them so much?"

"Hmm," he says. "I think it's actually the same reason you don't like them—that loss of control. I spend so much of my life worrying about what people think of me—whether it's my parents or a casting director or someone who posted a picture of me cramming an entire Egg McMuffin in my face—"

"Wait, someone actually did that?" I goggle at him, remembering how he used this as a "hypothetical" example of celebrity during our first meal together. "That was a real thing that happened? But why?"

"Why do people do anything?" he says with an easy shrug. "The next day, some gossip site ran a full spread analyzing all paparazzi photos of me from the last couple weeks, trying to determine if I was filling the emptiness I must feel inside with junk food, and how much weight I might have gained because of that—because what is Hank Chen without his abs, hmm? My parents reminded me that I always have to be mindful about what I'm doing in public. Otherwise, everything I have could go away—just like that."

"And you support them," I murmur. "Send them money. So that would mean, like, *everything*. For your family."

He shrugs again, but it's less easy. "Not eating an Egg McMuffin in public seems like a small price to pay, considering everything that I have."

"But it's another thing that doesn't let you be the whole you," I say. "You have to flatten yourself out again, because everyone in your life expects a certain kind of perfect."

He nods, squeezing my hand. "Everyone except you," he says, trying to make his voice light.

I squeeze back and study him as we shuffle forward in line. I got it so wrong. I thought he was so comfortable with himself, so at home in his body. I flash back to him dancing through the park, making faces at those kids. I'd assumed he didn't care what anyone thought of him. I flash back again, to another moment—him looking around nervously before our Grand Central Market meal, making sure no one was photographing him. Taking the smallest, most delicate bite of a taco possible when all he wanted to do was dive in with gusto.

The truth is, he cares maybe too much. Because he has to.

"So that moment when the roller coaster drops off—that moment when everything comes out," I say. "That feels freeing to you?"

"Yeah," he says, shooting me a grin. "It's the only time I'm not hyperaware of what I look like, how I must seem. Maybe one of the only times I can let go and just feel."

"What are the other times?" I can't help but ask.

He meets my gaze and looks at me for a long moment, his expression unreadable. Then his mouth quirks into the softest of half smiles and he leans in close, his lips brushing my hair again.

"The alley," he murmurs. "By Jitlada."

"Oh" is all I can say. And despite the warm summer air, a shiver runs through me.

We make it to the front of the line, and the ticket taker ushers us into our little car and instructs us to pull down the big foam bar that's supposed to keep us secure. Personally, I've always thought these things are way too flimsy. How does a simple piece of *foam* protect you from flying into the Pacific Ocean if this creaky-ass roller coaster makes a wrong move?

I breathe deeply and try to slow my rapidly beating heart. I'm all buckled in now, there's no turning back. And I want to do this. *I do.*

I grab on to the big foam bar and curl my fingers tightly around it.

"You okay?" Henry asks, his gaze falling to my white knuckles. He's tucked his incognito baseball cap into his back pocket, totally set for the coaster.

"Fine!" I say, trying to make my voice sound all easy-breezy. It comes out more like a pathetic yelp.

"You want to hold my hand?" he says, a trace of a smile in his voice.

"Um, *no*," I snap at him. "I said I'm fine. Just getting ready for this super-thrilling roller coaster. I don't need you to baby me."

"Wouldn't dream of it," he says—and that smile in his voice just keeps getting bigger.

Irritation flares in my chest, my nure-onna hissing at him. It's enough to calm my nerves, and my hands relax a little on the foam bar. Then the roller coaster takes off, shooting us into the first loop, and they tighten right back up again.

"Yesssss!" Henry yells, waving his arms in the air.

I keep my hands latched to the bar, not willing to risk being tossed into the Pacific for even a second.

We speed through a couple of loops, a mild drop or two. Henry shouts and cheers through all of it. I sneak a sidelong look at him and can't help but feel a little flutter at how *goofy* he looks, his eyes lit up with pure delight. He is truly himself right now, and there's something beautiful about that. This is the Henry I know, the one who *would* cram an entire Egg McMuffin into his mouth without a second thought. If he didn't have to worry about the cameras, that is, and everything that shattering his perfect image might lead to.

As we start the slow climb to the top of the coaster, the biggest drop, I hunker down over the bar, my eyes trained forward, my mouth set in a grim line. I must look ridiculous, like I am absolutely set on not having any fun at all. But at least I'm *here*.

Our little car creaks its way to the height of the drop, then grinds to a stop. I grip the bar harder, my palms slippery with sweat. I swear I can feel every rusty gear in this contraption, rattling through my bones.

I want to close my eyes, but I make myself look down and my stomach heaves. Okay, we are *really* high up. All the people at the carnival look like tiny ants, bustling through their tunnels on the ground below. The expanse of the ocean stretches out in front of us, endless blue. We're so *unprotected*. We're about to be flung into the sea. My sweaty hands slide against the bar, suddenly feeling desperately insecure.

And then I hear those rusty gears grinding together again as the coaster prepares to let us go.

"Henry," I gasp. "Hold my hand."

I shove my sweaty hand in his direction, and he grabs it just in time. Just as the coaster dumps us over the edge.

And then we're falling, falling, fucking *falling* . . .

A scream tears itself from my throat.

As we career toward the ground, the ocean, where are we even going, I don't know anymore, I am flooded with every single feeling I've been trying to hold back all week.

My frustration and rage at not being able to find my mother. My desperate hope to *belong* with someone, to be wanted, to finally get that piece that will make me whole. My giddiness when Henry looks at me in that certain way.

All of these things course through my blood, through my bones, through my entire being. That door to my heart feels like it's flying open, reckless and free.

We keep falling, and I scream and I scream and I scream. I can't seem to stop. All of this has to come out.

And as tears stream down my cheeks, a realization hits me square in the chest.

I *do* want that happy ending, goddammit.

I want to feel whole, complete. I want that dreamy moment that ends every Grace Kimura movie. I want it *so badly*, and as we plunge to our possible deaths in the sea, I can no longer deny that. Not even a little bit.

I want it with all I have, everything that's in my heart, all of these feelings that are flooding through me.

I throw my head back and scream again, and Henry squeezes my hand tight.

We finally hit the bottom of the drop, and the car shifts to a flatter track, towing us back to the start.

"Amazing," Henry says, pumping his fist as we exit the car. His other hand is still clasping mine—I can't seem to let go.

"Are you okay?" he says, as we make our way back to the boardwalk area. "Was that . . ." He stops and faces me, his expression concerned. "Was that all right?"

I meet his eyes. Take in a few deep breaths. Reach up and smooth his hair, hopelessly mussed from the coaster.

"It was more than all right," I say slowly. My voice is hoarse, my throat raw. I nearly screamed myself into oblivion. "It was so . . . exhilarating. Liberating." I give him a small smile. "I can't really explain *how* I feel about anything specific right now, but I do feel like I let some things out that needed to get out."

I raise our clasped hands between us.

"Thank you for holding my hand."

He smiles and brushes his lips against my knuckles.

"Come on," he says. "We've definitely earned some fried cheese."

✤

The Hot Dog on a Stick stand—which is apparently the *original* Hot Dog on a Stick stand; all mall kiosks are mere pale imitations—is a bit off the pier and the boardwalk, a cheery red-and-yellow hut plonked down right next to the beach.

It's so weird—I've lived in LA all my life and never been to the pier, or this stand. I always assumed it would be annoying and loud and touristy and that I'd hate every second. And maybe I would have, if I hadn't come here with Henry.

We get a cheese stick for him and a corndog for me (I can't quite bring myself to commit to his fried-cheese lifestyle) and a giant lemonade to share. Then we walk out into the sand, and he spreads his jacket on the ground for us to sit on.

"I'll give you this," Henry says, waving his cheese stick at the ocean. "New York does *not* have sunsets like this. This is incredible."

He takes a bite of his cheese, settles himself back on his elbows, and grins at the horizon. The sun isn't really fighting to stay today. It's more like she's trying to put on the most majestic show she can manage. Sinking toward the ground with her brilliance painting the sky glorious shades of pink and yellow and orange. Showing us her beauty in one all-consuming explosion of light.

I take a bite of my corndog, reveling in the greasy mix of slightly sweet bread and salty hot dog. And for a moment, we just watch, easy silence settling between us like the softest of blankets. I slip my shoes off and let my toes sink into the sand, still warm from baking all day.

There's a sense of calm at my center, after screaming all my feelings out on the roller coaster. Like the door to my heart is just sitting there now, open. And the nure-onna doesn't seem to mind at all.

My gaze slides to Henry.

"Hey," I murmur to him. "I was just thinking: What if I don't find Grace?"

He flips onto his side, his brows drawing together. "You will."

"But what if I don't?" I say. "I . . ." I play with my now hot-dog-less stick, twirling it through my fingers. That sense of calm surges through me again. "I think maybe it would be okay."

"What do you mean?" he asks.

I turn back to the brilliant sunset, taking it in. "I keep looking for her," I say slowly, "but I think I've been look-ing for something else this whole time. Something bigger.

And it was easy to put that all into one person, this mysterious figure who I actually know nothing about."

"Like she represented something?" Henry says.

"Yes. Because like I said before, I thought finding her would magically solve all my problems. I'd feel like I belonged somewhere, with someone. I wouldn't stick out so much, because everyone would know who I belonged with. I'd stop feeling like the only one with a bad temper, like a constant disruption, like . . ." My throat thickens, and I swallow. "Like a mistake," I manage. "But . . ." The beginnings of tears burn my eyes, and I swallow again. "I don't know. The past few days . . . Sensei Mary and Eliza welcoming me back with open arms. My sisters telling me all the ways they feel like they don't fit in either. Meeting Joanna and all the others at the Asian Hollywood thing . . ."

"Halfie Club," Henry murmurs, and I smile.

"Joanna especially . . . I don't know, there's something about seeing this person who looks so much like me, who understands me on this weirdly deep level, and who's leading this awesome full life and thriving . . . and doing all that because she's embracing who she is so fully . . ."

"Not trying to hide any piece of herself," Henry agrees.

"And . . ." My voice catches, and a tear slips down my cheek. But I have to keep going. "Being with you," I whisper. "I feel safe with you. But not like I have to, I don't know, be *less*. I can get angry. I can admit when I'm sad. I can feel all these things I'm usually afraid to let out, because I know you're *there*." The tears are flowing down my cheeks with wild abandon now. I don't even make an attempt to brush them away. "Maybe it's okay if I don't find Grace," I repeat. "Because there are already places where I belong. People I belong to. I couldn't see it before because I was so focused on . . . on protecting myself."

Henry sits up, reaches over, and takes my hand. "Are you saying you finally believe in your own happy ending?"

I laugh, surprised, my voice still thick with tears. "I don't know about *that*. But maybe I finally believe I deserve one."

Comfortable silence falls between us again as the sun continues to put on a show, the colors she's painted the sky turning wild and dusky. Henry strokes his thumb down my palm.

"I've never met anyone like you," he finally says. "I wish you could see the way I see . . . well, what you seem to think of as faults. I think all your passion—what you think is just rage—is beautiful. So is the way you love your family, the way you support them no matter what, even if they're driving you up the wall. You can never give anything less than everything. Even when you shove all those feelings down, you still live so *fully*. Whether you're defending Rory from the busybody Aunties at the mochi demonstration or going on a high-speed chase in the library or crashing into me on the streets of Little Tokyo. You do everything *fiercely*. And that's beautiful, too."

I look down at my sad little stick, which is becoming more twisted and wilty as I play with it. How does he see all these things I never have?

"You've made me see that I belong places, too," he continues. "That there are people who will let me be my whole self—all my Asian Hollywood friends, that community we've built. The folks making this new movie I'm gonna be in. And . . ." He pauses, looking out at the sunset. "I *am* going to talk to my parents about how I feel. About how I can't be their version of perfect all the time, and I love them, but I want them to see every piece of me." He turns to me and smiles, almost shyly. "I never would have even thought about doing that without you. And you're the one I can be my whole self with *the most*."

I swallow my tears—I can't quite look at him yet, but my heart suddenly feels too big for my body, impossible to contain.

"I believe in your happy ending," he says, and the certainty in his voice makes my heart skip several beats. "Because I believe in *you*."

I turn to him, tears streaming down my face. I love studying *all* of him. Those dark eyes that can sparkle with sly mischief or intense passion. That grin that I thought was too cute—because it *knew* it was too cute. Now I realize he was hiding under that facade, trying to project the image he needed to. But he's so perfectly imperfect, the real Henry can't help but shine through.

"Henry," I whisper.

I lean in and kiss him, the sun finally drifting off behind us.

His hands cup my face, always so urgent against my skin. He runs his fingers through my hair, and then his hands stroke lower, smoothing their way down my neck, my shoulders, my waist, leaving little sparks of electricity in their wake.

He presses against the small of my back, urging me closer, and I slide into his lap, straddling him at the waist. He feathers kisses over my cheeks, taking my tears away. Then he moves lower, his mouth brushing against my ear, my jaw, my neck. When he gets to *that* spot—that particularly sensitive patch right above my collarbone—heat flashes through me and I lean into it. I want more. I want everything. I want to feel his skin against mine.

I slip my hands under his T-shirt, stroking my fingertips over the delicious muscles of his back, wanting to be as close to him as possible—

"Rika." He breaks the kiss, his breathing ragged, his eyes wild. "Maybe we should . . ." He shakes his head, like he's trying to clear it. "Actually, I have no idea what we should do."

His hand has found its way under my shirt, and his fingertips are tracing the most irresistible patterns along my spine. He seems to be doing it unconsciously, which makes it even hotter.

I flush—but honestly it just feels like my *entire body* is flushed at this point.

"I . . . I want to," I say, pressing myself more firmly against him. His eyes nearly roll back into his head. "I want to, um, be naked with you."

A cool breeze whips through the air, bringing me back to reality. The sun has fully set now, it's dark out, and we're in a very compromising position. If someone took a photo of us right now, it would blow the McMuffin scandal out of the water.

"But it's a little sandy and a little *public* out here," I say. "So we should go be naked somewhere else."

"I . . ." He shakes his head again, like he still can't get a handle on what's happening. "I want that, too. But . . . are you sure? Have you, um, done this before?"

"No," I say hastily. "I haven't. Have you?"

"Yes," he says slowly. "A . . . a few times. But this should be . . ." He hesitates, stroking my hair off my face. "It should be special."

"It will be," I say. "I've never been more sure of anything in my entire life."

"W-we could go back to my apartment," Henry stutters. "I don't know if any of my roommates are there, but—"

"No." I cup his face in my hands and lean forward. "I can't wait that long. Let's go to the car."

I kiss him and his hands slide under my shirt again, and we are very close to making a very public spectacle of ourselves. But then he breaks the kiss, his breathing even more ragged than before.

"Okay," he manages. "I . . . I have, um, protection. In the car."

Somehow, we collect ourselves long enough to gather our things and haul them back to the darkened beach parking lot. Only a few cars are left, making it feel extra desolate.

I push him up against the car and kiss him again, my arms winding around his neck, *want* coursing through me like wildfire.

"Wait . . ." he gasps. "*In* the car. Not up against it."

He manages to get the back door open, and we tumble inside. I toss my Cinderella dress into the front seat, and then it's just . . . us. A tangle of limbs and lips and his hands sliding under my shirt again, tracing those sweet patterns along my spine.

"Rika . . ." he murmurs.

And then he says my name again and again and again. Peppering it between kisses, whispering it against my skin.

He makes it sound so precious—two syllables to be treasured, to be treated carefully. To be kept *safe*.

He just keeps saying it, and it brings tears to my eyes every time.

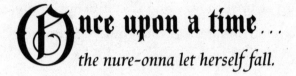

Once upon a time...

the nure-onna let herself fall.

EIGHTEEN

My eyes drift open to hazy light, scraps of sun filtering in through the window.

The *car* window.

I open my eyes more fully. I'm curled in the back seat, Henry wrapped around me, various jackets pulled over us in a makeshift blanket. He's still asleep, snoring softly against my neck. His arm is draped over my waist and his chest is pressed against my back and I feel warm all over. I revel for a moment in the rhythm of his breathing, the way his gentle exhales tickle the curve of my neck.

I can't get over last night. The way he looked at me. How there were parts that were kind of awkward, but *I* never felt awkward because he kept asking if I was okay. I trusted him, I let myself fall into the moment with him. He makes me feel like . . . not like my nure-onna or my temper are tamed or quieted. More like they've been given space to flourish and be powerful, and I don't have to repress anything. I can fully be myself with him. My *whole* self.

Like we belong to each other.

And then I guess we fell asleep. I don't exactly remember falling asleep. I can only recall him pulling me close afterward, brushing light kisses against my cheekbones. Still murmuring my name. Everything blurring into hazy, dreamlike sweetness where the only thing that mattered was him touching me. I felt so peaceful, cradled against him. I felt . . . safe.

I wonder if this is what Joanna meant about letting yourself *feel* things, making space for those feelings instead of trying to deny them. Because right now I feel something I've never felt before—a glow in my chest, a brilliant burst of vibrant color, just like last night's sunset.

And I want to relive every moment, every sensation from last night. His lips, soft against my bare skin. His hands, tangling in my hair. And the way he said my name . . .

I close my eyes, let bliss overtake me . . .

And then remember it's now morning and we've apparently fallen asleep in the back seat of his car and . . . crap.

Trying to move slowly so as not to disturb Henry, I fumble around for my phone, still contained in the pocket of my shorts—which are part of a jumble of clothes on the car floor. The screen is lit up like the Fourth of July, a cavalcade of messages from every single person I know. The Aunties, Belle, Rory. All wanting to know where I am. I am definitely going to be in big trouble when I get home. But there are also messages from other people: Eliza, Sensei Mary, even Joanna. I frown, scrolling through, trying to make sense of the mess of words and furious exclamation points.

Respond!!! one of Eliza's messages reads. **And please tell me when you've seen this.**

"This" is a link that nearly everyone seems to have flung my way. So I click on it. It leads to some kind of celebrity gossip website trumpeting about an all-caps EXCLUSIVE.

GRACE KIMURA SECRET LOVE CHILD SCANDAL!!!

My heart plummets, and it feels like all the blood drains from my body.

With shaking fingers, I scroll down. I can't process any of the words, can barely wrap my brain around what the article's saying . . . except I already know exactly what it's saying.

I shake my head, like that will somehow make all of this go away.

I scroll back up and force myself to sound out every word. The person who wrote this is practically foaming at the mouth, playing up every minute detail for maximum juiciness. But the facts are clear.

1. Years ago, Grace Kimura, Hollywood's squeaky-clean rom-com queen and perfect princess, had an illicit baby when she was only a teenager.

2. Said illicit baby—the SECRET LOVE CHILD—is none other than Rika Rakuyama, who has been identified as the girl Grace plowed into at the Nikkei Week parade.

3. This "Rika" "Rakuyama" (if that is, in fact, her real name) is the *same person* who was spotted with heart-throb Hank Chen at the library a few days ago. What is Hank Chen's connection to this scandal?!

I scroll further to see the reporter's key pieces of "evidence": photographs of teenage Grace holding baby me and the photos of young Grace and Auntie Suzy.

The photos I thought I'd lost. The photos I apparently did lose, only to see them turn up . . . here.

My body goes numb. My mind turns blank.

What do I do?

What do I even . . .

Adrenaline kicks in, forcing me to pull myself into a sitting position and scrabble around on the floor for my clothes. I can't think, and my breath is coming and going in short little gasps.

I have to . . . I have to . . . *I can't . . .*

How could I be so foolish? Why did I ever think this would end any other way for me? How did I *ever* believe anything resembling a happy ending was possible?

All these years, I've been trying to make myself small, to hide, to not stick out the way I naturally do . . . and now that's all been blown apart by a single breathless headline.

This could destroy my family; the brunt of the scandal will land squarely on them. Anyone who's ever been looking for a reason to toss all of us out of the community has it now, plastered in big block letters across the internet.

So many things are about to be destroyed, all because of me. All that hard work Auntie Suzy and Auntie Och have put into the restaurant for so many years, all the passion Belle's put into being crowned Nikkei Week queen, the one thing she's wanted forever . . . and Henry . . . Henry just landed the most important role of his career, may be about to get everything he wants and deserves . . . and that could be destroyed by this scandal, too.

I'm not a princess, about to float on dreamy clouds to her happy ending. I don't know how I tricked myself into thinking I was anything other than a SECRET LOVE CHILD.

"Mmm?" Henry stirs behind me. His arm is still kind of draped over my waist, even though I'm sitting up, trying to pull my shirt over my head. "Rika?" he murmurs, utterly confused. "What are you doing?"

I shake my head, unable to string two words together. I

don't know where to even begin, so I hand him my phone and continue scrambling to get my shirt onto my body.

"What is this?" Henry says, sounding more awake now. He sits up, and I scootch a little to the left so we're sitting side by side in the back seat.

"What does it look like?" I manage, my voice cracking on the last word. "I have to go."

I finally manage to get my shirt on and shimmy into my shorts. Then I throw open the door, preparing to eject myself.

"Wait!" Henry cries, swiveling toward me. "What are you doing?!"

"I just said I had to go," I snap. "So I'm going."

"Not like this," he fires back, shaking his head vehemently. "Try to calm down, *breathe*—"

"I don't *want* to calm down," I say, a sob cutting through my words. I don't even feel any tears, just this rising panic in my chest. Like I'm about to explode.

"I know, I get it—" he begins.

"No, you don't!"

"Okay, maybe I don't understand *exactly*," he says, holding up his hands. Somehow, his tone is perfectly even. *How* can it be even? How can *he* be so calm? "But let's talk about this. Let me take you home and—"

"*No.*" It comes out in a roar, my temper bursting to

the surface. The fire, the *rage*, is consuming my entire body, and I can't stop it. It burns through me, obliterating all that's in its path. If I don't catapult myself away from him, it will destroy everything. "Just . . . stop," I say, my voice ragged. "Stop being so calm and stop trying to get *me* to be calm—"

"I'm just trying to—"

"Didn't you hear me? *Stop trying.*" I snatch my phone away from him. "Do you not get how serious this is?"

"Of course I do," he says, his brows drawing together. "But—"

"Because it's also serious for *you*," I barrel on. "You just landed this incredible part that you wanted so badly, you're on the verge of finally being taken seriously, and now you're associated with this big, gossipy, trashy scandal. You're associated with *me*. The secret love child."

I grab my shoes and my giant Cinderella dress. I don't even know where I'm going. I just know I have to get *out*.

"*Rika.*"

I heave myself out of the car, not listening. He follows me, somehow managing to haphazardly yank on his jeans. Then he tries to grab my hand, but I pull away.

"Will you please just . . . stop for a minute," he says, his voice tight with frustration. "Listen to me, we're in this together—"

"We're *not* together," I snarl, crumpling all that tulle against my chest. It scratches my skin, aggravating me even further. My kaiju-temper is *roaring* now, smashing anything that gets in its way with giant fists. "I don't know why you would even want that. This could ruin your career. It could ruin *everything*—"

"*I don't care!*" he bellows.

My mouth snaps shut. I don't think I've ever heard Henry Chen yell before.

"I don't care about that," he says, taking a step toward me. "How could I care about that more than I care about you?"

"Because you *should*," I spit out.

He shakes his head, his face overtaken with disbelief. "Why do you make it so hard for people to love you?"

I clutch my dress tightly, the tulle scratching even more aggressively against my arms. "What?" It comes out as the most pathetic of whispers.

He takes another step toward me. I can't seem to stop trembling, even though the summer sun is already on full blast. I want to cry. I want to scream. I want to run. Somehow I can't do any of those things.

He meets my gaze, so earnest and open. Just like he always is.

"I love you," he says, his voice strong and sure in a way that touches something deep inside of me. "And I won't let you throw yourself away again."

Those tears I thought I wanted prick my eyes. My head is empty again, everything is just blank. I ache to close the space between us, melt against him. How can this person—the kindest, warmest, most infuriating person I've ever met—love *me*?

He can't. He shouldn't. He doesn't. He's saying that because we spent the night together and he's just so noble, so *good* . . .

And that means I have to shove him away as hard as I can.

The door to my heart slams shut.

"You don't get a say in that," I say, sounding as steady as I can even though I want to fall apart. "I know you're probably used to girls pledging their undying devotion to you after sex, but that's not me. I just want you to leave me alone."

I turn and stomp away, still clutching my dress to my chest, tears streaming down my face.

"Rika . . ." he calls after me, his voice breaking.

I don't turn around. I don't want to see everything I've destroyed.

❀

I walk until I can catch a bus, dragging my giant princess dress behind me. I don't know why I still have it or why I even took it with me in the first place. I imagine how I must look, a sad girl hauling a mass of sparkly tulle down the streets of LA.

It takes three buses and the whole morning to get back to Little Tokyo. When I finally get there, I start to instinctively walk home.

But then I see the huge mob assembled outside Katsu That. There are paparazzi, cameras at the ready. Clusters of girls craning their necks to try to see inside. I swear I see the denizens of the Becky table in there. A buzz of excitement floats through the air, surrounding the restaurant like an overeager swarm of bees. For the first time ever, the windows are dark. The place is closed.

After struggling and sacrificing and fighting like hell for so many years, Auntie Suzy and Auntie Och actually had to close their beloved restaurant for the day. All because of me.

Before all this, I was a scandalous mistake who could disappear into the shadows. Now I'm a scandalous mistake who's going to ruin her family.

My Aunties, who worked so hard for their place in

this community. Belle, who yearns for her own happy ending. Rory, who is destined to do something brilliant one day.

I will never belong here. It would be better if I left, if they didn't have to deal with me anymore.

I don't know exactly where I'm going, so I start wandering in the opposite direction of the restaurant. In the back of my mind, I'm all too aware that this giant-ass dress makes me super conspicuous and I probably need a place to hide while I plan my next move.

I need a good shadow to sink into.

My legs take me to the place they were meant to go all along: the JACCC garden and the onryo tree. A place where I feel hidden and safe—and where my mother apparently did, too, all those years ago.

Luckily, the building and the garden are deserted today. I guess everyone's too busy trying to ferret out the Secret Love Child.

I crawl under the tree, trying to let its long, drooping branches soothe me. For some reason, I wrap my Cinderella dress around me, like some kind of shield. I sit there for a long while and make myself very, very still—completely hidden from view. And I wait. For what, I'm not sure. I just know that I can hide here. I watch the patterns of the sun change as light filters through the tree, casting shards of brightness on my dark little nook. I don't know how much time passes. Seconds. Minutes. Hours.

Before I know it, my body starts to feel heavy, all the adrenaline from the day leeching into the soft grass beneath me. Then my eyes are fluttering closed and I'm asleep, my beautiful ball gown spreading over me like a blanket made of fairy dust.

❀

It's dusk when I wake up. The light has stopped filtering in through the tree, and the sky is beginning to darken. My head feels muzzy, like it's stuffed with cotton. I rub my eyes and note that my cheek probably has some very interesting patterns dented into it after being pressed to the grass for so long.

I pull my phone out and check the screen. Endless messages. A long scroll of notifications. I dismiss them all.

I decide to check social media, just to get a read on what's happening. Unsurprisingly, the story has blown up there, too, speculation flying about the SECRET LOVE CHILD. Uncle Taki and Craig Shimizu have already posted long, rambling comments on the Nikkei Week website about how Grace Kimura's entire family should be banned from the festivities for this disgraceful scandal.

That ban should start NOW, Craig's comment reads. **Belle Rakuyama and her family do not embody our values or the Japanese American pride that our sacred festival is supposed to celebrate. She should be decrowned immediately and should not be allowed to claim the title in any way whatsoever. Rest assured that my father and the rest of the board are taking this matter very seriously.**

We cannot allow our traditions to be tarnished, Uncle Taki's comment insists. **The Rakuyamas should not simply be banned from this year's Nikkei Week. They should be banned FOR LIFE.**

And there's more. Of course there are plenty of comments about *me*, how I've always been a disruptive force, a sour mark on the community. I don't care about that. It is, after all, nothing new.

But there's also stuff about how Belle doesn't fit the image Nikkei Week is trying to project, does not seem like the classic Japanese American princess for *reasons*. A snarky comment about Rory's failure to make perfect mochi at the demonstration and how she always "dresses like a weirdo." A very pointed screed about my Aunties' restaurant, how it should be boycotted, how they also do not fit with Little Tokyo's traditions or image.

That last one sends me over the edge and I feel my blood heat to the boiling point, a red haze descending over my vision.

How fucking dare they say *any of that* about my family?

There's no one in Little Tokyo more queenly than Belle—and no one who works harder to be that fabulous. There's no one more brilliant than Rory, an actual genius in so many ways. And my Aunties . . . angry tears prick my eyes, my kaiju-temper snarling like mad. They've worked *so hard*. Just to be accepted by a community that should have embraced them from the beginning.

The rage burns through my body, and my hands shake with fury.

I put down the phone, my nure-onna brain crafting a cunning plan. The Nikkei Week gala is tonight. And despite all my protests to the contrary, I'm going to go.

I'm going to use all this rage to proclaim myself publicly disowned from the Rakuyama family. I will tell all of Little Tokyo that they should never be tainted by me again.

I will throw myself away in *the most public way possible*.

Then maybe my family can get the happily ever afters they deserve.

I'm not dressed for a gala . . . and I guess this is why I insisted on hauling this ridiculous princess dress with me.

I scoop it up and get to my feet, marching toward the JACCC bathroom. I change quickly, wrapping myself in all that tulle, all those sparkles.

It fits perfectly.

I bunch my other clothes into a tight ball, cram it under my arm, and turn to the mirror next to the bathroom's entrance.

The girl looking back at me is not a girl I've seen before. She's in that big princess dress, those sparkles swirling over her body like pixie dust. The tulle looks like fluffy clouds sewn into place. The full skirt shimmers under the dim bathroom light, its magic refusing to be muted. The skirt is a little torn at the bottom and spotted with patches of dirt and grass stains, but there's no denying it: this is a girl in a princess dress.

But she's an *angry* girl in a princess dress. Her hair is tangled and festooned with leaves and other bits of garden greenery. Her eyes are wild, flashing with rage, and she looks like she's ready to breathe fire on whoever wronged her.

She looks like a princess. She looks like the nure-onna. She looks like a bunch of things that should not go together, but somehow do.

And for perhaps the first time ever, I feel something settle in my chest. A click into a place. An acknowledgment of the power I see, staring back at that girl.

Because that girl makes sense to me. She feels *whole*.

I'm not just living in my own skin, I'm celebrating it.

Celebrating it with *rage*, that is.

I remember what Joanna said about anger pushing you forward. Giving you *power*.

I feel that power right now, bright and alive and thrumming through my veins. No one is going to mess with the Rakuyamas—I'll make sure of it.

I stomp out of the bathroom, clothes clutched under my arm—I'm still wearing my gold Adidas, since Grace's dress didn't come with any glass slippers. I march through the garden and back to Little Tokyo's main drag. The gala always takes place in the courtyard of the Japanese American National Museum, which is at the end of the street. In the distance, I see twinkle lights and colorful lanterns strung through the trees, beckoning me.

It doesn't look like anyone's there yet, which is odd. Dusk is about to give way to night, and people should be starting to gather. At the very least, Belle's court should be assembling for photo ops.

Unless she's been decrowned already.

That sets my blood boiling all over again, and my

marching gets more forceful. My shoulders bunch up, my posture goes ramrod straight. That haze of red swims over my vision again, and I'm just . . . so . . . *angry* . . .

"Rika . . . Rika-chan!"

A voice punctures my angry bubble. At first I think it's some kind of auditory hallucination, me hearing things because my brain is burning up with so much rage, concocting things out of thin air.

But then it's joined by other voices. All yelling my name. They sound so far away . . .

I stop in my tracks and whip around, my princess dress swirling dramatically. I see Belle running toward me, her face a mask of distress. I notice that she's not all gussied up in her queen attire; she's wearing her pink sweatsuit, and her hair is stuffed into a messy topknot. Her eyes are red and puffy.

And then I look just beyond her—and I see that she's not alone.

Rory's trying to catch up to Belle, her tiny legs not quite getting the job done. Auntie Suzy and Auntie Och hustle alongside her. Sensei Mary's there. Eliza. Uncle Hikaru. And, like . . . a good portion of Little Tokyo.

It's another parade, just like the one that kicked off Nikkei Week. Only way more haphazard and distressed-looking, all the joy and festive facade stripped away.

I shake my head, trying to make sense of it. I'm so confused . . .

Belle reaches me first and sweeps me into a suffocating bear hug.

"Rika! Chan!" she exclaims, sounding like she's about to either cry or yell at me. She buries her face against my shoulder and squeezes me so hard, all breath leaves my body.

I still don't know exactly what's happening—my brain cannot seem to process it. But suddenly everyone else is piling on top of Belle, surrounding me in a very weird group embrace.

"We've been looking for you *all day*!" Rory cries, her voice plaintive.

"Where were you?" Auntie Suzy demands. "Why aren't you answering your phone?!"

"Or answering, like, anything!" Eliza adds.

"Worried sick!" Auntie Och proclaims. "All of us! You cannot just disappear like that, Rika-chan, I know from watching news that the detectives only care when white girls are missing!"

"Wait, wait, *wait*," I manage to yelp.

I carefully disentangle myself from the crush of people and face them, trying to figure out how to put my words together. So many feelings are crashing through me all at once.

"I don't understand," I say. "None of you are mad?"

"What?!" Belle says, looking at me like I've grown another head. "Why would anyone be mad?"

"B-because," I splutter. "The scandal, the Secret Love Child! All the stuff that's been simmering underneath the surface for all these years, the scandal centered around *me*, has finally blown all the way up. I . . ." Tears fill my eyes again, and my voice shakes. I don't want to cry, but I'm just so overwhelmed. I can't seem to control anything my body's doing, not even a little bit. "I've never belonged here," I manage, my voice breaking. "I've never belonged to *anyone*. Not really. I've always been a mistake, and this just proves it. That *is* what I am. What I'll always be. I can't deny it, no matter how much it hurts. I can't deny *the truth* . . ." My tears spill over and turn into sobs, and now I can't talk anymore.

In a way, it's a relief to say all of that. Finally.

"Rika-chan." Auntie Och's formidable eyebrows draw together, her piercing black eyes taking me in. "What you saying? That sounds like some kind of garbage. You are family. *Of course* you belong to us."

"Hai, yes," Uncle Hikaru says, crossing his arms over

his chest. "And all of Little Tokyo is family in some way. We take care of each other."

That only makes me cry harder. Auntie Suzy steps forward—and for the first time ever, she doesn't look tired. She looks like something has awoken inside of her, just enough for her heart to break.

"Oh, Rika—my Rika-chan." She pulls me against her, wrapping me in the tightest hug she's ever given me. "I'm so sorry. This is my fault. I never . . ." She strokes my hair, and I can hear the tears in her voice. She keeps doing that until my sobs quiet, my tears start to dry. Then she pulls back and puts her hands on my shoulders, her eyes glinting with something I've never seen before. A certain kind of resolve. I am struck with an eerie feeling, like I've gone back in time and am seeing the Auntie Suzy I've heard so much about—the one who stood up to her father all those years ago and married Auntie Och. "It's time to tell you the truth," she says. "All of it."

NINETEEN

We all pile into Katsu That—yes, the whole crowd. As people situate themselves in booths and at tables, I spot a familiar face I didn't notice before.

"Joanna?" I say, surprised. "What are you doing here?"

"I told you, I'm your fairy godmother," she says with a wink. "I saw the gossip this morning, obviously, and tried texting you. But you didn't answer, so I came down here to see if I could find you. And then happened upon all these *other* people trying to find you." She smiles. "So many people care about you, Sweet Rika."

I don't quite know what to do with that, so I smile back and then cram myself into a booth next to Belle and Rory, my nure-onna T-shirt clutched in my fists.

"Well," Auntie Suzy says, surveying the assembled crowd. "I was picturing this as a more, mmm, intimate discussion where I only shared this story with Rika—"

"It's all right," I manage to say. "You can tell it in front of everyone."

I'm not sure why, but it feels like the whole community needs to hear this story, some of their shared secrets finally emerging from the shadows.

"All right, then," Auntie Suzy says. She draws herself up tall, that defiant glint returning to her eyes. "I guess it's time we *all* talked about this properly."

She trains her gaze on me, so many emotions passing over her face. "Rika-chan. I know you hate a lot of fairy tales. But maybe you'll like this one — because the ending is so bittersweet."

She stays standing and turns to gaze out the window, a faraway look overtaking her expression.

"Once upon a time, my sister, Grace Kimura . . . no. Grace *Rakuyama*." She smiles slightly to herself. "She and I were as close as two people can be. Our father was strict and often cruel. Our mother was scared of him and rarely said anything — she faded into the background so much, eventually she faded away to nothing. She died of some kind of heart condition — my father would never tell us exactly what — when I was ten and Grace was only three."

My heart is beating so fast and so loudly, I'm convinced everyone in the restaurant can hear it. A hush has fallen over the crowd as Auntie Suzy tells her tale, her voice clear and strong.

"I remember loving Grace from the moment she was born—I thought that's what everyone meant when they talked about love at first sight. This sudden full-body pull toward another person. The first time I got to hold her, she looked up at me with the biggest smile, like she somehow knew to trust me completely—and I was gone. When our mother passed, my first urge was to take care of her. To protect her with everything I had."

Auntie Suzy pauses, her eyes going a little glassy. She's still looking out the window. Like she can't quite look at *me*.

"We were so tightly bonded together—as we got older, sometimes I didn't know where I ended and she began. Did we both love this certain kind of curry because one of us had first? Or had we developed a taste for it simultaneously, being so in sync? My father never wanted to have girls. He had very little use for us— except when we were fulfilling some kind of outdated notion of what femininity should be. I don't think Grace ever truly thought that he loved her. So I made sure she *knew* she was loved by someone. Every day. I was determined that she would never lose that big smile she'd given me when she was a baby."

My eyes have already filled with tears. I feel like I know where this is going, where it will end up. I want to cry for Auntie Suzy, who has been taking care of other people so selflessly since she was just a child herself. And for my mother, who began a hard life with such joy.

It doesn't feel like I can cry yet, though. So I hold my breath and fight back the tears, waiting for Auntie Suzy to continue.

"Even when our father disapproved of the things we did, we always had each other. When I became Nikkei Week Queen and fell in love with Och, Grace helped me. Covered for me when we went on dates, things like that. She was convinced that one day our father would approve and we'd all live happily ever after, as a family." Auntie Suzy's jaw tightens, her smile twisting. "I knew that would *never* happen. And when Grace started acting, started having these fanciful dreams of pursuing it as a career . . . well, I knew our father wouldn't like that, either. But I helped her however I could. At that point, Och and I had gotten married and opened our restaurant, so I would give her money for school play costumes and acting classes, things like that. And I always sent her flowers on opening night."

I picture my mother, only fifteen, her eyes lighting up as she's handed a dreamy bouquet of pink flowers. Somehow I just know they were pink.

"And then . . ." Auntie Suzy's gaze darkens. "She got pregnant. Some boy who was in the play with her—and

I'm so sorry, Rika-chan, but I don't know who he was. Rumor has it that he and his family moved away right after, wanting a fresh start. But there was no fresh start for Grace." Auntie Suzy takes a deep breath, and I feel like I can practically see inside her brain—all the memories she's tried to forget for so many years.

"I told her not to tell our father," Auntie Suzy continues. "I knew that would only end badly. But one of the things about Grace . . . she was always so convinced of people's inherent goodness. She thought that if he loved her, he'd come around. But of course, he didn't. Instead of giving her a safe place to land, he threatened to disown us both. He couldn't believe he'd raised . . ." Her voice catches, but she shakes it off, soldiering on. "Two *degenerates*," she spits out. "I wanted to stand up to him, to tell him I was sick of how he'd made both of us feel worthless. To disown *him*. But Grace . . ." She shakes her head. "She knew that would be catastrophic for me and Och and our little fledgling restaurant. Our father was a powerful elder figure in the Little Tokyo community, and he could very likely get other elders to boycott the restaurant—which would only spread until we had no business at all. He could have gotten all of Little Tokyo to turn their backs on us—something he'd certainly threatened to do before."

I feel a small hand take mine, forcing me to let go of

my shirt. I look over to see Rory, her eyes as big as dinner plates. She's so invested in where this is going. Belle is sitting on her other side, so she's kind of sandwiched in between us. I see Belle take Rory's other hand and look up to catch her eye. We share a small, impulsive smile. I can't help but feel like we're cradling Rory, holding her close to us—like Auntie Suzy tried to do with Grace.

"Grace told me she'd give the baby up for adoption," Auntie Suzy continues. "But I could tell that would break her heart—shatter her beyond fixing." She turns away from the window and meets my gaze, and there is something so tender lighting her eyes. Something I've never really seen before from her. "She *always* wanted you, Rika-chan. That was never in doubt."

Something twists in my chest, and I can only nod quickly, my eyes going to the floor.

"So we came up with a plan. Och and I would take the baby in. Grace would disappear. We'd say she died in childbirth. And as outlandish as this sounds, it actually wasn't that hard to do. At that point, everyone knew she was pregnant, and everyone was talking. But no one showed up to support. As much as we go on around here about family being so important, I guess a pregnant fifteen-year-old was just too much for people to handle."

A few of the older people in the room hang their

heads, shamed. And rightfully so, I think.

"Many people shunned her, just pretended she didn't exist. I had gotten her set up at a hospital that wasn't anywhere near Little Tokyo—the same hospital where I had Belle, just months before. My father never came with us. So when I returned from the hospital with a baby and a story about how my little sister had died . . . well. I think he was *relieved*, to be honest." Auntie Suzy's eyes flash with anger. This particular rage has never left her— it's just been buried very deeply for the past seventeen years. "Grace and I decided that she would set herself up with a new last name and a different life and hide out until either the taint of scandal faded or our father passed away. She lied about her age and got odd jobs waitress- ing and cleaning houses, and of course I sent her money whenever I could. Strangely, because I had taken in the baby"—she frowns, turning back to the window—"my father decided he could tolerate my other . . . 'transgres- sions.' I guess it was just *such* a good Japanese-daughter thing to do. Perhaps the *only* time in my life I was ever a good Japanese daughter, in his estimation."

Her face twists into a bitter smile.

"Our father did pass away eventually, but the scandal never quite died down. And Grace, after several years of working herself to the bone and going on whatever auditions she could . . . well, she finally landed her first big role. The one that would make her a star."

"An Asian Hollywood princess," Belle murmurs.

"Over the years, she kept asking when she could come back," Auntie Suzy says. "When she could finally be a mother to you. I always said the time wasn't right."

Auntie Suzy pauses again, taking deep breaths. Then she forces herself to turn and meet my eyes.

"This is where I went wrong, Rika-chan, but you must understand that it didn't seem that way at the time. The years stretched on and . . . it was *never* the right time. I'd finally made a place in the community for myself—for our family. Our restaurant was thriving. I felt like I belonged, at last. And you seemed to be doing so well—you had judo and your sisters, and you were so"—she smiles a little—"so *fierce*. Your spirit was one of the boldest I'd ever seen. I didn't want to disrupt any of that—I couldn't bring myself to rock the boat. We'd fought so hard . . ." She trails off, bowing her head. "And there were other complications as well. The backstory Grace's Hollywood people invented for her was completely made up, no mention of Little Tokyo or her secret child. She kept talking about how this would have to be done a certain way—there would be some kind of big-deal publicity photo shoot, revealing you. You would suddenly be in the public eye, exposed. Everything about you would be scrutinized, picked apart. You were still so little, I couldn't imagine . . ." She shakes her head, her eyes shiny with unshed tears. "I could not see how that would be good for you. Grace and I finally had a huge fight when you were five. Twelve years ago. And I told her that she could keep the money she had started to send back, we didn't need it. We haven't spoken since."

Auntie Suzy pauses for so long, I think maybe that's the end of the story—appropriately bittersweet. But then her mouth curves into the most wistful of smiles.

"But I could never resist watching her movies. I felt like I was finally seeing her get the happy ending she'd always deserved. And that I was still connected to the person I'd once been closer to than anyone in the world."

I think of how Auntie Suzy always looks at the end of a Grace Kimura movie—tears in her eyes, that same wistful smile lighting her face. I always thought she was crying because of the cheesy romantic beauty of it all— but she was crying for so much more.

Auntie Suzy meets my eyes again. "I'm so sorry, Rika-chan. I don't think I can ever make up for what I've cost you. You must know that I always did what I thought was best for you. You were your mother's complete opposite when you came out—red-faced, screaming, always so angry. But I knew you were going to fight hard for everything, just like she did. And I loved you as immediately and fiercely as I loved her."

Auntie Suzy's eyes fill with tears again, and she gives me a wavery smile.

"I'm sorry," she whispers.

Silence falls over the crowd, enveloping us like a blanket. I just stare at Auntie Suzy. I barely remember anyone else is in the room.

I don't know what to do next, so I let pure instinct guide me. I give Rory's hand a squeeze and pass her my nure-onna shirt, then slip out of the booth, gathering my big skirts around me. I slowly cross the room to Auntie Suzy, my eyes never leaving hers. I stand in front of her for a long moment, still not sure exactly what I'm doing. She draws herself up a little taller, like she's bracing herself. Waiting for a fight. Because she knows I'm *always* ready for a fight.

I *should* be angry with her. After hearing that story, my kaiju-temper should be raging to get out. But all I see when I look at her is the girl she used to be, the girl who fought like hell for *everything*. Who fought like hell for *me*. And yes, who's made a bunch of mistakes along the way, but mistakes always tend to happen when you're fighting so damn hard. I know that better than anyone.

I thought I was waiting for someone to want me. But all this time, someone *did*.

I take another step forward, closing the distance between us.

And then I collapse against her, throwing my arms around her waist and burying my face in her shoulder. I let out a long, shuddering sob—something that feels like it's been bottled up inside me for the past seventeen years.

"I love you so much," I whisper.

"Oh, Rika," she says, stroking my hair. "Rika-chan."

"Wait, I have a question!" a little voice yells, puncturing the moment.

Auntie Suzy and I look up from our embrace to see Rory jumping to her feet, planting her hands on her hips in indignation.

"Why didn't anyone in Little Tokyo recognize Grace when she became a big star?" She narrows her eyes at some of the older people in the room. "I mean, none of you thought it was odd that this supposedly dead outcast girl was suddenly on all your movie screens?"

"Years had passed by then," Auntie Suzy says. "She looked just different enough that people could pretend like they'd forgotten about tragic little Grace Rakuyama."

"Hmph," Auntie Och snorts, getting to her feet. "It

was also *shame*." She glares at everyone else. "This community was ashamed of that lost girl who got pregnant, ne? They treat her like garbage, then she die. When she shows up again in the movies . . ." Auntie Och shrugs. "Easier to act like they never see her before. Easier to pretend she's a whole new person." Her glare intensifies, and some people in the room can't help but shrink away from it. "We have too many secrets. Too much shame in our secrets."

"Sounds like the Asian way," I mutter under my breath. I'm surprised to hear Auntie Suzy snort at that, like she's on the verge of a laugh.

"What is going on here?"

We all swivel toward the piercing voice that's broken into our sanctum, a dissonant disruption to all the crying.

And there, standing in the doorway of Katsu That, is the last person I expected to see.

Craig Shimizu. Glowering at the assembled crowd.

And then his gaze lands on me, and that glower turns to pure hate.

TWENTY

"What are you doing here?" Craig demands of me. "Haven't you caused enough trouble?"

My temper stirs—I swear I can feel my nure-onna waking up, lifting her head.

But before it can fully ignite, Auntie Suzy steps in front of me.

"She hasn't done anything," she says—and her voice has so much steel in it, I do a double take. I have never heard Auntie Suzy—permanently exhausted, absent-minded, "don't rock the boat" Auntie Suzy—address someone with so much fire. "And if you want to talk about 'trouble,' Craig Shimizu, I would suggest you take a good, hard look at your own actions and delete all the bullshit you've been spewing online about my family."

The room falls completely silent—save for Rory murmuring "Daaaaaamn" under her breath.

I'm with her, but I'm way too shocked to say anything. Auntie Suzy's hands are planted on her hips, her spine is ramrod straight, and her eyes flash with some-thing I've never quite seen before. It's like she's regaining all her witchy powers right before my eyes.

Surprise crosses Craig's face, then he quickly coaxes his expression back into its usual smirk.

"Everything I posted is true—and for the sake of our community, I'm just so relieved all your family's disgust-ing scandals are finally exposed. That none of you will be part of Nikkei Week and our great traditions now." He sneers at me. "I *knew* you'd disgrace us all at some point—didn't realize you'd be so stupid about it, though, toting the proof around in your pocket, where it could just"—his eyes drift to the floor of Katsu That—"fall out. Right where anyone could see it."

"You . . . you took my pictures," I murmur, the puzzle pieces snapping together. "They must have fallen out of my pocket that day when Henry was here and . . ." I shake my head. "You gave them to some gossip site?"

He shrugs, his smile widening. Clearly enjoying him-self. "Just doing my part to take out the trash."

A piercing cry rings out through the restaurant—and before I know what's happening, a tiny figure zips through the crowd and launches herself directly at Craig Shimizu.

"No, Rory!" I shriek, throwing my arms around her and pulling her back before she makes contact.

"Don't!" she screams, thrashing in my embrace. "I'm going to *kill him*!"

"No, you're not," I say, shoving her squirming form toward Auntie Och, who gathers her up.

I turn back to Craig and step forward, as if shielding my family, still clad in my ridiculous princess dress.

"Your problem is with me," I say, rage sparking in my chest. But I don't try to suppress it this time. I let myself *feel* it. "Don't take it out on them."

"It's not just you," he says, taking a step toward me, so we're practically nose to nose. I refuse to step back, to give an inch. "It's your whole fucked-up family. You just happen to be the *most* fucked-up. And no matter how badly you want it"—he smirks again—"you will *never* belong here."

My kaiju-temper *roars*, and I'm about to fully let him have it . . . when I feel Auntie Suzy's hand, squeezing mine.

"Your *hate* doesn't belong here," she says to Craig, that steel in her voice again. "*That's* what hurts our community more than anything."

"You need to watch your tone," Craig warns—and now his eyes flash with something beyond his usual smirk. Something cold and mean. "My father can make sure all of you are banned for life—"

"No, he can't." Belle appears on my other side, drawing

herself up tall—like the queen she is. "One person doesn't have that kind of power—we are a community, are we not?" She casts an imperious look around the room.

"Hai—yes!" Auntie Och says, her arms still wrapped around Rory, who has stopped squirming and is now leveling Craig with a death-glare. "And communities need to change and grow along with the people in them. Your father need to learn that, too."

"That's right," Sensei Mary says, getting to her feet. "And he might want to remember that head of the Nikkei Week board is an elected position." She gives him a wry smile. "Which means we can *elect* someone else next year."

"Hear, hear!" Uncle Hikaru says, nodding emphatically. "What about Suzy? She cares more about Little Tokyo than anyone!"

"Mmm, it's about time we had a woman in charge anyway," an Auntie chimes in—and I recognize her as one of the gossiping Aunties from the mochi demonstration. "The Shimizus always want Nikkei Week to stay *exactly* the same—"

"Because of *tradition*," Craig spits out. "W-we can't corrupt that. And besides, my father has always been elected head of Nikkei Week—"

"Not *always*," Eliza says, rolling her eyes. "Nikkei

Week existed long before your father did. And we can preserve tradition while still updating it, right?"

"That's part of community, too," Sensei Mary agrees.

"I'll be more than happy to accept your votes," Auntie Suzy says, her eyes flashing.

"You can go tell your father we'll *all* be at the gala tonight," Belle says defiantly. "And if he wants to kick up a fuss . . ."

"There's nothing he can really do about it," Uncle Hikaru says.

"Unless he wants to ban *all* of us," Rory says, gesturing around the room.

"And it really won't be much of a gala with no one there, will it?" the mochi-demo Auntie says with a perfectly judgmental eyebrow raise.

Craig sputters, unable to get a single word out, his face turning bright red. I keep waiting for someone in the room to break ranks, to denounce me or all the Rakuyamas . . . but no one does. Everyone stands behind me, staring Craig down.

He sputters for a few moments more, his gaze finally landing on me.

"This is all your fault," he hisses, his eyes filled with ice-cold hate. "Fucking half-breed mistake."

My kaiju-temper sparks, sending fresh waves of rage coursing through my bloodstream. I imagine myself as the nure-onna, flames rising around me, my anger sure and true.

"No, it's not," I snarl. I step forward and feel a vicious twist of satisfaction when he steps back, panic crossing his face. "And I am not a mistake—that is so . . . *fucked-up* to even say that. A *person* can't be a mistake."

The truth of that hits me right as the words come out of my mouth. The image I saw in the JACCC mirror—that monster princess who felt so *whole*—swims through my consciousness. I am *real*. I am who I'm meant to be.

"And if you ever spew your disgusting hate at me or anyone in this family—this *community*—ever again, I won't hold back," I declare.

"What, you'll bite me again?" he says—but his words don't have the same heat behind them. It's like whatever spell was keeping his noble-prince persona in place is melting away, layer by layer, and now I can see him for what he really is. First he morphs into a fairy tale villain, a sneering troll under a bridge. And then a sad little boy who isn't doing anything with his life except drumming up drama, obeying his father's toxic wishes, and bullying everyone "beneath" him so he can feel important.

"Any power you thought you had over me—over

anyone—is *gone*," I say, the fire in my chest burning brighter with every word. I bare my fangs at him, just as the nure-onna would. "I don't have to bite you—but you know what? *Don't test me.*"

I take another step forward, and he steps back again, stumbling into the entryway. I get right in his face—and despite my giant princess gown, I don't stumble at all. In fact, the sheer grandeur of the dress makes me feel powerful—like the monster princess I am.

"Get out," I growl. *"Now."*

He stumbles out the door and into the street, his face getting redder by the second. I picture the nure-onna, smiling with the satisfaction—and a glow forms around my pulsing rage.

"Bad. *Ass!*" Rory shrieks, breaking loose from Auntie Och and running up to me. She throws her spindly arms around my waist and hugs me hard. "Wow, he fucking sucks!" She claps a hand over her mouth. "Oops. Sorry, Moms!"

"No, Rory-chan, you are correct," Auntie Och says, nodding vigorously. "He *does* fucking suck."

"He's no match for our Rika," Belle says, beaming at me.

"Still fighting as hard as the day she was born," Auntie Suzy says, her eyes lit with pride.

"Mmm, what a rude boy," the mochi-demo Auntie murmurs. "I've been wanting to tell him off for years."

I smile at all of them, my nure-onna hissing contentedly. I feel so *powerful*.

I slayed some kind of fairy-tale villain. And as I look around the room, I realize: I didn't do it alone. They all stood with me. They *fought* with me.

They wouldn't let me throw myself away.

"It shouldn't have taken *years* to condemn such hateful attitudes!" Auntie Och exclaims, slamming a hand on one of the tables. "This nonsense we put up with for so long—all the secrets, all the shame in our community, all this making people feel like they don't belong—it need to end *now*." She crosses her arms over her chest, her regal white-streaked mane twitching indignantly. "We shouldn't have lost Grace the way we did. Suzy always used to want us to stay hidden, make sure we don't rock that boat. But sometimes the boat—it need to be rocked!"

"Wait . . ." I murmur, realization flashing through me. I'm remembering the day of the parade, how Auntie Och agreed way too easily to my scheme. "You put me in that yukata—in *my mother's old yukata*—on purpose!"

"Hai," she says, grinning proudly. "I knew Suzy was trying to keep you away from Grace—she wanted you working that restaurant shift because she was afraid your mother would see you."

I shake my head, trying to process. "You both knew she was grand marshal. You thought she might recognize me . . ."

"Why this such a surprise?" Auntie Och says, giving me a look. "Listen, Rika-chan, when I put you in that yukata, I didn't necessarily guess there would be all this chaos. But . . ." Her gaze turns sly, and now I can really see the hell-raiser she used to be. "I also don't think chaos is bad. Like I said, communities need to change and grow along with the people in them, ne?"

"Yes," Auntie Suzy says. "And our community needs to be way, way better about condemning attitudes like Craig's and Uncle Taki's."

"That's right," Uncle Hikaru says, nodding at Auntie Och and Auntie Suzy. "When I think of how we all treated Grace back then, I am ashamed. She was a child, and she was *ours*. She deserved better."

"We need to strike back against those who try to cast people out," the mochi-demo Auntie says. "I can see now how this damages all of us in so many ways."

"It tears the very fabric of the community," Sensei Mary says. She beams at me. "I've always said that."

My heart swells as I look at each person in the room in turn. Sensei Mary, who always let me take lessons at the dojo, even when I started shit with other kids and my family was short on money. Uncle Hikaru, who never batted an eye when I sat in the back of his mochi shop for hours, reading my monster stories. My family, who has always loved me unconditionally—even when they couldn't express it exactly right.

I do belong here, and I do belong to them. I always have.

But my heart was shut up too tight to ever see it. And the more I was hurt by someone's words . . . the more I was convinced that I was a mistake . . . the more closed-off I became.

"We need to try harder," I say. "All of us." I meet Belle's eyes and smile at her, remembering her telling me that she also feels out of place sometimes—and how hard it was for me to believe that. "We all have to come together and rock the boat—so no matter how out of place people feel, they'll never have to question whether they belong here or not."

Auntie Suzy pulls me into another tight hug—like she's afraid I'll disappear all over again.

"We need to let Grace—my mother—know she's welcome at the gala tonight," I say. "And in Little Tokyo,

period. We need to let her know that she's part of this."
I gesture around the room. "That she always has been.
And that we won't let her go again."

"I agree," Uncle Hikaru says.

"Let's welcome her home with open arms," the
mochi-demo Auntie says, jabbing a finger in the air.

"But how we find her?" Auntie Och says, frowning.
"She's in hiding."

"Maybe I can help with that," Joanna says, waving
her phone around. In all the chaos with Craig, I'd forgotten she was here—but I feel a little jolt of pride realizing
that she saw me finally channel all that anger. I meet her
eyes and give her a small smile—and she beams back at
me in a way that says she totally understands.

"I have a pretty big social media following," she continues. "And hey, Rika, you do, too, now!" She gestures
to her screen.

"The Secret Love Child business must have gotten
me so many more followers," I mutter, not sure how I
feel about that.

"So we can blast it out there," Joanna says, tapping on
her screen. "But we're gonna need everyone's help—you
all have to boost these posts, make sure as many people as
possible see them. So we know Grace will see them, too."

The room explodes with activity, everyone grabbing

their phones and getting to work. I see Belle trying to teach Uncle Hikaru how Twitter works.

I hug Auntie Suzy one more time and slump into a chair, all the layers of my dress crumpling under me. I still can't even process everything that's happened today. Or even in the last hour.

I pull out my phone and make my post, urging Grace to come to the gala. I keep it short and simple: **Dear Mom, please come home. We're all waiting for you.** I add the time and location of the gala, just in case she's forgotten. Then I stare at the screen for a few minutes, as if this will make her magically appear.

As everyone buzzes around me, I feel that door to my heart crack open once more, the tiniest bit of light spilling out.

I *do* belong here.

I still can't get over that.

I scan the room and catch Joanna's eye again. She smiles at me, then goes back to her phone, brow furrowing with concentration.

I remember her telling me I don't believe in happy endings because I don't think I deserve one.

That's only part of the truth, though. The other part is that I've always been scared to hope for one because

I secretly knew it meant putting my whole heart at risk. It was so much easier to be . . . well, what I thought was the nure-onna. The nure-onna *before* she claimed her power, lashing out and wishing for revenge.

But now I'm starting to see that princesses and nure-onnas can be what you make of them. What you really feel inside—not just what you think you're supposed to feel.

And I feel like I'm ready to open my heart.

There's one more person I need to open it to. The only person who knew what was *really* there, buried deep inside.

I take my phone out again and tap Henry's name in my contacts. My index finger hovers over the text window, trying to find the words.

But they won't come. When I think of Henry, all that comes to mind are the horrible things I said to him right before abandoning him at the beach. He scared me so much . . . because he truly *saw* me. And he was relentless in trying to see me. He wouldn't allow my usual armor to deflect him, refused to be cowed by my lashing out.

No matter what, he wouldn't let me scare him away. He loved me, even though I make it so hard for people to love me. He loved me *because* of all the things I've always thought of as flaws. Not in spite of them.

And I . . .

"Are you trying to find Henry?"

Suddenly Rory appears right behind me, peering over my shoulder. I yelp and nearly drop my phone.

"I . . . yes," I say. "But it doesn't matter. I was awful to him. I pushed him away so hard, I—"

"He's at the beach," Rory interrupts.

I shake my head at her. "What?"

"We became *friends*," Rory says, rolling her eyes at me. "That day he worked at Katsu That. We text each other 'proof of life' pictures sometimes. That's our thing." She grins to herself. "So I texted him this morning after the whole scandal broke and *insisted* he send me proof-of-life photos every hour to make sure he was safe." She holds up her phone so I can see the screen. "See? He's down by the Santa Monica Pier."

I take the phone and scrutinize the screen. The photo is of the ocean, framed by sky and sand. The lights of the carnival reflect off the water, a kaleidoscope of bright colors. His face isn't in the picture, but he's jutting a hand into frame, as if waving to Rory.

Every feeling I've ever had courses through me, over-whelming all my senses—I'm at the top of the roller coaster again, right before the drop. And I know what I have to do.

"Hey, Auntie Och," I say, waving the phone at her. "Can I borrow the car—or can you drive me to the beach?"

"What's this?" she says, her eyes narrowing suspiciously. "I thought we all going to the gala . . . ?"

"We are," I say hastily. "But I need to . . . I really want to . . ."

"Rika's in love with Henry Chen!!!" Rory bellows. "And she has to go to him!"

Everyone falls silent, all eyes turning in my direction.

"Oh," Auntie Och says. "Why you not just say so? I take you. I love young love!"

"I have to go, too!" Rory proclaims, grabbing my hand. "It's because of me that she even knows where he is!"

"And I am definitely not missing any opportunity to see Rika get in touch with her mushy side," Belle says, sidling up to me.

"Well, if everyone's going . . ." Auntie Suzy grins, her eyes sparkling with mischief. "Then I suppose I should as well."

I know there's no arguing with them, so I throw up my hands in surrender. "Let's go, Rakuyamas."

Auntie Och orders Uncle Hikaru to keep an eye on the restaurant, and Joanna promises to keep the Get Grace to the Gala campaign going strong. And then all the Rakuyamas pile into Auntie Och's Mustang—Auntie Och driving, Auntie Suzy in the passenger seat, and me and my sisters crammed in the back. Belle insists on bringing Nak, and I notice that Rory is now wearing my nure-onna shirt—which still looks better on her. My big princess dress squishes all around us, enveloping us in a cloud of sparkles.

"Look at you," Belle says, stroking my dress admiringly. "You're finally Team Princess."

"I'd say Team My Own Kind of Princess," I retort.

"We're *all* our own kind of princess, Rika-chan," she says, rolling her eyes at me. "It just took you forever to figure out yours."

I open my mouth to argue—and then I just smile at her. Because, hey, she's right. She clasps my hand, and then we face forward. Nak faces forward with us, determined.

My gaze lands on Auntie Suzy reaching over the gearshift to take Auntie Och's hand. Auntie Och turns and smiles at her—and suddenly I can see them so clearly. The them of twenty years ago, when they fell in love. Soft and sweet and knowing that they can fight through anything, because they'll fight through it together. It's as if a glow surrounds them, creating something magical and precious.

"Hey, Suzy," Auntie Och says very quietly—like they're the only two people in the car. "We do all right, ne? Create successful business, raise three beautiful daughters, maybe just start a revolution in our staid old community. I know it's been hard, but we're living our own happily ever after."

Auntie Suzy squeezes her hand, her smile turning brilliant. "We are," she says fervently. "And our story isn't over yet."

TWENTY-ONE

Auntie Och drives like a bat out of hell, honking and yelling at people and taking sketchy side-street shortcuts to route us around traffic. Belle keeps throwing out the "mom arm" to keep Rory and me from jouncing forward every time Auntie Och makes another screechy hairpin turn. Nak somehow manages to pass out, snoring in Belle's lap. We arrive at the Santa Monica Pier in almost no time, which is quite a feat.

Auntie Och forgoes the more civilized official parking lot, angling her Mustang right up to the edge of the sand. I'm pretty sure parking here is illegal, but my heart is beating way too fast to even think about that.

"You ready, Rika-chan?" Auntie Och says, whipping around to face me. "You want us to come with you?"

"God, Ma Och, *no*," Belle says, shaking her head vehemently. "The whole family does not need to be part of this big romantic gesture."

"I'd say the whole family already *is* part of this big

romantic gesture," Auntie Suzy counters.

"There he is!" Rory yells, gesturing wildly at a lone figure whose back is to us, looking out at the water.

"How can you tell that's him?" Belle protests, clutching Nak to her chest. "It could be any random dude checking out the ocean!"

"It's him," I murmur, my gaze locking on the figure. I can't even explain how I know. It has something to do with the way he's standing—that inherent dancer's grace.

"Wait, is he leaving?" Auntie Suzy says, frowning as the figure starts to lope away from the ocean.

"Oh no!" Rory exclaims. And before I can stop her, she's rolling down the window and sticking her little head out. "*Henry!!!*" she bellows. "Don't go!"

"Oh my god," I mutter, sinking lower in my seat. This is really not how I imagined my fairy-tale ending.

Then again, if this week has taught me anything, it's that sometimes your fairy-tale ending is *not at all* what you thought it would be.

The figure stops and looks around, trying to discern where the voice is coming from.

"Go, Rika-chan," Auntie Suzy murmurs. She smiles at me, her eyes lit with that hope I haven't seen in . . . well, maybe ever.

Rory opens the car door and jumps out, making a

sweeping gesture toward the beach. I eject myself from the car, gathering my big skirts around me.

And I run. I run toward him, this lone figure on the beach who's starting to walk away from me.

"Henry!" I call out. "Please! Wait!"

He stops and turns—and his eyes nearly bug out of his head. If I wasn't feeling so desperate, burning up with this desire to get to him, I might laugh. I picture how I must look to him, a girl in a giant sparkly princess dress who's a complete mess from the neck up. Well, and the ankles down, considering my sneakers. And actually, my princess dress is kind of ripped and dirty, so I'm a mess all over.

I look wild. I look terrified . . . angry . . .

Passionate.

I look like the monster princess that I am. I have never felt more like myself, and I have never loved it so much.

"Run, Rika-chan!" I hear Belle cry out in the distance.

When I finally reach him, I'm out of breath. Running through the sand in a cumbersome ball gown is much harder than it looks.

"Henry," I gasp out.

"Rika?" he says, looking utterly confused.

We take each other in as I catch my breath. His dark eyes look so sad. His posture is droopy. Even his perfect movie star hair appears to be slouching a little. I want nothing more than to gather him close and never let go. But first, I have to speak.

"I'm sorry," I blurt out. "About leaving you here this morning. And about the things I said to you. I just . . . I freaked out. I've been so scared and defensive and closed-off my entire life. I made it hard to love me because I didn't believe anyone ever would. I put up so many walls to protect myself—even though doing that made me hurt even more. And . . ." My voice catches and I swallow my tears, determined to keep going. "You're the only one who saw through it. Like, *immediately*. You wouldn't let me put up those walls. You just kept being so . . . so . . ." I blink hard, unable to find all the right words. "You're so *good*, Henry. You really see people. You saw me in a way I don't think I've ever been seen before. That made me so uncomfortable at first, but now . . ." I shake my head, and a tear slips down my cheek. "I feel safe with you. Like I'm home. Like I belong. I love your dorky snorty laugh. I love the way you see beauty everywhere. I love that you've always believed in my happy ending, even when I haven't."

I take a step toward him and put my hand on his chest. It's the opening move for our judo throw. I'm just waiting to see if he'll catch me gently or throw me away.

"I love . . . *you*."

He stares at me for a moment, his expression unreadable.

His gaze goes to my hand on his chest. I can feel his heartbeat through the thin cotton of his T-shirt. Even if he does throw me away, I'm not sorry I'm opening my heart so fully. I wouldn't trade this last week with him for anything.

Slowly, he raises his head and meets my eyes again. I still can't tell what he's thinking. Like, at all.

Then . . . he raises a hand and very gently tucks that unruly lock of bright red hair behind my ear.

"Rika," he murmurs—in that way that makes me melt. "Weren't you listening this morning? *Of course* I love you, too."

"Oh . . ." I breathe. It comes out as a sob. "I—I did hear you. I was just so *angry*—"

He catches my mouth with a kiss.

I sink into it, tears flowing down my cheeks as he pulls me close. In the distance, I can hear my family cheering.

When we finally pull apart, he touches his forehead to mine, his hands cupping my face. Holding me like I'm precious.

"Angry," he breathes out, a smile in his voice. "*Passionate.* And all the fierce, tender parts underneath. I *do* see you. The whole you. And I love everything I see."

He raises his head and looks around, taking in the luminous moon reflected in the ocean, the sounds of the waves lapping against the shore.

"Look at us," he says, a smile playing over his lips. "It's just like the end of *Meet Me Again*."

"If you throw anything of mine into the ocean, I'll kill you," I say.

"We showed up for each other," he says, refusing to be cowed. "And *you* came for *me*—so I guess I'm the princess in this scenario?"

I grin and pull him in for another kiss. "We both are."

❀

The Nikkei Week gala is in full swing when the Raku-yamas plus Henry return to Little Tokyo. Belle is still in her sweatsuit but decides to forego her usual finery because "I look like a queen, no matter what." I feel a surge of joy as she tucks Nak under her arm and runs up to the rest of her court, who greet her with a giant group hug.

In fact, after all the excitement of the day, it appears that no one's really going for the usual super-fancy gala wear. Rory wraps another one of Auntie Suzy's dresses around her shoulders like a cape. Eliza and Sensei Mary are in their judogi, showing some of the kids how to do simple tumbles. Uncle Hikaru has just plopped a bow tie on over his T-shirt. Auntie Suzy and Auntie Och don yukata from Auntie Suzy's collection—paired with Adidas slides, of course.

Craig Shimizu, I notice, is nowhere in sight.

The spirit of the gala feels *freer* than usual. Like instead of keeping constant watch to see who's doing something inappropriate or who's worth gossiping about or who needs to be the target of so many disapproving stares, everyone in the community's actually enjoying the party.

There is, of course, a heightened buzz crackling through the airy courtyard—will Grace Kimura show?

Despite the community's best efforts, no one's heard from her. Henry's tried texting her, to no avail. I can't stop the constant nervous skitter through my gut. I've already been through an entire decade's worth of emotions in a single day. If she doesn't show up . . . will it ruin everything?

"Still nothing?" I say, peering over his shoulder as he glances at his phone screen.

"Sorry," he says, shaking his head. He stuffs his phone back in his pocket, giving me a soft smile. "Let's think about something else." He extends a hand and gives me a courtly bow. "Time for your dance lesson."

"Oh no," I say, holding up a finger. "Little Tokyo's gone through enough already today. Nobody needs to see that."

"You promised," he says, grinning mischievously as he takes my hand and tugs me insistently toward the dance floor. "A judo lesson for a dance lesson."

"Ugh," I say—but I'm smiling. "Fine."

I allow him to take me in his arms, pulling me into a slow dance.

"Just move with me," Henry says. "Trust me."

So I do. He leads me around the floor, making it easy for me to follow his moves. He's so graceful, so light on his feet. And even though I'm stiff and awkward at first, I find myself melting against him, my gaze drifting up to the twinkle lights sparkling above our heads. And beyond that, the starry sky. It really does feel like we're in some sort of fairyland. I picture our feet floating off the ground, Henry and me spinning into the air. Not caring about anything but this beautiful world we're existing in—and each other.

As the song draws to a close, I feel a tiny stab of disappointment. Do I actually want to dance *more*?

"One more song," Henry murmurs into my hair. "I don't want to let you go just yet."

I rest my head against his chest, the biggest, goofiest smile spreading over my face.

Then, out of the corner of my eye, I spot something . . . and my happy smile freezes.

It's just a flutter of something. A dreamy bit of pale blue chiffon, floating away from the party like a scarf caught in the wind. It's someone's dress, I realize—and that person is leaving the party, running across the street . . .

A prickle of intuition runs up my spine. There's something *familiar* about that figure, even though I don't remember seeing anyone in a pale blue chiffon dress. I can't seem to stop staring at it as it gets smaller in the distance, disappearing into the plaza . . .

"Rika?" Henry says.

But I'm too stuck on this chiffon, this tiny fairy floating farther and farther away from me.

And then I realize, with a shock that jolts my whole being, that the thing I'm feeling, that ping of connection . . . is the exact same feeling I got at the Nikkei Week parade. When Grace Kimura and I locked eyes and she crashed right into me.

"I have to go," I say, raising my head from Henry's chest.

"What?" He shakes his head and gives me a teasing grin. "Why? What did I do now?"

"Nothing," I say hastily. "Sorry. I should have said: I'll be right back. Just . . . excuse me for a minute."

"I'll be waiting," Henry says, sounding thoroughly puzzled as I gather my skirts around me and run.

I dash across the street and through the plaza, searching in vain for that flutter of pale blue. It's completely out of sight now—vanished into thin air.

Luckily, I know exactly where to go.

I blaze through the plaza in a cloud of sparkles, dart over to the JACCC, and duck into the garden. I'm headed straight for the onryo tree—the one I hid under just a few short hours ago.

I know I'll find her there, I just *know* it . . .

Except . . . I don't.

She's not under the tree. The tree is just sitting there, existing, its branches reaching out to the night sky.

My shoulders slump. Did I hallucinate that blue-clad figure? Why am I still so intent on chasing something that's never going to appear, that's never going to . . . to . . .

Wait.

My eyes are drawn to a spot shrouded in darkness, the grass blending into the tree. And there, sticking out from underneath that green canopy of leaves, is a tiny scrap of blue chiffon.

I kneel down, my heart beating so loudly, I swear I can hear it puncturing the silence of the garden.

When I finally see her, crumpled under that tree in a wilting pile of blue, all the breath leaves my body.

Her head jerks up as I peer under the tree, her eyes widening in shock and recognition. Just like they did at the parade.

"Rika?" she says, her voice barely a whisper.

And I can only say, "Mom."

TWENTY-TWO

I bunch my giant skirt up and crawl under the tree with her. She's still staring at me as if I'm not quite real.

"Of course," she murmurs, almost to herself. "Of course you knew to find me here. This is where I used to escape to when I was little and I wanted to feel safe."

"Me too," I say softly.

I'm trying to take her in, but my senses are overwhelmed, and it feels like my brain's short-circuiting. Her cheeks are tearstained, and her eye makeup runs down her face in messy rivulets. Her glossy black mane of hair is swirling around her shoulders, unkempt. And it looks like she, too, has torn the hem of her dress.

None of this makes her less beautiful. She looks heartbreakingly *real*.

"Oh, *Rika*," she says, her voice tremulous. "I dreamed of this moment so many times. I . . ." She trails off and lifts her hand, like she wants to touch me. Then seems to think better of it and drops her hand back in her lap. "I saw your message," she says. "And I knew I had to come—I had to finally face you. But as soon as I got to that courtyard . . ." She shakes her head vigorously. "I couldn't do it. I've gotten so confident being Grace Kimura. Did you know, I haven't actually set foot in Little Tokyo in . . . well, since I left. When they asked me to be grand marshal, I figured enough time had passed. That I'm a different person now, and no one would recognize Grace Rakuyama. But . . . then the parade happened. *You* happened." She gives me a shaky smile. "I haven't seen you since you were a baby—I always wondered if I'd recognize you, all these years later. But of course I did. And when I got to the gala, I just knew. As soon as the community saw me, I'd be Grace Rakuyama again. The disgraced teenager who could never find the strength to stand up for herself."

We let that sit between us, the soft summer breeze rustling through the garden, whispering all of its secrets. I don't know exactly what I feel. I've been picturing this moment all week—maybe not as long as Grace has. I'd thought our reunion would be instantly magical, a connection neither of us could explain.

And it is. There is some kind of bond between us, that same bond that drew us both to the onryo tree. But there's also an undeniable thread of melancholy weaving through all of that. Like every kind of fairy tale coming together—Belle and Rory's princess stories, my Japanese folklore, and just plain old real life. I feel so much for my mother, who was so immediately and viciously denied a certain kind of love—by her father, her community, her daughter she was never allowed to know. And I also feel . . . for me. For the girl who's spent her entire life lunging at everyone in her path with her fangs bared, because she didn't quite know how to love. Or how to be loved.

We both needed each other so badly, without even knowing it.

I reach out across the space between us—the space that is not just this garden but the span of the seventeen years we've been apart.

"Why don't you just talk to me," I say. "About anything at all."

She takes a deep breath and gives me a grateful smile.

"Let me tell you my side of the story from this past week," she says, her voice halting. "After the parade . . ." She shakes her head, the memories rising up. "I tried to go into hiding. But no matter what, I knew I had to find you. So I tried to get back in touch with my sister—with Suzy. I left a message behind that loose tile in the library. That's where we used to leave secret messages for each other, after I faked my death and was exiled from Little

Tokyo. I thought . . . after everything that happened at the parade, she'd know I needed to talk to her. But then you and Henry found it instead." She meets my eyes and gives me a hesitant smile. "And I knew you had, because everyone posted those photos of the two of you on social media."

"Then why didn't you show up?" I can't help but ask. "At the old zoo. I . . . I wanted to meet you so badly."

"I was scared," she says, squeezing my hand. "I was ready to talk to Suzy, but oh, Rika-chan—I couldn't face you. Not yet. I couldn't imagine how you could possibly ever forgive me for being gone all those years. Just thinking about seeing you brought back all those things I felt when I was fifteen—how scared and ashamed I was, how alone." Her voice catches, her eyes going glossy with tears. "I went deeper into hiding. I didn't go to the zoo or to the Asian Hollywood meetup. And I pushed off finishing my movie again. I've never felt so mixed-up—not since I was that terrified girl. I've spent so many years building up my walls, trying to give myself armor so I couldn't be hurt again."

I feel that ping of connection soaring through me again. I squeeze her hand back.

"When I saw your message today, I knew I had to come," she continues. "I *had* to see you, even if you hated me. And I would not blame you for hating me."

"I could never," I whisper.

"But once I got there, I realized I hadn't actually figured out what I was going to do," she says. "I had this image of a perfect, happy fairy-tale ending—like one of my movies. And then I just couldn't imagine it *actually* happening."

"I get that," I say. "You . . . you can't know *how much* I get that." I look down at our clasped hands, so many feelings surging through me. And I try to find the right words. "Wishing for a happy ending is terrifying," I say slowly. "It means tearing down those walls and putting your heart at risk. It means letting in *hope*. And hope always has the potential to let us down, to leave us crushed and broken and . . . and hurting." My voice cracks, and I try to breathe evenly. "You've gone through so much to get here. So have I. I used to never hope at all. But this past week . . ." I shake my head, my eyes filling with tears. "I've learned that you can make your own happy ending. And it doesn't have to look like the ones in rom-coms or fairy tales or . . . or . . . sad Japanese folklore stories about fierce monster women. It can look like none of those things—or all of them at once. It can look however you want it to look. It's *yours*."

"Rika-chan," she murmurs, her voice thick with emotion. "You are . . . you're so incredible. I can't believe I missed so much . . ."

"You did," I say, my voice very soft. "And I can't lie, I'm angry about that. I never knew that you wanted me. And I think I really, really needed to know that."

"I'm sorry," she says. "I fought for you so hard—but I should have fought harder. I made so many mistakes, and then I wouldn't listen to Suzy, even when she knew how bad it would be for you to suddenly be brought into the public eye with me . . ."

"Auntie Suzy made her fair share of mistakes, too. And I'm happy you're here now," I say, squeezing her hand again. "I would like to . . . to have something with you. Whatever that ends up being. I'm not sure yet. But I've heard so much about you now, from Henry and Auntie Suzy, and you sound pretty amazing."

"I want that," she says fervently. "More than anything."

"Then as a first step—come with me back to the gala." I meet her gaze and give her a hopeful smile. "There are so many people who want to see you. One in particular."

Grace hesitates and looks off into the distance. For a moment, she looks just like the lost teenager she was in that photo I found of her sitting under this tree. My heart twists.

After what seems like forever, she turns back to me and gives me that brilliant smile—the one I've heard about all my life. The one everyone—from her fans to the Little Tokyo denizens who remember her as a sweet, hopeful girl—loves so much.

"Yes, Rika-chan," she says, finally pulling me in for an embrace. "Let's go."

❀

I can tell Grace is nervous. Her grip on my hand tightens as we get closer and closer to the courtyard, her palm slick with sweat. When we reach the courtyard entrance, I give her an encouraging nod. And then we enter hand in hand.

Total silence falls over the courtyard. There's not even so much as a gasp. Just pure shock. All eyes are on us.

"People of Little Tokyo," I say, my heart ready to pound right out of my chest, "please welcome back Grace Kim—Grace *Rakuyama*."

A single cry pierces the air, something that sounds like a cross between a teenager meeting their idol for the first time and a wounded animal. A brightly colored blur streaks through the crowd, barreling straight toward us—Auntie Suzy, her yukata flapping around her.

"Suzy," Grace whispers, her eyes widening.

But she doesn't get any further, because Auntie Suzy

sweeps her into a bone-crunching hug. Grace collapses against her, both of them sobbing. They're so fused, I can't tell where one begins and the other ends.

Finally, Auntie Suzy pulls back, taking Grace's face in her hands. Studying her like she can't believe she's real.

"I'm sorry," she says. "For everything. And I'm so happy you're home."

And then everyone's crowding around Grace, shouting things, asking the kind of nosy Auntie questions they all love so much.

Belle and Rory jump up and down, trying to get her attention—asking if they can call her Auntie Grace and if she can show them how to do winged eyeliner and also if she'll bring them to one of her movie sets.

Somehow this devolves into a messy dance party, the gigantic group hug migrating to the dance floor and grooving with the music. And before I even have a chance to look for him, I feel Henry's hand reach through the crowd and take mine.

"Oh no," I say. "Are you really trying to get me to dance again? Wasn't I bad enough the first time?"

"Come on," he says, grinning and pulling me against him.

"Mmm," I murmur, as we sway in time to the music. "Well, even with the arrival of the long-lost daughter of

Little Tokyo, I'm pretty sure my general appearance is about to attract everyone's attention—for all the wrong reasons. Maybe I should go change?" I gesture to my dirty, torn princess dress. "Or at least fix my hair." I point to the tangled mass of waves, a snarl that I don't think even the most determined of tiaras would adhere to.

He draws me closer, one hand going to the small of my back, his mouth brushing my ear and sending a delicious shiver down my spine. "You look beautiful," he says. "You look like *you*."

He pulls back and gives me one of his smiles—hopeful and genuine. So Henry.

"What do you think?" he says, gesturing all around us. "Is this your happily ever after?"

I drink in the scene. Those twinkle lights are still twinkling. Everyone's dancing and laughing. Auntie Suzy and Auntie Och, gazing deep into each other's eyes and looking more in love than ever. Eliza and Sensei Mary, showing Joanna a judo move—which she seems to be taking extremely seriously. Grace, twirling around the floor with Belle and Rory, all of them giggling so hard, they're about to topple over.

Everyone is so *themselves*.

I turn back to Henry and smile. And I realize I can still feel the nure-onna inside of me—fierce, protective, passionate. And yes, sometimes angry. Because there's nothing *wrong* with being angry. You need that anger, to tell you when something's not right. To tell you when you *care*. To show you when you need to fight hard for what you want and stand up for the people you love.

That door to my heart is wide open, and I know exactly where I belong.

"It's not the kind of happily ever after I imagined," I say. "But it's *mine*. And I'm finally ready for it."

Once upon a time, a beautiful monster princess undertook an epic quest throughout the magical kingdom of Los Angeles. She slayed many dragons, was blessed with wisdom from her fairy godmother, and reunited with her mother, the long-lost queen. She also met a handsome prince, and they learned how to truly save each other—even when they thought they didn't need saving.

After she returned to her village, triumphant, she partied until dawn at the Nikkei Week gala, surrounded by her wonderful family and all the love in the world. She and her fellow princess Eliza even did an impromptu judo demonstration at said gala—yes, in her giant princess dress—which many people recorded and posted, and somehow it went viral, leading to UCLA scholarships for both princesses.

There was much rejoicing throughout the land, especially since her handsome prince planned on staying in the kingdom of Los Angeles for months to come, shooting the starring role in his amazing new movie and visiting many enchanted alleys with her. And she and her mother could finally get to know each other as they were meant to.

The princess never thought her life could feel so full. So beautiful. So magical.

Just like a fairy tale.

And she lived . . .

She lives. Happily ever after.

Her story isn't over yet.

ACKNOWLEDGMENTS

Writing this book felt like magic, and I am grateful to so many people. But first, a special thank-you to one of my favorite places in LA—Little Tokyo, you are a beautiful wonderland that provided me with so much inspiration. The Little Tokyo in this book is, of course, a fictionalized version of the real Little Tokyo and the community therein—the annual summer festival is a little different, Katsu That is not a real restaurant, and there is no massive photo collage at Suehiro (which *is* one of the best places for Japanese comfort food—that part is true). Some of the other elements are real and some are imagined. There is, for example, no major scandal involving a movie star—at least not that I know of. But Mr. Sherman the cat totally exists.

Thank you to my many superhero teams: the Girl Gang(s), the Shamers, the Ripped Bodice crew, Heroine Club, Asian American Girl Club, Team Batgirl, the Kuhn-Chen-Coffey-Yoneyamas, the writing sprint squads, the Millsies, and the incredible Asian American arts community of LA. As always, I am so honored to be in your company.

The biggest, shiniest thank-you to my marvelous editor, Jenny Bak, who saw this book's potential and pushed me to take it to its most epic heights. I appreciate your passion for and insight into these characters more than I can say—and I double appreciate your cute couple moniker: Henrika.

Thank you to my agent, Diana Fox, for believing in Rika's adventures, and to artist Marcos Chin and designer Tony Sahara for bringing them to such glorious life—this cover makes me swoon. And thank you to everyone at Viking, Penguin Random House, and Fox Literary for bringing this book into the world.

Thank you to all the folks who drew me into the magic of Little Tokyo in the first place, especially Jenn Fujikawa, Keiko Agena, Jenny Yang, Naomi Hirahara, Traci Kato-Kiriyama, Scott and Geri Okamoto, Naomi Ko, Will Choi, Phil Yu, Sean Miura, Yumi Sakugawa, Julia Cho, and all the wonderful people involved in the many events I've been part of in the neighborhood.

Thank you to Diya Mishra and Liz Ho for the insightful early reads, to superstar Maurene Goo for important YA author counsel, and to Tom Wong for all the brainstorms.

And thank you to Jeff Chen for being my happily ever after—yes, I did name him after you.

ABOUT THE AUTHOR

SARAH KUHN is the author of the popular Heroine Complex novels—a series starring Asian American superheroines. The first book is a Locus bestseller, an RT Reviewers' Choice Award nominee, and one of the Barnes & Noble Sci-Fi & Fantasy Blog's Best Books of 2016. Her YA debut, the Japan-set romantic comedy *I Love You So Mochi*, is a Junior Library Guild selection and a nominee for YALSA's Best Fiction for Young Adults. She has also penned a variety of short fiction and comics, including the critically acclaimed graphic novel *Shadow of the Batgirl* for DC Comics and the *Star Wars* audiobook original *Doctor Aphra*. Additionally, she was a finalist for both the CAPE (Coalition of Asian Pacifics in Entertainment) New Writers Award and the Astounding Award for Best New Writer. A third-generation Japanese American, she lives in Los Angeles with her husband and an overflowing closet of vintage treasures. Find her at heroinecomplex.com